SOUND THE ALARM!

Geritsi slentAlin sat on the damp sward, her knees drawn up under her chin; Dosent, her *sokyum*, stretched beside her, thoroughly asleep. Overhead, the stars were a scattering of blazing pinheads, visible where the brilli   arms of The Ribbons thinned   heir eternal dance

Geritsi sig   ic of the dance.

She closed h   listen—and that was when s   mething—else. *Not* the music of the   s or the mutter of systemic rubbish. *Not* the self-satisfied humming of the ambient.

No, this was a . . . voice, and it was talking . . . not to her, not to the brilliant night. Beside her, Dosent growled, flexed her claws, and raised her head.

An animal.

The words were quite clear—and quite clearly dismissive. Contemptuous.

Then, the sense of another presence was gone, leaving Geritsi and Dosent alone on the hillside.

From below came a shout—another—and the sudden sound of youngers, crying. More windows brightened; doors slammed; an illumination bloomed over the square, back-lighting the shapes of the projectors, dashing across the square to the news-tree.

Geritsi and Dosent began to run.

BAEN BOOKS by
SHARON LEE & STEVE MILLER

To purchase any of these titles in e-book form,
please go to www.baen.com.

TRADER'S LEAP

A New
Liaden Universe®
Novel

SHARON LEE &
STEVE MILLER

BAEN

A Baen Books Original

Baen Publishing Enterprises
P.O. Box 1403
Riverdale, NY 10471
www.baen.com

ISBN: 978-1-9821-2567-7

Cover art by David Mattingly

First printing, December 2020
First mass market printing, October 2021

Distributed by Simon & Schuster
1230 Avenue of the Americas
New York, NY 10020

Library of Congress Control Number: 2020031318

Pages by Joy Freeman (www.pagesbyjoy.com)
Printed in the United States of America
10   9   8   7   6   5   4   3   2   1

Dedicated to all the men and women of NASA who are using science, blood, sweat, and tears to push our boundaries to the stars.

Thanks to . . .

Alexei Panshin for Wu and Fabricant's Guidebooks

Antoine de Saint-Exupéry for *The Little Prince*

Andre Norton for *The Zero Stone*

For everyone who participates in the
Scavenger Hunts—you guys rock!

❧

The Authors Also Thank Mighty Typo Hunters:

Lori Altmann, Laura Arlov, Sally Barto, Bev Brown,
Teresa Carrigan, Nickola Cooper, Andy Funk,
S. J. Gum, Rich Hanson, Irene Harrison, Julia Hart,
Suzanne Hediger, Chris Huning, Wolfram Jahn,
Hope Johnston, Amy Josephson, Melita Kennedy,
Berry Kercheval, Kathryn Kramer, Butler Lampson,
Evelyn Mellone, Bex O, David Picon, Maurita Plouff,
Marni Rachmiel, Kate Reynolds, Sheila in Texas,
Phyllis Shute, Lucian Stacy, Sarah Stapleton,
Julia Steinberg, Rob VandenBrink, Sidney Whitaker,
Ruth Woodgate, Leanne Wu, and Anne Young for
taking part in the Great *Trader's Leap* Typo Hunt!
Your grace, humor, and hunting skills
are very much appreciated!

Prologue

. . . .

AVIZ PANERVEKIN SAT STRAIGHT UP IN HER BED, GASPING aloud.

For a moment, she sat quiet in the dark, breath rasping in her ears, too disordered to reach for an illumination—

"Aviz?"

The room light snapped on, chasing every shadow.

"Are you ill?" asked Kawli, her sister. She stood in the doorway, one hand on the wall plate, the other holding a reader against her hip.

"No . . ." Aviz said slowly. She squinted 'round the room, her breathing back to normal now, chilly with the memory of the touch . . .

"No," she said again. "It was a dream."

"A dream," Kawli repeated, her tone neutral.

"I was being . . . stalked," Aviz said, feeling after the dream, though already it was beginning to fade. "Most unsettling."

She turned to meet her sister's eyes. "I beg pardon, for disturbing you at your studies."

"I had just finished the chapter," Kawli said, considering her out of shrewd brown eyes.

1

"Come downstairs, why not? I'll start the kettle for tea."

"Yes," Aviz said, throwing back the blankets and reaching for her robe. "A cup of tea will do me good."

· · · ✳ · · ·

Nersing carnYllum got up from behind his desk and crossed the room to the balcony door. He pushed it open, stepped out—and snatched the metal rail to steady himself. Eight stories below him the midday commuter had stopped at the station. The debarking passengers looked very small.

Nersing bit his lip, and glanced over his shoulder, into his office.

He had been writing the synopsis of the feasibility study for a proposed new train line out from Arthenton Vane in the warehouse district, to Peck's Market, at the edge of the Grid.

The project fairly crackled with political tension, as did any project or program that hinted at collaboration between Wilderness and Civilization. It had taken his office three years just to get approval and funding for the feasibility study. Now the results were in and it was his task to present them clearly and without bias, all the while he fervently hoped that the project would be approved at last.

He had left strict instructions at the front desk that he not be disturbed for anyone, be it the Warden himself. All such system alerts and rail-traffic memos that would normally come to him had been put on hold, so that he could concentrate.

And he had been concentrating. To the exclusion of everything else, his mind wholly on his task, until he had come to himself, one step onto a three-step-wide balcony and walking briskly forward.

Once more, he looked down at the trains, the traffic, the pedestrians and shops so far below his vantage. Then, he turned, and carefully walked back into his office.

He locked the balcony door, crossed to the comm, and called building maintenance. Then, feeling somewhat foolish, he called Security.

While he waited for the two individuals he had summoned to arrive, he reviewed the . . . incident.

It would require an in-depth reading from Security, but he thought—he was very nearly certain—that he had heard . . . something. Nothing so unsubtle as a voice, but . . . *some*thing, a whisper that had acted directly upon his muscles, bypassing his busy brain.

That, he thought, was . . . worrisome.

Uneasy, he went over to his desk, filed the report he'd been writing and blanked the screen. He was just straightening up when a buzzer sounded. He touched the intercom switch.

"Security Chief calpakVernil is here to see you, sir," his secretary said, somewhat breathlessly. "At your request."

"Thank you," he said, his own voice not quite steady. "Please send the chief in."

· · · · ❖ · · · ·

Geritsi slentAlin sat on the damp sward, her knees drawn up under her chin; Dosent, her *sokyum*, stretched beside her, thoroughly asleep. Overhead, the stars were a scattering of blazing pinheads, visible where the brilliant swirling arms of The Ribbons thinned in the progress of their eternal dance with the void.

Geritsi sighed gently, listening to the music of the dance. Tonight, too, the ambient glittered and sang, though they were still more than a month from the Festival of the Seedlings. If it kept on like this, she thought, the festival would be one for the ages.

She closed her eyes, the better to listen—and that was when she heard...something—else. *Not* the music of the stars or the mutter of systemic rubbish. *Not* the self-satisfied humming of the ambient.

No, this was a...voice, and it was talking...not to her, not to the brilliant night. Perhaps, it spoke to itself. Perhaps, she thought, straining to hear more clearly, it was speaking into a note taker—it had that kind of flatness about it. Beside her, Dosent growled, flexed her claws, and raised her head.

Teeth grit, Geritsi leaned into the ambient, allowing the voice to flow directly into her memory, bypassing her understanding altogether. Someone would have to sift them out, which might be embarrassing, but she felt instinctively that these words—these *intentions*— were of vital importance to the Haosa.

The voice paused; there was a sense, as of attention sharpening. Geritsi made herself as small and insignificant as possible, curling up inside her own shadow; shivering as she felt the cold regard pass over her—and linger...

...on Dosent.

Geritsi gritted her teeth even as the cat's growl deepened.

There came a flutter of what might have been— amusement.

An animal.

The words were quite clear—and quite clearly dismissive. Contemptuous.

Then, the sense of another presence was gone, leaving Geritsi and Dosent alone on the hillside. Above them, The Ribbons danced, obscuring the stars; the ambient hummed no longer, as if it, too, were trying to escape the attention of . . . whatever—*who*ever—was overlooking them.

She'd best tell someone, she thought, even though she'd get in trouble for being out so late by herself.

Rising, she made a small light and, Dosent at her side, walked up the hill. She paused at the summit, gazing down at the village, noting the unusual number of lighted windows in this hour of the night. Had the voice woken everybody in the Off-Grid?

From below came a shout—another—and the sudden sound of youngers, crying. More windows brightened; doors slammed; an illumination bloomed over the square, back-lighting the shapes of the projectors, dashing across the square to the news-tree.

Geritsi and Dosent began to run.

Dutiful Passage
Langlast Departure

· · · · · · · · · · · · · · · · · ·

I

IT STARTED WITH A WALK IN THE RAIN, HIMSELF AND HIS oathsworn, across a dim port plaza. Rounded paving stones made for treacherous footing, and he was preoccupied; impatient, his thoughts on the end of the mission, on the next day's joyous reunion with his lifemate and his ship.

Mincing across the wet stones, he knew how this would end; knew that the rain, the plaza, the man at his shoulder, were all part of a terrible memory, replayed as a dream, now that one of them was safe. Knowing that he dreamed, he tried to wake; felt the piercing agony of a headache behind his eyes, and redoubled his efforts.

"Right here, isn't it, sir?"

The voice pulled him back into the dream; he glanced up at the mosaic flower above the shop door.

"Thank you, Vanner," he heard himself say. "I think I must be more tired than I know."

He took a breath, and turned toward the door.

He panicked then, and threw himself wholesale

into the effort of trying to alter the future—shouting aloud at his dream-self to turn away, to run, to grab Vanner's arm and—

But it was no use. The dream rolled on, inexorable, toward its foreknown tragedy.

He opened the door, as he had done, awake, and was doomed to do, again, asleep: walking down the aisle lined by gem-filled cases, to the back of the store, where the proprietor awaited him.

Spirit and soul afire, he fell, though that had been the least of the things that had happened in that place—and lost consciousness.

He tried to shout himself into sense, but the dream rolled on, crushing his feeble attempts to wake back into a world where this was the past, and not the living present.

He did not scream when Vanner died, murdered by his own hand, though he surely did so when the links he had cut rebounded against his soul, and the lash struck—struck, and struck again.

"Shan."

Even as he felt his life ebbing, and the frail flutter of wings inside his chest... Even as another power, glittering dark and diamond-sharp, harried him toward defeat—even then, he heard her voice; grasped it and held to it with all of his remaining strength.

"Shan. Wake now, love."

So simple a thing, he thought, as a cool hand cupped his cheek. With her touch, the dream unraveled, and he was free.

Free to open his eyes; free to draw a deep, shuddering breath, as he looked up into her face. He had fallen asleep in his chair. Foolish thing to have done.

"Priscilla," he said, his voice raw. "I do beg your pardon."

"Because you had a nightmare?" she asked, slim eyebrows arching over black eyes.

He blew out a breath, nothing so humorous as a laugh.

"Because I had a nightmare, *again*," he told her. "Really, of all the bad habits you might have expected me to adopt, screaming in my sleep cannot have been among the first dozen."

"I don't know that I've ever wanted you to adopt any more bad habits at all," his lifemate said meditatively. "I'm perfectly satisfied with those that came with."

He did manage something nearer a laugh this time. "Wretch."

She smiled, and he was struck to the heart.

It was a weary thing, that smile, filigreed with worry he could See clearly even in his diminished state. He raised a hand to touch her face.

"Do not overspend yourself, Priscilla," he said gently.

"Now, how would I do that?" she asked, with almost credible lightness. "I'll have you know that no less a person than the first mate has informed me that my *melant'i* as *dramliza* and Healer stands before my *melant'i* as captain."

"There's an impertinence," he murmured, sliding his fingers into the storm-cloud curls over her ear.

"Well, yes; but she's right. For the moment. She's a perfectly competent officer, and an excellent pilot. I don't expect that anything very terrible will happen before we make the Jump point, do you? And she does have Lonan and Dil Nem as backup."

She gave him a slight smile. "Not to mention myself."

"Indeed." He closed his eyes, trying to recall the schedule, but it eluded him. Such forgetfulness was new since . . . well, and Lina had said that he might expect such lapses, had she not? He had taken wounds. In fact, he had nearly died. There were consequences to such adventures, such as low energy and a vulnerability to nightmares. He would recover, in time; his body would heal, his memory would rebound, the nightmares would fade, his gift would reassert itself as strong, or stronger, than ever.

All this, Lina promised, though she failed of committing to *when*. Pressed, she had obliged him with *vot'itzen*—in Low Liaden, as one might speak to a child—which meant *in good time*.

So, in the midst of acquiring new bad habits, he must exert himself to acquire a new, good habit.

Patience.

Priscilla bent, kissed his forehead, and straightened to glance about the office.

"May I give you a glass of wine?"

"Thank you," he said. "Wine would be welcome."

She moved across the room, and he stood, trying to shake himself into order or, at the very least, divest himself of the clinging strands of the dream.

The memory.

The shame.

"Here you are."

She offered him a glass of the red, and when he had taken it in hand, she raised her glass in salute.

"To your good health."

It was apt, he thought; certainly he would accept all and any assistance toward good health. He raised his glass a deal less jauntily.

"To the good health of all," he said.

They drank. Priscilla curled into a corner of the couch, and he sat beside her.

"How fares Padi?" he asked.

He was to have met Priscilla at the half-shift, for a glass of wine and a shared sleep period. Upon his arrival in the master trader's office, fresh from the war bridge, and a piloting sim, he'd found that Priscilla had left a message—she was stopping to visit Padi in sickbay, and would be a few minutes behind him, whereupon he had sat down in his chair and fallen asleep.

In truth, he would have liked to visit Padi—his child, his apprentice in trade, nascent wizard and none too happy with that newly realized state of her being. The Healers presiding over his case had declared it prudent that he and Padi not meet until she was released from quarantine. Padi therefore resided under Lina's care, in sickbay, another situation he was certain met with less than her full approval.

Still, it had been agreed among the ship's Healers— Lina, Priscilla, and himself—that it was best, given the sudden and forceful onset of Padi's gifts, and her first use of those gifts—that she remain under observation for three ship-days. It was an arbitrary number, as even the assembled Healers acknowledged, while also acknowledging that three days was very likely the limit of what Padi's patience would bear.

"Padi is testy, but well," Priscilla said in answer to his question, "and still terribly bright. She's mastered the basic control level, and has informed Lina that acquiring her trader's ring remains her first and most important life goal. Any instruction touching upon her newly manifest gifts must take second place."

"That," said Shan, "is what got her into trouble in the first place."

Priscilla looked at him blandly. "She promises, most faithfully, that she will not wall off her gifts a second time."

"Excellent. Learning has taken place."

Priscilla laughed, and raised her glass. They drank again, sharing a wry smile.

"On your topic," Priscilla said, "Padi does...strongly question the wisdom of severing her link to you."

"Surely Lina explained that she cannot nourish two forever."

"It's Padi's feeling that she has too much for one, *far* too much for her needs, and that she would willingly give all she has to you."

"A filial child," he said, bland in his turn. "I had hoped to show her the benefits of her gifts. She sees them only as a hindrance to her heart's desire."

He paused, staring for a moment into his wine.

"How if Lina were to confide that Healers are forever entangled with those they Heal? Padi cannot, in a word, be rid of me now."

Priscilla sipped consideringly.

"Padi might find the information interesting, though immaterial to her case."

"Likely correct," Shan said with a sigh.

They were quiet then, each occupied with their own thoughts. Shan's stayed with his daughter. Padi was going to require a skillful hand in her training. Coming into so much power after hiding from herself for so long, and now to be so grudging in its acceptance...

Lina was not inept. Priscilla was herself a Witch of Sintia—a lapsed Witch of Sintia, he corrected himself. She had power, training, and control within the spectrums available to Liaden *dramliz*, though Priscilla's gifts, so she believed, came to her from an all-knowing and compassionate Goddess. She had received rigorous training as a novice and was in her turn a meticulous teacher.

If it came to that, *he* was accounted a good teacher, though he might not be quite so effective while recovering from his near murder.

It was possible—perhaps even likely—he thought, without enthusiasm, that Padi was going to require the considerable resources of a full Healer Hall for Sorting.

And if she was found to be a *dramliza*, the Hall would train her for a life-work that did not include trade.

"Are there any full *dramliza* who are also traders?" Priscilla asked.

So their thoughts had been running in tandem, after all. Shan moved his shoulders.

"If there are, I have never heard of them. Which argues that they are very good at concealing their natures." He sighed, rueful. "And I have just made Padi's point for her."

"Yes." Priscilla paused, and put a gentle hand on his knee. "Matters will clarify, once we identify her spectrum. We only need to wait until her gift settles and we can See her properly."

He nodded, stared blankly at the glass in his hand before lifting it to finish the last of the wine.

"Shan, you should rest."

Yes, he admitted to himself; he *should* rest. But he was beginning to distrust sleep, knowing what awaited him there.

Before he had spent his talent dry in a desperate bid to Heal a dire enemy of his House, he might have taken himself to Healspace and woven a self-Heal, or put himself into a Healing sleep. Now, even those small things were beyond him, and his Sight—which he had depended upon since he had come halfling as a Healer—was depleted to the point of blindness.

Lina had also promised that these wounds would heal, *vot'itzen*. In the meanwhile, he bid fair to being useless—

No, he thought, catching himself up sternly. That was rankest self-pity. He was a pilot of Korval; he was a master of trade. He was the lifemate of Priscilla Delacroix y Mendoza. These were not trivialities. He was more—he was *other* than his gifts, though that argument again came perilously close to Padi's chosen line of rebellion.

Padi—in her ignorance, new-come to her powers, Seeing with Healer's eyes, as direct in her solving as any other born under Clan Korval's Tree-and-Dragon— had sought to Heal him of psychic exhaustion by the simple expedient of producing a link—say, rather, a conduit—between them, and feeding him her power. An intuitive act, so all three of the more experienced Healers had agreed—intuitive and dangerous, for both donor and recipient.

Never less than thorough in her undertakings, Padi had formed a sturdy, and more importantly, a *strong* connection. It had taken both Lina and Priscilla, working carefully, hours to dismantle it, after they had separated Padi's energies from his. Shan *thought* Padi had not actively worked against the Healers, though she certainly had not tried to assist them.

"I can," Priscilla said softly, "give you a dreamless rest."

He looked at her, curled into the corner of the couch, empty glass held loosely between long fingers. She was tired, even to non-Healer eyes, and his first thought was to decline her offer.

While dragons—most especially Korval Dragons— wished to protect those under their wing, they did not come easily to being protected. He knew that, though he was not accustomed to thinking himself so *very* much a Dragon.

Still, he took a deep breath, and thought a second time.

There were facts, to wit: He had been wounded, physically. Rest was necessary to recuperation. He was the clan's master trader and would soon be needed at his post, in good health and clear mind. Therefore...

He inclined his head.

"I accept the gift."

"Thank you," she said softly.

She put her glass, and his, on the table next to the couch. Then, she rose, and held a hand down to him. He took it, and tried not to be ashamed, that he needed her support to rise.

A few minutes later, they were together in their bed, she curled around him, so comfortable and usual that he was already drowsing, soothed by her warmth and her nearness. Sighing, he drifted toward sleep.

There came the splash of rain against his face; he tensed toward waking—

And relaxed, utterly, into deep and dreamless sleep.

• • • ✻ • • •

Shan went to sleep eagerly, like a starving man reaching for a crust of bread. Priscilla, however, lay awake, holding him against her, looking at him—at the unique tapestry of his soul—and thinking dire thoughts.

He had taken—no! he had *inflicted* horrific damage upon himself. She could see the half-healed lacerations, the bruising, the tears, where he had slashed through threads, bindings, the very fabric of his soul, in his frenzy to be certain that, should he be trapped and subverted, the enemy would take no other captives through him.

It was very true that a Healer formed a bond—became entangled—with every soul they Healed. There were a hundred and more such threads woven into the tapestry of Shan, each glowing with energies peculiar to itself, enriching, and enriched by, the mutual bond.

She could see the link that they shared—broad; weighted with love, trust, and their years together, as partners and lovers. It blazed bright, even now, after he had severed it in his need to keep her safe. Nothing could truly sever that link, which he must have known. But, there, he had been playing against time. If he had lost his gamble with death, it would not have mattered that the severing could only be temporary; that the link would reestablish itself stronger than ever before.

Priscilla sighed and curled closer to him in body, as she gazed more nearly upon his soul.

She could see the link he shared with Padi; and all the others of his kin, brighter than the threads of those he had Healed, if not so bright as the lifemate bond.

There was a new thread.

In fact, there were two—more slender than the

kin-links, yet more intimate; two black threads woven tightly into the endlessly fascinating tapestry that was Shan. Two threads that together had a name.

Tarona Rusk.

A powerful *dramliza*, Tarona Rusk, and a woman of great and abiding evil, who had it as her life's object to destroy Clan Korval.

A woman to whom Priscilla was indebted, for having snatched Shan back from the edge of his death.

After he had Healed *Tarona* of what may have been her...delusion. Priscilla doubted it was within even Shan's scope to Heal evil.

And now, these two threads, these two *very strong* threads, that linked her lifemate and her love to a woman lost in wickedness.

She thought, not for the first time, that she should excise the things, but upon looking closely, she conceded, as she had done before, that she could not be certain she would not harm Shan in the process.

It was, she thought, disquieting, even worrying. But she could not solve it tonight. Indeed, she could not—ought not—solve it herself. Shan kept his own soul, as she kept hers. If, when he was fully returned to himself, he wished to excise those threads, she would gladly give him what assistance he asked.

That settled once more, Priscilla sighed, closed her Inner Eyes, and breathed herself into sleep.

II

PADI HAD ASKED LINA IF SHE MIGHT RETURN TO HER OWN quarters. She had asked very politely, and without any ill temper.

Of course, demonstrating a sweet and reasonable temper was not at all the same as moderating one's so-called *gift*, but it did show good intent, especially as it was *control* which Lina was at such pains to teach her.

Despite it being a skill Padi needed to perfect quickly, for the safety of ship and crew, Lina was not happy to be teaching her control. Even Padi could see that. It had, so she thought, to do with Padi having confined her gift for so very long. Lina feared the damage that might have been done, and did not care to do more. So, Lina was cautious, and conflicted, and if they had been engaged in trade, Padi flattered herself that she could have used that to her own advantage.

Sadly, she and Lina were not at trade. Lina was a Healer, and it was her current task to give Padi a grounding in basic *dramliz* practice.

Padi had applied herself to her lessons. The result, so she was told, was a steady, implacable...*brightness*, which she understood was much to be preferred over the random sparking and flickering which had been the shape of her gift when it had first manifested. Lina had even said that she was managing nicely.

Which was when Padi had asked if she might be allowed to return to her own cabin, and to sleep in her own bed...

And, to say truth, Lina had considered the request, though she had at last denied it.

"I regret," she had said gently. "Given the manner in which your gift manifested at last, it is to the ship's best benefit that we proceed conservatively."

The manner in which her gift manifested—that meant that Padi had not only destroyed her beautiful unbreakable bowl, but flying shards from its destruction had killed two people.

Even worse, all that had happened while the bowl was in her cabin on the *Passage*, and Padi herself, and her intended assassins, had been on the planet surface.

That had been, as even Padi understood, something *quite* out of the ordinary. Grudgingly, she admitted that Lina was right to be conservative—even *very* conservative. She foresaw a lengthy course in the *dramliz* arts in her future, to which she must apply herself diligently if she ever had any hope of returning to her proper work as a trader.

That thought had fretted her, too, though she had been careful not to allow Lina to suspect, as they said their dream-wells.

Father—the *Passage*'s master trader . . . Father had been hurt—severely hurt—by a *dramliza*—by an *enemy dramliza*, if one could find a proper way to think of such a thing. But there, the Department of the Interior, who had taken Korval for its enemy, and whose operatives were not *uniformly* stupid, though that was hard to recall—the Department of the Interior had subverted to their cause not only pilots or Scouts, like Uncle Val Con; or anyone else they felt might be useful to them, but they had *stolen dramliz* and that . . . was something Padi didn't want to think about . . . much . . . just yet.

In any wise, Father had been wounded; he was the master trader, she was his apprentice; he not only required her assistance, it was her duty to give it. Certainly, *that* was plain to the dullest of intelligences—and no one could count Lina or Priscilla dull. They were intelligent, resourceful, and accomplished persons, and yet—

And yet—here she was, in sickbay, taking lessons to control a gift she did not want, instead of supporting the master trader and the ship.

Padi sighed, and folded back the blankets on her bed.

Priscilla—Father's lifemate and a powerful *dramliza* in her own right—Priscilla had come to see her, just as Lina was leaving for her rest period.

At Padi's invitation, she had taken the chair. Padi perched on the edge of the bed. Father, Priscilla said, was as well as possible. Not only had he been physically wounded, but he had spent far too much of his own energy Healing—Healing!—the DOI's *dramliza*. Priscilla had read her outrage and commented that it had been a complicated situation, but after all, the DOI's *dramliza* had behaved with honor, and had Healed Father of the wounds which would certainly have killed him, so Balance was served, leaving only consequences to be dealt with.

Padi did not offer her opinion of consequences, but inclined her head so that Priscilla went on.

It would be some time—how much time, neither she nor Lina could foretell—before Father regained the full use of his gifts. He was likely to regain his physical strength very quickly, Priscilla said, thanks to the intervention of the DOI's *dramliza*. He had taken one session in the autodoc, to stabilize him, with another session scheduled in twenty-four hours. If that second session failed to bring him fully up to his template, other therapies would be employed, in consultation with Keriana, their chief med tech.

That was all very well, Padi thought. Of course Priscilla would take care of Father, that was beyond questioning. It was only that *she*, Padi, could have— would have!—*returned* his gift completely, but Lina and Priscilla had broken the link she'd made.

She *quite* understood that it wasn't the prettiest or the best-crafted link; she had no training in such things. But she had *so much* energy, and she didn't want *any* of it. And Father—Father was a Healer; his talent was like breath to him; he *cared* about it—a sense that was as useful and as natural to him as his eyes—whereas her talent was—an intruder; at best an unwelcome guest.

"We understand," Priscilla murmured just then, as if she had read Padi's thoughts—which was not impossible. "You wanted to help. Your instincts do you honor. Unfortunately, neither Lina nor I could properly See what you had done or how the construct was made, or could understand how to regulate the flow. It was—in our opinions—all too possible that you would deplete yourself as Shan had depleted himself, giving us the same problem to solve, in unknown terrain. Lina and I *know* what Shan's gift *is*, what it looks like, its texture; its weight. You—we haven't even Seen your full pattern yet; you're so *very* bright. We might have hurt you—hurt you badly—if we were to attempt a Healing."

"You decided to be *conservative*," Padi said, not meaning it, perhaps, to sound *quite* that sour. Priscilla gave her a wry smile.

"I'm afraid so, yes."

"Lina says that I'm to stay here, because that's conservative."

"That was not Lina's decision alone," Priscilla told her. "We all three talked about it, and decided that a day or two of isolation would best serve the ship, the crew, the Healers—"

She smiled again.

"*And* you."

"Me," Padi repeated, thinking of her usual schedule, her studies, the reading—

"Yes, *you*," Priscilla said. "A few days to allow your gift to—settle—will help *you* settle. There's always a period of dislocation after a talent arrives—even a small and well-behaved talent."

Padi grinned, half unwilling.

"And I have *not* got a small and well-behaved talent."

"No," Priscilla admitted, and then, very Father-like, really, "though that can hardly surprise anyone."

"Now," she said briskly. "The master trader is concerned that you'll fall behind in your studies, which he won't allow. Tomorrow, you will resume your work—he has, I believe, sent a reading list to your screen. While he expects that you will complete the list, he cautions that you must not stint the exercises Lina brings to you."

Padi caught her breath.

A reading list. She had scarcely looked for such a gift! She inclined her head.

"I swear that Lina's lessons will come first," she said earnestly. Perhaps *too* earnestly.

In any case, Priscilla laughed and rose, bade her dream well—and left the cubicle.

So, that was that. Priscilla was gone, and Lina was sleeping in the next cubicle—and that was an inconvenience for Lina, too, who had her own quarters and bed-friends, which she would surely prefer to a cubicle in sickbay, while she kept close watch over a surly newborn *dramliza*.

Padi sighed and stretched out on the cot. The lights dimmed obligingly, and the music she'd chosen from the library wafted softly on the cooling air. She pulled the blanket up over her shoulder, tried to settle her head on the pillow—and sat bolt upright, staring at the man in the dark, much-patched cloak and breeches, who was leaning very much at his ease against the wall, moving a worn red gaming token over the back of his hand.

Her eye was drawn, and for a long moment, she could not look away.

Father played this game, with a marker very like. Across the back of his right hand, the red token would walk until it reached the end of its path, whereupon it would—vanish, only to appear again, walking along the back of the left hand.

The token vanished. Padi drew a breath and looked up into the stranger's face—

But he was *not* a stranger, or not entirely so. No matter his hair was black, and long enough to braid, instead of crisp and white; nor that his eyes were black, rather than silver blue; and his clothing tattered, when Father was never anything but impeccably groomed—the face, the stance, the way the token marched across his hand—one received the impression that the man before her *could have been* Father in only slightly different circumstances, and besides—

She had seen him before.

"You," she said quietly, aware of Lina in the next

cubicle, and the monitors, which would pick up her voice and also supply news of a third person in the unit.

"You never told me your name."

He looked to her, one eyebrow raised, a shade more sardonic than Father might be, as if, for this one, there had been too much strife, and too little food, too often in his life, which hardships had worn away a layer of gentleness, exposing a lean edginess.

"There was scarcely time for introductions," he said now, and his voice was precisely Father's, smooth and beautiful, like being wrapt in velvet silk.

"There's time now," she pointed out, when he said nothing further.

"Agreed. I am called Lute. What is your name?"

She considered him.

"I think you must know my name," she said carefully.

"Ah, do you? Have they taught you yet that names are to conjure by?"

Padi frowned. "That may be the case with the . . . tradition in which Priscilla came to terms with her gifts. Liaden *dramliz* receive their gifts from a different source."

There was an arrested pause.

"A different *source*," Lute mused, his eyes on the game token, which walked to the edge of his hand, tumbled off—and vanished. *Almost,* Padi saw where it went—felt, perhaps, a tiny flash of power as it displaced itself.

"That is an interesting question of philosophy, child. Do you argue that the source of talent, of energy, of magic . . . limits itself to the rules of culture?"

Padi bit her lip.

"I would argue that the *dramliza* shapes the power,

according to her character and her need," she said slowly. "You'll understand that I am ... unschooled. But the lessons I have thus far received suggest that there is no single rule set."

Lute nodded gravely. "There is something in what you say."

Padi sighed. "I did *say* I was unschooled."

He bowed his head.

"I was fairly warned. Heed me though, child, you are already past pretty games of philosophy. Yours was a wakening heard 'round infinity. You shattered the meditations of saints, brought senior practitioners to their knees, and felled novices like so many skittles. Possibly, you woke the dead. Surely, the Living Names, and others of their sort, heard you. We are all fortunate that the Iloheen failed the crossing to this universe, else that world would have been engulfed and every soul living there unmade."

She stared at him, stomach suddenly cramped, and fingers icy. She had endangered *a world*? Simply by doing what all of her elders assured her was the correct and responsible thing to have done?

"The Iloheen?" she whispered. "Who are they?"

He shook his head.

"No one who will vex you here, and I am a brute to bring that threat before you." He extended a long, supple hand. "Shall I take it away?"

"No." She took a deep breath. "Thank you. I think I'd better remember everything I can."

"Wise, as well as bold. To return to the point—you have given the entire waking universe notice of your power. Will you give them your true-name as well, or will you invest in another, as your shield and armor?"

"As I understand it, I erred greatly in hiding myself away," she said slowly. "If the . . . whole universe has already heard me, then I am identified, am I not?"

"You erred in hiding yourself from yourself," Lute said sternly. "*That* is never wise. Misdirecting an enemy is merely self-defense."

He tipped his head. "What *is* your name, child?"

She blinked at him thoughtfully. "Are you an enemy?"

"Would your father have sent an enemy to protect you in his absence, even in extremity?"

"He might have," Padi said seriously. "If he felt you would adhere to the terms."

Lute laughed.

"True enough. I strive not to be an enemy, and I take the task which was laid upon me seriously—to protect Shan yos'Galan's daughter."

He had, Padi admitted, helped her when she had been under attack by agents of the DOI. And Father had said he had asked him to go to her and do what he could to protect her.

She looked up to find him watching her out of night-black eyes.

"My name is Padi yos'Galan."

"Thank you," he said solemnly. "Will you allow me to give you a gift? I swear on my name that it will be entirely benign."

"What is my benefit?" she asked, trader-wise.

"You will sleep as sound and safe tonight as I may arrange, which will, in turn, allow me to pursue the task your father laid upon me." He put his hand over his heart and bowed slightly. "Heart's ease is *my* benefit."

"Surely, he can't have meant for you to guard me—forever," Padi objected.

"Very possibly he did not, but we cannot be completely certain. You will ask him as soon as may be, and we will make adjustments."

Padi weighed her ignorance, the past actions of this man, and the fact that Father had trusted him.

"Done," she said.

"Excellent. Lie down, please, close your eyes, and take three deep breaths."

She curled back under the blanket, closed her eyes, and opened them again to find him leaning close.

"Why hasn't Lina come in to find why you are here?" she asked.

He smiled slightly.

"Because I'm not here, of course. Close your eyes."

That was easy to do, when her lids were so heavy. Padi sighed, took a breath; another—

And slipped over into sleep.

Tarona Rusk
Langlast Departure

· · · · · · · · · · · · · · · · · ·

THE PILOT MET HER WITH WEAPON DRAWN, DESPITE SHE had given the correct codes. This comforted her, even as she reached into his heart and made him love her.

He lowered the weapon.

"The others?" he asked.

"Dead or taken," she replied. "We lift now."

"Yes, Section Head," he murmured, sealing the weapon into its holster. "Bound for?"

"Auxiliary Services."

Dizziness assailed her, unexpected and shocking. She put a hand out to brace herself against the wall and drew a steadying breath. It would not do for the pilot to see her weak.

"I will be in my cabin," she said. "Disturb me for nothing."

"No, Section Head," he agreed. He bowed and turned toward the piloting chamber.

She sighed shakily and went down the short corridor to her quarters.

With the door locked behind her, she allowed herself weakness, crumpling to the bunk and closing her eyes.

She was, she noted, shivering, faint, low of energy.

Instinctively, she reached inward, toward the web of lives bound to her—reached, even as she recalled her current estate, and heard Shan yos'Galan's voice, chiding her gently.

Do not drain yourself. You have nothing but your own resources to draw upon now.

She sighed. Habit was a cruel mistress. In fact, she *had* nothing to sustain her now, save her own energies. Those whose lives had supported her were no longer hers to draw upon.

She was, as it had been said in the vernacular of her youth . . . *on her own.*

Healed.

Somewhat weakly, she laughed.

Healed. Behold! She was herself again!

Her laughter died.

No. Of all the things her Healing might have brought her, it had not brought her that. She would never again be the proud daughter of a wealthy artisan house, sought after and spoilt. They had been half-clan, of course, but what did that matter on a mostly Terran world?

Nor would she again be the bitter halfling, pride ground into surliness, having been sent to the Healers of Solcintra to be trained—and discovering what it meant to be half-clan on *Liad.*

Oh, she had been ripe for plucking, all thanks to the Healers and the High Houses. And the Department had not been slow to extend its hand in flattery, all admiration of her talents, which were so far superior to those who pretended to be her betters and worthy to teach her. *She*, said the Department, had been made for great things.

Which the Department would gladly help her achieve.

Fool, she thought at her younger self—and laughed again, in contempt.

Why, indeed, *yes*—her Healing was true; and she was a fool once more.

"We lift on three, Section Head," the pilot said over the all-ship. "One . . ."

She stretched, grasped the webbing, and pulled it tight.

"Two . . ."

She closed her eyes, and deliberately relaxed into the bunk.

"Three."

Acceleration. She put it from her mind, and for the first time since her Healing, she opened her Inner Eyes, and looked . . . within.

For a moment, she forgot to breathe, time and space suspended while she beheld herself, Healed.

She had become accustomed to the bloated state of her core: overfull with the multitude of links of those who nourished her and maintained her powers. The last time she had regarded herself, those sustaining links, through which she controlled dozens, had been bundled, twisted, and knotted together into a thick cable.

Stretched now before her eyes was a threadbare and ashy tapestry, loosely woven with a handful of irregular threads. Where the nourishing cable had melded with her very core . . . there was a clean cut, and a few frazzled threads blowing, as if in a breeze.

She remembered at last to breathe, and forced herself to focus.

Little Healer, she had called him, in her arrogance. In her pride.

She sighed, considering again the state of her self. Credit to craft, she thought, was certainly due.

It could not be denied: The Little Healer had done good work. He had been precise and methodical despite the fact that he had himself been wounded near to death. Focusing, she saw that he had extended himself still further, taking care to cushion the shock of separation for the . . . less robust of her connections. He had been careful, he had been gentle; he had used no more force than what had been required.

More, he had *taken the time* to be careful, when time had been desperately short; extended himself to ease the pain of others, when he had been suffering; wielding necessity like a surgeon's knife, terrifying in his virtue.

Tarona Rusk sighed.

Shan yos'Galan was not a monster. In truth, she would rather have faced a monster, being one herself, and more likely would have prevailed in such an encounter of equals. However, that door had closed. The Little Healer had bested her.

He had Healed her.

Healed *her.*

She focused, brushing away ashy remnants with a careful thought, and searched through the uneven, childlike stitches until she found it: a new thread, pretty and silver-blue, as supple and as strong as spider silk. Unassuming, it wove closely through the pattern of her being, radiating a faint air of good will.

Tarona Rusk shivered.

There was nothing more true in the universe than that Healer and Healed were entangled. It was a simple matter of physics. She and Shan yos'Galan were linked, irrevocably—*twice*, for at the end of it, he *would have* died—and she, newly Healed and giddy with freedom . . . she had exerted herself to preserve him.

Her Inner Eyes found the second link, somewhat less substantial than the first. When she placed her regard upon it—it *rang*, a single pure note that stopped her breath in her throat.

Carefully, she withdrew her focus, and simply . . . rested in the blighted landscape.

Those links, she thought. They would require analysis.

But not . . . quite . . . yet. She had other business before.

Despite his gentleness and his care, she had taken wounds from her Healing. The most paltry of wounds, in comparison to those she had inflicted on him, and yet, *any* wound weakened.

She had plans; she could not afford weakness, and she would not fail.

Her first concern, therefore, must be to Heal herself. She had suffered multiple amputations—that was not trivial. She must accommodate herself to her new isolation, and ensure that she was stable in her mind.

After, she would analyze those links which bound them to each other—Healed and Healer.

And she would make her plans . . .

. . . for revenge.

It was not passion which ruled her, but a cold determination to destroy as much of the Department of the Interior as she was able, before she was stopped—for stopped, she would surely be. First, she would find and destroy those who had recruited, shattered, and re-formed her into their own particular monster.

Worthy targets all, the loss of which would cause serious damage to the Department and to the Plan.

As yet, no one within the Department suspected this. She had lost her team—to violence and to Scouts—but to outward observation, she had escaped uncompromised. Thus, she would return to her office, to the section of which she was head, holding her keys, her codes, and her contacts. And the devastation she intended to sow would be ... everything that was necessary.

In her, the Little Healer had loosed a potent weapon against the enemy of his clan. She wondered if he had known—and immediately realized that, *of course*, he had known. Shan yos'Galan was of Clan Korval, an enemy more than worthy of the Department of the Interior. Pity had not motivated his actions, no more than his own survival. He had forged a knife in the fires of their combined energies; and when it was fit for his hand, he had thrown it ...

... Directly at the Department's heart.

Civilization

· · · · · · · · · · ·

THE FIRST DUTY OF THIS DAY, AS EVERY DAY, WAS TO SPEAK with the Oracle. As every morning, Bentamin brought her a cup of tea, carried in his own hand. A courtesy, for there was a fully stocked kitchen in her apartment, and she wanted for no tea, common or exotic.

In addition to being well-appointed and staffed, the Oracle's apartment, on the top floor of the Wardian, was the most secure in all of The Redlands. Not that the Oracle was a prisoner—no one would say so. Only, she needed to be watched over; and Civilization needed to be...shielded from her gifts.

Historically, Oracles and Civilization mixed badly. Not for the first time, Bentamin regretted that this particular talent had manifested in their population. It hadn't been among those cataloged talents that had seen them banished from the homeworld, long years ago.

But there, many talents that existed now had not been cataloged, or even thought of then. Things, and people, changed, after all.

This morning, with the tea, he also carried flowers,

Jasy having produced something very much out of the common way.

He thought they might please his Aunt Asta.

The head of housekeeping let him in, with a smile and a bow.

"She's in the alcove, sir."

Bentamin inclined his head.

"Thank you," he said, and moved through the familiar rooms to the alcove, where the Oracle sat at a small table, surrounded on three sides by windows overlooking the civilization which needed to be protected from her as much as she needed to be protected from it.

When she had first taken up her duty as Oracle, she had used to meet him in other rooms—the parlor, the library, the kitchen. Now, though, it was the alcove always. Staff reported that she spent most of her days at this table, gazing down at the city below.

"Good morning, Asta," Bentamin said, pausing by the side of the table. "I trust I find you well?"

"As well as ever I am," she said, turning her head to smile at him. "Oh! Flowers. Now, whose?"

"Jasy," he said, putting the little bouquet of pale blooms into her hand. "He's coming along well, I think."

"Jasy," she repeated, running light fingers over the flowers. They purred slightly and followed her touch. "Sarrell's?"

"His youngest."

"Well, he is a very talented boy! Tell him that his Aunt Asta would like him to visit her someday."

"I will," he said, and thought that he actually might. Jasy was a kind boy who knew what was owed to kin. And while he was inarguably talented, he also had a core of cold iron which wouldn't likely be influenced by his aunt's—his grand-aunt's—energies.

He put the teacup on the table by her hand and took the seat across from her, retrieving his own cup from the kitchen counter in his apartment, one floor down, where he'd left it.

He sipped, deliberately relaxing into the chair. Asta had returned to gazing out the window, one hand absently stroking her flowers.

"Do you have anything to tell me this morning?" he asked eventually.

Asta sighed.

"The dark has risen," she said, turning away from the windows with visible reluctance. "The universe resides in its direst hour, though so few of us can know it."

Bentamin sighed to himself.

The universe, according to Aunt Asta, had been increasingly at risk from the darkness for some numbers of years. Asta's uncle, the previous Oracle, had spoken of the danger from time to time during Bentamin's mother's tenure as Warden. Over the last six years, however, Asta had grown increasingly more agitated on the topic, insisting that the darkness would eat them all—and now, it appeared that the universe had entered its inevitable moment of trial. It saddened him that Aunt Asta clung to this—delusion, as he must suppose it to be. Oracles were not, after all, immune to afflictions of reason—in fact, they were rather more susceptible, Seeing as they did down multiple lines of possibility.

Bentamin was no Oracle. He was, as his mother, the Warden before him, had been, only a very strong multi-talent. All the Wardens were so, and thus he was, very slightly, in comparison to Aunt Asta, Foresighted.

He had Looked, reasoning that so large an event as the end of the universe must be visible even to his limited Vision. He had Looked, more than once, and gained nothing for his Looking but several dreadful headaches.

That being so, the obvious conclusion was that Aunt Asta, Oracle to the Civilized, had acquired a delusion. These things happened. It was the Warden's part to do all and everything to ensure the Oracle's health, comfort, and peace of mind, until it became the Warden's duty to remove the Oracle from their post.

In service of preserving the Oracle's peace of mind, he inclined his head gravely and asked the approved follow-up question.

"How may the universe prevail in this, its hour of trial?"

"A hero must arise," she replied, as she always did, "and do what is needful."

Yes, well. Heroes, in Bentamin's experience, were not precisely thick on the ground. He counted that a blessing, heroes mixing less well with Civilization than even Oracles.

Still, the third question, too, had to be asked.

"Will this hero arise from among us?"

"Us?" Asta was frowning down at the busy streets; she extended a hand to her teacup, picking it up without even glancing aside.

"From among the populations of The Redlands," he clarified, and saw her brows draw closer.

"Oh. I do not See the hero, only a gleam of steel and gold among The Ribbons. Is this a hero, or merely the possibility of a hero? I do not know."

The same answer, always ambiguous, that half

persuaded Bentamin that ... perhaps this struggle between the dark universe and their own might, after all, have some basis in ... fact. Would not delusion, insisting that a hero arise, provide that hero to the deluded Sight?

This was an uncomfortable thought. If this were not delusion and the hero was to stand up from among themselves—Civilized or Haosa—it would then fall to the Warden to take the hero in hand once they had done what was needful, and sequester them, as the Oracle was sequestered.

For the good of Civilization.

Best for the hero, Bentamin thought, that they bought the continuation of the universe with their life.

He sipped his tea to the dregs, banished the cup to his kitchen counter, and considered the side of Asta's face. She was not, he thought, seeing the streets below, but some inner landscape. That likely meant she had something more to tell him this morning, and his mandated hour was nearly gone. If she did not speak soon, he would be constrained to ask, risky though that was.

He cleared his throat. Asta turned her head to look—*toward* him, her face pleasant and her eyes unfocused.

"Great Ones will arrive among us," she said matter-of-factly. "They desire of us a service."

He frowned.

"Great Ones," he repeated. "*Dramliz*?"

Before the Dust had claimed its long dance with The Redlands, *dramliz* had arrived, three times, to study the progress of their small-kin, the Least Talents, in the strange environment into which they had been introduced. Coincidentally, a new talent had arisen soon after the first such visit of *dramliz*, that inflicted a growing uneasiness in those who were not welcome—and the *dramliz* did not stay long among their cousins in exile.

To dignify *dramliz* as *great*, however—Bentamin did not think Aunt Asta would do so, even in irony.

"Not *dramliz*." Asta interrupted his thoughts. "Greater than *dramliz*."

That, he decided, was...unsettling. Had the *dramliz* evolved another level of talent, to which *they* stood as small-kin? Talents *did* evolve; new talents *did* arise, as they knew from their own experience. But, surely, any such...mega-*dramliz*—ah. No. The behemoth did not *ask* the mouse, but ordered. A service desired could easily be a service compelled.

He sat forward in his chair.

"The Reavers, they are not returning?"

One could scarcely call the Reavers *great*—at least not the Reavers they had seen before they had succumbed to their mysterious illness. The Reavers had been dangerous. But, in fairness, no more dangerous than their very own Haosa, in whom the Reavers had met their match.

But how if those sad, vanquished Reavers had been only small talents, in the context of their own lives? What if, lacking reports, with scheduled check-ins missed—what should the upper ranks do, but mobilize and come looking for their oathsworn?

The Haosa were formidable. Further, they had learned from the Reavers, or they were not the Haosa he knew them to be. Bentamin had no doubt that they had absorbed numerous new concepts, and were even now *playing* with them, as his cousin Tekelia styled it, thereby learning even more.

"The Reavers have been mown down, severed from their source. We will not see *their* like again." There was a certain amount of savage satisfaction there, appropriate to an Oracle sitting in defense of Civilization.

Though there did remain the question of the source, of which the Oracle seemed dismissive. And it was not, Bentamin told himself, the Oracle to whom that line of questioning ought to be addressed, but to the Haosa. He would make it a point to do that. Soon.

In the meanwhile...

"Also," Asta said, interrupting these thoughts, "another comes, in the train of the Great Ones, bringing static and disruption. She may be a tool to your hand, Bentamin. Or you may be a tool to hers."

That was disturbing, too, in its way. He did not care to use others as tools, though he had done so in the past and doubtless would do so again in future. He liked being a tool set to another's purpose even less. Still, that was of much less import than this other thing. Clearly, Asta had gone past his topic, and one disliked to insist... indeed, one knew very well what was likely to come from insisting. Yet, necessity was, and duty demanded.

"These Great Ones," he said lightly, carefully. "What service will they beg of us?"

Asta laughed, picked up her bouquet, and raised it above her head. The flowers struggled briefly—and fell still.

"See the Great Ones beg!" Asta cried, as if addressing the gods themselves. "Oh, yes. Very fine. Very fine they are, indeed, in their supplications!"

She lowered the flowers, and waved them at him like a wand.

"Go away, Bentamin. I'm tired of you."

Well, and he had known how it would be now, hadn't he?

He rose and bowed to her honor.

"Good-day to you, Aunt. I will carry your message to Jasy."

She said nothing, having turned again to the window.

He waited a polite minute, then went away, back to the constraints of Civilization.

Dutiful Passage
Approaching Jump

· · · · · · · · · · · · · · · · · ·

SHAN CONSIDERED HIS DESK WITH SOME TREPIDATION.

What with the travesty at Langlast, he had fallen behind in his correspondence. That would have to be dealt with first. Trade existed in a webwork of relationships; relationships were formed and sustained by communication.

He was particularly anxious to know if Trader Janifer Carresens-Denobli had replied to his "return thoughts" for a mutual trade route, partaking equally of routes developed by the Syndicate and Tree-and-Dragon. Such a venture would be difficult. Perhaps even dangerous. Certainly, it would be exciting—and very possibly profitable.

The Looper Families and the Carresens Syndicate were old in trade. Their routes and Korval's had rarely brushed—before. Now, with Korval's master trader flailing like an inept 'prentice trying to design his first three-stop subroute—now, with Korval's base relocated to Surebleak in the Daiellen Sector—*now* they came much closer to the space and trade lanes the Carresens Syndicate was accustomed to considering their own. It would not have been wonderful, had Korval's initial overture to the Syndicate been rejected. Forcefully.

Instead, that overture had been met with serious thoughtfulness, and a beginning exploration of how a route might be built, serving both Korval's base on Surebleak and Nomi-Oxin-Rood, a Carresens port.

That had been unexpected and wonderful. Shan found himself eager to personally meet and entertain Trader-at-Large Janifer Carresens-Denobli. He could learn much of value from such a contact, and he flattered himself that he might teach, as well.

But for all these rose-colored dreams to become reality, there had to be more correspondence, open and frank, as it had begun.

He took a breath, half-smiling.

"Well, now," he told himself, "that's more the thing. Don't fear your work, Master Trader; anticipate it!"

He poured himself a cup of cold tea, strode over to the desk, sat down, and spun 'round to address the screen.

A finger tap woke it, and he considered the note he had left for himself.

Design a profitable new trade route, Shan.

Well, that hardly seemed difficult. He was, after all, a master trader. Designing profitable routes was what master traders did.

And, he acknowledged, taking a sip of tea, he did need to get on with that task—almost immediately.

But first . . . the mail.

The mail . . . was disappointing.

There was no letter from Trader Carresens-Denobli; the jolt of dismay telling him rather too clearly how much he had been depending on the trader to solve his problems for him.

Worse, there *was* a letter from his foster-son—which was to say Trader Gordon Arbuthnot, junior trader under Trader per'Cadmie on the tradeship *Sevyenti*. It was painfully stilted, which no doubt reflected his correspondent's dismay at being forced to the point of having to write such a letter, either to his master trader or to his foster-father.

Shan accessed the record of Trader Arbuthnot's recent trades, brows drawn into a frown. The frown grew more decided when he brought up the record of Trader per'Cadmie's most recent trades.

Yes, well . . .

Tapping up a screen, Shan wrote to his distressed trader, counseling both patience and an attitude of alert waiting. He also thanked the trader for having provided information so that his master trader could act appropriately.

The last letter in-queue was the worst yet.

It was in fact a memo from Minh Velkesa of Keyrz and Pearholder, Economic Analysts and Advisors to the Trade, one of several such firms utilized by Tree-and-Dragon Trading. Shan had some experience of Minh Velkesa, and respected both his analytical powers and the scope of his information network. Analyst Velkesa did not presume to advise, so much as he placed his information—arranged by fact, rumor, gossip, and fiction—in a mosaic designed to lead the mind to certain conclusions.

Sadly, the analyst never wrote when there was good news, though it might not be anything so dire as *bad* news that motivated him to publish a memo.

"Send it's interesting," Shan murmured, and tapped the screen.

Hugglelans Increasing Pressure on Tree-and-Dragon Markets, read the subject line.

Shan sighed. Hugglelans Galactica was a respected force in trade; had been so for more than a hundred Standards. Their profits were made in base-point trade, and they were known to be conservative in their dealings, which had been the wisdom of the elders.

Lately, however, it seemed that the wisdom of the elders had given way before the ambition of the rising youth. There had been a move to expand opportunity. There had been, one might say, a move to...*manipulate* opportunity.

While there were many advantages to base-point trading—notably, lesser investment, lesser risk, and the support of the community surrounding the base—there were other advantages attached to free-market trade and semi-Loops. The risks were not inconsiderable, and the rewards not always comparable; still, there was only so much growth available in the base-point model. One could scarcely find fault with ambition or with a conservative expansion into a Loop or two.

There is, however, always an element of luck to the business of trade. Unforeseen events occur and rewards loom large for those with the boldness to act.

Korval's recent actions having resulted in its ships and contractors being banned from a half-dozen or more ports had created...an opportunity for the bold. Shan had wondered who might aspire to fill the gap.

According to Analyst Velkesa, Hugglelans had thrown itself into the breach.

The good analyst had, according to his nature,

provided graphs, facts, and copies of documents. He had also supplied rumor, and a commentary.

It would seem that Hugglelans agents had twice signed *in support* of a complaint brought against a Korval contractor incoming to a port where ship, captain, and crew were well known. The original complainants had in each case been one of several names, as Analyst Velkesa put it so delicately, that they had seen previously.

There was, Analyst Velkesa felt compelled to add, no evidence that the Hugglelans' agent was involved with the originating complainant, only that they had seen—and seized—opportunity.

There were also some . . . disquieting threads of intelligence slightly more substantial than rumor—that Hugglelans had been noted targeting the chains that supplied various Korval, and Korval-affiliated, yards, bases, and repair stations. Analyst Velkesa was pursuing those threads and would send a supplemental report.

And that—was the awful whole.

Shan sighed, closed the memo, shut his eyes and reached for a simple balancing exercise. He experienced yet another jolt of dismay when the exercise proved to be . . . rather difficult to accomplish.

That was simply absurd. Balancing exercises were among the first taught to nascent Healers: a necessity, given that nascent Healers tended to arrive at their talents riding a wave of strong emotion.

Truly, the arrival of talent was an unsettling experience. He still recalled the noise and dismay surrounding the manifestation of his own gift, and his gratitude when the House shields closed 'round him, after his father had brought him to Healer Hall.

He recalled also the sharp eyes of Master Healer Iselle, looking at and into him, her voice cool enough to make him shiver.

"Attend me, boy. I am going to show you something. I cannot say how it will appear to you, but appear it will. Attend *closely*, for it will become one of your most-used techniques."

Certainly, it had been his most-used—and very nearly only—technique, during those first days in the Hall, when he was taught how to understand, and accept his gift. In those days, he had learned, as all scarcely budded Healers learned, many patterns, the building blocks of useful tools that were now woven so tightly into the tapestry of himself that they were merely facets of his own skills.

Until just this moment, when he found the most basic tool of all came but slowly to his hand, and only after he had deliberately formed its outlines in his mind.

It did come, however, and he was, with the application of entirely too much effort, able to access it for its intended use.

His feelings of dismay and turmoil faded, leaving him—

Exhausted.

Which was absurd, not to say . . . counterproductive.

No, he thought. Wait.

Shan sat with his eyes closed and simply—breathed. Carefully, he emptied his mind of every thought, every emotion, *every*thing, save the sensation of his breathing; the air flowing in and out of his lungs; the unlabored rise and fall of his chest. He felt a twitch along trained nerves—an instinctive reach for

Healspace. Gently, he denied instinct, breathing it into calmness.

When he felt that he had achieved calmness and clarity, he opened his Inner Eyes—breathing down a start of relief, when he was able to do so—and considered himself.

His pattern was whole, but sadly faded. The lifemate link he shared with Priscilla, and those smaller, gem-like intimate weavings, had reestablished themselves, as well as those natural connections he shared with Padi. Notably, the link he had built between them at Langlastport, before his adventure with Tarona Rusk, was not present, but that had never been meant to be anything but a short-term therapy.

Several new threads drew his eye—iridescent and dark. He stifled an urge to examine them more nearly; simply breathing calmly—in . . . out—accepting their place in the pattern of himself. There was no need to touch them, after all. Logic told him that these were the threads he shared with the woman he had Healed; the woman who had in turn Healed him.

Tarona Rusk.

He sighed. When last seen, Tarona Rusk had been bent on a mission of mayhem against Korval's enemy, the Department of the Interior. He wished her well in all the harm she might do. The Department of the Interior was proving remarkably tenacious and difficult to dismantle, as even the Scouts admitted. Of course, the Scouts, like Korval, must need come at the enemy from the outside. Tarona Rusk had the advantage of being able to strike from within.

He breathed gently, simply sitting with his pattern, allowing thought and emotion to slide past him like so many fishes, unregarded, save to notice how bright and fluid they were.

After some time of this, he stepped back and focused on himself from a distance, as he might consider someone who had proposed themselves for a Healing.

He saw immediately that his proposed client was physically depleted and exhausted on the psychic level. There was a protocol in treating such injuries.

All and any physical damage must be fully healed.

That done, the client must embrace the sovereign cure.

Rest.

Healing required energy—not only from the Healer, but from the one to be Healed. Ultimately, energy came from the physical being. To attempt a psychic Healing before the physical body was in perfect health was to invite a relapse, or perhaps an even greater disaster.

Shan sighed.

His physical injuries had been tended. However, it could not be denied that he was at low strength.

As a Healer, his duty—and his prescription—to his proposed client was—

Rest.

It was not so difficult a prescription.

Shan sighed again, and opened his eyes.

Except when it was given to oneself, of course.

Ruefully, he shook his head, and deliberately sat back in his chair.

Rest, he told himself, and this time the exercise he called to mind was from another of his *melant'is.*

Pilots learned a number of methods for taking quick rests and increasing the benefits of those periods.

Board rest, they were called, as a general category, and it was board rest he called upon now.

Twelve minutes of sleep on the deepest levels, saving only a very small portion of one's mind, akin to a sleeping cat's alert ear, tuned for the rustle of a mouse in the larder—or, in the case of the pilot, a ping from the board.

Nothing occurred to disturb his rest, and precisely twelve minutes after he had closed his eyes, he opened them, feeling refreshed and focused.

He spun his chair around so that he once more faced his screen, sighed gently at the empty mail queue, and went on to the next task.

Design a profitable new trade route, Shan.

Well.

He tapped up his working file and read through his notes. His sparse, not precisely brilliant notes. He had sketched in a few connections with Langlast, should it have shown potential as a hub, or even a transshipping point. He read those notes, and the entries excerpted from TerraTrade's *Encyclopedia of Trade and Product*; the Pilots Guild's port book; and the world log maintained by the Scouts.

Then he sat back again in his chair, frowning slightly.

After a moment, he extended a hand, tapped a key, calling up the ship's schedule, from which he learned that *Dutiful Passage* was en route for Millsap.

He brought his notes forward, verifying what he already knew.

Millsap was not one of the ports he had been considering as possible support for a route including Langlast.

In point of actual fact, Millsap wasn't in his notes at all.

How odd.

There must be a reason that they were bound for Millsap.

Mustn't there?

Perhaps the *Passage* was in need of repairs. He couldn't off-hand recall if Millsap, wherever it specifically was, housed a repair facility. Nor could he recall anyone telling him that they were going aside for repairs.

On the other hand, his memory was at the moment rather uncertain, due to his various recent traumas. It was very likely, therefore, that someone had told him...something...and he had simply forgotten.

Still frowning, he tapped up the port book. The entry came forward—a sparse enough entry, of which he was quickly the master. Millsap was, indeed, a port. It was, in fact, a transshipping hub located between two modest, long-established Loops. According to the Pilots Guild, it was a busy enough place, and, as it served Liaden ships and Terran in almost equal numbers—Millsap rejoiced in the presence of a Healer Hall on-port.

He sat back in his chair, eyes narrowed.

Yes, he remembered now.

Lina had suggested it when they had first returned to the *Passage*, before, he thought, he and Padi had been disentangled.

Things had been rather...muddled at the time, but he recalled her saying very clearly to Priscilla, "Shan has taken a very great deal of damage, and we may do him more by severing this...artifact that Padi has constructed. Padi herself—"

Lina had gone quiet, he remembered that, too, as if perhaps she was shaking her head, or telling over her words with care.

"Padi is beyond me, old friend. We need the resources of a Hall, at least, to see her Sorted."

"I understand," Priscilla had said, which was what Priscilla said when she was not entirely in agreement with a suggestion.

"Let's talk about it after we've separated them, and we've had a chance to see what we have more clearly."

Lina's *yes* had been a sigh, after which she and Priscilla had labored together—labored for some time—he recalled that, too. Disentanglement had been an arduous process—nerve-wracking, one might say, especially for those experienced enough to know all the myriad things that might go wrong, and how much harm might be done to any or all of the parties involved.

Once the separation was completed, and after his first sojourn in the 'doc, Priscilla had brought the Millsap proposal to him.

"Lina doubts her ability to tutor Padi," she said, "given how much we don't know about her abilities. I think it's possible the sudden release of her talents, after having been repressed for so long, is creating an illusion of a strange and limitless gift. I believe that will sort itself, over time, and we will find ourselves confronted with a new *dramliza*, in need of training, which is perfectly within the abilities of the three of us to manage."

"But . . ." he'd murmured.

Priscilla sent him an amused glance.

"But—*you* have taken damage, my love. You've lost

the use of senses that have been part of you since your twelfth nameday. That's not trivial. Yes, you'll recover—all of our combined training and experience lead us to believe that. But, we have to deal with *now* before *then*, as Dil Nem has it. And *now*, your wound—and the manner of your taking it—has put you off-balance. You've lost your Sight. That's no less traumatic than if you had lost your physical eyes."

"It seems a dire case, put thus," he said solemnly. Priscilla had sighed then, and reached out to touch his cheek.

"It's recoverable," she murmured. "But—given the nature of that damage, neither Lina nor I are certain that we ought to attempt a Healing—which you will notice we are not attempting. We feel we would all benefit from an examination done by other Healers, who are..."

She hesitated, perhaps uncertain of the best way to frame these "other Healers." Shan offered his assistance.

"Other Healers," he said, "who are not so tender of me?"

Priscilla shook her head.

"You must allow that we three are entangled on every level. It's possible that Lina and I may be erring on the side of tenderness—though I can't imagine why that would be so."

"Nor can I," he assured her seriously. "It is possible that these *other Healers* may have suggestions for interim protocols that may be useful in the case. And, since we will already be disturbing them with our problems, they might also be invited to cast an eye over Padi, in the context of trauma, and other hurts perhaps hidden by this brilliant aura of newly released powers."

"Exactly." Priscilla nodded.

Well, it had been a reasonable suggestion, given what he and Padi had suffered, not to mention Lina's misgivings. Millsap was not so far off their course—had they happened to possess anything so dignified as a course to be off of. As the third of the ship's three Healers, he had agreed to visit the Healers of Millsap.

He remembered that.

He did *not* remember that the prospect of being examined by "other Healers" had wakened any sense of uneasiness in him at the time. Quite possibly, he hadn't spent much consideration on that aspect of the matter. He rather thought, in fact, that he had framed the expedition as being for the benefit of Padi and Lina.

Considering it now, however, he was aware of a twinge of dismay at the prospect of being examined. There should be no difficulty in a routine examination done by competent members of the Healers Guild. No one was going to hurt him—and if they did, well. That was precisely the sort of thing they needed most to know.

He reached to his screen and called up the Healers Guild Register, speedily locating the entry for the Hall on Millsap.

Millsap Healer Hall was long established, serving a diverse, transient population. There were two masters, four Healers, and two journeymen on staff.

There had been three complaints brought against the Hall in the last twelve Standards, all filed by Terrans, who were later found to have not entirely understood what a Healing might accomplish—and that a Healing could not be reversed.

That was perhaps troubling. A Healer had a duty to explain the proposed course to her client, and the intended results of that course.

On the other hand, he was not an ignorant Terran. He was a mature Healer trained in the Liaden mode, as was Lina. Misunderstandings of process or outcome were extremely unlikely to occur.

So he, Padi, and their attending Healer would call at the Hall on Millsap, and avail themselves of such wisdom and suggestions as might be on offer. Well and good.

However.

The *Dutiful Passage* was a tradeship, a tradeship which was soon to approach a challenging port. Transit time to Millsap was not very long. Which meant that Master Trader yos'Galan and his 'prentice had best get to work.

He reached to the screen one more time and typed in a quick message, desiring Trader yos'Galan to attend him within the hour, if her schedule allowed.

· · · ·❖· · · ·

If her schedule allowed!

Padi closed the text on the theory of profit she had been reading, and leapt to her feet.

Of course her schedule allowed! *Finally*, to be properly working again—and even better, the *master trader* was working again. Father must be very much better, she thought—and realized of a sudden that she was breathing rather too quickly.

She closed her eyes and ran a calming exercise, which had the added benefit of sharpening her wits, which she would *surely* need when meeting with the master trader after having sat here dull and beset by lessons in control—well, and no one could object to her attending the master trader *at once*, could they? Not when it was his specific desire that she should do so?

Quickly, she stepped into the 'fresher, washed her face, combed her hair, and pulled it into a tail. She spared another moment to be certain that her collar was straight and her shirt and pants unrumpled. Satisfied that she was seemly and neat, she went in search of Keriana, who at this shift was in charge of sickbay, to give her news of the master trader's summons.

· · · ✳ · · ·

Padi arrived with commendable promptness, her face slightly flushed and her eyes wide. Shan resisted the urge to look at her through Healer senses, and merely accepted that she was delighted at the prospect of proper work coming into her hands.

She bowed—apprentice to master—and straightened rather more quickly than was perfectly proper.

"Good shift to you, Master Trader," she said.

"And good shift to you, Trader," he returned affably. "Pray provide yourself with a glass of whatever you may like. I fear we have something of a challenge before us."

Padi did not actually shout aloud; she scarcely needed to. Her eyes fairly sparkled, and there was a positive spring in her step as she crossed the room to pour a glass of cold tea.

She returned to the desk, set the tea to one side, and sat down.

"What sort of challenge?" she asked eagerly.

"We are en route to Millsap, on the necessity of the

Healers," he said, leaning back in his chair. "There is a Hall on-port, which, given recent events, is a fact that interests them considerably."

Padi bit her lip. Shan paused, but she said nothing. Nodding, he continued.

"Of interest to the traders is the fact that Millsap has trade. However, most of its trade falls in the realm of transshipment. It lies between two well-established long-Loops, which is very much to their benefit, and clever they were to have seized the opportunity to become a hub."

He paused. This time, Padi did speak.

"Does the master trader foresee that Millsap will be of use to us, as a transshipper?"

"Certainly, that is possible," he admitted. "But, to know that, we must understand the routes it services."

Padi nodded.

"Two established long-Loops," she said. "Have they been recorded?"

"In fact, they have. Which, as I know you will agree, is useful to our purpose. However, they *are* long-Loops, and we come to them as fresh and as ignorant as children. We will be arriving at Millsap space in a mere two ship-days, which does not give us very much time to become better informed."

"Unless you take one Loop, and I take the other," Padi said quickly. "We can research and compare."

"That seems very sensible," Shan said gravely. "How do you suggest we proceed?"

It might have said something about her state of mind that she didn't bother to acknowledge his show of naivete. Merely, she tipped her head, eyes narrowing somewhat as she marshalled necessities.

"We will each of us draw up a list of those ships which match our more usual cargoes. We will wish to note higher profit items, and . . ." She frowned then—rather ferociously. "The traders who ply those Loops—we would need to make agreements; be certain that we're not . . . inconvenient to them . . ."

The frown grew fiercer.

Shan waited.

Padi looked up.

"How long," she asked, "will the Healers need at Millsap?"

"That has not yet been determined. Also, you will have apprehended that you, and I, will be required to spend some time in-Hall, being inspected and possibly taken up to Heal."

"Yes," she said, still frowning. She reached for her glass and sipped cold tea briefly.

She met his eyes again.

"Millsap is not conveniently placed to any Korval routes," she said slowly. "If we had decided upon Langlast, and had been able to invest a quantity of time with the agents on-port . . ."

He nodded, well pleased with her.

"We did not decide upon Langlast," he agreed. "Do you counsel that the study of those routes feeding Millsap would be a waste of the traders' time?"

"Oh, no, never that!" Padi said, eyes widening. "We should at least—pardon me, Master Trader!—*I* should at least strive to understand the systems in place and the subtleties that sustain them." A pause, a conscious look. "Unless, we have a target, after Millsap?"

"Sadly, we do not," Shan said. "And you were neither impertinent nor amiss to suggest that the master

trader might also benefit from the study of the trade
economy which supports Millsap and two Loops."

He leaned forward, took up his glass, and raised it.

"Let us adopt your initial course. You will take
one Loop; I will take the other. We will meet here
again in one ship-day, compare our notes, and share
our conclusions."

It was very little more than a game—a trading
sim, Shan thought. But it would give them both an
opportunity to concentrate on trade, and recall their
powers in that arena. Most especially, it would give
Padi's thought a turn away from the vexed arrival of
her talents and the upcoming visit to Millsap Healer
Hall, of which she could not be sanguine.

"One ship-day," she agreed. "How shall we pick
our routes?"

Shan opened his desk drawer and produced a plain
Terran bit, which he tossed over to her lightly.

"The names of the Loops are Conway Primary and
ve'Atra Syme. Pray toss the coin to learn which is
yours, Trader. Old Sol in the ascendant will give you
Conway; the obverse will net ve'Atra Syme."

"Yes," said Padi, and flipped the coin into the air.

Off-Grid

. . . .

I

TWELVE OF THEM ASSEMBLED ATOP RIBBON DANCE HILL, six to quest and six to guard. That was the ancient formula, the Balance, and like so many other ancient things, it had no virtue beyond a pleasing symmetry. Those who quested were easier, Tekelia thought, knowing that each had a cousin at their back, ready to shield and to strike.

This attempt—this was no part of the agreement they had made with the Warden. They might, in fact, be understood to be placing the whole of Civilization at peril by making these inquiries of the ambient. Civilization would, Tekelia knew from experience, take that stand. After all, Civilization depended on rules, and on order, and on pretending, politely, that dead predators had no living sisters.

They, the gathered Haosa, understood their undertaking not as a foolish risk, but as a basic act of prudence. The Reavers had come out of the dancing Dust on purpose to harvest the small talents—Dreamers, Lucks, Back-Seers, Hearth-Makers, Finders—not for their talents, but because they *had* talent. It had been the purpose of the Reavers to attach those weaker and to subsume their wills, chaining their energies, so that they became no more than human batteries, augmenting another's power.

That was clearly terrible, but what made the intent of the Reavers yet more terrifying was the fact that—

They had not themselves been free. Every one of them, so far as the Haosa had been able to determine— *every* one of them had been enslaved as they had intended to enslave others.

It was the opinion of the Warden, and also of the Haosa, that the puppetmaster had not, themselves, come to Civilization on this mission of subjugation. That comforted Civilization, though not, thought Tekelia, who knew him well, the Warden.

Certainly, the notion that the puppetmaster was alive somewhere, and beginning to miss their puppets could not be anything but distressing. Surely, they had not sent all they had in the way of slavers. Yet, they had lost agents, and it was not inconceivable that they might be moved to come themselves, to see what the Dust-bound Redlands bred that were the equals of those they had deployed.

There also remained the puzzle.

*Some*thing had killed the Reavers, and it had not been the Haosa. No, it had been the part of the Haosa to collect the bodies, after the Reavers had died in their numbers, falling where they stood; passing from sleep into death with no waking between.

The Warden had held out the theory that it was the puppetmaster who had been struck down, taking their puppets into oblivion with them.

That was, to Tekelia's mind, a possibility—a strong possibility, given that other anomaly that had recently impressed Haosa senses.

Near to the time that the Reavers had died, there had been...an event. An explosion of bright noise, such as had not been seen before. There had been reports of some of the less-well-shielded in Civilization falling into a faint; among the Haosa the most common effect had been a headache, and a momentary Deafness.

That event could well have been the cause of the Reavers' fall, only—why had the Reavers *died* when all the rest who had been struck recovered handily, with no lasting ill effect?

Clearly, these were questions for the ambient.

So it was that twelve Haosa were gathered this night on Ribbon Dance Hill, just past the center of dark, when The Ribbons were the brightest, and the night mist swirling 'round their knees—six to search; six to guard. In theory, the ambient would itself hide them from their enemies, should there be any enemies present with eyes to See.

It was upon that theory that Tekelia's own faith foundered. For Tekelia, as with any other of the Haosa, to question the ambient was akin to questioning the air.

Exactly akin to questioning the air.

Yet the Reavers had come through the Dust, *through the ambient*, Haosa and the Civilized all unaware until the attempt was made to attach a Dreamer named Sylk ezinGaril, who had screamed her defiance into the ambient for all and everyone to hear.

Which was why Tekelia, on this bright and brilliant night, stood atop Ribbon Dance Hill, one among six of the inner circle—a quester.

Tekelia had questions—*several* questions, and serious—to ask the ambient.

"Cousins," called Banedra, who had a flawless sense of timing. "Now is our moment!"

II

THE QUESTING HAD BEEN EXHILARATING, BUT FUTILE.
The ambient—had not been helpful. That was worrisome, and even more worrisome when Banedra
called the questers back to themselves, to dance off
the accumulated energies; afterward to sit, eat, and
compare their results.

Tekelia's questions had been specific, not to say
pointed, a method that had produced success in previous inquiries. This time, however, the ambient had
been unforthcoming—even bored. Perhaps, Tekelia
thought, the questions had been *too* pointed.

Except Yferen, who specialized in questions so
broad as to be meaningless, reported the same lack
of interest, not to say success.

In fact, each of the six questers reported the ambient . . . distant, as if they and their concerns were of
secondary importance, behind some other, more highly
anticipated event.

That was worrisome.

Were more Reavers on the way? If so, the Haosa
had to alert Civilization. The last visitation had taught
them that Civilization had some worth in the discovery
and containment of enemies, and a valuable lesson it
had been.

However, the quest had left them uncertain on
the point of more Reavers, and their discussions grew
heated. It was at last agreed among the twelve that to
go to Civilization with vague uneasiness and maybes
would not only cause unproductive worry, it would

put Civilization's eye firmly onto the Haosa, which the Haosa very much did not prefer.

No, the twelve decided—there was but one course open to them. They must quest again, and ask more boldly. They needed answers, and evidence in hand, before they disturbed Civilization's peace. Indeed, they needed a particular *class* of evidence—but that was a discussion for later, after they had reaped answers.

In the meantime, there was the village meeting upcoming, and while the Haosa had no compunctions about hiding certain matters from Civilization, their own cousins were served the truth.

Eventually, the talk had run down, and the food had run out. The twelve left the hilltop together. At the base of the hill, they parted, most following the path to the village; others following the stream; and Tekelia, following no path at all, or so it seemed.

III

TEKELIA REACHED THE HOUSE AT THE EDGE OF THE WILD and ascended the ramp, thinking with a certain amount of wistfulness of a nap. It had been a long night, and while a dance with the ambient was energizing, eventually even Haosa must sleep.

A chime sounded, sweet and pure, when Tekelia reached the door—the particular chime set to alert one to the presence of Cousin Bentamin. And, indeed, there he was at the desk, papers and comp to hand, head bent in concentration.

"What are you doing here?"

Not the most gracious greeting for one's cousin-by-blood, who had a genius for knowing when he was most unwanted.

Cousin Bentamin looked up from his work, blue eyes wide and guileless.

"Tekelia, good-day to you as well."

Ah; a second chance to be courteous. Tekelia inclined from the waist.

"Good-day, Bentamin. Why are you here?"

"The Warden has some serious matters to discuss with the Speaker for the Haosa."

The Speaker for the Haosa being, according to Civilization and the Warden, Tekelia vesterGranz.

The notion that Civilization ought to work *with* the Haosa, the barbarian outcasts who lived Off-Grid, had been the particular brainstorm of Bentamin's mother in her later years. Having thought the thought, she had immediately set forth to locate an appropriate elder who was willing to act as her contact, hear her concerns and ideas, and take them to the rest of the Haosa. The Speaker was not—had never been—the leader of the Haosa. The Haosa had no leader; rather, there were those who were more attuned to the ambient. The former Speaker and the present had both been Children of Chaos, as the Haosa had it. It was precisely the sort of Haosa joke that terrified the Civilized, but the fact was that Chaos's Children were *especially* favored by the ambient.

It had taken some amount of time, patience, and white-knuckled effort to shape the relationship between Warden and Speaker, but both had seen benefit; they had persevered, and matters between Haosa and Civilization had, in fact, improved. Somewhat.

During this time of relationship-building between Warden and the very first Speaker for the Haosa, Tekelia had been born to a Civilized family, found wanting, and banished Off-Grid.

The Speaker died when Tekelia had been a dozen years among the Haosa. Soon after, Bentamin's mother had done the same.

Bentamin became Warden, and it was the most natural thing possible that he would contact his cousin Tekelia, inquiring after an appropriate Child of Chaos.

When the question was put, the larger community of Haosa as one stepped back from the honor—even the minority who thought that there ought to be open lines of communication between Off-Grid and Civilization. The Warden's cousin by that time was known to be close to the ambient. There was no need to look further.

Tekelia, one of that minority, had, without enthusiasm, accepted the duty.

"What serious matters have you to discuss, O Great Warden of the Civilized?" Tekelia asked sourly. A nap was becoming an imperative, followed by a period of meditation. However, neither was going to happen until Cousin Bentamin had his say and went away.

Which meant that an offer, at least, of hospitality was in order.

"Would you like some tea?" Tekelia asked.

"Tea would be very welcome, thank you. I'll contribute some of Entilly's cookies that you favor."

"Thank you," said Tekelia, and went into the kitchen to fill and start the kettle.

Bentamin's papers and comp were gone by the time Tekelia carried the tea tray out. The desk was orderly, and the table had been set on the back porch, chairs placed so that they could both look out over the trees. Bentamin had already claimed the right-side chair. A tin of Entilly's cookies was open among the cups and saucers, leaving enough room in the center of the table for the tea things.

Tekelia disposed those, poured, and settled into the left-side chair with a sigh.

"Long night?" Bentamin asked.

Tekelia sipped strong morning tea and flung him a baleful look.

"Did you come to talk about my night?"

"Merely a pleasantry, though we may need to speak about your night," Bentamin answered, offering the tin. "Have a cookie; you'll be better for it."

That was nothing but pure truth, Entilly's way with cookies being what it was. Tekelia reached to the tin and took up a wafer iced in lavender blue. It was delicious, of course, and devoured in three bites. Bentamin ate his pink-iced treat in two. They both sipped tea, and Tekelia sighed.

"Let's have them then, Cousin. These serious matters of yours."

Bentamin took up the pot and poured for both. Then he settled back, cup cradled in his hands, looking out over the Wild.

"I've been to see the Oracle," he said, which was surely no news. It was the Warden's job to see the Oracle, and to keep her safe—or, as the Haosa saw it, to keep her a prisoner, locked away from the vaunted benefits of Civilization, kept apart from her kin, the Haosa; her household comprised entirely of the Deaf, and her only real society the daily visit from the Warden.

"And how fares our Aunt Asta?" Tekelia asked when another of Entilly's cookies had been devoured, and Bentamin had spoken no further.

"She is, perhaps, beginning to grow weary," Bentamin said, his eyes still on the forest, "though very pleased to accept a bouquet of Jasy's flowers—" A conscious look from deep blue eyes. "You'll not have met Jasy. Sarrell's youngest. Quite talented, in a botanical way."

Tekelia waited.

"Yes, well," Bentamin said, reaching to the tin for another cookie. "You may be interested to know that the darkness has grown to such an extent that it is now an active threat to the universe entire. In fact, the universe has entered the arena, and the testing is at hand."

"Well, that's alarming," Tekelia said, half flippant before the entire sense of this statement unfolded. "Wait. She has Seen this? Has she Seen the outcome?"

"As I understand it, she has not. She has *perhaps* Seen that the universe will be saved by the rising of a hero who is prepared to do the needful. Mind you, it is equally possible that she has not Seen these things at all."

Tekelia took a careful breath, understanding him, but intent upon another line of questioning. "Has she Seen the hero?"

"She has Seen something that may be the hero, or perhaps only the *possibility* of a hero."

Tekelia reached for a cookie while Bentamin refreshed the cups.

"This is not a solid Seeing," Tekelia said eventually. "Though I admit to you, Cousin, that this shadow of a hero almost persuades me."

"And I. We were known as a wayward Line even on the old world."

"True."

Bentamin drank tea.

"I think," he said at last, "that this business of the universe's testing—even should it be a true Seeing, which . . . I am obliged, you understand, Cousin, to doubt . . ."

He paused, apparently wishing an answer.

"I understand," Tekelia assured him.

"Yes. Even if this is a true Seeing—it is beyond us. Civilized, Haosa, and the Dust together cannot prevent the destruction of the universe, though it be our most earnest desire to do so. If it is a true Seeing, then we have no choice but to put our coin on this hero, pray for them strength, success, and an honorable death."

"I agree."

"Excellent. That clears the path, and we may now discuss our more pressing problem."

Tekelia eyed him.

"And that is?"

"The Oracle reports—and *this* I believe to be a True Seeing—that we may expect the arrival of Great Ones, who will require from us—a service."

Tekelia stared.

"Great Ones?"

"Greater, so I am given to know, than *dramliz*." He inclined his head courteously. "I fear it is here that we may need to address your late night. You may of course speak freely, as I know that your actions, whatever they may have been, were in the service of Civilization as well as the Haosa."

Tekelia took a hard breath and put the cup down. Great Ones, greater even than *dramliz*?

Could this be the answer the ambient had not given?

"Last night," Tekelia said slowly, "twelve danced with the ambient, and asked of it our questions. We were most concerned with the puppetmaster—the one who controlled the Reavers and sent them to us. The ambient was—not helpful, and we resolved to dance again, soon. Now, we have heard the Oracle. I fear that these Great Ones *must* be the puppetmaster—coming to find what has happened to their toys."

Bentamin looked as if he had bitten into something sour. He glanced at the cookie tin—and looked away.

"A moment," he murmured, placing his teacup carefully on the table. He closed his eyes, and took a deep breath.

Tekelia nodded as the flow and texture of the energies in the room altered. Bentamin was Recalling his conversation with Aunt Asta. Prudent. Bentamin was always prudent.

Tekelia refreshed the cups, and put the pot down, empty.

With a blink of blue eyes, Bentamin returned. He nodded thanks for the warmed cup, lifted it, and drank off half in a single swallow.

"I believe that this morning's Great Ones are distinct from the Reavers," he said. "These Great Ones are said to be coming to ask of us a service. I pressed for more information, but I was found inept, and mocked." He paused, and added, "The Reavers, as I know you recall, had come to enslave us."

"*However*," Tekelia said, "it is nothing more nor less than a service, to ask that lost puppets be returned. The Reavers sent to us were not insignificant talents; most had the ability to attach a weaker and bind them."

Bentamin sighed.

"You are not a comfortable person," he observed.

"Nor do Oracles speak straightly. Admit that it is likely."

"I admit," Bentamin said. "It is all too likely."

"My regrets, for tearing up your peace," Tekelia said, which was proper, and even true. The Warden had peace in small enough measure, after all.

"The ambient was unhelpful, you said."

"Yes. We had already determined to dance again. Now we have these Great Ones and their service to task the ambient with, in addition to the Reavers. It may produce results."

"Let us hope so. A timeline would be . . . useful," Bentamin said wryly, and moved one shoulder. "Truthfully, *any*thing concrete would be useful. Keep me informed?"

"I will. Let me know if Aunt Asta speaks more—or more to the point."

"Of course. Well." He sighed. "I am wanted in the city," he said. "I thank you for a pleasant tea, and an interesting exchange of ideas. Shall I leave the cookies?"

"Take them," Tekelia answered, reaching to cover the tin, and offering it across the table. "How is it that Entilly is allowed by Civilization to produce these?"

"For family use only," Bentamin said promptly. "Most of her baking is quite . . . unexceptionable."

Tin in hand, Bentamin produced a stern stare. Tekelia met his eyes calmly. Bentamin might be Warden, but Tekelia was Haosa—Wild Talent, barbarian, bright Child of Chaos. Tekelia cooperated with Civilization from free choice—and the conviction that Civilization would founder without the Haosa. Much as the Haosa would become Lost, indeed, without Civilization to give stability to their lives.

"Be careful," Bentamin said now. "Tekelia. Swear that you will not risk yourself."

Tekelia laughed.

"Cousin, I risk myself every day. I am Haosa; there is no shield or wall between me and the ambient."

Bentamin sighed, and rose abruptly from the table, which was nothing more than his way. He was, after all, wanted in the city; he was an important person, and it had been quite a long visit, out here, Off-Grid.

"Keep me apprised," he said again.

And he was gone, teleporting back to the Wardian, the center of Civilization, the wash of energies filling Tekelia's senses for a moment, then draining tidily away into the ambient field.

Tarona Rusk
Auxiliary Services

· · · · · · · · · · · · · · · ·

MESSAGES BEGAN FLOWING THE MOMENT HER SHIP HIT
normal space. Tarona Rusk scanned them, but the
expected damage reports were not among the incoming. There was one memorandum—one!—forwarded by
Commander of Agents herself, indicating that several
dramliz had of a sudden fallen ill. The Commander
directed her to look into it, but not in any such terms
that might indicate... alarm, or even very great concern.

Tarona Rusk considered this memorandum closely.
No deaths? That could not be accurate. The Lucks
and the Brights to whom she had been linked were
fragile. No matter the care the Little Healer had
taken to be gentle, the separation must have been
traumatic in the extreme. Some *would have* died; it
was inevitable.

Frowning, she sorted through the rest of the incoming mail, finding another odd lack.

There was no summary report, nor greeting, from
her department sub-chief. She had sent ahead, allowing
him to know that she was returning; that she would

want him, with full reports in hand, the moment she was arrived. There had been no acknowledgment of that communication, which was not like his efficiency. Unless...was it possible that Fel Pin had succumbed to separation trauma? But, no; *that* she would have marked—no matter what else had occupied her.

She reached to the comm and sent a brief message, that she was on approach, and that she desired he meet her in her office at the twenty-seventh hour.

She felt his presence through the door; his determination, and his intent—and smiled as she placed her palm against the reader. The instant the light came green, she extended her will and *pushed* the door back on its track, ignoring the scream of the abused mechanism, and swung through the opening.

Her shields turned the first strike; she parried the second, even as she threw a bolt of her own, shattering his defenses and taking control of his autonomous systems. She squeezed his lungs, just a little, to get his attention; saw his eyes widen, and tasted his fear.

"Fel Pin, well met," she said pleasantly. "I offer you revenge. Look deeply—am I lying? Am I ensorcelled?"

She allowed him more air, opened her shields— enough; felt the familiar sweep of his scrutiny—once. Twice.

"How?" he gasped.

"I will tell the tale to my ally," she answered. "If you cannot accommodate yourself, I will, with reluctance, kill you now. I have work that I must see finished and, I fear, a shrinking window. I cannot be distracted by the need to continually guard myself against assassination."

"Give me revenge and I am yours in all things," he told her, truth ringing so brightly that it nearly deafened her outer ears.

"We are in agreement," she said, and released her hold on him, stepping farther into her office.

"Sit," she told him. "Tend to yourself. I will make tea."

He dropped into the chair he so often occupied, rubbing his chest, a web of healing energies taking shape around him.

"So," she murmured, moving to the buffet and the teapot, "I have been Healed, Fel Pin, is it not diverting? In the process, my Healer severed my links with—all of the network."

"The moment reverberated . . . strongly," he said. "Who was the Healer? Not—yos'Galan?"

"Indeed, yos'Galan," she said, and smiled at the flicker of his disbelief.

Well, and who would not disbelieve it? Shan yos'Galan—the *gentle* Korval; soft-hearted and foolish; a mere Healer, and no threat to the Department. The very Department which had taken him at face value, failing to recall that a master trader cannot be a fool, and *Korval's* master trader least of all.

"The half-breed fool has placed one—now two— potent weapons into the Department's very core, which the Scouts, for all their cleverness, have not been able to do. As I said—diverting."

"Ah," said Fel Pin flatly.

She considered him on every level available to her. *Trust* had no place in the Department of the Interior, where control was everything. She had controlled Fel Pin, but they were also *dramliz*, and therefore she *knew* him in ways which were simply unavailable to those who lacked their gifts.

"There is news?" she asked him now.

He moved his shoulders.

"Not news. I only recall that Val Con yos'Phelium was a Scout, and that the Scouts did not protest his recruitment."

The kettle whistled; she poured tea into cups and brought them to her desk.

"You believe that the Scouts placed all their tokens on one square?"

"I think it not impossible, and find it... amusing to dwell upon the data, which show us that the Plan had been proceeding with few setbacks... until Agent of Change yos'Phelium was placed into the field."

He took his cup with a small, seated bow.

"I will forward my study set, if you have an interest."

"Thank you," she said, and sat down.

They sipped tea, and Fel Pin lowered his cup.

"Returning to your topic," he said, "I fear that you have not the full count of our current knives. We hold many more than two."

She froze in the act of putting her cup down, and brought her gaze to his face.

"Tell me," she said.

"Yes," he said. He took a deep drink of tea, and leaned to put the cup on her desk.

"Zaylana, who had been stationed at the Ozpart Quick Strike Center, killed her section chief and ten of the strike team before she was neutralized. Veesha, who had been on-station to assist in retraining, influenced the surviving eight of the team to report a Scout attack which had been turned aside, though at cost. She is continuing to influence the survivors, awaiting, as she has it, orders."

"Orders?"

"From yourself," he said. "She—when the separation occurred, it was accompanied by a feeling that it had been you who had . . . liberated us. Veesha awaits your plan."

"You did not think that I had a plan?"

"I—" He met her eyes. "*I* did not wish to be enslaved again."

Truth once more, from the very core of him.

She inclined her head. "Well enough. What else?"

"The network is not intact. There are quiet zones; operatives who have yet to report. I have not sent out a general inquiry, fearing this might call attention from the shadows. An unusual number of attacks by Scouts has been reported, which, in turn, were unusually effective. One supposes from this that Zaylana was not the only one to have slaughtered those in her care, merely the only one who did so in the presence of a colleague who was moved to stop her."

Tarona Rusk forced herself to pick up the cup, to sip tea; to remain serene, despite the excitement roiling in her blood.

"We have reports, through normal channels, that various of the . . . more vulnerable succumbed to separation trauma," Fel Pin continued. "There may be one Luck left to us—or it may simply be that his team has not yet noticed his absence. We fare little better in our inventory of those talents who had been contributing their energies to the common core. The dormitory here was blighted, though the majority of our high-level talents survived the trauma with little more than a headache, accompanied by a fracture, which quickly healed itself."

The higher levels would of course have had the ability to Heal themselves—in many of the higher talents, the ability was innate. But—

"You say the majority," she said to Fel Pin.

He bowed his head.

"We lost two: Aei Vin and Sondi."

Tarona Rusk frowned.

Aei Vin had been the first she had recruited to the Department's cause; a Healer, but not strong. The ties that bound them had been close; yos'Galan's Healing would have acted upon him as powerfully as it had upon her. It was entirely possible that the trauma had overcome him. Indeed, he must have dropped where he stood, never knowing that he had been struck.

This other loss, however . . .

"*Sondi* succumbed to separation trauma?" she asked, hearing disbelief in her voice. In terms of talent, and sheer power, Sondi had been very nearly her equal. That had been why Tarona had been so very careful to bind her, and with all of the strongest cords: passion, sex.

Love.

Fel Pin reached for his cup, keeping his eyes averted, and drank the tea to the dregs. She could feel his distress. *Distress*. Those in her network had not been so cold as the operatives in their care. They could not be and do what the Department required of them. But it had been a very long time since any of them had been . . . *distressed*.

"She . . ."

Fel Pin met her eyes.

"She survived the trauma, Mistress. She survived the

break, and Healed herself. What she did not survive was her memory."

Tarona Rusk closed her eyes.

After a moment, Fel Pin cleared his throat. "She left a message, Mistress."

"Did she? What was it?"

"'You lied to me, Tarona.'"

It was said in all of Sondi's voice, mimicry being one of Fel Pin's lesser talents, and it stabbed her through the heart. Oh, yes, she had lied; she had rewoven reality and perception; she had made the bonds sweet, and tight.

And there was never a Healing or a linkage made that did not bind both.

"She killed herself, then."

"Mistress, she did."

She took a deep breath, shuddering, and deliberately put the pain aside. She was the author of a thousand and more betrayals, and what she had done to bind Sondi had not been the greatest of them.

"So then," she said, straightening, "we move on. The Commander forwards a report concerning the sudden illness of *dramliz* corresponding with the shattering of the network. She suspects nothing?"

"Commander of Agents has given complete responsibility for the *dramliz* into the care of this department," Fel Pin said slowly. "She is fully occupied in mobilizing an invasion. Also..."

She considered him with interest.

"Go on."

"The...current Commander has been experiencing some difficulty maintaining the transfer. She has called a Healer to her on several occasions."

She stared at him.

"A Healer."

"Just so." Fel Pin returned her stare with a smile. "She has been very careful to ensure the loyalty of the Healer, and has not called the same twice. However, the Healer she had with her soon after the separation deemed it prudent that the Commander not take too much interest in the business of *dramliz*, and was able to influence her to be very busy with the invasion, and even more invested in Korval's destruction."

"She was able to do that? The Commander Template . . ."

". . . made it, as I understood the message, very difficult to plant the suggestion, and the Healer was constrained to build onto a passion already in place. This she was able to do, however, and so we are, for the moment at least, beneath the Commander's notice."

"Where is she now, this Healer?" Tarona Rusk demanded. "I must see her, understand what she has learned. If we can subvert the Commander—"

But Fel Pin was holding up his hands, palms out.

"The Healer—Hosilee ver'Fonat—was of course put to death after the Commander was done with her. She happened also to be a match-telepath, so was able to transmit to her partner before she died."

Of course, she thought. The new Commander might be troubled, undertrained, and unable to manage the download, but she would not be so foolish as to ignore basic security protocols.

She drew a breath.

"I see. I will wish to speak with Healer ver'Fonat's partner, as soon as it may be safely arranged. What news of our teams sent to Colemeno?"

"No news, Mistress. I think we must assume that they did not survive."

"Hah." She closed her eyes briefly.

"Very well," she said, after a moment. "We must ascertain how many we are, and where we are situated. I want reports from all *dramliz* in the network, including their condition, the condition of those under their care, and their operating plans, if any. If we attract shadows, we shall not hesitate to use extreme measures.

"It would seem, from the information in hand, that the larger enclaves of techs and support personnel, as well as the rest of the lightly conditioned, are in our hands. The agents and field operatives remain a challenge, but let us consolidate our victories first."

"Yes, Mistress."

Fel Pin rose, bowed, and left her, the door closing smoothly behind him.

Alone, she leaned back in her chair, hearing Sondi's voice once more:

You lied to me, Tarona.

Millsapport

· · · · · · · · · · ·

I

MILLSAP WAS NOT A BEAUTIFUL PORT.

It was understood that not all ports were beautiful, Padi thought. But it might at least have made a push to be *interesting*.

But, no. Millsapport was merely a semicircular monotone of samples houses along the outer edge, through which the port omnibus moved at a fair speed, slowing somewhat as it entered the second ring—agent offices, each exactly the same as all the others, with only the names—centered precisely over each door—different.

In fairness, the research she and the master trader had hurriedly completed had not promised anything else. Millsapport and its numerous outyards—which had made the *Passage*'s approach to its docking orbit more of a challenge than it strictly needed to be— Millsapport was about safe storage and the orderly transfer of cargo. The samples houses existed in case there should be a question regarding the quality of the contents of a particular pod awaiting pickup by its contracted ship. The agent offices were there to make certain the paperwork was in order, and that the port received its just and proper fees.

There was no need to catch the eye of newcomers, or entice fresh traders into a deal, and no effort was made to do so.

Millsapport, in a word, was bound, caught tight and trapped by its own system, which functioned well, as it had done for dozens and dozens of years. Padi had wondered aloud to the master trader, during their analysis session, what might happen to the port, to the agents, if a new trader arrived, offering a fresh trade.

"Possibly, they would turn it away," Master Trader yos'Galan said. "After all, they don't *need* new custom. What they need most is to not disturb the custom they have."

The port omnibus paused to take on a passenger— another agent, Padi supposed—dressed in grey business robes that matched the grey façades of the offices.

This one spared them a glance as he passed to a seat in the back. He looked tired, Padi thought, and felt something flicker along a set of nerves she hadn't known she'd had until this second.

Not *just* tired, but anxious, even—

"Your pardon, Trader," Father said from the seat beside her. "I wonder if you would honor me with your opinion of that structure?"

Padi turned toward the window, following the angle of his chin, but truly, the line of offices they were passing, now that the omnibus was moving once more, looked precisely the same as—

She felt her cheeks heat, and looked up to meet Father's eyes.

"It just . . . *happened*," she said softly.

"One may catch a glimpse," he replied, "and that is an accident. To continue to stare, however..."

"Yes, sir."

Determinedly, she turned her attention to the window.

Shan gazed out the window as the omnibus lumbered on. He was not deploring the view, though it was certainly deplorable, but rather considering those other things he and Padi had discovered in the course of researching the port, and the systems which supported it.

Millsap lived—and lived well—because of the balance between its two Loops. One might argue their methods, but one could not argue that those methods failed of producing profit. Millsap had been profitable for a long time, and would continue to be so just exactly as long as its client Loops profited.

And there lay the rub.

The Terran Loop was, to his eye, beginning to falter, though he could, as he had several times reminded himself, be wrong. The data he had was too sparse to support an in-depth analysis. He *could* buy more data and study the matter in the fullness it deserved. After all, he was a master trader; process and the ongoing health of ports were his legitimate concerns. Indeed, it might well be his duty to file a notice with the Guild, but he hesitated to do so on the basis of such flimsy evidence as was now in his hand. Master traders were, after all, held to a certain standard.

And a *Liaden* master trader bringing a Terran trade enterprise to the attention of the Guild—there would be politics to cope with, no question, and his taste for politics was even less acute than usual. But, after all, politics could be finessed, when necessary. The question therefore became—*Was it necessary?*

He took a breath, seeking to clarify his thoughts and settle his stomach, as the omnibus turned right down a thoroughfare that seemed to be lined with—could it be shops? Good gods, so they were.

He glanced at the seat just ahead of them, where Lina sat next to Karna Tivit of ship's security. Hands folded on her knee, face serene, shoulders loose and level, she made a pretty picture of modest patience, quintessentially Liaden.

It had been decided by the ship's three Healers that there was nothing to be gained by startling the Healers of Millsap. From there, it had been a very short step to deciding that Lina should act as their Healer-escort while Priscilla remained with the ship. Lina was a good, solid Healer trained in the Liaden style. There was nothing about her to raise eyebrows.

Priscilla, on the other hand, would have had the eyebrows of the entire Hall arcing into hairlines before they were ever admitted.

Even presented as *dramliza*, rather than Healer, there were too many odd energies roiling about Priscilla and her methods—especially if one were a Healer trained in the Liaden style.

It had therefore seemed best, after discussion, not to tax the Healers of Millsap with questions when what was wanted—were answers.

So, Priscilla had stayed with the ship—their reserve force, as she styled it, in the unlikely event that the Healers of Millsap proved to be pirates or brigands— while Lina accompanied the wounded Healer and the Emergent in need of Sorting.

It was perfectly straightforward, he told himself, not for the first, or even the sixth, time. Nonetheless, his stomach, foolish organ, remained unsettled.

As if she had heard his ruminations, Lina turned her head and smiled at him briefly. It might have reassured him, if he hadn't known her for so long that her smiles hid no secrets from him.

Lina was worried, too.

Shan sighed.

Padi kept her attention on the window as the omnibus made its awkward way down the track and the boring port moved past.

Really, she thought, how could they put up with all this...greyness? Would it have done any harm to have painted the occasional building red, or even pale blue?

She bit her lip. Ordinarily, she liked to explore ports, though she preferred walking to port transport. Ordinarily, she would have dismissed the grey-on-grey color scheme as local custom, but today...

Today, she wished she were back on the *Passage*, even if the only thing she had to occupy herself with were exercises to help her become better acquainted with her gift.

She was not at all certain that she wanted strange Healers...*looking* at her. She had expressed this to Lina, who had agreed that it was very natural to feel uneasy. She had also said that no one would hurt her, and if someone *did* hurt her, she was to say so, immediately, for nothing the Healers would be doing during their examinations ought to be in the least uncomfortable.

Which did not...precisely...address Padi's unease.

One could not See oneself—not in that way. At least, she hadn't yet discovered in her private explorations any sort of interior mirror where she might regard this...brightness that was her talent.

She had received the impression, however, that it was not...quite...pleasing. That it was *too* bright— that *had been* said, though followed with a hasty reassurance that new talent often arrived in a burst of energy that might dazzle Healer eyes.

Unfortunately, she had begun to receive the impression that her brightness ought to have started to subside by now—and that this was not the case.

Aside all that, she had glimpsed in Lina's reticence to answer certain questions regarding Padi's *specific* gift, that it had become...misshapen, perhaps, as a result of her mistaken attempt to keep it locked away.

So, she wished—she *very much* wished—that she might dispense with the Healers altogether. Father, of course, *must* have an examination to be certain, among other things, that his heir had not hurt him in what she now knew to have been a foolhardy attempt to help him.

"I believe I see our stop," Father said.

Padi blinked out of her thoughts, and leaned closer to the window.

This section of the port boasted perhaps half-a-dozen dormitories, grab-a-bites, bars, restaurants, what might have been a house of pleasure, and another half-dozen general supply houses. And here, Padi saw, someone among the shopkeepers or the hosts had heard of paint, though they might have done well to coordinate the colors. Still, that was a small thing, and after the tedium of the journey through the warehousing and office districts, to come upon this small area was rather like stumbling into a meadow of wildflowers after wandering the desert.

The Healer Hall—she saw it immediately, situated on the corner of a small street between the hospitality and retail areas, as if no one could quite decide on its function. It was a modest 'crete square surrounded by a fence. Both the building and the fence were painted a soft, pleasing shade of pink, and the front yard, which at ho— *on Liad* would have been a modest garden, was here artfully decorated with bright mosaic sculptures, many with wind-catchers at the apex.

The wind-catchers, Padi thought, might have been an exercise in wishcraft, which might or not be an actual *dramliz* craft. It was sometimes difficult for her to know when Priscilla was having a joke.

In any case, the wind-catchers were catching no wind today, their blades as still as the petals of the flowers they were perhaps meant to counterfeit.

The omnibus groaned to a halt. Two seats ahead, Third Mate Dil Nem Tiazan, who made one of their security pair today, rose and moved toward the hatch.

Lina followed him, Padi following her, then Father, and Karna Tivit, the second of their security pair, bringing up the rear.

Karna's feet had scarcely touched the pavement when the door shut, and the omnibus rolled off, groaning loudly. The five of them stood for a moment, orienting themselves to the bright, windless day, before confronting the glittering front garden.

"Well," Lina said briskly after a long moment had passed and no one of them had made a move toward the gate. "We are well arrived. Let us allow the Hall to know that we are here."

The door was opened by a plump boy with curly yellow hair and soft grey eyes. He was dressed in an emerald green tunic and bright red pants, which was, Padi thought, certainly understandable, given the larger port environment, but perhaps a trifle too bold in terms of the House he served.

"Good-day to you," Lina said, from her position at the front of their group—the order being Lina at center, Father a step behind and to her right; Padi to his left, looking over Lina's shoulder.

"I am Lina Faaldom, Healer on *Dutiful Passage*, come with my clients to confer with the elders."

The boy...said nothing. His eyes narrowed slightly, as if he were looking into a very bright light.

"I had sent a message ahead," Lina said, and Padi had the impression that she had subtly done...*some*thing, which had the happy effect of bringing the doorkeeper's attention back to her.

"Yes, Healer!" he said, suddenly brisk. "We have been looking for you, and for your clients. May the House know the identity of these two persons below you?"

That was not as rude as it sounded. Dil Nem ánd Karna were standing on the path at the bottom of the short stairs so as not to crowd the door, while at the same time bearing witness to all that was said and done.

"Those are our security team," Lina said calmly.

The doorkeeper frowned somewhat.

"Those who do not seek Healing are not admitted to the House," he said.

Which, Padi thought, *was* rude.

Father shifted slightly, drawing the boy's eyes to him.

"At Solcintra Hall, where Healer Faaldom and I trained, kin, colleagues, and comrades of those come to seek Healing were allowed to wait in the inner garden, where they did not disturb the House."

He paused. The boy inclined his head.

"Sir," he said hastily. "I—of course, your oathsworn may enjoy the comfort of our garden. It is the House from which . . . the work . . ."

"I understand entirely," Father assured him gently, and added, "At Solcintra Hall, light refreshment is provided to those who wait. If that is not the custom here, perhaps you will advise us on the proper way to have a tray sent over from one of the restaurants nearby?"

The boy . . . blinked.

"Sir," he said, after a moment. "I am at a loss. The seniors await, and we ought not tarry longer. If you will permit, I will call my second to show your oathsworn to the garden, while I guide you to my elders. Once that is done, I will find from the Hall manager what the custom is in the matter of guests in the garden, and I myself will see that everything proper is done."

Father inclined his head, and produced a quarter-cantra, which he held out to the doorkeeper.

"If it should be that the Hall's custom does not permit of light refreshment, please do send for a tray from the restaurant you favor most, of those just there."

He used his chin to point down the street.

The boy hesitated a moment before he took the coin with a small bow.

"A moment, Gentles, if you please," he murmured, and stepped back from the door. Padi heard him speak, very briefly—the name of his second, perhaps, for a shadow moved in the hallway, and a girl some years younger than the doorkeeper, also yellow-haired but wearing pale blue tunic and pants, came forward to bow.

Father stepped closer to Padi and the girl padded lightly past them, down the stairs to where Dil Nem and Karna waited. Padi turned her head slightly and saw the girl bow again, everything that was polite, from a younger to elders.

Her voice was soft and pretty, somehow seeming to match the light blue of her garments.

"I am Yissi, an apprentice in the House. I will be pleased to take you to the garden, Gentles. It is a very nice garden, quite the best on Millsapport. Everyone says so."

It was not, Padi thought, a very high bar, but she hoped their security would be tolerably comfortable.

"Thank you, young Healer," Dil Nem said in his punctilious way. "My comrade and I will be very pleased to enjoy the comforts of the garden."

"Please," she said, "follow me."

She stepped 'round them, toward the side of the house, Karna following. Dil Nem paused a moment to look up the stairs, catching Father's eye.

"Sir?" he murmured.

"As ever, Dil Nem," Father murmured, and Padi saw the dour Third Mate smile slightly before he turned to follow the others.

"If the Healer and her clients will follow me, please," the doorkeeper said. "The elders are waiting."

II

THEY WERE GUIDED DOWN A SHORT HALL TO A ROOM
that erred on the side of austerity. Shan would have
preferred a more parlorlike setting, if only to soothe
Padi's sensibilities, but a glance at her face gave him
to understand that she had expected an examination
room, and found this austere little area worthy of an
appreciative lift of eyebrows.

Shan sighed. Padi, he recalled, had never before
been in a Healer Hall. She had not expected a consultation parlor holding comfortable chairs and small
comforts, or anything other than a room set up to
host the business negotiations of traders.

The Healers of Millsap had met those very modest
expectations, and Shan supposed he ought to be grateful.

"Master Healer Ferin, Healer Osit, here is Healer
Lina Faaldom of the *Dutiful Passage*, with her clients,
Healer Shan yos'Galan, and Emergent Padi yos'Galan."

Master Healer Ferin was female and grey-haired;
her eyes were stern blue. Healer Osit was some years
younger than Shan, male, and possessed of a pair of
merry brown eyes. Both rose and bowed welcome.
Shan bowed, and Lina did, and Padi. Healer Ferin
dismissed their escort.

"Please, sit," she said coolly, "and let us become
acquainted with your situations."

There was a small but important concession to the
traditional comfort of the consultation parlor—a tea
service sat in the center of the table. Healer Osit
poured for them all—Healer Ferin's cup first, his

own, then Lina's, Shan's, and Padi's. Apparently, the Healers of Millsapport did not honor those in need as guests of the House, but as petitioners for favor.

That, Shan thought, was interesting.

He accepted his cup with a small bow of the head. A moment later, Padi accepted hers with a murmured word of thanks.

Comfort dispensed, Healer Osit sat down. Healer Ferin raised her cup to sip, all doing the same. Teacups returned to the tabletop, and the elder Healer looked to Lina.

"We understand from your correspondence that you bring us two clients for assessment, with a request that we consult with you in their proper treatment."

She moved a hand, indicating Shan and Padi without actually looking at them.

"Is there a reason, Healer, that you chose not to shield the Emergent?"

"There is," Lina said composedly. "She resisted the arrival of her gift to the point of building a wall to separate herself from its fullness. I hesitate to subject her to another walling away until she is Sorted."

"One doubts that there can be a Sorting," Healer Ferin said. "She is altogether too chaotic. For the sake of those who are less overbearing, but more orderly of mind, she should be shielded."

Shan felt Padi shift beside him, and dared a look at the side of her face, which was entirely without expression.

Oh, dear, he thought.

"If I am discommoding the Healers," she said, stringently calm, "I will happily remove myself from the meeting, and wait with our oathsworn in the garden."

"If that is the best you are able to do, in respect of your elders," Healer Ferin began—and Healer Osit spoke quickly.

"If I might make the attempt, Master Healer? She *is* very bright and—disparate—but I believe I discern a line which may be worked upon. I will attempt to demonstrate a simple shield, which she may be able to reproduce. It will naturally fall to Healer Faaldom to instruct her in best practice."

"Very well," Healer Ferin said, sharply dismissive of both Padi and her colleague. "Take her down the hall. If I am to examine this wounded Healer with any amount of understanding, I must have my Sight clear."

"Yes." Healer Osit stood. "Emergent yos'Galan. Pray attend me. We may at the very least show you how to properly care for your colleagues."

Padi looked to Lina.

Lina, who had access to all of her talent, and presumably had taken the full measure of these, their colleagues, nodded at Padi.

"We had discussed how bright you seem to me, when I look at you with my Eyes wide open. Healer Ferin must make a detailed examination of Healer yos'Galan, which will require her to be most fully open."

"And I will distract her, if I remain," Padi finished, low-voiced. "I understand. I in no way wish to impede the Healer's examination." She rose and inclined her head. "Master Osit, I am at your command."

Shan let his breath out, and extended a hand to touch hers reassuringly, he hoped. She looked into his eyes and smiled slightly, then moved away from the table to follow the Healer from the room.

✳   ✳   ✳

The door closed. Healer Ferin sighed.

"Now," she said, "let us consider what we have here, Healer yos'Galan. I See that you have forensic shielding in place. That is very wise. However, in order to observe the damage you have taken, and form a diagnosis, I must be allowed inside your shields.

"Open to me, if you please."

Ice ran Shan's veins; his breath stopped in his chest, while his heart slammed into overdrive.

Open to me!

The sound of Tarona Rusk's voice in Command mode, the lash of her will, slicing open his forearm.

"What have we here?" He heard the question at a distance, beyond the pounding of his heart. "Panic? Healer Faaldom, is this a usual response?"

"It is atypical." Lina's voice was clear, calm. "I believe it may be associated with his other wounds. There was an attempt at forceful entry, using physical torture as an incentive."

"You have examined him since this episode?"

"I have, but we are long known to each other. You, on the other hand—"

"Yes, I see. Another stranger demanding entry—the horror surfaces once more."

Shan's breath broke free in a gasp that was nearly a sob. Instinctively, he reached for Healspace—and found that he was . . . not blocked. Not *quite* blocked. But met.

And held.

Warmth flowed between that soft connection; warmth, and an offer of assistance.

"I think you know, Healer," the voice that was not Lina's said, "that to attempt Healspace at this moment is likely not in your best interest. We have here myself, Ferin, a master in our craft. I have pledged my assistance to your colleague, whom you trust; so much I may See, though you hold your shields close. I also See that you are exhausted in spirit, which is in turn trying you physically. If you will open your shields, I may learn what you have endured, and how we might ease you."

"Shan," Lina said, from quite nearby. "I am here; I am watching. This our colleague is none such as she who harmed you."

No, of course, she wasn't. They had spoken about this at length, he and Priscilla, and Lina. The spike of terror had surprised him as much as it had surprised the others. Having such horror hidden even from himself—it would not do, if he intended to resume as a Healer, once his strength was returned. No. He had worked with past-trauma victims, who had no idea that panic still lived in their souls. Left unHealed, such lurking horror had the power to warp a soul, bend honor, break kindness...

He breathed in, carefully, accepting the warmth offered by Healer Ferin, using it to calm the last of the panic. He considered the labor of his lungs, the beat of his heart... and finding all within normal ranges, he formed the thought and deliberately opened his shields.

There was a long, long moment of profound silence. With his shields down, Shan could see the other Healer's dismay, taste her shock.

"Healer yos'Galan," said Healer Ferin at last, her voice rough. "You have endured much. Primary linkages were cut—cut much too close to the fabric of

your soul! I see rebound lacerations, bruising, and ...
the scorch marks of another will ..."

She sat back, and Shan tasted her disgust.

"Healer yos'Galan, I must know: What did you do,
to deserve this—this *carnage*?"

He took a hard breath, forcing himself to answer
evenly.

"I Healed a *dramliza* of considerable power of the
damage which had perverted her gift and made her
the willing puppet of evil."

"She *fought* your intervention."

"She did, yes. As I had fought against her attempted
rape." He sighed, suddenly weary. "I tricked her. But
I Healed her. And when I was done, I was spent unto
death. In her turn, she Healed me, thus proving my
treatment effective."

Another silence, then Healer Ferin's voice again,
controlled and tasting of steel.

"That the severed links have reestablished themselves
is well. The lacerations have been slower to heal, and
the bruising is still livid—indicative, perhaps, of your
general state of low energy. I may do something for
you there, Healer, if you permit."

She looked to Lina.

"Unless there is a reason that Healer Faaldom does
not wish them Healed?"

"Truth told, Healer, I was not certain that I might
not exacerbate the situation. Healer yos'Galan and I
are entangled on many levels. This is why I wished
the assessment of another Healer."

"Prudent," murmured Healer Ferin. "Of course,
you would wish to be certain that you did no harm."

"Do you," Lina said, "feel that these may be addressed, without risk?"

Healer Ferin pursed her lips.

"I think," she said slowly, "that they may be addressed with *minimal* risk. Healer yos'Galan is perhaps not as robust as you would like, but there is a strong possibility that these minor wounds are leaching energy needed for a full recovery."

"Shan?" Lina said. "What would you?"

"I am willing to accept a Healing of those injuries which Healer Ferin mentions as obstacles to my return to full function."

"Understand me," Healer Ferin said, her disgust of him entirely obvious. "You still look to a long convalescence before your full Sight is returned."

"I understand," he assured her.

There was a small silence while the Healer collected herself, and managed to ask her next, necessary question.

"May I give you relief, Healer yos'Galan?" she said, coldly formal.

It would have been prudent to agree, but he shivered, the toothy beginnings of panic clawing at his throat...

"Softly," murmured Lina, and he felt her hand on his, warm and pressing gently.

"I will not insist," Healer Ferin said, her tone austere. "There are two Healers present, after all. Perhaps, Healer Faaldom, he will allow your touch."

"Shan?" she murmured.

Gritting his teeth, he managed to step aside from the panic, and looked into Lina's eyes.

"Of your goodness, old friend."

There was a swirl, as of mist; the merest glimpse of Healspace. He breathed in, tasting cedar and vanilla, felt a brief bright pain—and the welcome chill of relief.

The room solidified around him, and Healer Ferin, too, her eyes hard.

"It is done," said Lina.

"And done well," Healer Ferin said, sounding neither pleased nor impressed.

"Healer yos'Galan, may I continue my inspection?"

He took a breath and met her hard gaze with what frankness he could muster.

"Of your goodness, Healer. Allow me to express my gratitude for your keen Sight and your patience."

That failed to win her, though it did demonstrate that he had some passing acquaintance with proper behavior. She inclined her head and said coldly, "We continue."

Shan relaxed, deliberately, and turned his eyes aside, looking over the Healer's shoulders and focusing on the artwork framed on the wall behind her.

The painting was well-suited for his purpose, so well-suited that it *must* have been placed there precisely to distract those under examination. Yet the Healer had not directed his attention to it.

Possibly, she had been put off her stride; she had complained of being half-blinded by the rather extravagant display that was Padi. She might simply have for—

"Ah!"

An electric thrill focused his attention inward to a new scar, the area around it showing classic signs of emotional bruising.

"What is this?" demanded Healer Ferin. "A link forcefully removed?"

She was pressing on the bruise. He had no idea if she was doing it deliberately, to focus his attention, or if her own astonishment had again rendered her forgetful.

Shan took a breath, and brushed her will with his, moving her off of the bruised area.

"What!" she cried, and Shan met her eyes.

"You were hurting me," he said coolly, even as Lina began to speak.

"The arrival of Emergent yos'Galan's talent coincided with the event during which Healer yos'Galan was damaged. The first thing that met the Emergent's full Sight was her father, depleted and bleeding energy. She instinctively reached out and created a conduit so that she might transfer some of her plentiful energies to him, for support and healing."

Healer Ferin's shock and outrage sizzled across abused nerves. Shan thrust her back and slammed his shields shut. Beside him, Lina gasped, and he felt a spike of guilt that he had hurt her.

Healer Ferin, however, seemed not to have felt the pain of his rejection, so exalted was her outrage.

"She *only* reached out and smashed a hole in the wall of someone's psyche—without asking permission, I apprehend!—and forced herself onto a wounded person? Has no one taught this girl *any*thing? She might have done irreparable damage! She might have killed this Healer—her own father! In such a diminished state, without protection—"

"I hardly needed protection from my own daughter," Shan snapped. "She acted from the heart; there was no ill intent, nor—"

Someone screamed.

III

"NOW, EMERGENT YOS'GALAN, ONE HAS SEEN QUITE CLEARLY that you are the bearer of a large and, forgive me, unruly talent.

"Of course, we may none of us take credit for the nature or strength of our gifts. These things are as the gods, and genetics, will have them. We may, however, discipline ourselves, and show respect to our fellows. That is why the very first lesson taught an Emergent, no matter her strength or her station, is *control.*"

"I *had* controlled my gift," Padi said, as one would who was merely imparting information. She was reasonably certain that she did not sound sullen. "That technique very nearly proved fatal."

Actually, it *had* proved fatal, to two persons who had been trying to kill her, but that was *surely* a fact that Healer Osit did not need.

Indeed, it may have been well not to have spoken at all. Healer Osit positively frowned at her.

"If I have understood your attending Healer correctly, you had not controlled your gift so much as you had confined—even denied!—it. Our talents *may not* be denied, and they *cannot* be confined. They *are,* however, subject to discipline. Your gift is not your master; it is an additional aspect of yourself. As such, it is your responsibility to act with discipline, integrity, and respect with regard to your gift, as with all other aspects of your nature. Which brings us to the core of your problem, Emergent yos'Galan."

Padi arranged her face into the expression of faint

good humor which, as a trader, she had found suited her character and her talents far better than Father's look of affable stupidity. She said nothing, merely leaned forward slightly, as if breathless to hear what Healer Osit had to say...

...which was not quite a sham. She *did* want to learn what this stranger thought the core of her problem was, with regard to her stupid so-called gift. While it seemed unlikely to her that this mediocre person was capable of insight beyond that available to Father, Lina, and Priscilla, it was true that she was new to his eyes. An irregularity familiar to, and passed over by, her intimates might be obvious to him.

She waited.

Healer Osit's mouth pinched and he drew himself up, straight and stiff, directing a hard glance directly into her eyes.

"You, Emergent yos'Galan, are spoilt."

She did not laugh. She was...reasonably certain that her face did not betray her.

Healer Osit, however, had access to other senses, and he was impolite enough to use them.

"You're amused?" he asked icily.

"Healer, I am," she answered politely. There was clearly no point in lying.

"And yet you have been much indulged. We will leave aside that you are a member of what was until very recently the Highest of the High Houses seated upon the homeworld. Not even the fall into clanless outcast has diminished your pride or your expectations that everything will go as you wish."

"I am not," Padi said, when the Healer paused to take a breath, "clanless. Only the delm may dissolve a clan, and Korval has not done so. We are—" She held up a hand, forestalling the Healer when he would speak again—

"We are *banished from Liad*, forbidden to trade or to settle any of our business or our blood there, but we *remain* Clan Korval."

The Healer's eyes were angry, and his face was somewhat pale. He took a moment, and a visible breath.

"We wander from our topic," he said. "Which is that you have not learned to master yourself, or to regard the circumstances—or the persons—of those who are exposed to you.

"Even in this matter of the arrival of your gift, you have been indulged. You have not been taught the most rudimentary lessons, nor have you been schooled in the respect that is owed your elders. You will be found much more pleasing to those elders who are constrained by their own gifts and oaths to train you, when you have mastered shielding. Why this was not taught you immediately, I cannot venture to say. I suppose it is possible that you are inept. But, in the case, Healer Faaldom ought to have shielded you.

"Now, attend me. Open your Inner Eyes. Tell me what you See."

Padi bit her lip.

Using her Inner Eyes made her dizzy, at best, and most of the time she didn't know what she was looking at. Father—she had seen Father's wounds clearly, and had known exactly what he had needed. But the patterns and other subtleties that Lina had several times asked her to view with her Inner Eyes might as well have been meaningless smears of spinning colors. She did not, however, explain this to Healer

Osit, who, she felt certain, would merely have sneered at her for providing yet more proof that she was too spoilt to put her hand to hard work.

"Well?"

She closed her . . . well, her Outer Eyes, she supposed they were, and opened those Others.

"I see an expanse of hull plate," she said, and her heart quailed in her chest, recalling the room in which she had imprisoned the tentative beginnings of her gift. A room that she had, in her naivete, thought imaginary, and which she now was beginning to understand had existed in some reality available only to the new senses that had been forced upon her.

"Very good. Observe it closely. This is what a shield looks like from the outside. I will now demonstrate what a shield feels like from the inside."

The hull plate ran, widened, and curved. Padi started back, but it followed her; a panicked glance showed that it was sweeping around, about to seal her inside, and—

Padi *pushed*.

· · · ❖ · · ·

Shields wide open, Shan threw himself against the closed door. What he might have done, had it been locked—but it opened, and he was through, into and past a wall of bitter cold, the air tasting of hull plate. He paused, rapidly Sorting through terror, anger, dismay—

"Padi!"

"Father!"

She was there, she was safe. Dismayed and determined, but unharmed. He put a hand on her shoulder—

The screaming had not abated.

"Osit!" cried Healer Ferin, clearing the door belatedly. She stopped on the threshold, her hand clutching the front of her robe.

Shan followed her horrified stare, found the younger Healer, his eyes wide and not so merry as previously, back flat against the wall directly across from Padi, arms and legs wide, all of him seemingly pinned firmly to the wall.

He was, Shan calculated, about a meter off of the floor. Screaming. Well, and who could say that it was an overreaction, though he seemed in no imminent danger of falling.

"You are," Shan said sternly, "upsetting my daughter."

Healer Osit stopped screaming.

"Thank you. Padi, what has happened here?"

"Father, he was—it was a trap. He was going to, to enclose me, and I—" She swallowed and looked slightly shamefaced. "I pushed."

"And held, or so it appears."

"I don't want him near me."

"Perfectly understandable. I wonder, are you able to release the Healer, if he will grant your safety, and promises not to attempt to entrap you again?"

"I—" She hesitated, which was perhaps not as comforting to the Healer as one might wish, and whispered. "Yes. I—think so."

"Very well, then. Healer Osit!"

"Sir?" the Healer answered faintly.

"My daughter desires your good word as a Healer that you will not attempt to imprison her, should she release you to the floor and your own will."

"I give my word, Healers. I will attempt nothing."

"Excellent. Healer Ferin?"

"Healer yos'Galan?" Her voice was ice cold. Shan felt the tremor of her fury in his bones.

"My party and I are leaving. Pray grant us safe passage to the garden so that we may gather up our security and be gone."

"The House grants safe passage. The House, in fact, insists that you leave and never return."

"I believe that we have an accord. Lina?"

"I am here, Shan, unthreatened and ready to leave as soon as our arrangements are fixed."

"Excellent. Padi, please release Healer Osit from your displeasure. Do *try* to release him gently."

She swallowed, and nodded, and he saw her hands, which were fisted at her sides, begin to relax. Across the room, Healer Osit slid slowly down the wall.

The fact that he did not land on his feet was due entirely to his own lack of coordination, in Shan's estimation. That was understandable, as his nerves appeared to be entirely in disarray. He sat on the floor, tears running down his cheeks. His colleague went to him and knelt at his side.

"We go," Shan said, and took Padi's hand, pulling her with him toward the hallway.

Lina led the way to the front door, which was opened by a wide-eyed doorkeeper, and out into the front yard. Dil Nem and Karna were just rounding the corner of the building, and the five of them exited via the gate, Karna hurrying ahead to the curb, to wave down the approaching omnibus.

Off-Grid

· · · · · · · · ·

"GREAT ONES?" SAID KENCIA AFRINBORER. "OUR POOR
aunt grows weary in her bondage. There are no gods."

Tekelia looked at him with sudden interest. Kencia's
talent was chaotic in the extreme, to the point where
it was best to scrutinize any odd utterance closely.

"Who," Tekelia asked, "said anything of gods?"

Kencia frowned.

"I . . . did *I* say *gods*?"

"You said gods," Tekelia assured him. "What vaulted
you to that opinion?"

Kencia held up his hands. "The words came out of
my mouth, Cousin. Chaos speaking, I fear it."

"And yet it makes a certain sense," Emit torikSelter
said in her turn. "If we posit those who are more
powerful even than the *dramliz*, what can we have
but gods?" She moved her shoulders. "Small gods,
perhaps, but surely that is the next step?"

"Being gods—even small ones—what can they want
from such as us?" Kencia said. "No, it's as I've said,
our aunt is in need of a rest. The Civilized push her
too hard, and she's become confused."

There was great respect for the Oracle among the

Haosa. She was, after all, one of them—a chaotic talent who dealt directly with the ambient field. There was also anger among the Haosa on behalf of the Oracle, imprisoned by Civilization and *put to use* for its benefit. The Oracle belonged with *them*, that was the feeling among the Haosa, who felt a fondness for the *idea* of the Oracle, though most had never seen her, though she did join their celebrations and deliberations from time to time, in spirit, when the ambient favored them.

"My notion," Tekelia said carefully, "is that these Great Ones are the Reaver masters, and the service they will require from us is the return of their slaves."

There was a small silence.

"There is some weight there," murmured Emit, who had Sight of a sort which made Civilization uneasy. A Seer ought not, said the rule-bound Civilized, be able to judge the *most likely* future by weighing the lines of probability. "The question then comes: How do we answer?"

"I think the truth must be our best answer," Banedra said. "They died—and not at our hands. Surely, even Great Ones—gods or not-gods—must accept that mortal creatures die. The ambient will attest our innocence."

There was some murmuring at that, for the slaughter of Reavers had been discussed by the Haosa, who had supported employing other options—first. The ambient could not... always... be counted upon to differentiate between idea and action.

"Our innocence would be a deal more obvious if we could demonstrate a likely cause of their deaths," Tekelia murmured and held up a hand. "Whereupon we have my question, which I had placed before the ambient during our last dance, to resounding silence—"

Tekelia looked 'round at what Civilization understood to be the governing body of the Haosa—counselors, they called themselves, for they both gave and took counsel. They did not, however, govern. Haosa associated governance with Civilization, and Haosa were, at best, scornful of the Civilization which had determined that they were both dangerous and dismissible.

Until such a riddle as the Reavers arose, and the Warden called upon the Haosa to stand up as Civilization's champions.

The irony of this escaped none of the Haosa.

However . . .

"My question," Tekelia said now, "is very simple, Cousins. It is only, why did the Reavers die?"

Maradel arnFaelir, who was a medic and a Healer, leaned forward.

"They died of a massive shock to their autonomic systems," she said. "The signs were very clear upon those I examined." She moved her hand, rocking it back and forth slightly. "I did not examine all of them, but every Reaver I did examine had died of shock. We are, I think, within our rights, and the realm of what is reasonable, to assume that all fell thus."

She frowned at Tekelia. "I told you this."

"You did," Tekelia agreed. "I have perhaps phrased my question clumsily, and therefore earned the ambient's rebuff during our last dance. What I mean to ask is why did they die *here*? How *could* they have died here, Cousins—*particularly* here—where the ambient informs and supports us all?"

Maradel sat up sharply.

"You mean that the ambient ought to have—preserved them?"

"They were talents, every one," Tekelia answered. "Why would it not?"

"For one thing, their purpose was to enslave us!" Kencia cried.

Tekelia considered him thoughtfully.

"Now, that is so, but was that their own intent, or that of their master? Would it have mattered?" Tekelia paused, then spoke again into the disquieted silence. "Could the ambient have . . . *acted*?"

"To preserve *us*, you mean?" Yferen asked. "I don't know as I like that idea, Cousin."

"Nor I," said Maradel. She turned to Banedra. "Have we a precedent?"

The Rememberer held up a hand as she closed her eyes. The rest of them waited in respectful silence until she opened her eyes again, and turned both palms up, empty.

"No precedent. The ambient has never been observed to behave in any way that would suggest intent. It no more has the ability to withhold itself from select individuals than the atmosphere has."

"And yet—what caused this massive systemic shock which killed *only* Reavers?" Tekelia asked. "We need to identify the cause, Cousins, whether we are to host gods or puppetmaster."

"I see it!" Emit cried, her eyes fixed on something over Maradel's head.

She started to her feet, dancing, entranced, her gaze fixed on the lines of probability. Catching her thought, Tekelia leapt up to dance with her, open to the ambient, between it and the Seer's ecstasy.

"I see it!" Emit cried again. "A silver blade descending. Black ribbons part. They recoil, returning to those who are bound. Struck, they are stunned. They fall. And so quickly are they gone from us. Gone!" she shouted, her voice ringing against the roof beams. "Dead, and lost!"

She stumbled, dancing no more, going to her knees with a cry that became a wail of grief. Yferen went to her and brought her to her chair. He knelt and held her hands as she grieved a loss that was not theirs.

Tekelia went to the buffet, filled a cup with fruit juice, and returned. Yferen took the cup carefully, and lifted it to Emit's lips.

"Drink, Cousin," he murmured.

"Stunned," Maradel said. She was standing, turning slowly around so that she faced each of those gathered, one by one. "They had no time to reach out, or to open themselves, and be saved."

She took a hard breath and met Tekelia's eyes.

"This answers all," she said. "Why it was only Reavers who fell. Why they all died at once. The very shock to their nervous systems."

"The puppetmaster is dead, then?" said Kencia, halfway between a question and a statement.

Tekelia turned to face him.

"You don't sound certain, Cousin."

"Well, I'm not," Kencia returned, frowning at Emit, who was still sipping her juice. "The lines were cut, so we're told. What we're not told is that the master shared the fate of their playthings."

"But even if not," said Maradel, "they will have no reason to come here, demanding explanations and reparations."

"True enough," said Kencia, flapping his arms in

one of his characteristic gestures. "All that's needed is for them to send more."

"If they have more," Maradel snapped. "How many puppets do you imagine one master might hold?"

"We don't know that there is only one master," Kencia retorted.

Emit had finished her juice. Yferen rose and crossed the room to fetch her another, and something to eat.

"That's true," Tekelia said, and sighed. "Nor do we know if the puppetmaster has a master."

"But we have been told," said Banedra, "to expect gods."

Dutiful Passage
Millsap Orbit

. . . .

I

SHAN POURED A GLASS OF THE RED AND CARRIED IT TO
the desk.

The disappointment at Millsap—no. He had no
regrets to waste on the affair at Millsap. If Padi
remained unSorted, she had not been harmed—and
in fact had shown a gratifying amount of restraint in
her rebuttal of Healer Osit's temerity, merely holding
him against the wall, when Shan had received the
distinct impression that it was entirely within her
scope to have thrown him through it.

Really, it made a father's heart glow.

Their arrival back on the *Passage* having coincided
with her usual hours with Cargo Master ira'Barti,
Padi had taken herself off to that pleasurable duty.
Lina had gone to her station in the ship's library, and
Shan had returned to his office, his mind occupied
by two necessities.

He had finally put his finger on the very person
with whom he might profitably share his concerns
regarding the Terran route that nurtured Millsap.

Janifer Carresens-Denobli.

Of course.

Before he did so, however, he needed to complete one more, minor bit of research.

Leaning to the screen, he tapped in a series of three commands, calling up a star map of Millsap space, including the Terran Loop. Working carefully with the screen, he traced the route back from Millsap, to its point of origin—

"Hah!"

He grinned at the star map, increased the gain, made one more adjustment.

A dense field of purple triangles bloomed in the area of space he was studying, each triangle marking a note regarding navigational hazards and special conditions of local space.

Nodding, he moved his field of interest a trifle past Twidee, the planet where the Conway Primary Loop originated, increasing the optics only slightly...

An infobox bloomed, brilliantly orange.

Dust alert.

"Excellent," Shan crooned, and tapped the box.

NOTE: Check your programming! Rapid changes in density within Jump arrival and departure zones in Finashif Sector are expected to diminish as the proper motion of the greater Rostov's Dust Cloud and proper and radial motion of cha'Goolin's Star contribute to a return of system dynamics toward stable approach parameters. Jump approaches based on historic local and regional dust occlusion densities may result in substantial Jump offset. Use of Dust Avoidance tables or data older than two Standard Years for approaching this region is not recommended.

*Check your programming! Figures attached are based
on successful Jump reports within the last 1/10 Standard Year or less.*

Shan leaned back and picked up his glass, enjoying the momentary glow of having guessed correctly.

With the Dust taking a different direction, it would
be reasonable for the traders of Twidee to send ships
out to explore this newly accessible space in terms
of trade. Indeed, it would be foolish not to do so.
Naturally enough, they would have to draw on the
inventory of ships in hand, which meant one—or even
two—fewer available to the Conway Loop. The goods
delivered to Millsap would therefore be less—very
slightly so, in the scheme of things, but more than
enough to catch a master trader's eye—and present
him with an opportunity.

Leaning back in the chair, he considered the possibilities before him.

Trader Carresens-Denobli had not answered his
last letter. Here was an opportunity to continue
their contact without seeming to be too eager in
their discussion of the possible Ashlan-Surebleak-
Nomi-Oxin-Rood Loop proposed by the trader. The
seeming alteration of a long-established Terran Loop
must concern a man who was at once a trader-at-large
for the Carresens Syndicate, and a senior trade com-
missioner. Shan would, perhaps, be doing the trader
a good turn, if he had not already understood the
alteration in the motion of the Dust in Finashif Sector.

If Trader Carresens-Denobli *was* aware of the new
situation, a letter from Shan would demonstrate that
he was a worthy trade partner, observant and willing
to share information.

Yes...

He reached for the screen, paused with his fingers over the keys, and then began, gently, to type.

To Janifer Carresens-Denobli, I offer greeting and information of possible use, for the good of trade...

II

"ALLOW ME TO COMPLIMENT YOU ON YOUR DISPLAY OF good sense and fine control at Millsap," Lina said, speaking Liaden in the mode of instructor-to-student.

Padi, seated on the other side of the small worktable, did not bite her lip, but it was a near thing. Lina was—not *angry*. Not *exactly* angry. But she was... distressed. And she had been so since they had left the Healer Hall on Millsapport.

Indeed, she had been quite subdued during the entire return to the *Passage*. Padi had received the distinct impression that Lina was not only out of sorts with her, but that she was... displeased... with *Father*.

When they had boarded the shuttle, Lina and Father had gone to the backest seats possible. That much Padi had noticed before she had begun wheedling shuttle Pilot Kris Embrathiri to let her sit second, or at least observer, for the lift to the ship.

It had taken very little wheedling before Kris allowed her to observe, and Padi had not seen Father, or Lina, again until they had exited the shuttle, each with their own necessities in mind. Padi, having realized that she could be on time for Master ira'Barti, had made her bow to the master trader and dashed off for her scheduled session with the cargo master.

Master ira'Barti had put her to work running remote pod stabilization queries, and realignments, as necessary. She had embraced the dull task so willingly that, for the last hour of her work session, she had been assigned to inventory the tool kits attached to each hold.

All too soon, however, her session in Cargo was over, and she dutifully moved on to the next item...

...*dramliz* lessons with Lina.

And Lina was out of sorts. Worse, Padi wasn't quite able to tell if the compliment on her good sense and fine control might not be irony. The High Tongue was uniquely suited to both irony and ambiguity. Being able to parse such nuances was an important survival skill, in trade as much as in society—and to ask after the speaker's meaning was to display a weakness.

However...

Padi took a careful breath.

Lina, she reminded herself, was her teacher; she was Lina's student. Their relative *melant'i* allowed—insisted upon!—the asking and answering of questions. It was not weakness for a student to ask of her teacher; it was a mark of respect.

"Forgive me," Padi said, in the mode of student-to-instructor, "but I wonder what I may have done to displease you."

There was a pause before Lina inclined her head gently.

"You have done nothing to displease me," she said. "I had hoped for sweeping solutions or, at the least, unique insight from the Healers of Millsap, and I am dismayed to find my expectations dashed. As your tutor, I wish to teach you well; I wish to see you embrace your gift, to grow with it into the fullness of yourself." She smiled slightly. "In a word, I am not confident in myself. I have tutored many—Healers and *dramliz*—with success. However, it is very true that no one is the best tutor for all students. And it comes to me, forcefully, that I may not be the tutor you need."

Padi took a careful breath. "In truth, I have not been the most willing scholar."

"In truth," Lina agreed with a return of her usual humor. "However, you have not been *rebellious*. We have been working together, and if our pace has not been brisk, it has been tending in the correct direction..."

"But there's something about me, or my talent," Padi said, "that disturbs you. Instructor, if I may be frank..."

"By all means, let us both be frank," Lina said dryly. "What occurs to you?"

"It occurs to me that you *are* a Healer," Padi said slowly. "If you feel there is something amiss, then—perhaps it would be best to..." She paused, recalling the phrase that Lina used so often—"listen to your talent."

Lina laughed.

"Yes, I know this dagger—it is precisely my own!"

That was from a *melant'i* play, Padi knew, though she didn't quite place which—and in any case, Lina was sweeping on.

"You make a compelling case. However, we are pinned by necessity. You must become proficient in the basic forms, for your own safety even more than for the comfort of your elders-in-craft who so concerned the Healers at Millsap. We do not give weapons into untrained hands, nor do we allow Emergent Healers and just-fledged wizards to ply their gifts, untrained. There are traps for us as there are for anyone else, and you must at least learn how to protect yourself."

There was nothing to argue with in that, nor did Padi argue. Instead, she put forth the thought that had caught her, fresh as she was from testing tolerances, measuring stresses, and realigning pod loads.

"How am I unlike?" she asked.

Lina frowned.

"Unlike—whom?"

"No—in what way do I differ from your other students—in general formation, I mean. Are there... benchmarks? Skills that are generally mastered in the first three days, six days, twelve?"

"I see."

Lina's frown deepened somewhat as she took counsel with herself.

"Most," she said slowly, "grasp the basic forms very quickly—within hours of being shown, as if they instinctively knew that there was system and pattern, and needed only to be shown a shape..."

She looked at Padi thoughtfully.

"Perhaps it had been like that for you, when you were made known to your first piloting equation."

Padi remembered that moment; she had adored the star map rugs that were part of the décor of a nursery for pilots. She remembered the moment she realized that the equation set she had just solved was *the key to the map*; that if she only applied herself and learned all the variables...

"Yes," she told Lina. "I do know what you mean."

"Excellent. And—we have come 'round again to my opening gambit. I am quite sincerely impressed by your accomplishment at Millsap, which spoke of a cool control of your gift. I wonder if you will repeat what you did there, for me, here, now."

Padi blinked.

"You want me to hold you against the wall? I—with all respect—"

Lina held up her hand.

"Forgive me. What I would like is an opportunity to observe your technique. I think that a demonstration, where Healer Osit is replaced by something inanimate, might inform both of us."

"I see," Padi said, not quite truthfully. "What should we—"

Lina reached into her pocket and, with a flourish, placed a red stylus on the table between them.

"Here we have an exceptionally impertinent writing instrument. It has scolded you and bullied you and may be preparing to entrap you. How do you answer, Emergent yos'Galan?"

Padi's lips twitched. It was too ridiculous, the bright pretty thing reposing innocently in the center of the table, the antithesis of Healer Osit with his disdain and his self-importance, and the stink of metal as hull plate expanded, curving left, curving right—and she would be trapped!

Padi—pushed.

The red stylus shot upward.

"Oh, no!" she cried, leaping to her feet, to do what, she scarcely knew—and it fell, after all, to ship's gravity for solving.

There was a hollow *thud*—and in the center of the table was Lina's stylus, pretty no more, but rather . . . singed . . . and—was . . . it?

Padi leaned forward and winced.

Yes. It was definitely smoking.

"Well," Lina said carefully. "I see there is some

emotion tied to the memory of Healer Osit's attempted tutoring." She looked up. "It appears that the ceiling escaped damage," she said.

"But your stylus!" Padi said, sitting down weakly. Gods, gods, if the stylus had been Healer Osit in truth...

"I might have killed him," she whispered.

"Perhaps. It is to remove this sort of uncertainty that we train. In the case, however, I believe what we have seen is a proportional error, in which you brought the precise amount of force necessary to push and hold a grown Healer to the wall, against my unfortunate stylus. One must be certain the equation is properly scaled to the task. This concept is familiar to you, I think."

"Yes," Padi said slowly. "Relativity is key."

"Exactly."

Lina paused, her face set in that expression which meant that her instructor was weighing options and best possible methods.

Padi waited, trying not to look at the sad, singed thing in the center of the table.

"I regret," Lina said.

Padi blinked. "Regret?"

"Indeed. I regret that all I know is a path which I am increasingly persuaded is not suited for your feet. There is a thing that is said among Terrans—*Bad training is worse than none*, which in many cases is true, but not in this. I have consulted my feelings"—she offered Padi a brief smile—"and I remain convinced that the solution formed by the ship's three Healers is sound. It can do you no harm to have a grounding in the forms. They are universal. For instance, Priscilla's training differed—vastly—from my own. Yet, we may communicate as Healers and easily collaborate on such work as may require both of us."

She moved her shoulders, her smile fading.

"Therefore, we must return to the topic of precision, you and I. We are agreed that you must achieve proportion—there should be just enough energy spent to accomplish the task in hand, no more. This ensures that you do not set the table afire whilst attempting to light the candles."

"Or burn a stylus by using too much force."

"Yes. Also, you know, there is another facet to this exercise, tiresome as I know you find it. The more you work with your talent, the more you will come to terms with the fact of it. You have here an opportunity to build a relationship with your gifts."

"But my gifts *are me*," Padi protested. "They manifested in a particular way because of who I am."

"Your gifts are *one aspect* of who you are, and like the other aspects of your personality, they must be schooled and integrated into the whole. For instance, I warrant that you have had training in controlling your temper. You will, in fact, have had several tutors, beginning in the nursery. By now, you are quite accomplished in its regulation. Sometimes, you are angry, but you choose not to demonstrate the fact. Sometimes, you are *very* angry, and you allow the merest wisp of displeasure to be seen."

She smiled.

"In the many years I have known him, I have once seen your father entirely angry. It is something that I do not wish to see again. He had not, you understand, *lost his temper*; he had *unleashed his anger*: it was a weapon, and he wielded it so.

"Your gifts are multifaceted: properly applied, you may use them to assist those in need; to defend those under your protection; to restore those who have been wounded; and to elude those who wish to harm you. As you know which tool in your belt is suited to a particular job, so you must learn which aspect of your gift to call upon to aid you in a particular circumstance."

Lina paused, considering, so Padi thought, whether she ought to go on. After a moment she inclined her head.

"You must also learn *when* your gift is the best answer to a problem. You have power—a great deal of power—though it does, as everything, have limits. But, just as a dagger is not the best tool for signing a waybill, so, too, your talent is not always the best solution to an immediate problem.

"You must always recall that you have options, and you must take care not to become overdependent upon your gifts. They are an *enhancement*; they complement your other skills; they are subject to your intellect, and your judgment. *You* choose how—or if—to answer a perceived threat. In the case of Healer Osit—I do not mean to belittle your ultimate choice because I believe it was the best of several to hand. However, only consider what you might have done instead."

She held up her hand, thumb extended.

"You might have called out."

She extended her forefinger.

"You might have run."

Second finger: "You might have physically restrained him."

She paused before extending her third finger, expression wry.

"You might, in fact, have allowed the Healer to proceed.

"Some of those choices were better suited to the situation than others. But it is well to always remember that you *have* options, precisely as you did before your gift broke through. You have not been reduced to one answer; rather, you have been given an additional category of solutions."

Padi said nothing. Lina inclined her head, as if she had heard Padi's doubts, and continued.

"So, then, you will please allow me to link with you. I intend to demonstrate the formation and use of a simple lift-tool. This is a basic protocol, designed to help beginning practitioners rightly judge the amount of force required for particular tasks."

She extended her hand, palm up.

Padi drew a breath to calm the flutter in her belly. This was *Lina*, after all. They had linked several times since her gift had arrived, mostly so Lina could fully observe her process.

Lina would not, Padi told herself firmly, try to entrap her.

She placed her palm against the other woman's palm.

"Thank you. Now attend me."

There came a sensation of slight warming, and Padi saw a swirl of mist just above the tabletop, to the right of the scorched stylus. The mist coalesced, taking on a wedge shape.

Once the shape was set, Padi felt a shift in the air—a push, in fact.

"You see?" Lina murmured.

"I do . . ." Padi said, and wondered if she should mention that she had no clear idea how to produce a tool of her own, though she had just watched this one being formed.

"I will now transfer the wedge to you, so that you may learn its shape and essence," Lina said.

Padi felt a . . . weight approach, and instinctively—*reached* with something other than her hands, but which nonetheless felt perfectly natural. She sat, holding the wedge . . . somehow, feeling the shape and the weight, and the . . . intention behind its making.

"Excellent," Lina said eventually. "Return it to me, please."

Fumbling, Padi managed to push the thing in Lina's general direction, and was aware of its weight vanishing.

"We unlink now," Lina murmured, and Padi lifted her hand away, blinking to clear the wisps of mist from her eyes.

Across the table, Lina sat with hands folded, the scorched stylus somewhat removed from its original landing area. She inclined her head.

"For your off-shift practice," she said, "you will use the lift we have practiced together to raise a stylus fifteen centimeters from the top of your desk. You will hold it steady for a slow count to six, then lower the stylus to the desktop. You will do twelve repetitions. For the first, you will use as much energy as you believe is necessary for the task—no more. For each succeeding repetition, you will decrease the energy you bring to the task until you are unable to lift the stylus. When you reach that point, increase your output of energy as slowly as you are able, until the stylus rises. While you are doing this practice, pay especial attention to the quality of the energy that you raise, and note its characteristics: temperature, texture, weight, shape, and any other factor that arises to your notice. Do not rush through this exercise. Take time to observe the quality of each energy level."

She paused, and added, "When you have finished the twelve repetitions, open your Inner Eyes and observe the stylus. Be ready to recall and describe what you See.

"Do you have any questions?"

Padi did not sigh.

"No, Lina. Thank you."

The Healer laughed aloud.

"Yes, it *is* a tiresome exercise, fully as tedious as studying exchange rates, or dancing basic footwork in *menfri'at*! I ask your forgiveness for placing such a burden upon your gift, which I assure you is dazzling and complex and wholly beyond me. My only excuse is the one given by all tutors in the groundwork of a skill: You must be certain of the foundation which will support every thing that you will build upon it. Truly, it is best to go slowly, and test every joint and nail. Which I know is very little comfort to you, when you wish to open your wings and soar!"

Padi smiled, and bowed. "How should the student forgive the teacher?" She paused, and added wistfully, "Though I should *like* to soar, if only a little."

Lina frowned slightly.

"There is something in what you say. Allow me to consult with Priscilla and with Shan. Perhaps something may be arranged. In the meanwhile, Student, our lesson for this shift is done. Until our next meeting, be well, be attentive, and be strong."

III

HIS LETTER SENT, SHAN OPENED HIS RESEARCH FILE. THE information had not grown more hopeful in the time he had spent away from it. In fact, it seemed even more dismal than before, mere lines and columns of statistics and facts with no glow of interesting possibility to any of it.

If he had hoped to find that their side trip to Millsap had reshuffled possibility in a positive way—he would have been sorely disappointed. The next closest port of even small interest was Pommier, which . . . he called up the various indexes, confirming what he already knew. Of small interest to the *Passage* and to Korval, was Pommierport.

Shan spun his chair so that his back was to the screen, crossed his arms behind his head, and tipped back until he was staring at the ceiling.

He and the ceiling were old friends; he had many times sought its advice in the face of a knotty problem. Indeed, this was not the first time they had met together on the topic of designing a new route sufficient to the clan's necessities. If only it were to be the—

A chime sounded, sweet and brief. Shan dropped the chair to perpendicular, spun 'round to face the door, and stood.

"Come!" he called, as if the door wouldn't open to her hand. It was an old joke, comfortably worn in, like an old jacket.

But Priscilla, when she entered a moment later, was not smiling. She looked, Shan thought, weary, and there was an undercurrent of annoyance buzzing along the lifemate link.

He hoped, without much confidence, that he wasn't the cause of this ill mood. But, even if he was, it was clearly his part to offer her ease.

"Hello, Priscilla," he said gently. "Would you like a glass of wine?"

She smiled briefly. "I'll just have some tea. May I refresh your glass?"

"Thank you, no; I've only just filled it," he said, and watched her cross the room, pour, and return to settle into the chair opposite him.

He sank back into his own chair, raised his glass. She raised hers; they drank.

Replacing his glass, he considered his options. Best, he thought, just to ask. He cleared his throat.

"Lina tells me that the Healers of Millsap were . . . unhelpful," Priscilla said, interrupting him before he had fairly begun.

"*Unhelpful* scarcely brings us into far orbit around the Healers of Millsap," he said, startled by the bitterness in his own voice.

"They took leave to remonstrate with Padi regarding her lack of care for her elders, after which one of the pair attempted to surround her in his shields."

"Surely he had a reason," Priscilla murmured.

"Surely he did," he said sharply. "He wished to demonstrate to her what it felt like to be enclosed by shields. Padi, however, recalls most vividly the crisis she was brought to by locking her gifts away. Indeed, her elders have been at great pains to tell her—repeatedly—that her method was an error of some proportion."

He took a breath, and finished, more moderately.

"Also, I gather that she did not find him...reassuring."

Priscilla sighed. "Did she hurt him?"

Shan shook his head. "She startled him. She may have frightened him. But she did not *hurt* him."

He put the glass down.

"It's entirely possible that he found being held against the wall a meter or so above the floor...uncomfortable. He may have feared falling, though to my eye, he was being held very firmly."

He paused to catch his breath, which was absurd, and finished more quietly. "I asked her to release him, which she promptly did, allowing him to slide most gently down to the rug. I witnessed no harshness, no cruelty, no carelessness."

Priscilla sipped her tea thoughtfully.

"It takes considerable fine control," she said at last, "to lift and hold a man against a wall."

"So I was just remarking to myself. Even Lina allows it to be so."

"Does Lina think Padi overreacted?"

Shan sighed, recalling his last, rather tense conversation with Lina.

"Lina remains convinced—has become more convinced—that she is no fit tutor for Padi. The display of fine control that you and I find so admirable in the case...perturbs Lina. I gather she would be easier if Padi had left even a *small* dent in the wall."

Priscilla smiled, briefly, and sipped more tea.

"And yourself?" she asked eventually.

"Myself?" he repeated. "I am altogether distasteful

to the Healers of Millsap, an opinion I can't really dispute, given that I was so ill-natured as to entertain a panic attack in answer to a modest request that I drop my shields. In addition, I preferred Lina's touch, and was found to have taken my wounds from a forced Healing, which was nothing more, and possibly less, than I deserved."

"A panic attack," Priscilla murmured.

"Yes. Ridiculous of me. She was entirely civilized, and yet—"

He stopped, and looked into her eyes, turning his hands up to demonstrate precisely how empty they were.

"I believe that I may be experiencing a bit of post-trauma distress."

"I can help you with that, if you wish," Priscilla said softly.

He glanced aside.

"Unless," Priscilla said, after a moment, "there's some value to holding the trauma close."

Yes, well, trust Priscilla to lay her hand immediately on the dilemma.

He met her eyes again.

"It may be that there is," he said, which was nothing more than the truth given between lifemates. "I'm uncertain in my own mind, if you will have it."

"Healer Ferin did give as her professional opinion that the lingering cuts and bruises might be Healed with minimal risk, and some gain in overall health. That has been done..."

"Lina?" murmured Priscilla.

"Indeed. I believe it may be best, for clarity, to allow the new Healing a day or two to resolve, before making an in-depth evaluation."

"That seems wise," Priscilla agreed. "Let's talk again in a few days."

"Yes."

"In the meantime," Priscilla began—and paused.

Slowly, she straightened in her chair and glanced down at her hands, now folded on her knee. There was a flutter across the lifemate link, then a sense of decision taken.

Puzzled, Shan waited.

Priscilla lifted her face to his, her mobile features composed, very nearly Liaden in their smooth lack of emotion.

"The captain inquires of the master trader," she said in the High Tongue.

Shan blinked.

Over the years, Priscilla had gained near-native fluency in the High Tongue—no easy task for one not born to the burden—but they rarely spoke Liaden between themselves, preferring Terran, or the love language they had created together.

Certainly, they did not play *melant'i* games with each other—they were lifemates: one heart, one soul, one *melant'i*, so tradition had it.

Except . . . not precisely.

After all, Priscilla *was* the captain, and he . . . *was* the master trader.

He took another breath.

Really, Shan, he told himself, strive for some breeding.

Melant'i had been invoked, and at the highest level. He would insult the good captain if he sat silent and gaping even a moment longer.

Therefore, he inclined his head.

"The master trader awaits the captain's inquiry with interest."

It was shading the High Tongue, that *with interest*, lending it a cool semblance of warmth. And yet, he could not speak to Priscilla as if they shared nothing more than their relative *melant'is* of captain and trader.

Priscilla was in a fair way to winning this game, if game it was. Her expression was properly bland, she looked at his face, but did not make eye contact. Impeccable. One would scarcely be able to contain one's admiration were one not frightened half to death.

"The captain wonders after the master trader's proposed route," she said.

His route? Surely, she knew that he had no route, that he had been flailing in the muck, trying to find, shape or buy a route for the last—

Oh.

Suddenly, he saw where this was going. Into a minefield, that was where it was going, and very possibly into a quarrel. Priscilla was . . . not at high energy, while he—well, it had been recently established that he was emotionally at risk. Perfect starting material for a quarrel, especially if they remained in Terran, which was so charmingly . . . intimate.

The High Tongue, however, was chilly and distant, which made a . . . *heated* quarrel impossible, though the outcome of the conversation might yet be disappointing.

"The master trader," he said, his mode austere and impeccable, "continues his researches in regard to a route. Has the captain a suggestion?"

He might have properly ended his reply with *route*, but there was no point in prolonging this uncomfortable conversation by insisting that she petition him to entertain another inquiry.

"The captain suggests that the master trader might

combine two necessary tasks with care for kin and self. The captain is able to provide to the master trader a short list—three worlds, rated safe to very safe, with access to well-regarded Healer Halls large enough to accommodate a staff of teaching Healers.

"The captain is also able to provide the coordinates and a brief for a fourth world, also rated safe, which shelters an independent Circle of priestesses, a temple, and a school. Customized tutorial programs are also possible."

Oh, yes, Shan thought, so very, *very* much better to pursue this conversation in the High Tongue.

He inclined his head.

"One values the captain's good sense, and her advice. Please forward the particulars of these worlds and I will include them in my researches. When those researches are complete, the master trader will petition the captain to set course. As is proper."

Gods, that was cold, he thought, hearing himself. Only—cold was better—twelves better!—than hot.

Priscilla—the captain of *Dutiful Passage*, say rather— inclined her head, and stood.

"The captain thanks the master trader for his consideration."

She did not bow, perhaps being uncertain of the proper mode. Gods knew *he* was uncertain of the proper mode.

Therefore, he rose with a murmured, "Captain," and walked with her to the door, which he opened for her with his own hand.

He stood there, long after the door had closed, feeling breathless and without connection, trembling on the edge of weeping.

Gods abound, but he was a fool!

No, he corrected himself. No, he was *much* more than a mere fool.

Only count the ways.

He was a master trader failing in his duty to his clan...

A thodelm who had forgotten proper care of kin...

A Healer who could not Heal...

A father who imperiled his heir...

A man whose lifemate feared his temper...

Oh, it was a marvelous list, and it could, he thought, grow longer and more desperate yet, if he were willing to give in entirely to self-pity and despair.

Suddenly, he wanted, very much, to talk with his father.

His father, who had been master trader when Shan had been Padi's age, and a hopeful 'prentice.

His father, who had followed his lifemate into death twelve years ago.

Sadly, conversing with the dead was beyond the scope of any Healer or *dramliza*...

He blinked, and took a hard breath.

"No," he said aloud to the empty room. "Not quite."

Shan put the box in the center of his desk and considered it for a moment. It was not a large box; one might easily slip it into a sample case or a leave bag. There was a thumb lock set into the top. The rest was of the particular color and grain that told those who had grown up sheltered by its branches, that the box had been made from the wood of Jelaza Kazone itself.

He had seen it before—three times, exactly.

The first time, it had merely seemed an oversight, though Er Thom yos'Galan had not been the sort of man to overlook such details. The box had been in the center of the desk, much as now, and the master trader intent on some work on his screen when Shan had arrived for a consultation.

"My notes," he had said to Shan's carefully unquestioning glance. "I should say, my *flights*. On the rare occasion anything beneficial actually comes out of an exercise, I bring it forward into the master trader's files."

He then put the box away in the bottom-most drawer of the desk, and brought them to the subject of their consultation.

The second time Shan had seen the box...had been after Mother had died. Er Thom, haggard, weakened by the death of his lifemate, had called Shan to him. There again was the box, in the center of the desk.

"It should know you," his father had said, beckoning him closer. "Put your thumb against the plate."

The third time he had seen the box had been immediately after his father's death, when he had taken up the duties of the master trader attached to *Dutiful Passage*. It had been nestled in its drawer, and he had seen no need to disturb it then, nor even once in the years since he had stepped into the void left by his father's death.

So, now: the fourth encounter.

Gently, he pressed his thumb to the lock.

A soft chime sounded, followed by an even softer *click*. Shan raised the lid of the box.

Inside, two rows of personal tablets were tidily filed by date, earliest at the top left, most recent at the bottom right.

"Well, then," Shan murmured. "Where to start, I wonder?"

He closed his eyes, emptied his mind, and—breathed, witnessing the passage of each breath until, in response to what stimuli he could not have said, he opened his eyes—and saw that he was holding a tablet in his right hand.

He glanced at the box. He had drawn a book from the second row dated Standard Year 1374.

"Now, why this one?" he asked softly, but of course there was only one way to find out.

He reached to the screen and set his status to *do not disturb* for the next six hours.

That done, he settled more comfortably into his chair, and pressed the tablet's access switch.

A pearly glow rose from the depths of the screen, washing out to the margins. There was a subtle flicker, and words arrived, line after line in a neat, no-nonsense script, black and firm against the glowing background.

Shan gasped, tears rising for the second time in an hour. He blinked, closed his eyes, and once again merely sat, breathing, until the grief thinned, leaving him in what might be called peace.

He sat for another few minutes, to be certain of himself.

Then he opened his eyes, and began to read.

I want to speak with my brother, his father had written on Zeldra Eighthday in the sixth year after Aelliana Caylon had been murdered; five years after her lifemate, Er Thom's *cha'leket*, had left Liad, heart-reft and half-alive, to draw the enemies of Korval away from the clan.

It had been put about that Daav yos'Phelium had

died soon after his departure from the homeworld, though Shan had never heard his father say so. Indeed, Father, then *Korval-pernard'i*, holding the Ring in trust for Val Con—had never written Daav out of the clan book, nor made any notation of a death beyond Aunt Aelli's, until he had written the name of his own lifemate on that page.

He had, in the years after Daav's departure, developed an interest in the scholarly works of one Jen Sar Kiladi, a professor of cultural genetics teaching at Delgado University. Such an interest might seem out of the way for a mere merchant, master of trade though he was. However, Er Thom's interests had been wide-ranging, after his passion for trade.

It had taken Daav's return to the care of his clan, scarcely a Standard gone by—years after his *cha'leket's* death—to inspire Er Thom's heir to reconsider that particular collection of books and monographs.

Well.

Shan returned his attention to the tablet he held, the words written just so, the strokes of the stylus clean and sharp. Almost, it seemed to him he *could* hear his father's voice as he read.

In the old days, Daav and I would sit together over our wine and share our knottiest problems. Often, one saw what the other had not, and so a solution was made. Just as often, the telling was enough to see the difficulty melt away.

If only this matter would melt away. And perhaps it will, if only I tell the tale out.

So, my fancy is this: I say to my cha'leket, as we sit over our wine, just here and now, that I fear for the continued survival of the clan.

He will laugh, will Daav, and swear that he had known how it would be when he left Korval in my hands. Then he will invite me to show him those things that vex me.

These, then, Brother. These, I lay before you.

I hope—I confess it—that you will show me that I have brought you nothing more than fog and folly.

I truly wish that you may do so.

IV

PADI GLARED AT THE STYLUS, HER CHOSEN SUBJECT, AS it reposed peacefully on the surface of her desk. She had cleared the other things that normally occupied the area—extra styli, note taker, keyboard—to one side, so that there should be no question regarding which object she was focused upon.

She had taken a deep breath, to center herself, and consciously formed the object Lina had shown her. When it was firmly in mind, she laboriously slipped it under the stylus.

Which had risen, in a slow and seemly manner—not at all like Lina's poor stylus—and stopped when she ceased exerting pressure via the lifting tool.

There was one, entirely minor deviation in the expected result—the stylus was slowly turning on its axis, as if the lift had produced extra energy; or, as if the stylus were a bored child, shifting from one foot to another, flirting with an outright reprimand.

Still, Padi thought, with a small smile of satisfaction—already she had an improvement over her performance of this afternoon. Perhaps there was something to Lina's admonitions to go slowly, to be careful, to think twice . . .

She took another breath, centering herself, and focused her will on the stylus.

The rotation ceased.

Excellent.

Now, for the second part of the assignment.

She lowered the lifting tool, slowly, mindfully, to the desk.

The stylus, however, did not follow the tool. It remained floating in its original position with nothing but its own stubbornness to support it.

Well, perhaps she had disassociated the lift from its object. Since she was not entirely certain how the tool and the object acted upon each other, that seemed the likeliest explanation.

She focused on the tool, extended her will—and swore as it disintegrated into an untidy spangle of sparks.

After a moment, almost as an afterthought, the stylus clattered to the desktop, rolled and stopped.

Padi glared at it. Nothing in particular happened.

She closed her eyes and recruited her patience. When she felt quite calm, she carefully rebuilt the tool, watching it form in her mind's eye, and feeling a slow burn near the base of her spine, where Lina taught that her gift—the power that fueled her gift—was to be found.

Mindfully, carefully, she slipped the tool between the stylus and the desk, and using only the very slightest amount of energy, lifted.

The stylus remained on the desk, the tool passing through it as if it didn't exist.

More energy, Padi thought, bringing the tool down again.

She exerted herself slightly more, raised the tool—

And the stylus remained firmly on the desk.

Padi exhaled. Loudly.

"Fine," she muttered, "be coy, do."

She turned her attention to the notepad resting innocently at the side of the desk, slid the tool beneath it—and watched it rise with calm exactitude to stop its ascent precisely fifteen centimeters from the surface of the desk.

Holding her breath, Padi reversed her thought, and the notepad descended gently, returning to the desktop with a slight bump.

Padi took a deep breath. She wasn't supposed to hold her breath when she was using her talent; she knew that. Just, when she was working so slowly, it felt like she might spoil things if she breathed the wrong way. She never felt that way when—well, for instance, when she wasn't paying complete attention and small items around her began to spontaneously lift away from the surfaces on which they had been resting . . .

When that did occur, she just said something along the lines of—*all of you go back where you belong, now!*

There was no sensation of heat, or of her thought taking on a particular shape. It was very much as if she were talking to—well, to one of the cats at home, who had been misbehaving.

Which didn't help her with the stylus, she thought. Or did it?

"You might *try* to be convenable," she said to it, scolding just a little, as she were in fact speaking to a mischievous kitten. "My tutor specifically mentioned this exercise with regard to a stylus. I'd think you'd be pleased to be noticed."

The stylus . . . quivered, and suddenly, with no more help from her than that, it rose smoothly to a height of precisely fifteen centimeters, and stopped, as still as if it were resting on the desk.

"There," Padi said approvingly, "that's more the thing. Except, you know, it's my part in this to observe the quality of my gifts when the desired result is produced, and the only sensation I have is one of slight foolishness, because I'm talking to a pen."

The stylus began to rotate.

"Stop that," Padi snapped.

To her amazement, it obeyed.

Padi frowned at the stylus and thought.

What she practiced with Lina was akin to *daibri'at*, except instead of moving slowly and stretching every muscle, one engaged with one's gift and did a series of slow, precise mental stretches.

The reason for those exercises was precisely the same as for physical exercise: to work with a certain set of muscles, with the view to making them supple and strong.

Lina also had her practice seeing with the Inner Eyes. This was, in Padi's experience, far more difficult than even physical *daibri'at*, which did not come easily to her at all.

The Inner Eyes saw...auras. This was Lina's strength. Not only could she see someone's living aura, she was able to manipulate the personality, mending broken threads, reweaving sections which had been worn away by illness or trauma.

The only thing Padi saw when she tried to focus her Inner Eyes were smears of meaningless colors.

It was much the same with the Inner Ears.

Lina could hear what she described as *whisperings*. Not that she read minds; only, Lina had said lightly, emotions.

"Which is a great deal more useful, you know," she told Padi during their first lesson. "I do not need to know *why* a particular person is angry at me. All I need to know is the fact of her anger, so that I might prudently remove myself from her vicinity."

"But if you could hear her reasons..." Padi ventured, and Lina laughed.

"One of my colleagues at the Hall where I was 'prenticed could read minds. He described it to me as a vile confusion of noise. We do not, he said, have one thought at a time, but an unending, interwoven riot of thoughts. To pick out one thread and follow its progression, while all the other thoughts of all the other people in your immediate vicinity are beating against your mind—is not possible.

"Worse, prolonged exposure to unfiltered thought is known to be fatal to those who are vulnerable. The masters at the Hall therefore concentrated on teaching him how to build impenetrable shields and, after they were in place, to maintain them at the least cost possible, so that he was not constantly assaulted by the racket of other people, thinking.

"He was fortunate that Healers were often born to his House. He might have died screaming within a day of having come into his gift, save there was a kinswoman in-House who was a Healer. She immediately understood what had occurred, shielded him heavily and bore him to the Hall."

"Then he had a...useless gift?" asked Padi.

"Not in the least," said Lina. "He was a very skilled physical Healer, which is not at all useless. Empathy was not a strength, possibly because the shields which blocked the thoughts of others also blocked their emotions. But there are more than enough empaths to meet necessity."

She smiled.

"We really are quite common."

That had been a sort of bait, Padi had been certain, and she'd made no answer. It only occurred to her to wonder now if one could be a *dramliz* of a certain sort without also being a Healer, or at least, a common empath.

The thought was...oddly disturbing. Surely, Padi thought. *Surely* one required some mechanism by which to judge the...best use of one's gift?

Which brought one back 'round to the Inner Eyes.

Lina said that it was possible to See relationships— Father and Priscilla, for instance, were very clearly linked, if one had the eyes to See, and the wit to understand.

And Uncle Ren Zel, Padi thought, recalling something she had perhaps not been *meant* to hear—Uncle Ren Zel could—possibly—See the links that held worlds together. To her knowledge, she had never observed him doing so, but if such a thing were possible...

...could she be *linked* to her stylus?

It was, she thought, an interesting question.

She sat back in the desk chair, put her arms on the rests, and curled her fingers over the ends. It was best to be firmly anchored, as she tended to get dizzy when she opened her Inner Eyes. She focused as much as she was able on her gift, and on the place where her gift resided.

Then, she spoke to the stylus. "Come down to the desk, do," she said calmly.

Nothing happened. No, not true. There was the very faintest flicker of warmth along nerve endings she had never noticed before her gift had become manifest...

...and the stylus descended gently to the desk.

Padi took a deep breath, closed her outer eyes, and reluctantly opened her Inner Eyes onto the usual messy smear of color; like looking at a flower garden through a rain-slicked window.

She . . . squinted, straining to make sense out of nonsense . . .

. . . and quite suddenly, her Sight cleared—there was the desk; there the notebook; screen, keyboard—and the stylus too; all looking precisely as they did when beheld with more mundane vision.

But, no, she thought in the next instant. That wasn't exactly so. The difference was subtle, but it was there.

The stylus glowed faintly blueish, and the notebook, too. The desk seemed quite itself, as did the comm unit. Tentatively, keeping her Inner Eyes open, she extended her thought, and slipped it under the keyboard. Warmth built—just a little—and she applied a very small amount of pressure to the thought beneath the keyboard . . .

. . . which rose, smoothly and without fuss, and— kept rising.

Hurriedly, Padi extended another thought and placed it atop the keyboard. It stopped rising and sat in the air, held between the wedge of her will. The warmth at the base of her spine was steady now, noticeable, but not hot. Not *dangerous*.

She took a breath, and another, concentrating on her gift. In Inner Sight, the keyboard was held between two pale mauve paddles made out of . . . smoke perhaps. The quality of her will was . . . a little gritty, she thought, and smelled faintly of lavender.

The warmth in her chest increased. The keyboard began to waver slightly between its two poles. Padi took another breath, and let the top paddle grow heavier, and the bottom . . . less substantial, until the keyboard drifted gently back down to the desk, whereupon she withdrew her thought and glanced at the stylus.

"I'll wager you've forgotten how to do that," she said casually.

Once again, nothing . . . overtly . . . happened; there was no sense of extending, nor did she See or sense her will touching the stylus—which was now floating fifteen centimeters above the surface of the desk, apparently having performed an instantaneous translation from desktop to plain air.

"Show-off," she said—and the stylus dropped straight down to the desktop.

Padi laughed, opening her eyes.

Her desk was orderly: stylus, notepad, and keyboard were precisely where she had seen them last. There were no embarrassing singe marks or dents to be seen.

Very good.

It was then she noticed that she was breathing deeply, as if she'd been exercising hard, and her hand, when she picked the stylus up, was shaking.

· · · ❖ · · ·

Shan finished reading the first journal. After, it had been necessary to sit quietly for a time, until the echoes of his father's voice had faded from his mind and he had come to terms, again, after so many years, with the fact that Er Thom yos'Galan was dead, and his son Shan would never speak with him again.

Rather like Er Thom coming again, and at last, to the realization that the brother of his heart could give him neither advice nor comfort in his extremity.

And that even love was insufficient to bring them together again.

Well, and so.

Once he felt himself sufficiently settled, Shan reached into the box for a second journal. When he had finished reading that, he extended a hand and took up a third.

Eventually, he reached again to the box—

"You might, without loss," said a familiar voice, "lay down your cards for the night."

Shan sighed, and put his hand flat on the journals remaining in the box.

"Why would I do that?" he asked.

"In the service of your continued good health. You took dire wounds, of a kind which are treacherous and slow to heal. You would do best by being soft with yourself."

"Ah."

He spun his chair, turning to face the man sitting— seeming to sit—in the chair across the desk from him. A man perhaps of his own age, with a rough-hewn face; dark hair in a neat, long braid; his clothing tidy, if ragged. He was toying with a gaming counter—red, the paint worn off the edges, walking it over the knuckles of his big hand, until it came to an end and—

Vanished.

"I'm pleased to see you have that back," he said, using his chin to point at the counter, which was again walking across the other's hand. "Keep it, of your kindness."

"Now, there's a rare ill-temper," said his visitor, whose name was Lute. "You make my point for me, child. Take some rest now."

"There is business to be done," Shan told him, already making a list of research topics.

"In truth, I don't dispute it! Only I ask—does it need to be done *right now*? Will you not benefit from a deep and healing sleep?"

Shan closed his eyes and rubbed his arm.

"The Witch had mended that damage, had she not?" Lute asked sharply.

Shan opened his eyes.

"What damage would that be?"

"The gash on thine arm, infant! Which was all but the death of thee."

"She did Heal it," Shan answered, at the same moment becoming conscious of the ache, just there, where she had flayed his skin to the bone.

He unsealed the sleeve and pushed it up, staring at the angry red scar, the skin around it inflamed and tender.

"Well . . ." he murmured, and nearly leapt to his feet in shock as Lute leaned over to take his arm in one gentle, calloused hand.

"I will do this," he said. "You will deplete yourself further, do you make the attempt, and the wound will become angrier still. Be still now."

Coolness washed over his tender skin. The scar faded; the ache leached away.

"There. That will keep you. Rise. Yes, and lean on me."

He found he needed the support to his bed, where he lay himself down fully clothed.

"When you wake, betake yourself to your lady, and ask her grace for your stupidity," Lute said sternly. "Close your eyes."

That last hardly needed to be said, Shan thought. The challenge had become to keep them open.

"You will pursue all necessary tasks tomorrow," Lute told him. "Nothing will be lost by caring for yourself. Learn some little wisdom while you sleep. You endanger all and everything by ignoring your hurts."

A large warm hand was placed on his forehead, and Lute's voice spoke again, gently but with such power the very air sparked blue.

"Sleep, Shan yos'Galan. Sleep and heal."

V

IN THE CAPTAIN'S OFFICE, PRISCILLA SAT BACK IN HER chair and closed her eyes.

She had just concluded a meeting with the Liaison Committee and the Ombudsone, and what she had heard...was not good.

In truth, they'd said nothing she hadn't already known. Only—she'd been hoping that the malady would heal itself.

Which, she told herself wearily, they hardly ever do—and who should know it better than you?

She had allowed the problem to fester, her attention centered on the damage done to Shan, and the riddle that was Padi. She, the captain, had—not quite *ignored* her crew. But she had allowed them to slip into third place.

"So," she said to the empty room. "Let's review."

The death of Vanner Higgs in the performance of his duty had been only one shock visited upon the *Passage* at Langlast, and it had been severe. They were a tradeship, not a privateer. One did not expect the death of a crewmate; especially not a violent death.

Nor did one look for the ship to be attacked by planetary administration while peacefully in orbit, nor for the kidnapping and torture of the master trader, or the attempted abduction of the apprentice trader.

Vanner had been well liked and, as shuttle pilot and security, known to every member of the ship's complement. Two gatherings had been held, to mark his passing and to celebrate his life, so that all might mourn properly.

As expected, some had also sought the Healer for

assistance in coming to terms with their loss. Additional classes in self-defense had been made available, and seminars reviewing the reasons Clan Korval had been banished from Liad, and the nature of their enemy.

The crew had known, before the *Passage* left Surebleak, that they would face challenges on new ports and why those challenges existed. They had signed their contracts fully informed.

And yet, to meet actual violence, to find a colleague, a friend, a comrade, a lover murdered—it shook the shared soul of the ship. So much the Liaison Committee and the Ombudsone had said. So much she had known for herself and—set aside.

They were, Priscilla thought carefully, a tradeship. Mutiny was unlikely. So the Liaison Committee had assured her.

Then there was the problem of their next port.

They *were* a tradeship; not unreasonably, the crew expected that they would trade. The contract outlined several payouts to crew if the trade hit certain markers—which had never, in the years Priscilla had been with the *Passage*, been in doubt. *Dutiful Passage* was a profitable ship.

Had been a profitable ship.

The door chime sounded and she raised her head, feeling his presence on the other side.

"It's unlocked," she said dryly.

The door whisked open, and a tray was steered into her office by her tall and elegant lifemate. Clearing the door, he paused and straightened.

"Good my-morning and your-midshift, Captain. Will you join me for a meal? We may call it whatever you like."

Priscilla rose from behind her desk.

"Let's call it a welcome diversion," she said, with a wry smile.

Shan parked the cart at the end of the couch. They served themselves and settled side by side, he to break his fast, she to address . . . she supposed it might be lunch.

"I don't mean to sound ungrateful, but what brings you—and the diversion—to me?"

"Honor," Shan said solemnly. "One must keep one's word."

"Very true," she said, matching him for solemnness. "But I don't recall you promising to bring me—a meal."

"Well. The meal is an inspired last-minute improvisation. My word was given to Lute."

Priscilla paused briefly in the act of choosing a cheese roll. Shan did not often talk about Lute. Shan did not *approve* of Lute, though he had, since their first meeting in Weapons Hall, come to tolerate him, while often wishing him—and the game counter that was, in the lexicon of Priscilla's youth, a sign of divine favor—at the devil.

Something had changed his attitude, as so many things had changed, at Langlastport. Shan, having seen Vanner murdered and himself held captive by Tarona Rusk, had dispatched Lute to protect Padi, who had been alone and about to be confronted by a team of operatives attached to the DOI.

"Does Lute think that we need to spend more time together?" she asked lightly.

"He wouldn't be the only one of us who did—but no. I had been working late, and was on course for later, when all at once and with no warning, Lute arrived and proceeded to ring such a peal down upon my head you would have thought him my elder kin. He took as his texts the importance of proper convalescence to continued survival, and the wisdom of taking one's own advice."

"I assume he had a reason," said Priscilla.

"In fact, he had. I had stupidly reopened a wound, which put him to the trouble of Healing it. To ensure that I would inconvenience him no further—at least, by the same route—he placed me into Heal-sleep. Before he did so, however, he elicited my solemn word that I would, upon waking, seek out my lady to confess my errors."

He inclined his head.

"Thus you find me before you, cowed and obedient."

In fact, Priscilla thought, considering him with all the senses available to her, he seemed rather more . . . vibrant than at any time since his return from Langlast, when he had been utterly exhausted, and very nearly without color. But, even then, he had not been *cowed*. The members of Clan Korval might occasionally repent, but they did so with heads high.

"Am I to take it that you find me insufficiently subdued?" Shan asked. "The silence is rather alarming."

She shook her head, smiling.

"I was lost in admiration of your obedient nature."

"As anyone would be," he said gravely.

She shook her head again.

"Which wound did you reopen?" she asked.

He raised an arm, unsealed the cuff and pushed the sleeve up, so she could see the white scar marring the brown skin of his forearm. It was, she thought, rather more prominent than it had been the last time she had seen it.

She extended a hand—and Shan pulled back.

"Do not risk yourself!" he snapped.

She raised her eyebrows, and considered him for a long moment until, sheepish, he extended his arm once more, murmuring.

"Your pardon, Priscilla."

"Thank you," she said, bracing his arm along her forearm. "I am scanning for infection, and for deliberate sabotage of the Healing process. I don't expect to find either, but if I do, my advice will be that you take yourself either to Lina, or to Keriana, as the case requires."

"Yes," he said, and he did, just for an instant, actually sound daunted. "Thank you."

"You're welcome."

Her scan discovered nothing, save a signature that seemed at first to be Shan's own. Closer scrutiny revealed a very slight difference in nuance, which would of course be Lute, near enough to be Shan's elder brother. She did not sigh. It was no easy thing, to be god-ridden. Even the Temple acknowledged that.

She removed her hand. He withdrew his arm, pushing the sleeve down and sealing the cuff.

"Shan, you *must* rest. Access your gift as little as possible. Overstress yourself, and that wound will open again—that *particular* wound, because it was inflicted on two planes."

"I understand," he said, and failed to look delighted, cowed, or even remotely compliant.

"I believe," he said slowly, "that I have found a downside to the Liaden method of conducting ourselves as

Healers. We're taught control, but we're also taught to use our shields as little as possible, to engage with the wide universe with as many of our senses as we may. We thereby, so we are taught, lead a complete life."

Priscilla lifted a hand to his cheek.

"I know," she said.

She had been trained in another tradition. A priestess of the Goddess lived chaste behind her shields, engaging the world with her talents only when it was required. She'd had to *learn* to remain open all the time, as Shan was accustomed to doing, and she thought that it would be . . . difficult to retreat entirely behind her shields again, now.

"*Try,*" she said softly.

He caught her hand and brought it to his lips.

"For you, Priscilla, I will try."

They returned their attention to breakfast-or-lunch, eating in companionable silence. In good time, Shan leaned back into the cushions; Priscilla put her cup on the tray to snuggle against his side, sighing gently when his arm came around her shoulders.

"If it can be told, from what knotty problem did my arrival rescue you?"

She leaned her head against his shoulder.

"Morale," she said, closing her eyes.

"Ah," he said softly.

"Had we not lost Vanner, or been attacked while going about our entirely lawful business . . ." Priscilla murmured. "Coming after Langlast, a side trip to a port where there was no possible profit to be had, and now with the route in doubt—it may be too much . . ." She let her voice drift off.

"You spoke to the crew Ombudsone?"

"And to the Liaison Committee."

"Do they offer solutions, or merely complaint?"

"They . . ."

Priscilla raised her head and looked into his eyes.

"They surprised me. They suggested that the crew be offered the chance to buy out their contracts at the next appropriate port."

Shan sighed.

"If I were inclined to be Liaden about this, I would note that the current crew each signed contracts, including the clause that specifically stated that this was an exploratory venture which would follow no certain route, and because of that might encounter both increased risk and lesser profit."

Priscilla stirred. There were Liadens who lived and died by the contract. Shan had never been so rigid. However, a trader must believe in the force of the contract, else he'd lose his profit and his advantage.

Shan had been known to modify contracts. When she had first come to the *Passage*, she thought his ability to see contracts as flexible was an artifact of his being a Healer.

"A Healer lives always in the world," she murmured now.

Shan laughed.

"Perhaps so; though I will point out that my father could very easily think outside of the clauses, and his mother before him. The question, naturally, is when is it advantageous to do so?"

"Are you," she asked, "inclined to be Surebleakean?"

"There is such a thing as going too far," he murmured, and Priscilla laughed softly.

"We may, however," he continued as if he hadn't

heard her, "compromise. My most recent research indicates that Pommier is within reach. One of the claims it makes for itself is that it is a Guild-certified crew reassignment station. Unless there is another port, nearer or more appropriate, I think we have our solution."

"The Liaison Committee specifically named Pommier," Priscilla said. "I haven't done the research, myself."

"If memory serves, which it must at some point, Pommier is quite reasonably civilized; an active port; at the intersection of at least two major trade routes, and a dozen lesser."

"Would you like me to pull the World Book entry?"

"If you have time now, we should review it together."

Priscilla rose and went to her desk, Shan following. She leaned over her console, tapping keys, then spun the screen so they could both see.

"A slight course adjustment," she said, "and we raise Pommier in three ship-days."

"Not impossible, though we shall have to bustle. I suggest that we call a meeting of all hands in six hours to remind them of the bailout clause. We are prepared to honor it at Pommier, and we are prepared to pay full wages to that point."

Priscilla did some basic arithmetic in her head.

"That will bring ship's cash reserves down—significantly."

"I'll supplement the buyout from personal funds," he said. "The ship needn't go below prescribed levels for this."

Priscilla did another sum in her head; stirred.

"We can't afford to lose more than—"

"Quite right. But I don't think we'll see a mass exodus. I may of course be wrong. And if I am wrong, we will consider our course carefully. If Pommier dares to do business with us, we might still come about."

"And if Pommier won't do business with us?" Priscilla asked.

"They are still bound by Guild law to take distressed crew," Shan said lightly. "And then—we'll see what happens."

VI

SHAN FINISHED READING THE LAST OF HIS FATHER'S JOURnals, repacked them, locked the box and returned it to the drawer.

Then, he sat down in his chair and leaned back with his arms crossed under his head, considering the ceiling. His heart was sore, and his thoughts were clamoring.

For the first time, he considered the possibility that the task set to him by his delm—the core of his duty as the clan's trader; the essence of being a master trader—was something that was beyond his ability to achieve.

He considered the possibility that he might fail.

The realization was simultaneously terrifying and liberating.

Korval contrived, after all. Korval *dared*. Korval erred, and occasionally made quite horrifying mistakes. But Korval did not *fail*. That...was unthinkable.

And yet, Er Thom yos'Galan had foreseen that he would fail the clan.

Now, in his turn, Er Thom's son and heir considered the unthinkable.

The unthinkable, Shan thought, his eyes on the ceiling, was by definition beyond solution. To think of a thing was to define it, to give it shape.

To make it vulnerable to solution.

Very well then. He would think the thought.

I might fail to construct a viable new trade route.

There, the thought had been formed; the problem had been named. A solution could now be sought.

If one failed of constructing a new trade route, what might one do *in its place* which would achieve the goal of providing cash flow and contacts sufficient to the clan's needs?

He took lengthy counsel of the ceiling; and, when they had at last come to an accord, he spun his chair around, reached to the screen, and began to open files. Research, some of it quite unusual—the various trade resources, piloting notifications, Scout reports—to which he added the most recent readouts from the Named Beacons. He became entangled with History, too, which had proved unexpectedly beguiling, until at last, he swept it all away, and called up a blank screen.

When the screen was no longer blank, and he was satisfied with the results, then he extended a hand, and placed a call to the captain.

"What," Priscilla asked, reasonably enough, "is the Redland System?"

"Three worlds," Shan answered, "collectively called The Redlands, clustered around a red dwarf. Liaden worlds, I should add."

They were sitting on the couch in his office, each holding a cup of cold tea. Priscilla was frowning.

"*Liaden* worlds?" she repeated. "At the edge of the Dust, orbiting a red dwarf?"

"It scarcely seems likely, does it? In actual fact, we ought say two parts Liaden and one part Terran, with a lovely, convoluted history, and what may be called an *interesting* location, now that the Dust is swirling in other patterns."

She considered him.

"*How* convoluted a history?"

He grinned and drank some tea.

"Moderately convoluted, I believe. The Scouts opened The Redlands for colonization at the end of the Terran AI Wars. Two of the three planets were quickly colonized, due to the discovery of minerals and plants and other things of interest to various small Liaden companies.

"The third planet attracted farmers—Liaden, and also ethnic Terrans who had been displaced by the war. Its population did not grow—in fact, it diminished—and in the fullness of time, another call was put out for colonists, which was fortunate, because at that time on Liad, the Council of Clans was involved in a purge."

Priscilla blinked.

"A purge?"

"Indeed. It had come to the attention of . . . some . . . that there was a class of people living in society who were . . . not precisely as they seemed. There they were, going to school, attending dinner parties, participating in contract marriages, and behaving as if they were *perfectly ordinary*. Which, alas, they were not, a circumstance to which some took very great exception. There was talk of removing whole clans from the Book, in order to keep society safe, you know, from those who might influence the unwary and exploit their *unnatural advantages*."

"Unnatural advantages?" Priscilla frowned again, then straightened as she recalled other lessons from the histories of other planets. "The Council of Clans tried to purge *the Healers*?"

"Did I say that? No, not the Healers. The Healers, you see, were *useful*. They might, the Council conceded, require *regulation*—even *oversight*!—but they scarcely needed to be *purged*. That would have been too much. Luckily, it happened that the Healers were closely aligned with Korval. Which is why there is today a Healer's Guild. Not even the Council dared tamper with Guild Law."

He sighed and turned his palms up.

"No, the Healers were safe enough, as were the more powerful of the *dramliz*, who knew very well how to hide.

"Those who stood in danger of losing their liberty and their lives were the small talents—the *vas'dramliz*— the Lucks and the Hearth-Makers; the Finders; the Rememberers; the Reversers, and all the rest of the little mutations of talent we see from time to time."

"Those are all *dramliz* talents," Priscilla protested.

"Well, yes, they are *now*—when the *dramliz* are accepted as a necessity, if not precisely loved. Then . . . it was a difficult time, and the Council needed a scapegoat, badly. The Healers were out of reach; the *dramliz* went into hiding, but the *vas'dramliz* . . .

"The *vas'dramliz* . . . simply *were*. They had no more control over their talents than they had over the color of their eyes."

He sighed.

"They were easy meat, and it was a bad time. If they were no danger to anyone—except, sometimes, themselves—they were certainly too diverse to bundle well into a guild.

"Some were killed, a few clans were broken—but most managed an escape from Liad. Korval helped them; Ixin did, and Tanitha.

"A few went to Irikwae; about as few went to Beezatra . . ."

"While the larger number went to The Redlands as colonists, and hoped never to hear from the homeworld again?" Priscilla suggested.

"Precisely the case, Priscilla, yes. Now, here is my reasoning, if it can be dignified as such: Korval is no longer of Liad. We have always been a friend of the gifted, and have assisted them in times of trouble. It is...*possible*, therefore, that we will be received at The Redlands with...patience, if not actual courtesy. They must trade—in fact, they *do* trade, as I find in the databases. It seems...not unreasonable that they might wish to expand, now that the Dust is thinning. And we are uniquely placed to assist them."

He leaned back into the couch and gave her a weary smile. "All of which means that—"

"There's opportunity," said Priscilla.

"It is, at least," Shan conceded, "a theory."

Priscilla nodded, frowning still.

"Will you take Padi into this?" she asked. "Do we know how—or if—the small talents have grown?"

He half-laughed.

"I think the proper question is, how will I prevent Padi from accompanying her ship and her master trader into this opportunity?"

He moved his shoulders. "Another question would be—will I take my lifemate, and our to-be-born, into this?"

Priscilla considered him. "I think that is not wholly your choice."

"And so," he said, leaning forward to brush his lips across her cheek, "we both have our answers."

She turned a hand palm up, giving him the point. "Schedule changes," she said, and he nodded.

"I agree."

A moment of silence before Priscilla finished her tea, and met his eyes, her own perfectly calm.

"So, the route—first to Pommier to deliver our buyouts to the proper authorities. Then to The Redlands. Auxiliary stops, or quickest route?"

"Quickest route," he said, and gave her a smile. "Understand, Priscilla, that this is my last throw. If The Redlands will not have us, then we will be returning, quickest route, to Surebleak, so that I may make my bow to the delm and inform them of my failure."

"What, exactly, will that mean?"

"*That* . . . lies with the delm," he said, which was true. He did not add that delms had wide latitude with regard to the members of their clans. And, really, he did not expect Korval to execute him, lease him to another clan, or find him gainful employment as a big-ship captain. Priscilla herself might be subject to that last, but he trusted that the delm would see the wisdom in keeping them together.

Mostly together.

"I see." Priscilla took a deep breath.

"We'll hope that your last die is your luckiest, my dear," she said, and kissed him.

VII

PADI ALWAYS CHECKED HER SCHEDULE FIRST THING UPON rising. Schedule changes were the lot of a 'prentice, and it was her responsibility to be on time to her assigned duties. One could only imagine Cargo Master ira'Barti's response to an apprentice presenting *but my schedule was changed!* as her reason for tardiness.

This morning, however...

This morning, her schedule had not been changed so much as it had been utterly demolished and something new and wholly astonishing built from the ashes.

Her shifts were always busy—but this...new...iteration of her day had entered the realm of the frenetic.

It was, she apprehended, scrolling down through the day—it was an *accelerated* program, that shortened her sleep shift...significantly. That wasn't necessarily a problem; she was accustomed to using two, or even three, hours of her sleep shift for work, but, given the demands of the new schedule, one wondered when she was expected to *study*, or even to answer her correspondence.

Indeed, rather than her research hour, she was, immediately after breaking her fast, to attend the master trader in his office, after which she went to Healer Faaldom for tutoring, followed by a session with *Dramliza* Mendoza; then her usual session with Cargo Master ira'Barti, and nuncheon.

After that, piloting lessons on sim; *menfri'at* training with Arms Master Schneider; two hours guided study; one hour—*one* hour!—of free trade research, a second session with Lina and, in the early hours of her sleep shift, another meeting with the master trader.

Padi blinked; ran down the new schedule a third time, and leapt to her feet. The window of opportunity for breaking her fast was shrinking—rapidly. If she took a quick shower, she'd be able to grab a protein cookie from the cafeteria on her way past, and eat it while she walked—quickly—to the master trader's office.

Father—which was to say, Master Trader yos'Galan— was at his desk, all of his attention seemingly on the screen. An empty wine glass stood by his hand. Padi refreshed it at the bar, poured herself a glass of cold tea, and returned to the desk.

The master trader still entranced by his screen, she put the glass on the green-and-blue coaster and took her accustomed seat on the opposite side of the desk, sipping tea, and cultivating patience. A trader, so Father had said more than once, did well to have a store of patience set by, to be deployed at need. Wielded with skill, patience was a potent trading tool.

Regrettably, Padi was not accomplished in the art, though she flattered herself that she had made strides in becoming less *im*patient. She had found that it went better with her if she directed her thought to some useful topic while she waited, reviewing conversion tables, perhaps, or solving piloting equations.

At the moment, it occurred to her that she would next be meeting with Lina, who would expect that she had something rational to say about one's Inner Sight. It might, she thought, be prudent to practice.

This would be tricky. Lina allowed her the crutch

of closing her outer eyes before she opened her Inner. It would not, however, *do* for the master trader to find her sitting with eyes closed, apparently having a nap while she awaited his attention.

She therefore fixed her eyes on the desktop, concentrated, and managed after a few fumbling breaths to open her Inner Eyes.

Merely, she had intended to regard the desk while paying attention to how the Seeing made her feel, and what vagaries she detected in her gift, so that she might articulate these things to her teacher.

The desk blurred, showing layer upon layer, an interweaving of complexity that overbore her in an instant—a bustle of thread and texture—a pattern, surely? Only it went beyond mere Seeing. She felt herself caught up, *drawn in*—and with a strong effort, she wrenched her Sight aside, to be caught and held against a blare of silver so bright that she cried out, and—

"Padi! Close your eyes!"

Father's voice, sharp with command. She jumped, Inner Eyes snapping shut, and his face coming into sharp focus—stern, eyes glinting silver.

"I beg your pardon," she said, her voice not quite steady.

Slanting white brows lifted.

"The last I had heard from Lina, you were yet encountering some difficulty in focusing your Inner Sight."

"I—yes, sir. Which is why I took it in mind to practice while I . . . awaited the master trader's attention. I had only meant to look at the desk, so that I could describe—"

She took a hard breath.

"I am afraid that I am not very skilled."

He glanced down, then back to her eyes.

"Only to look at the desk," he said softly, and shook his head. "Child . . . this desk—say that this desk has seen much. I own myself impressed that you weren't beguiled."

"I—was," she said. "That is—I was being drawn in, and I moved my gaze. Only then, I caught a—mirror, silver and so very bright—"

"Ah. Likely you Saw my shields, though I don't believe them to be so very bright. Possibly, you caught a reflected image of yourself."

"If *that* is what I look like, no wonder the Healers at Millsap complained," Padi said, with feeling.

"The Healers at Millsap," Father said, rather sharply, "had resources available to them. They did not have to bear the whole of your brightness, though they chose to make complaint rather than accommodation."

Padi sighed.

"I . . ." she began—and stopped, recalling that she was in the master trader's office, and on business.

"Ask," Father said.

"Yes. I only wonder how—how can you possibly *make sense* of all that?"

To have been taken in by a *desk*, no matter how much it *had seen*—had there ever been *any*one so inept?

"Practice," Father said gravely. "Dull as it is, practice is the key to mastery in all things, from piloting to *menfri'at* to Healing. And to trade. My mother your grandmother had used to say, *practice makes perfect.* As a musician, practice was her most constant companion."

Padi nodded, and had recourse to her tea. And Lina, she thought, was *only* a Healer?

"I fear that Healer Osit's explanation was cut short," she said carefully. "It would be helpful if I knew what shields . . . *are*."

Father nodded.

"Shields are what we rest behind. They are a protection in uncertain situations. For the moment, I am shielded so that I may direct what energy I have toward healing."

He paused, and extended a hand toward his wine glass, though he failed of picking it up before he met her eyes again with a wry smile. "Which I will allow to be even duller than practice."

She met his smile with hers. He nodded, and moved his hand.

"I suggest that time is wearing on. Shall we take up the master trader's topic, Trader?"

"Yes," Padi said, sitting straighter in her chair and bringing trader's *melant'i* to the fore.

"One assumes," said the master trader, "that you have seen your new schedule."

"I have," she acknowledged. "I wonder what the adjusted focus of my lessons portends."

He nodded.

"An astute question. We—by which I mean the *Dutiful Passage* and all her crew—are en route to the Redland System, in search of trade and allies. I have forwarded such information as has come to my hand regarding The Redlands to your screen. I look forward to discussing your thoughts and suggestions regarding them when we meet again, later.

"In the meanwhile, Trader, you have a choice before you. I realize that the amended schedule is challenging. It may well be too challenging. You and I have spoken frankly and at length regarding your goals and aspirations. I am fully aware that your first priority is to win the garnet as quickly as possible, and to set up as a trader on your own route."

Yes, certainly: her *goals*. Padi did not sigh. A trader would not reveal so much, though the master trader had courteously paused to allow her opportunity to speak. But, really, what was there to say? Her *goal* had been the garnet before her eighteenth nameday, which she might have easily managed, but for the *idiot* Department of the Interior escalating its insults against Korval until there had been nothing for it, but that Plan B should be called into effect.

Well.

She inclined her head, indicating that the master trader might resume.

"You will have noted that the new schedule does not honor your goals," he continued briskly. "If you accept it, you will be doing more *dramliz* training, at the expense of work that will move you toward your first priority. I am in error, that I did not immediately make it plain that there is a choice available."

Padi considered him.

"One assumes the master trader has made these adjustments to my schedule from necessity, rather than whim," she said slowly. "May I know the reason for the changes that were made?"

"Indeed. As you will learn from the material I have forwarded to you, the population of The Redlands was increased by a significant number of *vas'dramliz* many years ago. The reason for their emigration from Liad was painful, and they did not seek further contact with the homeworld. Talents, even small talents, being what they are—which is to say, open to mutation and personal style—we simply do not know what we will be meeting there. It is, frankly, not the best place to bring a neophyte whose abilities have not yet been cataloged, much less honed."

Padi bit her lip.

"What is the alternative?"

"I have been in contact with Trader Veshtin, who is willing to have you with her on *Maribel's* long route. I will mention that this is a very interesting route, rife with ongoing challenges of the sort that will delightfully test the mettle of an aspiring trader. It is not impossible that you will have that garnet, Trader, by the end of the route."

He paused. Padi said nothing, and after a moment he continued.

"I have also forwarded information on Trader Veshtin and *Maribel's* route to your screen. I look forward to hearing your thoughts on those as well, at our next meeting."

Padi inclined her head.

"Thank you, Master Trader," she said. "I look forward to reviewing the information."

"Very proper," he murmured. "Have you any questions?"

"No, sir."

He nodded.

"Excellent. You're just in time to find Lina for your lesson. Jet."

"You will perform, please, the board drill which increases concentration and mental acuity," Lina said.

Padi, who had scarcely arrived in her office, and

had not yet bowed to the honor of the teacher, much less taken a seat at the table—blinked.

"Your pardon?"

Lina raised her eyebrows.

"You will perform the board drill which renews the pilot's focus. I believe that there *is* such a drill, and that it is commonly taught to pilot candidates at the very beginning of their training. Perhaps I have been misinformed?"

"Yes—no!" Padi said, off-balance. Her cheeks warmed. Really, she scolded herself; that was scarcely up to one of Father's most mundane flights, and you're cast off-balance? She sighed, focused, and bowed slightly.

"Forgive me. I mean to say that no, Instructor, you have not been misinformed; there is indeed such an exercise, which is taught with the earliest board drills."

"I am gratified," Lina said dryly. "Perhaps you will be so good as to demonstrate this exercise?"

That was rather sharp for Lina, thought Padi. On the other hand, Padi had already shown herself to be stupid this shift.

"Yes, Instructor," she said. She closed her eyes, easily accessing the familiar exercise, which imparted all the benefits of a deep sleep to a weary pilot's mind and body.

Exercise complete, she opened her eyes, noting that she did feel somewhat more energetic, though she had not been aware of being tired.

"I see," Lina said, her eyes narrowed as if she had, indeed, observed the process taking place inside Padi's head.

As, Padi realized, she had done.

"Do you recall the discussion we had, regarding the proper tool for the job?"

"Yes, Instructor."

"This tool which you have just demonstrated will be of great use to you during the upcoming time of increased and accelerated study. Remember it, and use it wisely."

Padi bowed as one with additional information to impart.

"Yes?"

"We—that is, beginning pilots—are warned not to overuse this exercise. It does not *create* energy, but only borrows from the future, creating a debt that will be called in by the body."

"Another excellent lesson!" Lina said, bringing her palms together lightly. "In fact, there *is* no boundless source of energy. You may borrow on future reserves, but eventually, the loan will come due."

She raised a finger.

"There is a corollary to this—pilotkind typically know their physical limitations to a fine edge. We are not always so wise. Even very experienced Healers may overspend their resources and their reserves. There is no limitless well of energy from which we may draw with impunity. Willpower, focus—these are tools to our hands. Ultimately, however, even the most powerful *dramliz* is only as strong as muscle and bone. Your gifts can kill you. Respect them, and use them sparingly."

Padi bowed again, somewhat baffled. Why this now—again? She wondered, even as she straightened.

"Yes, Instructor. I understand."

Lina's face softened, losing the fierce, unaccustomed lines.

"I know that you do, child. I make the point repeatedly because the danger is greatest where the gifts are strongest. This new schedule you have been given is—challenging. And it is made even more challenging by the fact that the end of the course will not bring relief, or relaxation, but increased demands upon your gifts."

"Surely," Padi said slowly, "the additional work will act on my gifts as exercise does on muscle? I will grow stronger as I meet and surmount increased challenge."

Lina sighed.

"To a degree. In your particular case, I note that your will is adamantine. No amount of exercise will render your body its equal."

She stood. "So! You have practiced control on your off-shift. Show me what you have learned."

Carefully, Padi took her stylus out of a pocket and put in on Lina's table. It lay there, perfectly convenable and well-behaved. Padi cleared her throat.

"Rise, do," she said.

Obligingly, the stylus rose into the air. When it had reached fifteen centimeters, she said, "Stop, now."

The stylus stopped, reposing in the air quite calmly.

Padi turned to look at Lina, who was considering the stylus closely.

"Describe to me what you felt—what you are feeling—at the seat of your power," she said.

Padi hesitated, and Lina brought that narrow gaze to her.

"Your feelings are indescribable?" she asked politely.

"My feelings are—nonexistent," Padi said. "I don't think that it's drawing on me—on my energy—at all. It's as if I—*taught it* to float, and now it . . . does."

"I . . . see." Lina took a breath. "May I?"

Padi hesitated.

"I—cannot be certain what will happen. To the best of my understanding, I'm not holding it there..."

"You did not utilize a construct," Lina said. "It seems to me that this is exactly what you describe. The stylus has learned how to float, and now does so upon request."

She gave Padi a sharp look.

"Does it *require* your request?"

"I—don't know," Padi confessed. "Perhaps not. They all *do* float, sometimes..."

She stopped, recalling too late that she had failed to share this detail previously.

Lina eyed her speculatively.

"Ah, do they so? What method do you employ in grounding them?"

"I just tell them to behave," Padi confessed, not quite meeting Lina's eye.

"I see. Well then."

She took one step back from the table.

"Please, Trader, recall your stylus to more seemly comportment."

"Yes," Padi said, and to the stylus, "On the table now, quickly!"

The stylus hit with a muted thud, and remained where it had struck.

"That was...interesting," Lina said. "I understand you are to see Priscilla after we are done here. Please demonstrate this. Tell her that I particularly wanted her to see how it was done."

"Yes, Instructor," Padi said.

"So. We have other work before us. Let us determine your aptitude for shielding."

VIII

PADI LIKED TO BE BUSY; FURTHER, SHE WAS ACCUSTOMED to being busy. She very rarely tired, being young and of energetic stock. It was therefore with no small sense of alarm that she found herself yawning profoundly and very nearly staggering as she approached the master trader's office for the last meeting on her schedule.

The time was two hours into her sleep shift, but it was not unusual for her to work so long, catching up on technical reading, researching trade opportunities, or completing such off-shift work as her various tutors and supervisors might have required of her.

It was true that today's schedule had been heavily weighted toward tasks that she found difficult, and which tired her all out of proportion with the actual, physical energy expended. But she had several times during the shift accessed the board drill recommended by Lina and had not thought she had overspent to the point of making a spectacle of herself in the hallways.

Well, that would *never* do, and especially not when one was about to engage with the master trader. One needed sharp wits with the master trader, who suffered dullards not at all—or worse, he suffered them *kindly*. Besides, she wanted to discuss with him in depth this new trade scheme he had found. However *had* he found it? She had attempted to follow his research, and had become lost within seconds, though *she* already knew The Redlands existed! Whatever had prompted him to *go looking* for them? Had he been considering a section of space, and providentially come across a . . . news item, a market report, the breath of a hint of *some*thing?

In any case, she certainly could not come before the master trader in a disordered condition, and she absolutely would not cast herself in the role of fool. Tonight—*now*—she must be quick, clever, and persuasive. Nothing else would do.

That being so, there was only one course open to her.

She swung to the side of the hall, closed her eyes and accessed the simple board rest exercise one more time.

Energy flowed into her, buoying her spirit and sharpening her wits. Padi sighed. *Now* she was of an order to engage the master trader on his own field.

She stretched her legs, eager to meet him there.

Father was standing in front of the couch, glaring down at the chessboard set out on the occasional table.

He sighed as she entered the room, and looked up, sweeping out one big brown hand.

"I believe that the longer I play this game, the more inept I become."

"Practice," Padi said, recognizing the theme on which they had parted, "is said to make perfect."

His eyes glinted silver.

"Yes, it is, isn't it?"

He stepped 'round the table and threw her a glance over his shoulder.

"Sit, do, Trader. What refreshment may I be pleased to offer you?"

She had already drunk too much tea on the day, and she did not dare to have wine.

"A glass of cold water, of your goodness," she said, moving to her usual chair at the master trader's desk.

"Now, there's a perfect prudence," Father said.

A moment later, he joined her at the desk, placing a tall glass by her hand. There were slivers of ice floating in the water, and the glass glistened with condensation.

"Thank you," she said, and drank carefully.

He inclined his head and took a single sip of his wine, which was everything that was proper, and put the glass aside.

"So, Trader, you've had a long day."

She inclined her head.

"A long day and a surprising one," she allowed.

"Surprising in what way?"

"Well, for an example, I had not expected Priscilla and Lina to be so...*unalike* in their methods," she said slowly. "I suppose, had I...*considered* the matter, I would have realized that of course it must be so, with Lina a Healer and Priscilla of the *dramliz*. It is merely that...Lina does not *use* her talent, no more than she *uses* her eyes or her ears. But Priscilla... takes up her gift, like a tool in her hand; she uses it, and then she puts it aside."

"That is an apt observation. The difference you note has to do with their basic training. Lina was trained in the Liaden style where one's talent is, as you've said, merely another sense to be used in concert with the others. Liaden Healers and *dramliz*, as far as their gifts allow, remain open to the world; the *melant'i* of a Healer is always of a Healer. Shields are used only in extremity."

He paused and added, with a wry look, "And, sometimes, not even then.

"Priscilla was trained in the Sintian style, which

requires the *dramliza* to live shielded, opening only when her gift is called upon. When the task which called her fully into the world is completed, she again steps into isolation."

He tipped his head slightly to the side.

"Some of the Liaden *dramliz* have likened this method to tying a scarf over one's eyes before going for a walk in a garden."

Padi laughed.

"Indeed. What else did you find surprising upon the day?"

"I wouldn't say surprising," Padi said, "but rather *astonishing*. However did you *find* The Redlands?"

"Why, by luck, of course."

Padi eyed him.

"Luck?" she repeated, and then, not quite managing to keep her voice level, *"Our* Luck?"

Father laughed.

"Spoken like a true child of the clan," he said, "and it is my sad task to tell you that it might well have been *our* Luck."

He lifted an eyebrow, and it was the master trader present now.

"Tell me, Trader: What do you think of The Redlands?"

Padi had been trying to determine just that since she'd read the files he'd sent her. Rostov's Dust was, according to almost everyone, dangerous, though that hardly mattered in the scheme of things. Runig's Rock was supposed to have been safe—and only see what had transpired there! Besides, The Redlands weren't *in* the Dust, only at the edge.

Which marked her first concern.

"They are not very conveniently situated," she said carefully, "with regard to Surebleak."

He had leaned back in his chair and was watching her with interest.

"No," he said now. "They could scarcely be less convenient, with regard to Surebleak."

There was, after all, no reason that Surebleak must have a direct route for The Redlands, but Padi's research—admittedly rushed—had not revealed *any* existing trade, convenient or not.

"I checked the Guild's records, and TerraTrade's," she said. "There are no routes serving The Redlands. One wonders why."

"I participate fully in your wonder. Though I feel compelled to point out that not all trade routes are recorded with the guilds."

That of course was very true. Perhaps there were local indie Loops operating in Redlands space which might benefit from consolidation, and the support of a master trader, to the profit of all. It was worthy of exploration.

"Have you other thoughts?" asked the master trader.

Padi sighed.

"Far too many, I fear," she confessed, "and none which are to the point."

She bit her lip, and met his eyes. "I do have a question, if I may ask it?"

"Only one question? I am astonished. By all means, ask."

She drew a breath. She rather feared that her question was impertinent, which she did not intend. It would only be very good to know if . . .

"Are we desperate?" she asked.

Father might have laughed. The master trader merely inclined his head.

"An apt question. I would say that we are not . . . *quite* desperate, though we are sorely tried. My own master's instruction was that, when one is sorely tried, and the wisdom of the past has failed, it is our duty to find new wisdom from which to shape the future."

Father's master had been *his* father, Padi's grandfather, Er Thom. During his tenure as master trader, Korval's trade had expanded via the Loops he had built and integrated into the existing routes of small contractors. On the face of it, that would not seem bold enough to alter the future. All of those routes were in far-flung systems, the contractors largely Terran; Korval goods were delivered to them, and thence to their proper markets via a system of intersecting Loops, from Korval ships. It was a very good system, as Padi knew, having spent very nearly a Standard studying it. And only now was it revealed as far-seeing. Korval had lost many trade partners and allies in the so-called core worlds upon their banishment from Liad. The outspace Terran contractors, however, simply continued as they had been doing, and it was Master Er Thom's system of interlocked and intersecting routes that was the main source of the clan's income now.

"Master Er Thom," Padi said to her own master's interested eyes. "Had he been working his way out to the Dust?"

"Excellent," the master trader murmured, with a slight smile, "and—perhaps. I recently had reason to reread his personal logs. Certainly, he had an interest, as a pilot and as a trader. He took updates on the movement and condition of Rostov's Dust, and monitored the reports from such Beacons as could make themselves heard.

"All of us have of course made a study of Gobelyn's *Envidaria*, but his was intense. He built the outspace routes as stepping stones, interconnecting, one with the other, the next farther out than the last, until he seemed to meet an impasse, thwarted by observations of a new bubble of Dust building."

He reached for his glass, but did not pick it up. Rather, he sighed and briefly closed his eyes.

"He had another route sketched in—the veriest draft, though he had obviously returned to it several times over a period of years. The last mention of it was a memo revealing his belief that Korval might soon need a *place to go*—he called it Dragonhold—and that perhaps it might be wise to shape a route that included Edmonton Beacon, or even Spadoni Station, though at the time the memo was written, Spadoni was still embroiled in that wretched bubble.

"So you see," he continued, "I did not so much go looking for The Redlands, as I thought to revisit my master's work—which opened my eyes to a future. The Dust is taking a new direction, freeing The Redlands. In addition, the bubble which isolated Spadoni Station has burst. I realized—not quickly, you understand— that here was an opportunity to build directly upon my master's work and to expand it."

That was well, Padi thought, and yet . . .

"May I ask another question?"

"Certainly."

"Why did Master Er Thom believe that we would need . . . Dragonhold?"

"Recall that his *cha'leket's* lifemate had been assassinated, and attempts made afterward, on that *cha'leket's* life."

Padi knew that; it was why Uncle Daav, who had been delm, left Liad, leaving Grandfather Er Thom to hold Korval—Ring and clan—in trust for Uncle Val Con, Daav's heir.

"But that had been the Terran Party," she said, and stopped, brought up short. "It was the Department of the Interior? So long ago as that?"

"So I believe, looking at events through the lens of what we now know. Master Er Thom knew that the clan was a target. There were many reasons why we might be, after all, including the fact that Korval was wealthy, privileged, and too thin to adequately protect itself.

"Very possibly, Master Er Thom believed that one among the High or mobile Middle had identified an opportunity, and was moving to clear the field of obstacles. One could scarcely envision the Department, without prior introduction."

That was certainly true, Padi thought. A rare combination of determination, error, and deadly efficiency, the Department of the Interior—and it was *still* hunting Korval.

"And, you know, Korval had been dissatisfied with the homeworld since before Master Er Thom was born, and growing more so. Especially Line yos'Phelium who, despite all yos'Galan might do, longed to truly stretch their wings."

He gave her a too-earnest look.

"I do believe that any relocation envisioned by Master Er Thom would have been done in a more orderly fashion than our actual removal to Surebleak, though I find it…*interesting* that he looked toward *the Dust* for Korval's safe harbor. Rather puts Surebleak into perspective, doesn't it?"

It did at that, thought Padi. Compared to reports of planets and stations situated inside Rostov's Dust Cloud, Daiellen System was nothing worse than a rustic getaway for the citizens of the core worlds.

"It may be that The Redlands are every bit as luxurious as Surebleak," she said. "One could have wished for more data regarding the planets and societies we are likely to encounter. The world books are unhelpfully laconic, and TerraTrade doesn't bother with a rating at all."

"More data specific to our needs would be comforting," agreed the master trader. "However, we may make some extrapolations. For instance…" He extended a hand, fingers folded into his palm, thumb out. "One. We know that a large number of *vas'dramliz* emigrated to The Redlands, which had advertised for colonists 'of all genetic types' to bolster the struggling colony."

He extended his forefinger.

"Two, Korval provided transport for those of the *vas'dramliz* who wished to fly that route."

Second finger.

"Three, talent tends to evolve. The small talents may have grown into large ones, or they may have diversified. In either case, we are likely going to see things we have never seen before, *dramliza* and Healers alike."

Ring finger.

"It is not necessarily criminal to bring a nascent

dramliza into an environment rife with unknown talents, but a case may be made for lunatic. What say you, Trader?"

"I say," Padi answered, following this without effort, "that I most carefully reviewed the files you made available to me. Trader Veshtin is clearly experienced, bold, and able. Her previous apprentices and juniors have all praised her abilities as a teaching trader. At any other time, I would willingly place myself under her guidance. However, my master trader is on the edge of opening not only a new market, but very possibly a *new sector* to trade, and as my ultimate goal is to achieve the amethyst, I cannot in conscience turn my back on that experience."

There, it was said. She met her master's eyes, face composed and calm.

After a moment, he inclined his head.

"Allow me to compliment you; that was nicely phrased."

"Thank you," she said, with a composure she did not quite feel. She had given her opinion. The master trader was under no obligation to abide by her preferences. Nor, if it came to that, was Father so constrained. She was his heir, and while an heir *could be* placed at risk, it was not best practice.

"As you have chosen to accompany the *Passage* to The Redlands, there are certain studies you will be required to undertake, for your own safety," he said.

Padi sat up, breath-caught.

"Yes, sir," she murmured.

He smiled, slight and wry.

"You will see that I had anticipated you," he said, and raised a finger. "You will apply yourself wholeheartedly to your tutoring in the *dramliz* arts. Especially, you will learn to build and maintain shields."

"Yes, sir. Lina and Priscilla have already begun to train me in the art. Today, it was determined that I have the capacity to build shields, and that I have enough raw power to maintain them without tiring. It has also been determined that I need to acquire focus. Priscilla has given me exercises."

"One is gratified."

He sighed, picked up his glass and sipped.

"If you please," Padi murmured. "I have a question."

"One question. The hour grows late."

"Yes sir. I wonder if we will be taking on trade goods for The Redlands, and if so, what is our port?"

"That is two questions," he noted, replacing his glass.

Padi waited.

The master trader lifted his eyebrows.

"As you know," he said austerely, "our next port is Pommier, there to release those who no longer wish to stand crew on this ship. We shall, of course, consider what Pommier has to offer—in fact, I will welcome your opinion on that topic tomorrow. After Pommier—we shall see. Does that satisfy you, Trader?"

"Yes, Master Trader," Padi said evenly. "Thank you."

The master trader bowed his head; Father met her eyes.

"If a mere parent may suggest it," he said gently, "you have had a long and tiring day; the first of many long and tiring days, I daresay. I see from your face that you have been accessing board rest, and enhancing your concentration . . . rather often. That is not viable, long-term, as we both know. If you allow, I may give you a technique which will place you into a Healing sleep. Thus you will Balance your debt to your body, and also, perhaps, make it...less necessary to incur such a debt tomorrow."

It was, Padi thought, very tempting. Board rest would only serve her so far, and it would be good to have another knife in her belt. However, the benefits of her last exercise were already beginning to thin, and *dramliz* work was more tiring than most...

"Peace, my child. I would make you a gift."

"I...believe that I don't understand," she said. "Forgive me."

"There is nothing to forgive. I promise that it will be quite painless. All you need do is accept it."

Accept it was a technical term as she knew from her lessons with Lina. It required making her mind a still pool and releasing her emotions. Which sounded easy...

Still, she *had* had some practice, and if she did not approach perfect, she at least was not entirely without technique.

Carefully, deliberately, she calmed her thoughts, and breathed peace into her center.

"Admirable," Father murmured. "Only remain so, peaceful and calm. It is a very small thing I give; soft, sweet, and infinitely useful to you. You cannot make energy from nothing, and you cannot perpetually borrow against your future. You may, however, give your body leave to function at its most efficient. Here, now, in your hand."

She felt it, exactly as if he had slipped a sweet into her hand. She curled her fingers to hold it safe, and in that moment felt it dissolve, leaving a delightful taste on her tongue, and a brief glimpse of a pattern in lambent silver, spinning comfort at the back of her mind in the instant before it, too, dissolved.

She sighed and opened her eyes.

"Thank you," she said, feeling soothed and, yes, peaceful.

"You are most welcome," Father said, smiling. "Go now and find your rest. *Chiat'a bei kruzon*, my child."

"*Chiat'a bei kruzon*, Father," she said.

Rising, she leaned over the desk, kissed his cheek— and left him.

The door closed behind her, his bright blade of a daughter, and Shan slumped somewhat in his chair.

That last—that had been a rare foolishness, to open his shields even so small a bit, to pass one of the sweetest and most useful of a Healer's many tools on to someone in desperate need.

Well. He closed his eyes, and only breathed until the fine trembling stopped, and he felt he could be steady on his feet.

When he was thus certain of himself, he spun back to the screen, extended a hand...

...and closed his files.

IX

PRISCILLA FILED THE REPORT ON THE REDLANDS THAT Shan had forwarded to her.

It was, she thought, just as well that they had offered the buyout option, and were en route to deliver the most distressed of their crew to safety. She only hoped that The Redlands didn't give birth to another round of despair.

For a brief moment, she considered the possibility of making another offer before they hit Pommier, but—no. There was a limit to how many crew they could lose; and a limit, too, to available reserves, the ship's treasury as well as Shan's personal fortune.

And those were really worries for—tomorrow.

For now...

For this moment, when she had time to herself, with the most pressing of her tasks completed, and her shift, if the captain could fairly be said to have *a shift*, over—she had an impossibility to inspect.

Lina had proven Padi telekinetic. That was useful for the purposes of a final Sorting, but not surprising. Padi's aunt—Shan's sister, Anthora—also counted telekinesis among her numerous talents. Priscilla had once, years ago, seen Anthora tease her brother Val Con by moving his wineglass just ahead of his reaching hand. And she had Seen the extension of Anthora's will that she had used to push the glass. It had been the veriest whisper of will, a tool no more substantial than a cat's whisker. But there *had been* a tool—a form—involved.

A form *had to be* involved in the interface between the planes. The form focused the will, and insured that only the energy required for a given task was expended. Without a form, a *dramliza* might expend all of her talent on one simple task.

What Padi had shown her at Lina's instruction was, therefore, theoretically possible.

There had been no connection between Padi and the stylus. There had been, to Priscilla's Sight, a faint lavender nimbus around the little object, echoing Padi's aura, which gave some credence to the seemingly daft idea that she had "taught" the stylus to float. If she had, in fact, detached a pinch of her considerable power and bound it to the stylus, it might indeed seem as if there were no connection between the witch and the object. Padi's rather shamefaced confession that many of the objects in her quarters floated—but only when she was concentrating or perhaps a little warm in her emotions—lent credence to this theory.

Priscilla had traded Padi one of her own, non-floating, styli for the one that did tricks, and had set it aside to study later.

And now . . . it was later.

She opened the drawer where she had placed the stylus, against any sudden moment of aerial improvisation, placed it on the desk, and considered it with all the senses available to her.

Excepting the faint lavender aura, it was a perfectly ordinary stylus. The aura . . . Priscilla extended a thought—then pulled back.

Settling into herself, Inner Eyes open, and shields down, she said, very calmly, "Please rise, stylus."

The stylus remained only a stylus, and so very

innocent of any peculiarity, on the desk. Priscilla sighed, and extended her will. There was a spark, sudden, as her thought intersected the lavender aura, and Priscilla felt a faint thrill before she enclosed the stylus in her will.

It reposed inside her regard, cool, inanimate, and faintly mocking.

Priscilla frowned and held herself still, recalling once again that evening when Anthora had seen fit to tease her brother until he, no wizard, had simply decided that the glass would obey her prompting no more.

It had upon the instant stopped its coy game. Priscilla, who had been watching closely, Saw Anthora *push*, increase the weight and angle of her will, *shove*—

And Saw her intention bisected, flowing past the glass to dissipate in the room beyond.

In the meanwhile, young Val Con had casually put out his hand, picked up his glass, and wandered away, sipping.

"Pah!" Anthora had said, when Priscilla had asked what had happened.

"It is because he is the delm genetic."

She had sighed at Priscilla's frown, and elaborated.

"Clan members cannot circumvent the Delm's Word. He wished me to stop moving his glass—and it was so. I doubt I could have lifted it had I reached out my hand and took hold."

For years, Priscilla had simply assumed that the effect was as Anthora had described it, born of relationships and *melant'i* in-clan, and had nothing to do with the larger arena of *dramliz* talent.

And now here came Padi, disdaining forms, and merely *desiring* an object to float.

Well, Priscilla thought, and what if Val Con's wish

for a less peripatetic wine glass had not acted upon *Anthora*, but upon *the glass*?

She considered the stylus reposing within the bubble of her will, and carefully withdrew herself. Standing, she did inventory, making certain that she had not automatically created an artifact; that she was in no way in contact with the stylus, though her attention was certainly centered upon it.

It was something like making sure that she was standing with her hands behind her back, shoulders deliberately level, and not quite daring to breathe.

"Rise," she said, and *willed* it to be so.

The stylus rolled on the desk, two full revolutions, and then—

It rose.

This was not the easy wafting into the air that Padi had demonstrated, but a rather brisk ascension, nor did it stop at fifteen centimeters, but kept on rising, accelerating a little, until Priscilla said sharply, "That's enough!"

It paused then, and for all the worlds like a peevish apprentice, fell, striking the desk with a *boom*!

Priscilla's Sight jumped; golden lines spun, flared, coalesced. Off-center, she flung out a hand, glimpsed a black, yawning hunger—heard another *boom* that shook her heart in her chest—

And it was gone. Serenity reigned as far as her Senses extended. The hunger was dismissed. The song of the universe fell sweet upon her soul.

She felt a familiar touch, and there came the voice, Moonhawk's own, rising in jubilation.

The door has closed.

· · · · ❖ · · · ·

BOOM!

Padi twisted on her bunk, more than half asleep, brows pulled in protest of the echoes. A hand fell on her shoulder and she stilled, brow smoothing.

"What was that?" she muttered, and wasn't really surprised to hear Lute's voice in answer.

"A door closed, that was all. Sleep again, child; there's naught for you to do."

Civilization

· · · · · · · · · ·

"...DATA," TRADER ISFELM WAS TELLING THE TRADE COUN-
cil. "On our side, see you, we've got plenty too much
data. I make no argument; the best course, for yourselves and for us, too, is to go *out*. But to *go* out, we
need to know what's there. We need charts, navigation
updates..."

"We have charts, maps, and navigation tables in
our archives," Portmaster krogerSlyte said. "We'll be
more than pleased to open them to you."

Bentamin leaned back in his chair, watching Trader
Isfelm with all the senses available to him. The trader
was well-known, being their usual contact with the
Iverson Loop, a wiry, quick-talking woman, with a
sharp intelligence and seemingly endless patience with
the ignorance of the world-bound. What continued to
fascinate him, meeting after meeting, was her apparent natural ability to shield her thoughts and emotions
from even a determined auditor.

Right now, Trader Isfelm was being patient with
the portmaster.

She smiled, spread her hands, and ducked her
pointed chin slightly.

"That's free-handed, and I'm grateful," she said, sounding *exactly* grateful. "But the truth is—we have charts, maps and nav grids, same like you—likely from the same source, and every bit as old. The problem, in a word—is that in the spaceways, under Dust or in the Clear, things *move*. In fact, what we're calling routes are less like that fine avenue outside the window here, than a series of markers and suggestions. The routes, and the protocols for traveling along them—they're all adjusted as space moves."

She considered the faces 'round the table one by one, apparently not finding the ready understanding she had hoped for.

Glancing down, she picked up the mug before her and sipped tea, wondering, so Bentamin thought, how to get her concept through their thick heads.

The tea apparently had a restorative effect; when the trader put her mug down, she was smiling slightly.

"Well, here now—you'll have seen the Dust Warnings we bring in with our infopacks. Data gathered from the beacons, buoys, and stations along our route, that is. Those measurements were how we first knew the Dust was leaving us, the rate of its going, and where it might be tending. All of space is like that—moving, readjusting itself, always changing, fast or slow."

Another glance around the table. Bentamin gave the trader a nod of encouragement, and got a wry half-grin in return.

"Now, our information being as old as it is, past Redlands space, we might as well not have it; it's more a danger to navigation than any kind of help. We need updates from out there—clear, fresh data—that's what it comes down to. I'm *willing* to go *out*. Space! I'm *eager* to go *out*! But unless and until I can supply my captain and my nav rider with numbers better than two hundred Standards gone, they're not taking the risk. And nor do I blame them."

"These numbers, then," said the portmaster. "How do you suggest we gather them? Even before Dust, The Redlands were considered out of the way."

By design, Bentamin thought. The population of The Redlands specifically did not want to be found out by *dramliz*, the Liaden Council of Clans, or by any other persons who might see them and their talents worthy only of elimination.

Or, he thought, Reavers suddenly looming in his thoughts, exploitation.

"My thought was the research station," Isfelm said, and raised her hand, the big, showy ring she always wore catching the light from the windows. "The Dust is thinned enough now, signal distortion ought not be a problem. How if—"

A subtle chime sounded inside Bentamin's ear, followed by the voice of the portmaster's amanuensis.

"Begging your pardon, Warden, but the Oracle is calling for you on the emergency comm. You can take it in the privacy parlor."

"Thank you," he replied.

Trader Isfelm was still talking, the rest of the council concentrating on her proposal.

Bentamin rose and slipped quietly out of the room, moving quickly down the short hall to the privacy parlor.

The red light was blinking on the comm unit. Bentamin braced a hip against the table, and touched the button.

"Aunt Asta, it's Bentamin," he said, keeping his voice calm and gentle.

"Bentamin! I wanted you to know immediately! The universe has cut its final ties with darkness. We need have no more concerns on *that* head."

Bentamin blinked—and realized that he was relieved indeed. Aunt Asta was free of her private horror. The universe was no longer in danger. She could rest now, and be easy.

"That is excellent news!" he said enthusiastically.

He hesitated before deciding that he had to ask, if for no other reason than it would be unlike him not to ask. "How were these ties cut, if it can be told?"

"A hero arose," Aunt Asta said. "Battle was joined; the sacrifice was made; and the door was closed! Closed and sealed. We are unbreachable."

"Truly, we owe much to this hero," Bentamin said piously.

There was a pause, and for an instant he feared that he had gone too far and Aunt Asta, with her Far-Seeing eyes, had Seen entirely through him.

If so, she decided that mercy was in order, on this day when the hero's sacrifice had been made, and the universe was saved.

"It is the way of life," she said, as if she were delivering a lesson to a child. "Danger arises, and also the answer to danger. Balance is the rule."

An old lesson, that one, and not accurate, so far as Bentamin had observed. On the other hand, rules were a comfort to Civilization, as much as they were irksome to the Haosa. In between those two poles, surely a truth was balanced. And who could say, but that the universe depended upon that truth?

"I am going to take a nap," Aunt Asta told him. "Go back to your meeting, Bentamin."

The line went dead.

Bentamin's lips twitched. He closed the comm unit, and rested there a moment, hip against desk. A nap now...

A nap sounded infinitely attractive. He wondered, idly, how long it had been since he'd had one.

After a moment, he shook his head, stood...

And went back to the meeting.

Dutiful Passage

. . . .

I

ASTONISHINGLY, POMMIER WAS AGREEABLE TO TAKING their displaced crew—well, no. Padi corrected herself; that wasn't the astonishing part. *Of course*, Pommier would take displaced spacers. If they refused and a complaint was filed with the Guild, as it surely *would* be, given that Hepster si'Neest was among the eight leaving the *Passage*—they would be reprimanded, *and* fined *and* put on probation. Pommierport was important in this sector. They *certainly* wouldn't jeopardize their standing over the trivial burden of eight displaced spacers.

No, Padi thought, calling up her personal files, the *astonishing* thing had been that Pommier had agreed to let the *Passage* dock and trade. Port admin seemed perfectly oblivious to their supposed reputation as a violent ship. They'd not been immediately banned as pirates or outlaws. They'd been given an approach and an orbit. Father had received a trade packet and a port ID for himself as master trader; and also a packet and ID for her, which duly noted her status as an apprentice-in-trade.

Padi had read the packet while she ate her hasty nuncheon. Now, having just finished her shift in 'ponics, she was taking advantage of the common use station to access her inventory list.

The wood and the tinderfones were possibles, she thought, but that was light stuff, really, and only in her inventory at all because whimsy sometimes sold where serious goods did not.

Then there was the question of what she ought buy into for The Redlands, which remained frustratingly obscure. Well, perhaps there was information to be had at Pommier.

It was a puzzle, but not one that could have her whole attention now. Now, she had better be on her way, or she'd be late at the Pet Library.

She shut the screen down, and set out at a brisk walk for the ship's library. No one had found it necessary to tell her why two hours in the Pet Library had been added to her schedule, or why it replaced one of her scheduled sessions with Lina. Granted, Lina was Ship's Librarian, but the *melant'i* of that position did not include instructing barely emerged and uncatalogued *dramliz*.

Still, the schedule was the schedule and she kept to it though she was beginning to sorely miss her private research and study time. She was going to have to contrive some consecutive hours to compare the trade packet closely with her inventory. It was not something that could be done in stolen minutes at a public computer screen. She doubted even Master Trader yos'Galan could put together a profitable trade lot under such circumstances, though he might do *well enough*, given that he had so very much experience to inform him.

Her odds of doing even *well enough* were vanishingly small under such conditions, though with the opportunity to study and peace enough to allow her imagination scope, she felt she might manage to not utterly embarrass herself.

But all that was for later. Now, she must bring her mind to her next duty.

She took a deep breath, centering herself, and stepped into the library just as the hour chimed.

Waving her card at the reader, she saw that Lina was on the front desk, deep in consultation with Bonil Stemins, several screens open between them. She did not call a greeting, but turned her steps immediately to the Pet Library.

Just inside, she paused, blinking, vaguely aware of the door closing behind her.

Priscilla—her father's lifemate, captain of the *Dutiful Passage*, *dramliza*—was standing by the garden enclosure where the norbears lived. It was, Padi owned, a shock, though she couldn't think why it should be.

Many people visited the Pet Library, after all. Pets soothed people, lowered stress, and increased optimism. This being a Korval ship, and one designed by her great-grandmother Master Trader Petrella who, according to Father, never did anything save there was a profit in it, there was a pet library on the *Passage* for a *reason*. Not all Korval ships had a pet library, not even all the major ships, though three carried norbears, and four others had large aquarium rooms. All Korval tradeships had a garden room, featuring flowering plants and shrubberies. Great-Grandmother Petrella *must* have seen profit in providing a pet library to her crew, as had the master traders that came after.

Before this present scheduling adjustment, Padi had not herself been a frequent visitor to the Pet Library. She was busy, and while she liked the cats at home, she rarely felt their lack aboard ship. She might perhaps have come more often had there *been* cats, but cats and spaceships simply did not mix well. Cats did not care for Jump. They somehow *knew* when the ship had entered hyperspace, as if they were pilots sitting their boards, and would not be comforted until they were returned to normal space.

That might not have been so bad—there were, after all, rumors of cats who were the hundredth generation on Family Ships, like the Wildes, the Smiths, and the Tragers, who had been flying Loops since before the arrival of Rostov's Dust . . .

Korval might, indeed, have bred a line of cats who did not object to Jump, but that would probably not cure them of their curiosity, or their ability to get into places where they really ought not to be.

No, it had long been decided that cats and spaceships together were a disaster waiting to happen, and it was simply best not to take the risk.

So, there were no cats in the Pet Library. There were, however, fish, snakes, and turtles; pidogs; gerblits . . .

. . . and norbears.

Truth told, Padi did not care overmuch for norbears. She found them aloof and distantly polite, as if, indeed, norbears—at least, those norbears populating the Pet Library aboard *Dutiful Passage*—did not care overmuch for Padi yos'Galans.

Which was certainly fair enough.

On those rare occasions when she *had* visited the Pet Library on her own behalf, she had contented herself, in the absence of cats, with the pidogs, who were cheerful, if foolish, and made no demands other than a floppy ear be properly addressed.

Which was, of course, why she had been assigned *particularly* to the norbears.

Her obligations to them consisted of making certain that they were thriving, cleaning up any messes they might have made—though in their favor, norbears were much tidier than pidogs—making certain that their greenery was in order, and also their waterfall, and replenishing the nutrient pellets as required.

She was also to hold each one and talk to it. Norbears thrived on physical contact. She did the things required of her . . . punctiliously . . . and the norbears accepted her ministrations in the spirit in which they were offered.

Now, here was Priscilla, standing by the enclosure, with the norbear named Master Frodo on her shoulder. One of his furry handlike paws was gripping a lock of Priscilla's hair where it curled 'round her ear; in the other, he clutched a slice of apple.

Priscilla's face was angled downward, as if she were listening to some conversation the creature was whispering into her ear.

Padi hesitated, uncertain if approaching would be an interruption—an intrusion. There was something . . . intimate in the scene before her, as if they were two old friends, telling over the points of their affection.

As if she had heard Padi's hesitation, which she may well have done, Priscilla raised her head and smiled.

"Hello, Padi. I hope I'm not disrupting your schedule. I had a few uncommitted minutes, and I thought I'd revisit my roots, and Master Frodo, of course. I'd forgotten what a dreadful gossip he is!"

She paused, head tipped slightly toward the norbear.

"Yes, sir, you *are* a dreadful gossip!" she reiterated. "And you have been from our first meeting."

Padi was somewhat taken aback. She knew of course that norbears were functioning empaths who shared memory dreams with those who were able to understand them. Padi could not see the norbears' dreams, though it didn't surprise her that Priscilla could. What *did* surprise her was the caressing tone; almost as if the little animal *was* speaking into her ear.

"To be truthful," she said, recovering herself and moving toward the enclosure, "you're doing my work for me. I'm grateful."

Glancing at the feeding station, she considered the supply of nutrient pellets on offer. Probably the bowl ought to be topped up, though they were in no danger of starving. The norbears preferred greenery and seeds to the pellets which, indeed, they seemed to regard as emergency rations, to be held in case some tragedy rendered the real food rare.

She reached for the bowl...and paused, looking over her shoulder.

"Your roots?" she asked.

"Exactly my roots," Priscilla said with a grin. "This was my first duty station on the *Passage*. I was hired to be Pet Librarian."

Padi blinked.

Lina, of course, had assistants in the library, including those who—as Padi now—tended the various residents of the Pet Library. But to have a Pet Librarian as a unique position...

"It was your father, being a Healer," Priscilla said, interrupting these thoughts. "I was badly in need of

Healing by the time I found the *Passage*. So he put me into the care of the Librarian and ship's Healer— and also into the care of the norbears. Master Frodo in particular took an interest in my case, and it was precisely what I needed."

Padi stared, recalling how the assignment to the Pet Library had appeared, with no notation...

"Am I," she said slowly, "in need of Healing? Because I will be plain—the norbears do not like me."

Priscilla's eyebrows rose over black eyes.

"Don't they?" she said, and paused again as if she were listening to advice from the creature on her shoulder.

"I see," she said, and looked Padi in the eye. "They remember your wall, and while they see you no longer wear it, they don't want to be shut out again. If they make an effort, they want it to be worth their time, you might say."

Padi eyed the little creature, who was nibbling energetically on his slice of apple.

"Am I," she said again, "in need of Healing?"

Priscilla sighed lightly.

"It's no secret, I think," she said, meeting Padi's eye, "that you're in need of Sorting."

"Sorting," Padi repeated.

"Norbears are particularly good at Sorting," Priscilla said mildly. "They're also amusing, if you don't mind a tendency to gossip."

Padi frowned at the norbear. The apple was gone, and the creature met her eyes with an intelligent directness. There was a certain air of overdone innocence about it, rather like Father when he was pretending to pull a fast one.

"Of course," Priscilla continued, reaching to her

shoulder and gathering Master Frodo close, "if you're not inclined to make the connection, that's up to you. Some people don't like norbears, and as you've noted, they don't warm to everyone. You'll decide how much, or how little, you want to interact with them."

She bent and placed Master Frodo into the enclosure, pausing when the creature placed his handlike paw on her wrist.

"Yes, I will tell her that," she murmured. "Thank you. I'm glad we had time to visit."

She straightened and faced Padi.

"Frodo asks me to tell you that they appreciate your care. He hopes, purely on his own part, that you won't go back behind your wall. He says you're much more attractive without it."

Padi took a breath. *Attractive?*

Priscilla smiled slightly.

"He does mention that you look underfed. I wouldn't mind that, particularly; he's been telling me the same thing for years."

She bowed her head. "I'm afraid duty calls. Thank you for your patience."

Padi watched her stride long-legged and graceful out of the Pet Library, the door closing gently behind her; sighed, and turned back to the norbear enclosure.

She refilled the pellet bowl, made certain that nothing impeded the waterfall's flow, raked the sand, trimmed away a dry stalk of vegetation, and added some fresh slices of carrot to the greens mix.

Those tasks complete, she stood looking down into the enclosure, thinking.

She was being *Sorted*—which the Healers at Millsapport had not been able to do—by norbears.

The norbears in question were presently being social with each other, gathered in a loose circle on the sand, comfortably touching. Tiny and Delm Briat were sharing a leaf, while Master Frodo leaned companionably against Lady Selph, who appeared to be drowsing.

"Well," she said, addressing the group. "Since there seems to be some interest, I can tell you that I will not be rebuilding the closet. In retrospect, it was a singularly bad idea. Had I thought to seek counsel, it would very likely never have been built. Life was perilous, however, and informed counsel . . . difficult to achieve. It just . . ."

She raised her hands and let them fall.

". . . it just seemed like a good idea at the time."

Feeling slightly foolish, she began to turn away— and turned back at the sound of what could only be described as a sharp command. Despite being somewhat high-pitched, the tone reminded Padi forcefully of her cousin Kareen.

The norbear circle had broken. Tiny and Delm Briat were still placidly chewing on their leaf, but Master Frodo now sat a little apart, watching Lady Selph with interest.

That one was standing on her hind legs a little forward of the other three, forearms raised. Padi was abruptly convinced that the norbear wished to be brought out of the enclosure. After all, it was part of her job to hold the norbears.

There came another firm squeak, Lady Selph sounding more than a trifle annoyed with the slowness of Padi's wit.

Well, then.

She bent, got a careful grip around the creature's ample furry middle, and raised her gingerly, meaning to cradle her against a shoulder, as had become her custom. This move, however, earned her a sharp rebuke. Padi hesitated, and glanced back at the enclosure, where the remaining norbears were observing the proceedings intently.

"All right then," she said, and holding Lady Selph firmly, moved two steps to the end of the enclosure, and sat in the chair there. She put the creature on her knee, as if it were a cat, and received a rather surprising trill, as if she were being praised for having— *finally*—done something right.

The next moment, the norbear squirmed, and Padi loosened the grip she'd kept around the creature's middle, though she was not so foolish as to let her go.

"What do you want?" Padi asked.

Lady Selph abruptly came down on all four paws, adjusted herself for balance, and began to purr.

It wasn't quite a cat's purr, thought Padi. This was more of a throaty hum, with trills interspersed—so very comforting. Much *more* comforting, in fact, than a cat's purring, though she would be certain not to mention that to the cats at home.

In fact, thought Padi, there was Paizel now, from home, and that—why, that was Fondi, though she wasn't at all certain who *that* was, perhaps a cat had been added to the household while she was away. Jeeves did accept new applicants after careful screen—

No, *that* wasn't Jeeves, that was *Father.* Jeeves was . . . yes, *that* was Jeeves; indeed, yes, Father knew him well, Jeeves being the yos'Galan butler. And that was Aunt Anthora. Yes, of course Father knew her, too—his very sister! And Aunt Nova, his other sister, elder of Anthora—and Uncle Val Con—yes, *that* was

Uncle Val Con, too, but much younger, doubtless when he was cabin boy on this very—

And, oh, yes, that was Uncle Ren Zel, who had been first mate; lifemated now to Aunt Anthora—and that? Why, that was Master Trader Er Thom, Padi's grandfather, and his lady, Thawlana Anne...

There was a pause then, filled by the norbear's trilling. Padi sighed, stirred—and stilled as another face appeared before her mind's eyes.

But this was not the comforting, familiar face of one of her kin. This face was...not quite civilized. Certainly, it was not Liaden, not with that scowl showing openly. She had never seen them before, and truly, she hoped they never met. In fact, the longer she considered the face—round and tan; with fierce mismatched eyes, one gold, the other black, and straight-set angry mouth—the more agitated she became, until all at once, she pulled on her power and thrust the intruder away with all the strength in her.

She opened her eyes then, breathing hard and shivering somewhat as she met Lady Selph's knowing bright gaze.

"Messages for you, Padi," Hilfi Tawler said from behind the reference desk as Padi emerged from the Pet Library.

"Thank you."

She slipped behind the desk, and input her comm code. There was only one message in-queue. From the master trader.

I note that we both have some preparation to make as we approach Pommier. I wonder if we

*might agree to postpone our meeting this eve-
ning, and plan instead to have breakfast together
in my office tomorrow. We may then usefully
compare strategies for success at this new port.*

Padi felt some of the tension leave her shoulders.
Yes, that was precisely what would do her the most
good—as he would know.

Your father being a Healer, she heard Priscilla say
in the back of mind—but really, in this case, it was far
more likely that the master trader was being pragmatic.

She reached to the keyboard.

I agree, she typed. *A few hours to prepare myself
would be most welcome. I look forward to speaking
with you over breakfast.*

That done, she cleared the screen and set off at
very nearly a run for her session with Cargo Master
ira'Barti.

II

"WHY," PADI ASKED LINA WHEN THEY MET FOR THEIR NEXT session . . . "Why do the norbears care about who I know?"

"It is how they shape the universe," Lina answered. "They seek connections. Whom did you speak with?"

It took Padi a moment to realize that Lina meant which of the norbears had dreamed faces at her.

"Lady Selph."

"Ah. You are in the care of an expert. Lady Selph is quite elderly, and was well-traveled before she came into the service of your grandfather. No doubt you will learn much from her."

Padi frowned slightly, and moved a shoulder in slight confusion.

"She may be beyond me," she said ruefully.

"Oh? What was her opening?"

"Paizel—a cat from home—and another, Fondi. Then, a cat I didn't know—dark ears and stripes. Then Father, though I think Lady Selph thought he was Jeeves. Then Jeeves, Aunt Anthora, and Aunt Nova, Uncle Val Con, Uncle Ren Zel, Grandfather Er Thom and Grandmother Anne . . ."

Lina was nodding.

"In my experience, the usual progression of norbear communication is from near to far. Aside the striped cat, did she show you anyone you did not know?"

"Yes. A . . . stranger; someone I had certainly never seen—and very unnerving, too. *Quite* ferocious."

"Ah. And who else, beyond this stranger?"

Padi shook her head.

"No one. I was, as I said, unnerved, and I pushed the . . . person . . . away, whereupon I . . . woke up . . ."

It occurred to her now that she had not so much *woken up* as shattered a delicate rapport with a master of her craft, in mid working.

"Well," she added. "After that, Lady Selph wished to return to the enclosure. I suspect I had been rude. I picked up each of the others, but no one of them cared to . . . share. Then the hour turned."

"Well, then, Lady Selph will dream with her cuddle. Do not doubt she will have more matches for you to make, when next you meet. She has apparently determined to take you in paw, and—I will not hide the worst from you—she is a very determined person."

"So, she'll Sort me properly?" Padi asked, with some irony.

Lina didn't even blink.

"It is not impossible that she will succeed where others have not. She is, as I said, quite old, and not accustomed to putting up with impertinence."

Padi sighed, and was about to put another question regarding this *Sorting out*, but Lina at that moment brought her palms lightly together, saying briskly:

"Now, if you please! Let us work on your shields!"

· · ·❄· · ·

There were letters in-queue, according to the light on the comm screen. Shan crossed to the wine table, pouring a glass of the red more out of habit than desire, and carried it with him to the desk.

Possibly, he thought, as he put the glass down and settled into his chair, there was a letter from Janifer

Carresens-Denobli. He was becoming quite anxious for word from that trader...

He touched the screen...

Messages in-queue, indeed.

In fact, *three* messages in-queue, arrived within moments of each other.

One letter from his delm.

One letter from Security Officer Jeeves.

One letter from his brother Val Con.

Shan leaned forward and tapped open the letter from Val Con.

Brother of my heart, I greet you with all joy.

I will first do brother's duty and save you the necessity of scolding me. Freely I admit that I ought to have written sooner. Indeed, I had on several occasions wished to do so. My poor excuse is that, while they fill our days and hours, news of committee meetings, weather calculations, and social experimentation could hardly arrest your interest, engaged as you are in establishing the clan's future.

However, I no longer have the excuse of being dull, for much has happened of which you must be made aware.

There is news of kin.

Firstly, our sister Anthora has conceived a child with her lifemate Ren Zel.

Secondly, Anthora and our brother Ren Zel have taken injury in a desperate venture to preserve the universe as we know it. For long minutes, we feared that Ren Zel had given himself in Balance, but matters were not so dire as that.

*They are together with the Healers as I write
this. I cannot say what outcome may be given
us, but they are alive, and know themselves.
Anthora was not at the front, and Ren Zel's
memory of the event is unsteady. Indeed, I fear
it has abandoned him utterly, so we may never
have the whole tale. Suffice us that the universe
continues, or so I take leave to believe.*

*Line yos'Phelium rejoices in a new daughter—
Tocohl Lorlin, Jeeves's heir by his own devising.
On that head, a warning—he chose for her the
voice of our mother, which gave me pause on
first hearing. On questioning, he would have it
that he had observed Mother's voice to have been
remarkably soothing to any who heard it, which
is certainly true. Given the task the delm put on
her, mere hours after her birth, supplying Tocohl
with such a weapon as Mother's voice can only be
seen as prudence on the part of a caring parent.*

*You will, I know, be gratified to learn that
our young cousins Kor Vid yos'Phelium and
Daaneka tey'Doshi have returned from their
negotiations with our good Uncle. They arrive,
alas, shipless, and have petitioned the delm for
a courier class. I believe the delm is disposed to
grant that petition, but has required them both
to submit to licensing tests.*

*yos'Phelium also rejoices in the return of our
cousin Jen Sin, whom we had long thought lost.*

Shan tapped the screen.

"Jen Sin yos'Phelium is dead," he informed the
empty air. "*Two hundred Standards* dead."

The air vouchsafed no reply, which Shan supposed was just as well. Val Con's letter was upsetting enough. Uncle Daav *and* Aunt Aelli returned? Well, that was expectable, even necessary, given their situation, which, the last time Shan had seen them, was that each was resident as their own person inside Uncle Daav's head, Aunt Aelli having been so careless as to have mislain hers two dozen Standards ago. Only now there were new names, and a new license required from each...

Which could only mean that *our good Uncle* had somehow separated them out of Daav's head, and into...*young* cousins. Clones. Clones grown by the puppetmaster of the universe, for his own use, generously given instead to needy Korval pilots.

Clones, so Shan strongly suspected, were not cheap commodities. One was therefore compelled to wonder what *our good Uncle* might call as Balance for such sweet courtesy.

He shivered and reached for his wine.

Truly, set alongside the return of the clan's elders as *young cousins*, the other points of Val Con's letter hardly held luster—no, wait. Anthora stricken in her powers, and Ren Zel, too? Between them, they had the potential to unmake the universe—or to preserve it. The latter had apparently been Ren Zel's choosing, gentle lad that he was. One hesitated to predict what the outcome might have been, had the choice fallen to Anthora.

Send that the trauma had not harmed the babe— the Healers would do their most for all, of course.

He sipped his wine, and put the glass down.

Well. Best see what other news his brother had sent him.

He tapped the screen again.

We have the felicity of receiving Theo, her ship, and her crew; Norbear Ambassador Hevelin; two Pathfinders from the Old Universe, who had fallen behind during the removal; and Spiral Dance, intact, piloted by a small, but one fears strong-minded, Tree.

I would not have you think that Theo returned to us in response to the entreaties of a worried brother. Nothing like! In keeping with the tradition of her House, she came because she was in a scrape. Also, she had some notion that Scout Commander yos'Phelium might be of use to her.

Which, I fear, he was. You will know more, and of course be properly horrified, when you read the delm's letter.

Nova prospers in the city, as Boss Conrad's administrator and a Boss in her own right. My Aunt Kareen is also located in the city, where she is deeply engaged in a task assigned by the delm: to produce a Surebleak Code acceptable to the native and the immigrant populations.

Past the news of kin, there are one or two other items which you may find amusing.

The survey team from TerraTrade is with us, and very thorough they are. One of their number holds the opinions expressed so eloquently in news sources such as Taggerth's, but the team leader swears they are committed to an objective study.

The delm will doubtless enlarge upon this theme, but I feel it is a brother's duty to inform you that the clan has very recently acquired a *space station. It is said to be in good general repair, though the keepers—of which my cousin Jen Sin signs himself chief—provide a list of desirable upgrades to bring it into modern times.*

Talizea your niece my daughter grows wiser and more beautiful every day—which my lifemate pronounces a father's partiality, and further states that I am wrapt 'round Lizzie's fingers. I object to this, on condition that I had already been wrapt thoroughly 'round her mother's fingers.

Now, there is the news, as succinct as you might wish it, and you may now read the delm's letter with some degree of comprehension.

Miri sends her love, and desires you to return to us as quickly as may be. In fact, she goes so far to declare that she misses you, and Priscilla, often. She says of Padi that she will soon find a new route for herself. Miri does occasionally Dream True, and there had seemed a certain weight to this last. Make of it what you will.

As you have long held my heart, there is no need for further discourse on that head. Come back to us when you may, and take what care you might.

Val Con

P.S. I had nearly forgot. Lady yo'Lanna, finding herself temporarily bereft of handwork, has announced her intention of traveling, with her household, to Surebleak, in the very near future.

Shan shouted aloud with laughter.

"It needed only that! Forgot, is it? Wretch."

The door chimed through his hilarity. In fact, he

was still grinning broadly when Padi entered the office and paused, head tipped slightly to one side.

"Is there something amusing?" she asked.

"Only your uncle Val Con coming the clown," he told her. "Please, serve yourself."

He scanned the letter again while she poured out a glass of tea, and settled into the chair across the desk.

"There is news of kin," he said. "Your aunt Anthora and Uncle Ren Zel have put themselves in the path of disaster. Both took blows to their talents and are with the Healers. Also, they have between them conceived a child."

Padi bit her lip. "We seem to be traveling parallel paths."

"There is a certain similarity, isn't there?" Shan said, glancing back at the letter. "Clever of you; I hadn't marked that.

"In other news of kin, Theo has returned to Surebleak, with crew and ship. One doubts that she will be long content to remain on Surebleak, but perhaps Val Con—I should say, Miri—may persuade her."

"Theo is not very persuadable, is she?" Padi asked, sipping her tea. "Perhaps, if she is given a task, so that she needn't find her own trouble, that would answer."

"Perhaps it might. Padi, you are thinking like a *thodelm*."

"Surely not! And if I were, it would be very improper in me. Theo looks to Line yos'Phelium."

Shan grinned.

"Theo would doubtless tell you that she looks to neither Line, nor to Korval. I therefore amend myself—you are thinking like a trader who wishes to preserve a talented contractor so that she may be of profit to Korval, and to herself, in future. My compliments."

"Thank you," she said, very proper indeed. "Does Uncle Val Con have other news?"

"In fact, he does! He allows us to know that Jeeves has produced a child, who has come into yos'Phelium, and was sent off by the Delm's Word scant hours past birth."

He picked up his glass.

"He of course writes no details of this mission, so all we are left to say is: *Poor child! Grant she has her parent's resourcefulness to sustain her.*"

"Which she will have," Padi pointed out, frowning slightly. "Does the judgment upon Jeeves convey to his offspring?"

"An excellent question. Jeeves is quite canny, and I don't believe he would have produced a child only to see her murdered or set into slavery. However, you may have put your finger upon the reason for the delm's quick action on her behalf."

"Get her out of the way until something may be contrived?"

"Some respect for the delm, if you please, daughter, but—yes. Exactly so."

He moved a hand toward the screen.

"Leaving kin aside for the moment, I am gratified to learn that TerraTrade did, indeed, dispatch a survey team to Surebleak, and they are even now undertaking a thorough survey.

"Also—and the reason for my unseemly mirth upon your arrival—Lady yo'Lanna has stated her intention to come to Surebleak, household in train, which fact your uncle my brother wishes us to believe that he had utterly forgotten until the instant before he was to dispatch his letter."

Padi grinned.

"No, that's not very likely, is it?" she said. "But Lady yo'Lanna—she's so very old, Father! What can she want on Surebleak?"

"Novelty, I would expect; and an escape from faces too familiar, while the face she longs most to see is forever denied her."

Padi glanced aside.

"I have no way to judge so venerable a lady," she said at last. "But—her household? Can she be bringing Maelin and Wal Ter with her?"

"She might. Neither has been named an heir. Clan Justus might very well wish to establish a cadet house on a growth world."

He frowned slightly, weighing the matter.

"We may have the felicity of seeing Master Ken Rik again, if Justus cares to fill his grandmother's household from the ranks of the extras. She might have all classes of kin to support her, as well as a modest staff."

"So many? Can Surebleak City accommodate her?"

"A telling question. I'm certain that your Uncle Val Con is equal to the task of locating a suitable residence, for if she's not already given him the commission, you may depend that she will do so in her next letter."

Padi laughed.

"If all of that is to fall on him, it's little wonder he tried to forget her arrival!"

"Very true. I own myself impressed that he hasn't yet left the planet."

"Are we called home?" Padi asked, after a moment.

"By Val Con? Hardly."

"By the delm," Padi amended patiently.

"Ah. Well, we may be. There is a letter in-queue from the delm, which I haven't yet read. For the moment, we are entirely on course.

"So"—he spun his chair to face her fully—"honor me, Trader, do, with your thoughts regarding Pommierport."

III

THE NORBEARS WERE GATHERED ON THE SAND WHEN
Padi approached the habitat. Four furry faces were
turned up to her, as if wondering how rude she was
going to be this time.

"Good-day," she said. "You will perhaps be relieved
to know that I have received a lesson in manners, and
will better comport myself in future."

She paused, surveying the enclosure.

Emergency rations were full; the waterfall was running merrily, the stones around its basin rather damp,
as if someone had had a hasty wash.

The growing greens were a trifle ragged, and the
feeding platform was empty.

Padi bent to the keeper, and brought out some
apple slices and a few berin nuts, arranging them
attractively on the platform, before replenishing the
greens' bowl.

The norbears watched this with interest, but did
not get up to inspect, as was their usual habit.

Padi sighed.

"Would anyone like a moment?" she asked, and put
her hand into the enclosure.

Nothing moved; even the waterfall seemed to sus-
pend itself. Then, Delm Briat came up onto his back
feet and raised his paws toward her.

She gathered him up and brought him against her
shoulder, smoothing the fur between his ears with
careful fingers. He purred softly, which he had never
done before. She thought she saw a flicker of color

behind her eyes before he abruptly squirmed, and she received the impression that he would welcome being set down among the others now.

She accommodated him, of course, and straightened again with Tiny—who was not—cuddled against her. The pattern repeated. She stroked him; he purred, seeming content, but then quickly signaled his willingness to return to the enclosure.

Master Frodo was standing on his back legs when she replaced Tiny on the sand, but when she would have gathered him up, he instead extended a paw and held tightly to her finger.

She stood very still, closed her eyes, and waited.

Eventually, an image formed in her head.

"That is Priscilla," she said. "My father's lifemate, captain of the ship, and as I know, your very good friend."

She received a sensation of warmth, as if Master Frodo was pleased with her quickness.

Another image formed—that of Lady Selph. Padi frowned slightly.

"That is Lady Selph," she said. "I fear that I was rude when last we spoke. I do intend to make amends. However, just now, it is your turn."

But, no. Through some protocol that was neither speech nor dreaming, she was allowed to understand that Master Frodo was ceding his place to Lady Selph, who very much wished to have a long coze with Padi.

That . . . was unsettling though, Padi thought wryly, Lina had tried to warn her. Lady Selph had taken on the task of Sorting Padi yos'Galan, and she was going to see the thing through properly.

"I don't want to slight you," she said, but Master Frodo would have none of it. Lady Selph, so she was given to understand, was Master Frodo's extremely dear friend, and he was delighted to stand in support of her efforts. He was not so poor a thing that he would lose weight for one missed hug—not that he didn't find Padi's hugs pleasant, of course.

She chuckled.

"That was quite a nice recover," she told him, and received the *idea* of a chuckle from him.

"Very well then," she said. "Lady Selph may do her worst. I hope you will give a good report of me to Priscilla, if I cannot be saved."

Master Frodo loosed her finger, patting her wrist gently before he dropped to all fours and moved away toward the fresh treats which had already lured Delm Briat and Tiny.

Lady Selph remained tucked up on the sand, quite alone and making no move to bring herself to Padi's attention.

Well, of course not, thought Padi. It is the student's part to place herself at the feet of the master.

"Lady Selph," she said, with as much gravity as she could muster, "I am come for my lessons. I will do my utmost to be attentive and to refrain from any... unseemly displays."

There was a long moment, as if her words and attitude were being evaluated for any want of sincerity.

Just when Padi was certain she was to be dismissed from the master's sight as unworthy, Lady Selph rolled to four feet, then two, standing quite straight and dignified; once again putting Padi forcibly in mind of Cousin Kareen.

She bent, settled her hands around the lady's middle and raised her.

As before, she retired to the chair and sat, norbear on knee, hands lightly bracketing, to prevent any possibility of a fall.

The session again began with faces—crew, this time, rather than kin. Padi was astonished to discover how many of her crewmates visited the norbears—at least, she was until her lapse of attention was noted with a surprisingly sharp flicker of discomfort, rather as if Lady Selph had put a ruler across her knuckles.

After that, she did not allow her mind to wander, but gave all of her attention to the faces proposed to her, naming names until they had accounted for the crew entire, saving only—

There.

Yes, she thought; that is Lina, and that . . . well, but that is my stylus, floating—yes, floating; I taught it to do that. Yes, Lina's stylus, worse for my attentions, I allow. I had no idea it was so . . . susceptible.

There came the impression of austere amusement then, before the image of a bowl came before her mind's eye.

Ah, *such* a bowl! Dark blue at the center and lighter blue swirled with green rushing up toward the rim, where it broke into a froth of white and cream . . .

Padi felt her eyes fill with tears.

"That was mine," she said. "It was given me by a potter on Andireeport . . ."

No need for sadness then, came the suggestion from the master.

Padi shook her head, taking a deep breath against the sharp sense of loss. She tried to explain, her thoughts perhaps not as orderly as they might be . . .

The bowl—it had been broken. Assassins had been trying to kill her, and she had needed something... so*me*thing to hide in, and Lute—

Inquiry.

Lute—Father sent him to keep me safe, because he—Father—was in the gravest danger. And Lute had said that it was a very fine thing to hide under, this *idea* of the bowl, which was, after all, indestructible in its own right—only it had not been; she, Padi had broken it. She hadn't understood—well, and how could she have understood?—that by using the idea of the bowl—by stretching the essence of the bowl so... very... far, she had made it vulnerable.

Fragile.

An image of Father interrupted this recitation of failure, bearing the taste of inquiry.

"Yes, that's Father—oh! Lute? Well..."

Laboriously, she formed the image: the lean, brown, long person who *might have been* Father in some strange manner, despite his hair was dark and braided down his back, where Father's was white and crisp cut. Father's clothes were those of a prosperous trader; Lute's were worn, patched in places, thin in others. They both had the same big, clever hands, but really, there was no mistaking them one for the other; it was merely a chance resemblance...

The image of Lute hung between her and Lady Selph, as if it were a holograph. Then, with a little sound of satisfaction, the norbear...*accepted*... the image, and it vanished from Padi's ken, to be replaced by an image of Priscilla— No...*not* Priscilla, Padi thought, but someone—some*thing*—*wearing* her seeming.

Priscilla's eyes were fine, but they did not glow from within, luminous as ebony stars. Priscilla's skin was pale, her face mobile and lovely. This . . . other woman wore an alabaster mask, translucent and emotionless.

"Who is that?" Padi whispered.

The image of Lute reappeared, standing beside the luminous lady. They were partners, then; lifemates, perhaps, as Father and Priscilla.

"Her name?" she asked, but Lady Selph did not answer. Eventually, the joined images faded, and nothing else arose. Padi felt a definite sense of . . . patient waiting.

"I don't understand," she said, even as another image began to form.

It was the stranger from the session before. Padi felt her muscles clench, but she controlled herself and did not thrust them away. Instead, she held herself ready to receive whomever it was, as if she were at a trade show, waiting upon a customer new-arrived at the table.

The face was not, she thought, so rough this time; the eyes were green and blue—more puzzled than fierce. For a moment, they were merely a static image, like the others Lady Selph had dealt her.

Then, the mismatched eyes moved; the rough head turned—the stranger met her gaze, and *saw her*.

IV

Korval greets Thodelm yos'Galan and Master Trader yos'Galan.

Thodelm yos'Galan is advised that Anthora and Ren Zel, of the Line, have become in need of Healing. The clan is seeing to their proper care.

Master Trader yos'Galan's attention is directed to the documents sent under separate cover by House Security, particularly the field judgment rendered by Scout Commander yos'Phelium.

Master Trader yos'Galan is advised that Tinsori Light is a Korval property and open for trade. At your earliest convenience, please inspect the station with an eye to including it in any new routes you may build. It is expected that the station will receive significant traffic from Independent Logics.

Korval

Priscilla glanced up from the screen, eyes crinkled at the corners.

"At least they say, *at your earliest convenience.*"

"A concession, I allow it," Shan said, from his slouch in the chair on the far side of her desk. "Truly is it said that every problem carries within it the seeds of its own solving. You will, I know, be pleased to learn that Master Trader yos'Galan did most sprightly direct his attention to the documents provided by House Security."

"That would have been the field judgment rendered by Scout Commander yos'Phelium?"

"That, and also letters of introduction. At least now I know what to do with Theo."

Priscilla frowned at him.

"With *Theo*?"

"More accurately, I should say, *with Theo's ship*. If most of our expected clients will be Complex Logics, then it behooves us—wouldn't you say?—to have at least one Complex Logic on our side of the equation?"

"There's Tocohl—Tinsori Light," Priscilla pointed out.

"Tinsori Light is Station," Shan said, "and must be objective. Tocohl has been Seen by the delm and looks to Line yos'Phelium. If you were . . . a Free Ship, let us say, accustomed to living hidden, would you place yourself in the hands of Line yos'Phelium?"

"I might," Priscilla said. "There's Jeeves, after all. But I take your point: Someone who is objective, to represent Korval's interests and meet equally with AI clients, would be more likely to foster trust."

"If anything can foster trust in the community of Independent Logics. Though I suppose . . ." He sighed and rubbed his eyes. "I suppose that those who dare Tinsori Light first will be the boldest, and the canniest. The less bold will be watching, judging, and forming their own conclusions. I fear it will be a project that we will pass on to the succeeding generation, undone. However!"

He pushed himself to his feet.

"As Jeeves has been kind enough to supply me with an introduction to Tinsori Light and to Tocohl, I shall write to each, and also to Light Keeper yos'Phelium, soliciting such particulars and advice as they may have available. Also, I will write to Theo, and desire her to bring her crew and *Bechimo* to Tinsori Light to set up as emissaries of Tree-and-Dragon Trading until we can join them there."

"Which may not be soon."

"*At our earliest convenience*, recall. We shall trust that the combined good sense of Tocohl and the light keepers will be sufficient to contain Theo, her ship, and crew, while we continue to The Redlands."

Priscilla frowned.

"Is Tinsori Light convenient to The Redlands?" she asked.

Shan moved his shoulders. "To my recollection, Tinsori Light is convenient to nothing—and a good job that was, too.

"The information supplied by Jeeves reinforces my recollection, but I think—just as a first consideration— that we may want to build some security into any routes we craft with the Light in our thoughts. Tinsori Light is out of the way, which will suit the smart-ships well. It will suit them less well, if we should immediately highlight the station, and start bringing in—well! What shall we call ourselves now, I wonder? Traditional tradeships?"

He turned his hands up.

"In any case, it may suit the situation better to put some Loops and small-routes between Tinsori Light and—everywhere."

"That may work," Priscilla said, sounding only slight dubious.

"Clearly, it requires additional consideration," Shan agreed.

The comm buzzed, and Priscilla touched the button.

"Mendoza," she said crisply. Then, "Yes, thank you. I'm on my way."

"To the bridge with you, Captain!" Shan said, rising from his chair with a bow.

"I'm afraid so. For some reason, the first mate wants me near at hand when we begin our approach to Pommier."

"Your presence buoys their spirits," Shan told her, and followed her out of the office.

Off-Grid

·········

THERE ARE DREAMS—AND THEN THERE ARE DREAMS.

All dreams are distinct from Seeing.

Seeing is an act of probability; in essence, the Seer's talent and unconscious mind collaborate in a string of extrapolations, the outcomes of which have root in various highly probable scenarios.

Dreams, on the other hand, have no use for reality, probability, or even logic. While a Seer, or an Oracle, may misunderstand or misinterpret what they have Seen, what they See is always *possible*.

Dreams—even True Dreams—speak their own language, and they are not confined to linear narration. A dream, therefore, may as easily be addressing the finale of a particular event, as the start, or the middle.

Dreams—even True Dreams—tend to prove that the human mind is closer to chaos than order, even when rigorously trained.

Lacking the framework of rules and proven technique, each of the Haosa developed their own, unique relationship with the ambient. Some worked ceaselessly to hone their skills; others worked only enough to be certain that they would not accidentally cause harm to another.

Tekelia had trained rigorously, in so far as the Haosa could be said to train. The Haosa, let it be known, believed in training by doing. The ones best trained were the boldest—or as may be, the most foolish—who went back to the ambient again and again, no matter how many times they were hit in the head by strange young women, or their efforts ended in broken bones.

Tekelia's approach to the ambient and the acquisition of skill had been—determined. Possibly even stoic. Power was well enough, but for one seeking a life of relative peace, nuance was desirable, not to mention acuity of thought and purpose. Civilization thought that the ability to form and use tools made the Civilized superior.

It was Tekelia's opinion, shared by many of the Haosa, that dependence on tools and ritual made one less nimble in defense, as well as offense, and thus made one vulnerable.

Which was why Civilization needed the Haosa, no matter how much that equation horrified both sides.

Tekelia had been born to Civilization. After a series of tutors and counselors had thrown up their hands in despair of teaching the child one thing that a proper person ought to know, Tekelia had been pronounced Unteachable.

It was naturally a blow; no family wishes to discover that one of its children has been found wanting by the highest rank of society. To Tekelia's family, the judgment had not been a surprise. Tekelia was by no means the first Wild Talent the family had produced; however, the verdict of Unteachable did mean that there was a decision to be made.

There were those families who had their Unteachables Deafened—a small matter of specialized shielding, painless. As their memories were also adjusted so that they were not borne down by the weight of their failure, this was seen as kindness and proper care of kin.

Tekelia's family had always produced unpredictable talents. As far back as Liad, they had birthed both greater and lesser talents, with no regard for decorum or propriety. What they did not produce were *no-talents*, and that the clan elders had taken as a heart-lesson. It had happened that a Deafened child had overcome their shielding, to the sorrow of all involved, and also thereby increasing the store of bitter wisdom available to the elders. A living child, so said the elders, was superior to one who died in agony, knowing themselves betrayed. Banishing the Unteachable was therefore a kindness and best care of kin.

Which is how it came to pass that there were members of Tekelia's family residing both in Civilization and in Chaos.

There was Cousin Bentamin, the very Warden, whose duty was nothing more nor less than the preservation of Civilization; the Oracle, Aunt Asta, a Wild Talent confined and pressed into the service of Civilization; and Tekelia, of course, who might fairly be said to be not merely chaotic, but an instance of Chaos Itself.

Back in the classroom, it had only needed that Tekelia be told a rule to see it shattered. It could not be—in fact, was never said—that the child had no aptitude: Tekelia was extraordinarily apt, even brilliant. Show Tekelia one of the tools Civilization required in order to interface with the ambient, and that tool would be skillfully reproduced on the instant.

The rub was that—Tekelia's tools, elegant as they were, did not function.

There was no need to use tools to access the ambient, after all. On this, the Haosa, and Tekelia, were clear. The ambient existed. In fact, it was *ambient*. To reach the ambient—to interface with it or to influence it—all one needed to do was—open one's self...

... not too far, naturally, and not without taking appropriate care in the matter of shielding and spotters. While the ambient supported and sustained Civilized and Haosa alike, it did have—as the air—the power to harm those who were too trusting of it.

Trust had claimed more than half of Colemeno's original settlers, who had neither training, nor shields, nor knowledgeable kin to protect them. They had therefore succumbed to hallucination and the effects of Chaos, and thereby died. It had been the sheerest good luck that the second wave of colonists had been the *vas'dramliz*, relocated to Colemeno from Liad at a time of mutual need.

Or, as history suggested, perhaps not. Clan Korval, which had an... interesting relationship with probability, had been part of the relocation effort after all.

Now, though...

Now, Tekelia settled into the chair, and took a moment to order turbulent thoughts. It was useful to have a goal in mind when treating with the ambient. Yes.

Today's goal was to achieve a... more satisfying... contact with the young woman who had thrust Tekelia away with so much authority on their first meeting, coincidentally leaving behind a blazing headache.

Some of the Haosa played at hide 'n seek in

the ambient. It was not a game Tekelia cared for overmuch—and in any case, the woman had not been playing. Tekelia was under the impression that she had been startled, and had acted instinctively to protect herself from a potentially dangerous stranger.

That, at least, was more comforting than to think she had been specifically hunting, or that she was connected in some way with the Reavers.

Tekelia sighed. To have an enemy in the ambient was no good thing. To have a friend though...

Clarity was required. It was prudent, if not imperative, that another contact be made so that they might each fairly take the measure of the other, and know themselves for who they were.

So. Tekelia shifted slightly in the chair, eyes closed, open to possibility.

Bentamin would have initiated a search protocol to locate a person of interest, but Tekelia's way was much simpler. Merely, one stepped outside of one's shields, and whispered to the ambient.

I am here.

The echoes of the words faded. Dreams and phantoms drifted past, some familiar, others not. Tekelia felt interest, curiosity, wariness...and sat, open, but not engaging, watching the flickering parade slip past...

And there she was.

Pale hair drawn back from an angular face; lavender eyes; bold nose; decisive chin—startled once again. Her shields were open, and she made a reflexive move, as if she would close them. Then she stilled, holding herself in wary silence.

The ambient revealed her pattern, the texture of her

spirit, the weight of her will—no Reaver, she. Tekelia felt relief; really absurd amounts of relief.

Tekelia carefully paid out a thread of goodwill.

She bit her lip, her shields quivering, as if they might snap closed of their own volition. Such a display of timidity was . . . puzzling, and drew Tekelia's attention more closely to those shields.

They were bulky—businesslike—with edges sharp enough to cut, and an air of wary alertness about them. Attack shields, one might almost say, save that went against the very nature of shields and shielding.

Only, look how quick she had been to strike out on their first meeting. Perhaps she was in a position of peril, or lived in a moment of ongoing threat. One might easily find it prudent to strike first and ask particulars later. Such shields might fit that situation.

She seemed calmer, this meeting. Perhaps she realized that no one need be cut in this contact; in fact, no one need be afraid.

Tekelia wove warmth and hopeful friendship into the modest line of goodwill, the while subjecting those shields to closer scrutiny.

Bulky, yes, but not ill-formed; there was in fact a certain whimsy about them. Still, they felt . . . laborious, as if they had been built by one who was uncomfortable with the protocols she had been taught.

She was a student then; perhaps a student who was not so apt as her tutors would prefer, which Tekelia found oddly pleasing. Mayhap it was this trait that had drawn them together—strangers, but each, perhaps, a Child of Chaos.

"Who is that?" the woman asked, possibly of her tutor, and Tekelia felt . . . a touch, and the sense of someone who was more dream than voice. The information came through the ambient, directly to Tekelia's understanding—ears and whiskers; age, curiosity, purpose; a suggestion of green leaves and growing things . . .

A norbear, Tekelia realized. One's fierce and comely contact was tutored by a norbear.

That . . . was interesting.

Tekelia held very still, open to the ambient, accepting of anything and all that might come.

What came was a . . . feeling . . . a . . . designation—nothing that the mind might make sense from, though intuition did—a particular and unique signature, which could be confused with no other.

Carefully, Tekelia offered their own signature; felt it accepted by the norbear—who withdrew, leaving the student alone, hesitant and growing warier by the heartbeat, on the very edge of shutting down their rapport.

Once again, Tekelia offered their signature; felt the other catch it; felt, too, her startled amaze.

Nothing else came through, the silence stretching so long that their delicate connection began to tremble. The ambient . . . tightened . . . flickered, as if with lightning or with rage. Smoke swirled, or fog.

Tekelia looked to their own shields, anticipating a strike; the smoke thickened, swirled, and blew away, leaving the ambient as clear as a drop of amber, against which a signature began, tentatively, to form.

Fierce it was, and winged and . . . definite, like an etching in the very fabric of time and space.

Tekelia felt the signature strike, quartz to fire-steel, and looked into the dragon's eyes.

The ambient warmed . . . considerably.

It might have been horror at her own boldness; it might have been exhaustion—that quickly, the woman was gone; sharp shields folding shut as gently as the petals of a flower; and the ambient was smaller without her.

Dutiful Passage
Pommierport

· · · · · · · · · · · · ·

I

IT WAS A SUBDUED GROUP OF EIGHT WHO ACCOMPANIED Captain Mendoza and the 'prentice trader onto the shuttle. Even once away from the *Passage*, there was scarcely any talk, much less the chatter one would expect between crewmates.

Possibly, thought Padi, that was the problem. Very soon, they would cease to be crewmates, and would instead be eight individuals with varying skill sets, each looking for a new berth.

Pommierport would house them in dormitories, and feed them from the transients' cafeteria until they had either found new berths, or thirty Standard Days had elapsed, all according to Guild regs. There was no guarantee that the eight would be housed in the same dorm, nor share a common mealtime. Once they were accepted as wards of the port, it was probable that they would never see each other again.

Padi wondered if they were sad, second-guessing perhaps their choice to leave the *Passage* and their mates, or if they would welcome the final break. Her curiosity on that point was surely unseemly, yet she longed to open her Inner Eyes to take just one very quick look, assuming that she would be able to make sense of anything she saw...but, no.

Aside her poor Sight, which made it doubtful that she would learn anything instructive, it was rude to Look without permission.

Also, to even make the attempt would require her to drop her shields, which was *absolutely forbidden*.

Padi sighed lightly.

Let it be known that she did not *like* her shields. After much practice with Lina, and promptings from Lady Selph, she had managed something not *quite* so evocative of hull plate, but nor did they approach Father's supple silver, Priscilla's lambent lapis, nor even Lina's cheerful multihued door.

According to Lina, in fact, Padi's shields were rather...sinister.

"No, you must not look so downcast!" Lina had said, catching Padi's hand between both of hers. "They are very plainly shields; they not only do the job you intended them to do, they give what may be termed *fair warning*. Anyone attempting those shields *must* know that there will be a cost."

Padi herself wasn't so certain of that. On the other hand, if the mere aspect of her shields discouraged attack, that was all to the good.

For the rest of it, now that they were in place, it took—well, it took no effort at all to *keep* them in place, which Lina said was just as it ought to be. Only they...itched, to which Lina had nothing to say save, "Perhaps they will not, once you become accustomed."

Also, having the shields up made Padi feel...distant,

rather as if she were wearing earplugs, which *Priscilla* found interesting.

"You must be hearing something of the ambient noise," she said. "Enough that you miss it when you're shielded. We'll test you, once we're back on the ship and unshielded, to find out how much awareness you have. It may be that you'll benefit from focusing exercises."

The trouble with being of the *dramliz*, Padi reflected, was that there was *always* something more to learn. That was also true of trading, of course, but she *wanted* to be a trader, so those lessons were not burdensome.

In the seat beside her, Priscilla had her portable unit open and was already at work. The eight soon-to-be-former crew members sat stoic, even grim, in their seats, some reading from handhelds, others with closed eyes, meditating or asleep.

Padi had also brought her portable, since she had not been scheduled at the board for this descent, despite needing both the flight time and the practice—in her opinion. No, for this trip, her *melant'i* was apprentice trader and captain's escort.

Therefore, she touched her screen, opened the study file in-queue and was very shortly absorbed.

II

"THANK YOU, CAPTAIN MENDOZA," SAID STATION INTAKE Specialist Hanssen. "The records you have provided are exemplary, and I have no further questions."

He extended a soft, freckled hand and tapped the recorder off. Then, instead of pushing his chair back and rising, or merely waving them toward the door—he sat, hand resting on the machine, head bent as if he were thinking very hard.

Or, Padi thought, annoyed, he had fallen asleep there.

"Is there some other way in which we may assist you?" Priscilla asked, when the silence had grown uncomfortably long.

A sigh escaped Specialist Hanssen; he raised his head to meet her eyes.

"You must understand that my next questions are not part of the formal interview," he said, folding his hands on the table before him. "You are under no obligation to answer."

He paused, to Padi's eye rather uneasy, as if he were breaking some small but important rule. Priscilla, for her part, considered him without comment, face expressionless. Once more, the silence stretched. This time, it was Padi who broke it.

"Will we place ourselves at a disadvantage, if we choose to answer or to not answer?"

He flashed her a startled look, then smiled slightly.

"Trust a trader," he murmured, and inclined his head. "Your answers will not place you in peril of any kind. Your ship will not suffer for the answers you give, nor will it be rewarded. If you do not wish to answer questions off the record, you only need say so, and the matter is concluded."

"Perhaps if we heard the question," Priscilla said gently. "If you are asking for confidential information, of course we are not at liberty to answer."

"Of course."

He cleared his throat, and once again met Priscilla's eyes, his face tense.

"On my way to our interview here, I was stopped by a colleague who had just concluded an intake interview with one of your former crew. The person interviewed stated that she had taken the offered buyout because of her concern that *Dutiful Passage* had been hounded by its enemies into adopting the very course those enemies claim for it—in short..."

He paused, ears red, but to his credit he did not look away from Priscilla's eyes.

"In short, it was the opinion of this person that *Dutiful Passage* had come to be a wandering ship; if not an outright pirate, then a trader of opportunity. If not black, then certainly grey."

He stopped, and Padi received the distinct impression that he was regretting his course of inquiry, and also that he had been given no choice but to pursue it.

"I must ask *Dutiful Passage* if this... allegation by former crew has merit."

"It does not," Priscilla answered serenely.

Padi was impressed; certainly, there was nothing to add to that calm denial. She kept her trade-face in place and remained modestly silent, even when Specialist Hanssen looked her way. Surely, there was no more he might feel compelled to say, having received the assurances of *Dutiful Passage*'s captain.

"Forgive me," he said, and cleared his throat. "May I know the route which *Dutiful Passage* pursues?"

Priscilla raised her eyebrows.

"You're aware that *Dutiful Passage* is a master trader's ship," she said, and there was an edge to her voice now. "Master Trader yos'Galan has been charged to develop new routes and to found new business alliances. What may look like wandering to general crew may have a place in the greater shape seen by the master trader."

Padi took a careful breath, not quite willing to draw Captain Mendoza's eye.

Specialist Hanssen's broad face was flushed. He licked his lips.

"Do you have any other questions for us?" Captain Mendoza asked him.

He pulled himself together with a deep breath.

"Captain, I do not. Thank you for your information . . . and for your consideration. I will apprise my colleague of your answer."

He rose, and they did, to follow him out of the conference room.

They had gathered their third, Security Officer Tima Fagen, from the waiting room, and moved out into Pommierport, pausing on the walk outside the administration building to survey their surroundings.

This, according to Lina, was the worst of remaining behind shields. One needed to depend far too much upon other, less efficient senses to scan for threat or anomaly in the area.

Padi, however, had not, until very recently, had access to any senses save those less reliable, so this pause to glance up and down the street seemed quite usual to her.

Tima scanned the street with professional competence, glanced at Priscilla, and nodded.

"Good to go, Cap'n," she said easily.

Priscilla, who had confided to Padi that it was much more difficult to go back behind shields after training herself to be open to all the nuances of life, returned the nod with a slight smile.

"The question being—where will we go? Trader? Have you a commission from the master trader perhaps?"

Padi sighed.

"The master trader asked me to especially look out for tourist guides to The Redlands," she said, and met Priscilla's eyes frankly, kin to kin.

"One is not *certain* that he was offering a jest."

Priscilla considered her. "Well," she said, "is it *likely* that there are tourist guides to The Redlands?"

"Were it anyone other than Master Trader yos'Galan asking me to look them out," Padi said, with feeling, "I would say, *oh, no; of course not.*"

Priscilla laughed. "I understand completely!"

Padi shook her head. "Then you will understand why I researched bookstores and infotainment kiosks once we had a map of the port available. All such resources are to be found in Enlightenment Square." She gave Priscilla a conscious glance. "We may, if you wish, hail a taxi."

Priscilla raised her eyebrows. "How far is Enlightenment Square?" she asked.

Padi swallowed.

"It's the next square," she admitted, beginning to fear that she'd been inept. "Across four avenues."

"Am I showing signs of being frail?" Priscilla pursued, and Padi sighed.

"Pommier enjoys heavier gravity than we maintain aboard," she said. "Med texts indicate that such conditions are more noticeable when one is pregnant."

"I see! You were trying to spare me discomfort. Thank you."

Priscilla smiled and took Padi's hand; a touch between kin, which was fitting, as Padi had been... *trying* to exercise care of kin.

"I *am* pregnant, but not yet so *very* pregnant, and the truth is that I had been looking forward to a walk after all that stuffiness inside." Priscilla pointed at the administration building with her chin.

"We don't have time to do a proper port ramble, but a stroll over to this Enlightenment Square sounds like what I was wishing for"—she glanced around—"unless Tima would prefer to take a taxi."

Tima grinned.

"I been looking forward to stretching my legs since we got on the shuttle, Captain."

"Well enough, then. Ramble we will."

Priscilla released Padi's hand.

"Lead on, Trader."

III

"HOW DOES HE *DO* IT?" PADI ASKED. SHE RAISED THE SLIM, carefully wrapped package over her head, and paused on the bookstore's front walk.

"When I've asked him, on similar occasions," Priscilla answered, "I've been told that he is, after all, a master of trade."

"Which properly put you in your place," said Padi, her voice carrying an undercurrent of laughter.

"It did indeed," Priscilla said seriously. She looked over her shoulder. "Tima, *you* pick our next destination."

"Well, I was kinda curious about that shop we passed just at the corner, with the—"

"Aid!" a man's voice cut across hers. A man's voice speaking Liaden. "A rescue, Tree-and-Dragon! My partner is wounded, and I beg your consideration!"

Padi turned, half-expecting untamed hair, fierce face, and mismatched, feral eyes. But the man who came forward two careful steps, hands held out at belt-height, showing fingers spread wide and empty palms, was ferocity's simple opposite. His hair was pale and close-trimmed; his skin dark brown and smooth; his eyes were lighter than his face, glowing like chips of amber. His clothing was unexceptional—a plain jacket over a dark sweater, crew-grade trousers, and good boots that had been worn into comfort. There was a gun on his belt, peace-bonded according to port regs, and a hook, where a comm should have hung.

He looked, Padi thought, a little undergrown, as

if he had known want in his early years, and had never caught himself up.

Tima matched his two steps forward, which put her in a position to intercept him should he make a sudden lunge. A flicker of his eyes acknowledged her, but it was to Priscilla that he spoke, respectfully, though his mode was a trifle uncertain, as if he did not speak the High Tongue often.

"Captain, of your kindness," he said, petitioner-to-authority.

Padi stood close enough that she heard Priscilla sigh before she answered him in kind.

"What is your name?"

"I am Mar Tyn pai'Fortana; my partner is Dyoli ven'Deelin Clan Ixin. I beg on her behalf, Captain, not mine."

pai'Fortana was not precisely a Line name—so much Padi knew. She had some vague notion of it having to do with gaming—and also that it was not, quite, respectable.

ven'Deelin, however—ven'Deelin was respectable in the extreme, and Clan Ixin as old in trade as Korval itself.

"Why have you not taken your partner to the port medics?" asked Priscilla. "Or have you?"

The man—Mar Tyn pai'Fortana—lowered his hands, one eye on Tima, who made no objection.

"Captain, the nature of her wounds would only baffle a Terran medic, and I find no Hall nor Healer inside the port."

That, Padi knew, was true. She had made the same discovery during her researches of Pommierport, and had noted it as . . . slightly odd.

In such sections of space where trade and worlds were clustered, and a port would expect to see Liaden crews and Terran, small Halls and individual Healers were frequently found.

Pommier, though, could be said to occupy a space of its own. While Liaden ships might occasionally stop, it was not so frequent a thing that the port saw profit in installing what it might think of as Liaden-specific comforts.

"Captain," Mar Tyn pai'Fortana said softly. "For *her life*, I beg you."

Priscilla...moved. Padi could not say precisely *how*, but she was suddenly in receipt of the very strong notion that Priscilla had stepped out from behind her shields. Before them, the man's pale eyes blazed in his dark face. He bent in a profound bow, and did not straighten.

"You have secrets," Priscilla said at last.

Mar Tyn pai'Fortana unfolded, slowly, from his bow, and stood with shoulders rounded and eyes averted, a humble mouse confronting a hawk.

"Captain, I do—who does not? I swear I mean no harm to you or to yours. Bind me, if you wish; I submit—to all and to anything. Only extend your care to Dyoli."

It was love, Padi realized at that moment. This insignificant and probably disreputable person loved his High House partner. She wondered if the esteem was returned, and if, perhaps, this explained the presence of a ven'Deelin so far from the orderly lanes Clan Ixin most usually plied.

Beside her, she felt Priscilla move once more, stepping back, so Padi was certain, behind her protections.

"I won't bind you," she said to Mar Tyn pai'Fortana. "But I *will* kill you, if one of your secrets is treachery."

Again, he bowed, and this time, when he straightened to his full meager height, he met Priscilla's eyes squarely.

"Yes," he said.

Priscilla inclined her head.

"Very well. Take us to your partner."

IV

LET IT BE KNOWN: SHAN WOULD HAVE RATHER BEEN ON Pommierport, even if he had no intention of trading. Ports were all of them unique, and who knew what small thing, chance-seen at this port, might spark a thought at some other, or influence a matter of trade.

However, it had been the opinion of no one less than the ship's medic that he could tolerate a little more rest, just to be certain that there were no relapses. Keriana took a dim view, indeed, of relapses.

So, Shan was—not resting. Not exactly. But he *was* sitting quietly at his desk, doing research and running sims and in general not striding about in the dirt, the heat, and the gravity, portside.

He had some time ago put out discreet inquiries on Lomar Fasholt, who had vanished from all of her usual ports and places about the time that Korval had quit Liad for their new homeworld of Surebleak.

A few more answers to his questions had arrived in his mail queue, all of them unsatisfactory in the extreme, just as the others had been. He was beginning to believe that Lomar, far from not wanting to be found, no longer existed to be found.

Sighing, he filed the unsatisfactory correspondence, rose, and walked over to the wine table. He poured a cup of cold water and stood sipping it, staring at nothing in particular.

From the desk came a sharp *ping*. Incoming mail that was—he stirred himself and turned. Incoming *pinbeam*.

He reached the desk in three long strides, leaned over to touch the screen and stared, breath-caught.

There was a letter in-queue from Janifer Carresens-Denobli.

I offer good greetings and fair profit to Shan yos'Galan.

I have your latest message in hand and I thank you for your observations of conditions at Millsap. I tell you frankly that Millsap has been a concern. The essence of Dust is change, as we who study the Envidaria are made aware. Millsapport rejects this in regard to itself. Its location does not allow it the comfort of fantasy, as you have noted. Work goes forth with the administrators of Millsapport. I tell you this because you have noticed what they will not, and I am grateful to you for this report of conditions made with a third eye, as we say it. With your permission, I will include your observations in our next discussions with the administrators.

In coincidence, I discovered your letter to me as I opened my desk to write to you. I am sad, that my topic cannot be so succinct of solving as yours. In truth, I think we must meet. There is much, of a sudden, for us to discuss, and that quickly. I see by the map that we are not too far distant, as the Jumps tend. I offer an immediate meeting at Eeshaybazi or Volmer, that choice falling to you.

My hope is to find a return letter in my lists when next I open my desk. My further hope is that we two will very soon sit across from each

*other and speak with great frankness, for the
good of the trade.*

  I remain Janifer Carresens-Denobli.

Shan read the letter twice. He got up, poured a
cup of cold tea, and returned with it to the desk.

He read the letter a third time.

Then, he reached to the screen to pull up a star
map and the current ship's schedule.

He split the screen, opened the coord book with
the flick of a finger, snapped open a calculation space,
and began to frame piloting equations.

Eventually, he leaned back in his chair to take brief
counsel of the ceiling, which was pleased to introduce
no second thoughts.

That understood, he bent again to his screen.

The first letter was to Denobli, very brief, naming his
choice of meeting place and expected arrival window.
He sent that into the pinbeam queue, marked *soonest*.

The second was a course change memo sent to the
attention of the captain, reflecting the master trader's
necessity to be at Volmer. Soon.

Off-Grid

· · · · · · · ·

WHILE TEKELIA HAD BEEN SENT TO THE HAOSA BY A FAM-
ily that valued talent in all its forms, the overwhelming
preference of the Civilized was to keep their defective
children with them, their talents sequestered, and
their memories erased.

It was therefore twice surprising to receive a
message—from no one less than the Warden!—stating
that two Wild Talents, siblings, would be arriving at
Peck's Market via the supplies caravan. The Warden's
personal interest extended so far as to solicit the
kindness of the Speaker for the Haosa on behalf of
the young people, who were provided with names.

Vaiza and Torin xinRood.

That, at least, explained Bentamin's interest. xinRood
as a family was prone to disaster, the most prominent
being their association with kezlBlythe. In fact, it could
be said with some accuracy that kezlBlythe was the
disaster from which all others sprang.

Vaiza and Torin were twins, quite young, and so,
one would imagine, apt to fall quite easily into mortal
peril. That they had not done so might be read as
kezlBlythe retaining some seed of decency.

However, Tekelia thought, considering Bentamin's laconic bit of correspondence, it might also be an indication that all of kezlBlythe's scheming could not undo a pair of fraternal twins who were barely past their eighth Name Days. Which fell somewhere between interesting and—terrifying.

If the twins were Wild Talents—*merely* Wild Talents—then the kezlBlythe had potentially made a costly error.

If they were *not* Wild Talents, then this banishment Off-Grid was the kezlBlythe move against their lives. Off-Grid was no place for Civilized children, who would certainly succumb quickly to the *rarification* of the atmosphere, as the ancestors had so charmingly had it.

And there was the Warden's personal interest explained. Tekelia was to determine the style and condition of these children, and report back. If they were Civilized, the Warden had something he had long yearned to find: cause to break kezlBlythe.

If the children were Wild Talents—well. Best to do things in order.

Which was why Tekelia was at Peck's Market at a time so early the mist still clung to the treetops that marked the boundary of the Off-Grid, in company with Maradel arnFaelir, their medic; Tanin karPelin, the baker; Arbour poginGeist, the village administrator; and Geritsi slentAlin and Dosent, who together could calm, gladden, and reassure any number of frightened children simply by their presence.

While they scarcely expected even the kezlBlythe to send children into the wilderness naked and starving, it was felt best not to take chances.

Tanin, therefore, carried a basket filled with all manner of sweet and savory foodstuffs, as well as bottles of hot tea, while Maradel had her full medkit slung on her back. Arbour and Geritsi carried warm clothes and boots in their backpacks, while Tekelia and Dosent walked a little ahead of the group, casting for trouble and projecting warn-aways.

They were barely arrived at Peck's receiving yard when a caravan came puffing up the hill and pulled up to the dock. Arbour and Maradel went to the passenger door, and after a moment, one of the caravan crew came 'round with the key.

By her easygoing smile and lack of either deference or alarm at the sight of them, she was Deaf, which was no surprise. Most of the caravan crews were.

"Hated to have to lock them in," she said to Arbour, as she put the device against the plate and tapped it. "Just wee little ones, they are. They have their pet, but I imagine still it was a long ride, with no windows to see from. Gave them the blanket from the cockpit, since they had none of their own. All else is theirs—and not much of it, too."

"Thank you," Arbour said, smiling, "for your care. We brought warm things in case they were underwrapped."

"That'll do, then," the crew woman said with satisfaction, and cast a look around. "They're only little bits," she said, as the key muttered to itself. "You got far to walk?"

"We can carry them, if needed," Maradel said. "Or they might like to ride the *sokyum*; she's quite gentle."

The key pinged, and the crew woman pulled the door wide, revealing two tiny people dressed in what looked to be tunics, a well-used blue blanket over their knees. There was a wide strap across the boy's chest—perhaps he had a bag.

"Here we are, now," said the crew woman. "Were you bored?"

"Eet told us stories," said the one nearest the door. She bundled the cover together in her arms and handed it down. "Thank you; it was very warm."

"Glad to be of use," the crew woman said, receiving the bundle and tucking it under one arm. She stepped back, urging Arbour forward with a jerk of her chin.

"Here's your friends come to take you to your new home. This gentle here has some warm clothes for you, so you see they mean to take proper care of you."

"Yes, Essy," said the boy-child. "Thank you very much for your care."

"You're welcome," she said, and might have said more, except a shout went up: "Essy! On the dock!" and instead she jerked her head down in a sort of general farewell to all, and ran for the back of the truck.

Arbour stepped forward and held up a hand.

"I am Arbour poginGeist, administrator of Ribbon Dance Village, your new home. I welcome you in the name of the village. May I know your names?"

Two pairs of wary blue eyes considered her, before the girl placed her palm against her chest.

"I am Torin xinRood, and this is my brother Vaiza."

"Welcome, Torin and Vaiza. Where is Eet?"

There was a moment of frozen silence, then Vaiza shifted. It was a bag on the strap, and he reached inside, bringing forth a furry, grey-striped creature. Tekelia looked sharp, and the creature resolved into a norbear, smaller than those that populated the woods and glades of Off-Grid, but immediately recognizable.

Arbour inclined her head gravely.

"Ribbon Dance Village also welcomes Eet."

Relief showed briefly on both faces, and Eet climbed back into the boy's bag.

Arbour held her arms up.

"May I help you alight?"

"Thank you," said Torin, catching the offered support and sliding to the ground. Her shoes were shiny and thin, Tekelia noted, not suitable even for the relatively short walk back to the village. Geritsi's Sight had not led her astray in the matter of boots. And there was, after all, Dosent, if she was feeling agreeable, and the children not too alarmed.

Maradel stepped forward and offered a dismount to Vaiza, who accepted the assistance, and kept a grip on her arm, even when he was firm on his feet.

"Come under the pavilion," Arbour said, keeping a firm grip on Torin. "We'll have a picnic and get to know each other."

"The Haosa," Maradel added, "do all our important business over food."

Vaiza actually grinned, blue eyes sparkling.

"I think I'll like being Haosa," he said.

· · · ❖ · · ·

The children had been both hungry and wary, which did not escape Tekelia's attention, and made Geritsi positively growl. However, they were sated for the moment, having each consumed one of Tanin's small and savory meat pies, two mugs of hot tea, and a cookie.

The caravan had driven off while they were eating, and it was for the moment quiet under the pavilion near the boundary trees.

Gauging the moment with her usual nicety, Arbour announced that they ought to see the twins dressed for conditions. Tekelia obligingly produced three opaque walls across the pavilion, so that modesty could be served, and the breeze somewhat blocked.

Tanin and Geritsi had taken Dosent for a stroll under the trees.

Arbour and Maradel accompanied the children into their dressing area, bags of boots and clothing in hand, leaving Tekelia alone to guard the remains of the picnic and consider the present situation.

Tekelia had Seen the medic examining Torin and Vaiza while they ate, apparently finding, as Tekelia did, two underfed, but basically sound children, who had been taught distrust too young—which could only be acknowledged a survival trait, given the presence of kezlBlythe in their lives.

That they were talents was obvious—whether they were Wild Talents had yet to be determined. Tekelia's preference was split on the point—if they were, in fact, Wild, then the Haosa would keep them as theirs by right. Which might very well open the Haosa to any future malice the kezlBlythe might hatch. If the twins were Civilized, then they fell into the very capable care of Cousin Bentamin, who, as Warden, could call upon all the resources of Civilization, and might thereby crush the kezlBlythe as they so richly deserved.

It was, now that Tekelia thought on it, a little chilling to suppose that the kezlBlythe had already done

these sums and concluded that they might more easily
have their way with the Haosa.

Which led to the next disturbing question:

What could the kezlBlythe want that the Haosa had?

A subtle movement brought Tekelia out of thought,
to look at the table where Eet the norbear sat quite
near, holding a piece of pie crust in one small hand.

Tekelia touched the ambient and established a rap-
prochement. The norbear considered it with interest,
and took a bite of his crust.

"Young Eet," Tekelia said slowly, "I wonder if you
might assist me."

An answer rippled the conduit between them, as
if the norbear had lifted a noncommittal shoulder.

"No, I quite see how it must be," Tekelia assured
him. "Your first duty is to the children. Indeed, I'll
lay odds you're the reason they have thus far survived
the tender regard of their cousins."

That earned a sharpening of the creature's regard.
Tekelia, seated, bowed.

"They are safe with me, fire eater. But, here, where
are my manners? I offer you thread for your web."

The signature of the old norbear tutor came easily
to mind; it scarcely required an effort to place it into
their shared consciousness.

Eet considered the signature with some interest,
and accepted it without acknowledging acquaintance.
He then placed a reciprocal offering into the conduit,
as was only polite.

"Zandir kezlBlythe, I thank you. It is pleasant that
we have an acquaintance in common, though I might
wish it to be a more pleasant acquaintance."

Eet acknowledged this sally with a chuckle that

rippled brightly along their connection, and offered another face, this one tasting like a query.

Tekelia considered carefully the dark-haired woman with the sparkling blue eyes. There was something familiar—yes, of course. The similarity to Torin and Vaiza—especially to Torin—was striking.

"I have not had the pleasure," Tekelia said gently.

Sadness flowed between them, and Tekelia gave the norbear a moment before producing another signature.

This was not the usual sort of signature, but rather the thread that had repeated in the signatures of all the Reavers who had been read by the Haosa. It was possible that it was too esoteric for present company, who might not recognize the truncated thing as a signature at all. Norbears in general did much better with faces than with—

Eet squeaked, dropping what was left of his crust, and sending a strong sense of negation through the ambient between them.

"My pardon," Tekelia said earnestly, "it was not my intention to distress you. Truly, I am pleased that we do not share this acquaintance. But, given the kezlBlythe..."

Comfortable understanding flowed across the conduit, the norbear equivalent of a pat on the hand.

"Thank you," Tekelia said, hearing Geritsi's voice coming closer. "One more, if you will indulge me."

The image of the old norbear's student filled the conduit, her signature, and her marvelous shields.

There came another squeak, though of different quality than the first, expressing wonder more than disgust. Eet muttered softly to himself and then, slowly, an image took shape, and Tekelia was looking at a strong-faced woman, dark brows and high cheeks, with the glitter of well-built shielding around her, and another glitter on one long, wiry hand—a ring of many jewels that might perhaps have been found gaudy on a person of less presence.

Tekelia bowed again.

"Interesting. She is very like. Thank you."

The norbear allowed it to be learned that he would welcome another session when they both had leisure, then turned toward the children's dressing room, ears pricked as the walls flowed away again into the ambient, and the twins stepped toward the table, looking much more the thing in warm, flat-woven sweaters, tough canvas trousers, and good boots.

"Well, then," said Tekelia standing up and away from the table as they approached. "That's more the style."

"Now you look like proper Haosa!" Geritsi added, coming 'round Tekelia's right side, with Dosent pacing at her knee.

"We have time to eat something more, to keep us on the walk," Tanin added, circling wide toward the table.

Torin smiled—somewhat less tightly than previously, and Tekelia saw a gleam of actual pleasure in her eyes as she found the norbear sitting in the center of the table, among the ruins from their previous snack.

"I don't think pie is good for you," she said, and Tanin laughed.

"I don't think I've ever seen a norbear eat anything that didn't make it rounder and sassier," he said. "I've got a bit of fruit here, though, which might be welcome?"

He and Tanin and the unrepentant Eet turned

toward the basket; Maradel and Arbour were walking lazily toward the table—

And Vaiza flung himself directly at Tekelia, arms wide and eyes blazing.

Tekelia blinked a pillow into existence between them. A very soft pillow, though it would still be seen as rejection by—the rush of emotion was searingly obvious at this proximity—a lonely and affection-starved child.

"Hey, there!"

Geritsi swooped down and close, just brushing the pillow with her elbow, scooping Vaiza into her arms. She pressed her cheek against his hair, rumpling it, and braced him against her hip.

"I want Tekelia!" Vaiza said.

"Of course you do," Geritsi said with a grin. "Anyone would. You show very good taste. However, we Haosa have rules—different rules from those I daresay you've been used to, but rules, just the same. And one of those rules is that no one touches Tekelia."

Vaiza blinked at her, and turned his head to address Tekelia.

"Are you being punished?"

"No," Tekelia said, leaving philosophy for another day. "My connection to the ambient is very strong. So strong that those who touch me, even if they are shielded, are sometimes wrenched out of themselves and into the ether. Then, we need to find them and help them reenter their bodies and rebuild their center. All of that is time-consuming, beside being frightening for the person thrust into the ether. Best for all if we avoid the possibility entirely."

Tekelia bowed.

"Among the Haosa, I am called a Child of Chaos. There are one or two born every generation."

"Is that why you sparkle?" Vaiza asked, and Tekelia Looked deeply at the child until—oh, yes. Wild Talent indeed.

"I did not realize that I sparkle," Tekelia said, "but I don't find it impossible."

Vaiza nodded. "Also, your eyes are different colors."

"That, I did know," Tekelia admitted. "What color are they now?"

"Amber," said Vaiza, "and purple."

"Thank you," Tekelia said.

"Now," said Geritsi, "it's time for a snack before we walk back to the village. If we hurry, we'll be home in time for dinner!"

Dutiful Passage

. . . .

I

PRISCILLA AND LINA WERE WITH DYOLI VEN'DEELIN, WHO
had neither stirred nor waked during her transport
from the tiny, airless cubicle in the day-worker dorms
to sickbay aboard *Dutiful Passage.*

Tima had taken charge of Mar Tyn pai'Fortana,
guiding him, so Padi assumed, to secure quarters,
there being no brig or holding cells on the *Passage,*
until the captain, or possibly the head of security,
had time for him.

Padi, returning to her quarters, tapped her screen
up on her way to the 'fresher. She was scheduled to
meet with Lina in ten minutes for another lesson on
how to be a wizard, but she would be very surprised,
she thought as she washed her face, if that session
hadn't been canceled.

She dried her face, combed her hair, and clasped
it with a hair ring before exiting the 'fresher.

She ought, she thought, contact the master trader
and ask when it might be convenient for him to accept
delivery of his book, but when she came again to
the screen, she found that she was behind time; the
master trader had already sent her a note.

Greetings, Trader! Please do me the honor of attending me in my office after you have refreshed yourself. I will provide tea and small-foods.

Of course, she thought, half amused. There were no other messages in-queue, so she closed her screen, picked up the wrapped book, and went to wait upon the master trader.

· · · · ✦ · · · ·

". . . separation trauma," Priscilla was saying, her distress obvious even over the comm, "and exhaustion. Keriana is with her now, doing an assessment. There are no physical injuries—though she is dehydrated and malnourished. After Keriana's done, we'll all three consult. It may be that a session in the 'doc will be of benefit to Healer ven'Deelin, but we're being"—a bare hint of laughter in Priscilla's voice—". . . conservative."

Conservative, Shan recalled, was one of the many concepts with which Padi took issue, when applied to herself. One hoped that she would not produce similar objections on behalf of Healer ven'Deelin.

"After she's physically stable," Priscilla continued, "Lina will do a more detailed examination, with an eye to performing a Healing. From our preliminary exam, it seems that Healer ven'Deelin depleted her talent and her resources by attempting a working that exceeded her abilities."

"Do you know if she completed the working?" Shan asked, watching the comm as if he could see Priscilla's face through it.

"We'll have to wait until she's stable to probe at

that level—or until she wakes up and tells us. If I were to guess, I'd say that she did complete it."

"Really? What leads you to that conclusion?"

"Mar Tyn pai'Fortana is alive."

"Ah. Where is Master pai'Fortana presently?"

"Tima took him to one of the guest rooms and put it under security lock. He's awaiting our questions, if any."

"As it happens, I have questions, which I will be very pleased to put to him, while you and Lina concentrate on more pressing matters."

Priscilla sighed.

"I seem to have gotten us into a scrape," she said ruefully.

"No, only think how much more terrifying if we had left a ven'Deelin in need," Shan said.

That, of course, could not be thought of. Ixin was not a particular ally, though they tended to move along orbits parallel to Korval's. Certainly, they were not an enemy, though they might have brought that about by ignoring one of the Rabbit's children in her extremity.

"There's that," Priscilla admitted; there was a short pause, and the sound of voices in the background, then she was back online.

"Keriana has completed her exam, and recommends that her patient be allowed six hours of physical therapy before we attempt to rouse, or Heal, her. It may be that she'll wake on her own, in which case Keriana will alert Lina. If she does not wake, we three will consult again as to the best course."

"Prudent," Shan agreed. "I will speak with Master pai'Fortana directly after Padi and I have had tea," he said, then—"Priscilla."

"Yes?"

"Will you sleep with me tonight?"

He didn't need to see her smile; he felt it in their link.

"I will arrange the schedule," she said.

"Excellent."

"Until soon," Priscilla murmured, and ended the call.

Shan closed his eyes, ran a relaxation exercise, and opened his eyes just as the annunciator sounded.

"Come!" he called.

The door opened to admit Padi, carrying a neatly wrapped package and looking . . . somewhat worn, despite a freshly clean face, and hair pulled back into a neat tail.

Well.

He rose, smiling, and came 'round the desk, arms wide. She walked into his embrace and leaned her head against his shoulder. Six heartbeats later, he heard her sigh, and felt her relax.

"Hello, Father," she said, voice muffled.

"Hello, Padi," he answered. "Come and have tea."

"How did you know it existed?" Padi demanded after the dainty stuffed pastries had been given their due and the second cup of tea had been poured.

Shan smiled. He reached for a pastry knife, slit the sealing tape, and pulled the book free of its wrappings.

"But I didn't know that it existed," he said. "I only *hoped* that it—or something like it—existed."

Padi shook her head slightly.

"Is that a—*dramliz* talent?"

"Now, that would be terrifying, wouldn't it? To be able to alter the universe and its furnishings with a thought or a wish? I sincerely hope that there's no such talent."

"Then—what? Just a guess?"

Shan finished his tea and put the cup aside.

"Perhaps a hunch—a minor Seeing. I'll note that I'm not often moved to ask that objects which don't exist be found for me; and that, on those occasions when I do, the requested object is only found about one time in four. One has better odds playing at Hazard."

Padi didn't answer, loudly. She finished her tea and put the cup away, then leaned forward to place her hand on the book—*Wu and Fabricant's Guide to The Redlands*.

"May I read it when you are done?" she asked.

"You will be required to read it, Trader, though the captain may wish to read it before either of us. Perhaps I will ask the library to make copies for the traders and all department heads. Yes, I'll do that."

She nodded and leaned back, brows drawn and a line etched vertically between them.

"Father," she said suddenly.

"Yes."

"What is—binding?"

Shan felt a shiver run his spine, as memory supplied an image of the hundreds of psychic links that had supported Tarona Rusk.

"In what context, I wonder?" he murmured.

Padi drew a breath.

"Mar Tyn pai'Fortana...he said that Priscilla might bind him; that he would submit so long as she agreed to help the Healer." She glanced aside, clearly agitated, and met his eyes again.

"He said it as if—as if it were quite usual; as if

it were something he—that had been done to him—
perhaps even done *often* to him. Priscilla...refused,
though she did say that she would kill him if he tried
to harm us."

"And Master pai'Fortana's reaction to that provision?"

"He seemed to find it quite fair. But... Priscilla
didn't care...at all...for the offer of binding..."

"No, I suppose she must have been horrified."

Shan sighed.

"Binding, in this context, is an extremely question-
able practice which good Healers and *dramliz* do not
employ. It involves depriving another person of their
free will and volition, therefore rendering them, if
you will, a mere extension of the binder."

He stopped. Padi, he noted, was looking rather ill.

"Do you think," she said, her voice not quite steady,
"that the ven'Deelin—"

"I think it unlikely that any of Ixin would take up
such tactics, no matter their necessity. They are, after
all, justly proud of their negotiating skills."

"Yes, of course." Padi sighed, her face still pale.

"I think that the question is best put to Master
pai'Fortana. You may be certain that I will do so,
when I speak with him. In the meanwhile, Trader,
I require several things from you—attend me well!"

Padi squared her shoulders.

"Yes, sir."

"Yes. First, I wish you to visit the norbears directly
you leave me, and share the events of your day with
Lady Selph. I believe she will be interested.

"Second, please check our progress at Pommierport
Trade and send me a report.

"Third, go to bed. Put yourself to sleep for five

hours. When you have waked and broken your fast, come to me here."

"Yes, sir."

He considered her, and added sternly: "You will sleep for *five hours*. Stint yourself and you will have the master trader *and* your father to contend with. Am I plain?"

Padi grinned.

"Yes, sir; extremely plain."

"I am gratified. Please assure Lady Selph of my respect and steadfast affection."

II

THEY HAD LOCKED HIM IN, OF COURSE. HE HAD NO COM-
plaint to make there; he was, in fact, disposed to be
grateful. The quarters were spacious, set beside most
he'd known: clean and tidy, with everything working
as it should. Well, the screen only offered books, and
vid, and puzzle-games, but that was surely intentional.

If it weren't for his fear for Dyoli, he might have
been well content in this pretty prison room; might
have opened a book, or taken a nap, or . . .

It had been hours now, since he'd been shown
inside and had the door locked upon him, with the
information that someone would be by to talk with
him soon.

Perhaps they'd forgotten him.

Perhaps Dyoli—but no. Surely, *surely* they would
have told him if Dyoli . . .

A chime interrupted this worrisome chain of thought,
followed by a man's voice.

"Master pai'Fortana, it is Shan yos'Galan, master
trader on-board. May I have a moment of your
time?"

yos'Galan. Mar Tyn took a deep breath. He had
expected a security person, or perhaps the captain,
again. He had not expected the master trader. Had
never expected yos'Galan *himself*.

It had not occurred to him that he would be
required to answer so high.

Another breath, and he found his courage again;
courage to speak as if the door obeyed his voice.

"Please enter, Master Trader," he said. "I am entirely at your service."

The door slid open, and his visitor stepped within, everything that was tall and elegant, with the sheen of High House sophistication upon him.

He had silver hair and silver eyes, yet he was not, Mar Tyn noted, beautiful. He was far more than beautiful; he was self-possessed, polished, well-dressed, and—as became apparent as he paused to bow welcome to the visitor—charming.

If his nose were a trifle bold, his skin more brown than gold, and his chin rather too pointed, what matter? Those were not the defects they would be counted in some lesser person, but rather marks of distinction.

Mar Tyn bowed as lesser to greater, showing his empty, upturned hands.

"I would bid you welcome, my lord, but it would be an impertinence."

"Would it? Well, perhaps you're correct. Allow me, then, to bid *you* welcome, and ask if you have time to sit and talk with me. I have, as you may suppose, some questions."

"Yes," said Mar Tyn. "I had supposed that . . . someone . . . would have questions."

yos'Galan tipped his head and sent a sharp glance at him.

"But you hadn't supposed that it would be me? I regret. We are short-handed, and all the crew is doing double duty."

He moved a graceful hand, showing Mar Tyn the room, the bunk, the single chair.

"Please, sit, and be as comfortable as you may be. I will do my best not to come the High House lordling."

Almost Mar Tyn smiled, remembering Dyoli's attempts to leave a like manner behind. He expected that this man might have somewhat more success than she had done, but he would never be mistaken for a Lowporter.

He sat on the edge of the bed, leaving the chair for the yos'Galan, who nodded slightly and settled himself.

"Do you want for anything?" he asked. "Have you been fed?"

"Master Trader, I want for nothing, save word that Dyoli—Healer ven'Deelin—is conscious and recovering herself."

"I regret that I am not able to give you that word... yet. I hope to be able to do so in the near future.

"In the meanwhile, you will wish to know that she is under the care of our med tech, and is receiving fluids and nutrients intravenously. The ship's Healers have performed a preliminary scan, and it is their opinion, bolstered by the med tech's findings, that Healer ven'Deelin reached for that which was beyond her grasp, thereby expending a great deal more energy than is usually considered wise or safe."

He paused, head tipped slightly.

"As one who has only recently erred in the same way, I can tell you that I have been advised that my abilities will return—eventually. You must hold yourself ready to assist—your partner, I believe you said to Captain Mendoza—in many small ways, and to remind her not to tax herself during recuperation."

Mar Tyn bowed his head.

"Of course, I will assist her in any way that I might," he said. "As to our relationship—we were partners by necessity. Now that our situation has... been altered, it is likely that the partnership will be put aside.

"Properly," he added, after a moment, "I am no fit partner for her."

Slanted white brows rose in polite disbelief.

"As you say. But I am remiss! You must allow me to congratulate you on your boldness!"

Mar Tyn considered him suspiciously.

"In what way have I been bold?" he asked, and hearing his tone, added more temperately, "Sir."

"Neatly caught," the yos'Galan said. "As for boldness—you are a Luck, are you not?"

Ah, here it came, then. He had for a moment hoped that so charming a person might refrain from open contempt of himself and his talent. Well, at least he knew how to meet derision.

"Indeed," he said calmly, "I am a Luck. I pay my dues to House Fortana."

In truth, he was many quarters arrears in his dues, and very likely Fortana had struck his name from the membership lists. But that was a worry for much further down the path he'd been forced onto, and in no case a life tragedy. If House Fortana would not take him back, there were others who would have him—and his dues—with joy.

For now, though . . .

"I fail to understand in what way I have been bold," he said, still a little more sharply than was perhaps wise. "I am not accustomed to being thought any such thing."

"And yet you have survived into adulthood, in Low Port, and have made your way into one of the guilds. I would think that bold enough—or perhaps I mean determined."

Mar Tyn waited.

The yos'Galan's lips twitched.

"Yes, well. My point is merely that you *are* a Luck, yet you allowed yourself to be brought onto a Korval ship, knowing, in a way that many cannot, our relationship with luck. Did that not give you pause?"

It took him a moment to regroup, to realize that he was being offered a sensible question, the sort that those who had enough energy left for debate at the end of the day might discuss among themselves, gathered in Fortana's common room, with drinks and snacks to hand.

"In truth, it did not occur to me, what coming aboard a Korval ship might do to—to my talent. It is, after all, a poor thing; hardly worth Dyoli—Healer ven'Deelin's—life."

"And yet . . ." prodded the master trader.

"And yet, it is thought, by those of us who care to consider it, that the luck with which Korval is known to interact is a—say, it is a *field*. The field of luck no more belongs to you than gravity belongs to a planet."

He moved his shoulders.

"Speaking to my own case, I am a talent; my abilities are inborn, precisely as other, more respectable talents are inborn. It is the same as having been born with brown eyes."

He drew a breath, aware that his voice had quickened in response to a topic that interested him.

"It is possible, I suppose, that the field of luck might move to consume me—my talent—for reasons or conditions peculiar to itself. But is it not true that the field of luck does not inevitably produce . . . good results for those of Korval?"

"Very true," said the yos'Galan. "Between us, Master

pai'Fortana, I strive to have as little to do with Korval's Luck as possible."

Mar Tyn looked at him seriously.

"You know that you cannot withhold yourself, surely?"

"I had suspected it. Still, perhaps some resistance is salutary."

Mar Tyn smiled slightly.

"Perhaps it might be, at that."

"So, you counted yourself safe enough—what little thought you gave to the matter at all—because random event is . . . random?"

"Something alike," Mar Tyn admitted. "And truly, I did not think of it overmuch. There were more pressing things in-queue."

"Indeed."

The master trader sat back in his chair and crossed his legs.

"Tell me," he said conversationally, "why did Healer ven'Deelin bind you?"

Shock brought him to his feet, staring at the man in the chair.

"*Dyoli* bind me? Are you mad?"

Silver eyes looked lazily up into his.

"Apparently so. Who did bind you, then?"

Mar Tyn drew a breath. The only thing that mattered, he reminded himself, was Dyoli's life; therefore . . .

"The truth, if you please, Master pai'Fortana," the yos'Galan said.

And such had his life been this last Standard and more that Mar Tyn drew in on himself, expecting the punishing lash across his talent—but there was nothing. Only interested silver eyes in a spare brown face. The yos'Galan, waiting for him to tell the truth.

Carefully, Mar Tyn resumed his seat on the edge of the bed.

"There had been rumors of hunters in the Low Port who were taking up Lucks. Four of House Fortana had gone missing in as many days, and those of us of the mid-ranking had been sent out to find what we might."

He drew a breath.

"I found the cause, but too late; they had already snared and ensorcelled me.

"I believe I had been unconscious, because suddenly I was aware . . . aware of kneeling in a vast, dark space. There was one source of light—the woman standing before me; she was . . . aflame, or so it seemed, and so tall.

"'Give me your name,' she said, and that quickly it flew out of my mouth, straight into her hand. She wrapped it in black thread, and stood for a moment, seeming caught in thought. I . . . I had no power to do anything beyond kneel at her feet. I had a moment of weakness, and I thought I might faint—but I was saved by a flash of energy.

"She looked at me then, and smiled, and I was suffused with love for her; and I knew I would do anything—anything at all—for her sake.

"'Excellent,' she said, and slipped my name away into her sleeve. 'You are mine now, Mar Tyn pai'Fortana. You wish for nothing, but what I wish for you, and because that is so, I will care for you as nearly as I care for myself. Stand now, and receive my kiss.'"

He moved his hands.

"I stood, and she kissed me as a delm kisses a child of the clan. I remember weeping with joy. Then she touched my cheek, and said, 'Sleep,' and when next I woke to myself, I was joining a strike team which had need of some luck. When that mission was accomplished, I was dealt out to others, as their need was seen."

"Did your mistress ride you hard?"

"I would not have you think it. Truly, I was content. Occasionally, I would be smitten with bouts of weakness, but I knew it for a sign of her regard—that she had chosen *me* to sustain her—and . . . I was . . . happy. Even when I did such things as were . . . strange to my nature, I was content."

"It sounds a perfect existence."

"And so it seemed, from within. Eventually, I was placed in a team with two others of higher talent. One was Dyoli ven'Deelin—our talents worked in tandem, and gradually our ties to the Mistress became . . . less encompassing."

He drew a breath—sighed it out.

"Luck, you see, had thrown us together, with our talents so nearly aligned. We were not unbound, but we knew ourselves, we knew that we had been violated and used against our own wills, we knew that we wished to escape the Mistress's control."

He looked to the yos'Galan, who made a motion with his hand, inviting him to continue.

"That became . . . difficult. But we knew that we had to obey, and behave as if we were yet extensions of her will. We also knew that we needed to wait for . . . the moment. The lucky moment.

"It came as we were on-route to our next assignment. We were on Pommierport to meet another team and proceed together to the target. There was pain—a great deal of pain, but I was free, and scarcely minded, even when I realized that I was free of all and everything, soaring up and away until there was no air. I remember that—my heart stopped.

"Then it began again, and I knew myself. I knew that Dyoli was holding me, in her arms and in her talent—Healing me, pouring her energy into me— pouring her *life* into me. I begged her to stop, but she did not—perhaps she could not. When my strength was greater than hers, I refused the gift, and brought her to the day-worker dorms, where she fell into a faint and since has been as Captain Mendoza found her."

"And the third of your party?"

"Aph Zed? Aph Zed was a strong general talent; he despised me, which was not unexpected—only weaklings, after all, depend upon luck—but he also despised Dyoli."

He moved his shoulders and met those silver eyes.

"She could only save one of us."

"I see. And the state of your soul at the moment?"

"Free. Unbound. My own self, and none other."

"Excellent." The yos'Galan paused. "I wonder—do you know the proper name of she who bound you?"

"Tarona Rusk, sir."

"Of course."

The master trader rose, his bow a thing of fluid beauty.

"I will leave you now, Master pai'Fortana. A meal will come shortly, and I swear to you that you will be kept current with Healer ven'Deelin's condition. Also—"

He paused, and made another bow, unexpectedly profound, and far beyond Mar Tyn's ability to read such things.

"I fear I must own myself the cause of your near death, and of Healer ven'Deelin's current state of depletion. I hope you will find it in you to forgive me."

Mar Tyn blinked.

"Forgive you for what?"

Shan yos'Galan smiled, very slightly.

"I cut the links that bound Tarona Rusk to her minions. Necessity was, but I knew, even so, that some would die."

The smile grew more pronounced.

"It was, as you say, only luck that you and Healer ven'Deelin were not among them."

III

REALLY, SHAN THOUGHT, IT WAS AMAZING HOW MUCH good it did one to sleep with one's lifemate, followed by a comfortable waking, shared shower, and a leisurely breakfast over which they discussed plans for the Line House they were to build on the new homeworld.

"We ought to do this more often," Priscilla said, echoing his thoughts as they approached the door to the captain's office.

"My thoughts take a similar direction," he answered. "I propose that we seriously approach the schedule with an eye toward balancing the needs of ship, captain, and master trader. The ship is entirely too greedy of us. It has competent crew. I suggest that there is no need for it to have a full Korval captain on at all shifts. Even if one of those captains has stepped back from active duty."

"I'll have the computer work up a couple of models. We can look at them together—over dinner?"

"Priscilla, you astonish me."

"Do I?" Her smile was wistful.

He leaned close and kissed her cheek, never caring who might be watching.

"Don't mind me, love," he murmured, for her ear alone. "I will be delighted to have dinner with you. How better to end a day which has begun so well?"

She laughed slightly, and kissed his cheek in turn, placing the pair of them beyond the ken of decent people—should those people happen to be Liaden.

"The war isn't behind us, but it'll be with us forever if we don't let ourselves trust our own crew."

"I agree. Let us take up that topic as well. Perhaps over wine."

"Until dinner then," Priscilla said.

Shan stood in the hallway until the door had closed behind her, then turned back toward his own office and his meeting with Padi.

Tarona Rusk
Meeting Space

· · · · · · · · · · · · · ·

THE MEETING SPACE WAS A CONSTRUCT HELD SIMULTANE-
ously in the minds of all there-gathered. In former days,
she would have simply pulled all who were attached
to her into the space she visualized and created with
their leashed energies.

Today . . . was the first time they had created the
space in collaboration, each individual willingly tith-
ing a portion of their energy, their talent, and their
perception to the tasks of creation and maintenance.

Tarona Rusk looked out over those gathered. Fel
Pin had not overstated their losses. A mere glance
down the room confirmed that their numbers were
greatly diminished. That most of those remaining were
mid- to high-level talents might at first be thought
fortunate. Until one recalled, as Tarona Rusk did
now, that the best use of the small talents and the
bright ones had been as reserves of energy for the
greater talents.

Every talent in this room had been accustomed to
having an extra tithe of power to draw upon at need,

even as she had been able to draw on the entire net of those who had been bound to her.

Every talent present, not forgetting to include herself, was diminished. All had suffered losses—the loss of self that had come with their recruitment only the first—they were mad, every one of them. It could scarcely be otherwise.

They would need to recalibrate, she thought, tasting the mood of the room. They would need to do many things.

But first, they must find where they stood with each other, and in relation to the Department that had destroyed their lives. She needed to know how many lusted for revenge—and how many would fight to achieve it.

She took a breath, looking out over those gathered once more. Her shields were open; she had never hidden herself from them. Among those who had been in her care, some few of the remaining greater talents were also fully open. Most had decided upon compromise—open enough to be seen and heard. Open enough to do their part in the maintaining of the space.

Open enough so that she could feel them—their anger, their grief; their hatred, and their love.

It was time.

She stood.

"It pleases me that we are able to gather together as colleagues," she said. "We have sustained losses, our numbers are fewer, but we are not weaker. The blow that sundered our closest ties has freed us to be many, working together for our mutual benefit."

She paused, in case there should be objection or

question. There was only silence, a sense of increased concentration. The boundaries of the meeting space seemed to grow more definite.

"We are met here to discuss what must yet be done, in the aftermath of our loss, using our new-found strength. While I am mistress no longer, I am eldest among us. I hope you will be guided by me in planning for the disposition of those who remain."

That produced a stir, as well it might. It warmed her to see so many invested in her topic.

"I must ask," she said quietly. "How many desire the destruction of the Department of the Interior?"

Every hand went up, and Tarona Rusk allowed herself a smile.

"We are of one mind," she said. "That is good.

"My suggestion for the destruction of the Department requires that we first rid ourselves of any remaining draws upon our power. When we are free of those remaining encumbrances, then we may move among the levels of command and eradicate them, unto the Commander herself—and the Department will be dead."

She looked out over the room.

"Are we agreed?"

"No," said a quiet voice, and the dissenting Healer stood.

Tarona recognized her—Kethi vay'Elin, a Master Healer in Solcintra Hall she had been before Tarona had attached her.

She inclined her head.

"Healer . . ." she began, but she got no further.

"No," said another voice, from the back of the room.

"No," came a third, louder; and people began to rise from their chairs in waves.

"No."

"No!"

"No!"

"No!"

The force of their denial struck her in a wave, another—and another, beating against her soul—she snatched for her shields—too late. She was immobilized, her will throttled, and she would have fallen, save there came an arm around her waist, and a warm breath against her hair.

"Mistress," said Kethi vay'Elin. "Mistress—no. Please, you must sit down. Listen to us."

A hand on her shoulder. She was pressed into a chair. Will-bound, furious, she sat, feeling her body trembling, hearing rough sounds, as if someone nearby was gasping for air.

"Release her!" Kethi vay'Elin snapped.

"She will enslave us!" came an angry shout, backed by another.

"There are dozens of us, and one only of her! If she had wished to reattach us, she would have come, one and one and one, as she did before," Kethi said. "She called all of us together, to work as colleagues—did any of you find a lie in that?"

There was silence save for the labored breathing.

"Valisa dea'Manz! Allow her breath, at least!"

There was a sense of easement; the painful gasping ceased.

"Yes," said Kethi. "The rest of you—release her. I take responsibility."

"I, too." That was Fel Pin. Distantly, Tarona felt a weight on her shoulder.

"Who here among us built no shielding against

slavery?" challenged a voice Tarona did not recognize. "Call aye!"

There was silence.

"So," said the voice that had called the challenge. "Let her go. She is no threat to us."

Her will returned, and with it her rage. She felt Fel Pin's hand press more firmly against her shoulder.

"Mistress."

She looked up to meet Kethi vay'Elin's eyes.

"You are not without friends here," the Healer told her gently. "We wish you no ill, but you must understand that the Commander—even now the Commander has access to a protocol which will disband the Department. It is horrific; it will drop every operative at every level. I and my colleagues at Headquarters have been doing our utmost to keep her attention away from that protocol, while we work to weaken her hold on the organization. We—there must be an orderly transfer, Mistress. We cannot just . . . rid ourselves of our remaining encumbrances."

"We are Healers!" a voice shouted from behind them. Tarona thought it might be the same voice that had shouted that she would enslave them.

"Yes," Kethi vay'Elin said gently. "We *are* Healers, Mistress. Nor is this the first time we have met together since our ties to you were broken. We have already formed a plan, and begun to carry it out."

Tarona sighed, and looked to Fel Pin.

"You might have said," she commented.

He bowed his head.

"In truth, Tarona, I did not know, until I began the process of arranging this meeting."

"We needed Fel Pin's ignorance, Mistress."

"Yes," Tarona said. "I see that. Now, if you please..."

She stood, Kethi and Fel Pin giving way before her.

"So," she said, looking out over those she had once held as...slaves. "You are Healers, you say. I would be honored to hear how you plan to proceed. I assume that the destruction of the Department is still a point of agreement between us all."

"The Department, yes," said the woman who had called for Tarona's release. "The Department is a blight, an illness—a cancer. But there is a difference, Mistress, between the Department and those who were forced to serve it." She bowed gently.

"We are *Healers*. Destruction is not our business, though we are merciful, and quick, when there is no other way."

She turned to address those gathered.

"Sisters and brothers, tell her. Tell Tarona Rusk what we have done thus far to further the excision of the Department of the Interior from the healthy body of the universe."

The stories came then, sweeping from one to the next, to the one after—stories which were different in detail, yet, at heart, the same.

Stitched into one narrative, the tale went thus: When the Healers had come to themselves, after the shock of separation, whole in their own wills, they had first reached for those in their care, to assess their situations. All were afflicted with the malaise of the Department, some more than others. There were, in fact, those who could not be Healed, who were truly broken, who would seek to visit violence and mayhem upon the innocent unless they were placed under constant supervision. Resources were limited—often, resources consisted of one Healer. The irredeemable could not be freed to themselves and allowed to compromise those who might yet be Healed—or those who had undertaken their care.

Healers did not take lives lightly, but all had been taught that it was sometimes necessary.

The necessary deaths had been handled as humanely as possible.

Whereupon, the Healers had turned their care to those who might be redeemed.

"Will you give your lives to this?" Tarona asked, as the last Healer finished his tale and sat down, tears running his face. "Sustaining those the Department has tainted even somewhat—I suspect that is a life-work, my children."

It was Kethi vay'Elin who answered.

"We believe you are correct," she said quietly. "But recall, Mistress—we are tainted, too."

That was a blow, the more so because it was true.

Tarona Rusk bowed.

"Yes. Forgive me."

"And you were also tainted," Kethi added. "Mistress, it was not your plan; it was *never* your heart."

"Yet, I did enslave you."

She swept her hand out over those gathered.

"A question, if I may?"

"Yes," Kethi said, answering for all.

"Are there any here who have none to care for, and who would consent to taking part in a further culling? There are those at the higher levels who may be truly evil; and others, who may require care."

There was a small hesitation before a man stood from the middle of the room.

"I am willing," he said.

More rose, as if emboldened by his frankness, and at the final count, she had eight, which was more than she had hoped for.

"Fel Pin will be in touch with you, and we will produce a proper plan," she said then. "Please, hold yourselves ready."

They bowed, and she looked to Kethi vay'Elin.

"I see that you have become the natural leader of the group," she said, then. "I will not dispute you. I will assist as I am able, but I have my own proper business to tend, and I will not be thwarted there."

Kethi bowed.

"I thank you, Mistress. May I suggest that we two meet within the next day to discuss your business and how you might assist us best. Now, we all have folk to tend to."

"Indeed, indeed."

She turned back to the gathering.

"I thank you," she said, her throat closing. "I thank you. Please, go where you are needed."

Dutiful Passage

. . . .

PADI POURED HERSELF A CUP OF COLD TEA AND RETURNED
to the desk, settling into the chair with a faint smile.

Shan leaned back in his chair and considered her.
She looked . . . well. The quick glance he allowed himself around the edge of his shields revealed a pattern
vibrant, alert, and receptive. Sleep had done her well.
Or perhaps there had been another influence.

"How did you find Lady Selph?" he asked.

"Everything that was polite," Padi responded promptly.
"She puts up with much, as you must know. She thinks
you very clever to have called for the proper book. Also,
she wishes to interview Mar Tyn pai'Fortana."

Shan blinked.

"*Does* she?"

"She was very clear, not to say adamant."

"It must of course be my first object to accommodate Lady Selph. I will see what I may do. I only
hope that she doesn't mean to attach him."

"I mean to cast no aspersions on the lady's worth,"
Padi said slowly, "but I . . . *think* that Mar Tyn pai'Fortana
is . . . in love . . . with Healer ven'Deelin."

"Yes," Shan said gently, "he is. Perhaps Lady Selph

merely wishes to set up a flirtation, to distract him from his cares."

He turned to the screen, and called up the trade report she had compiled.

Well, he thought, running his eye down the screen, they had doubtless received trade reports that had been more dire. He simply couldn't at this moment recall when.

"So, Trader," he said, glancing over to her. "It appears that Pommierport neither needs nor desires our commerce."

"We hardly put ourselves forward," Padi pointed out. "Had we held a reception, or even sent out cards and customized catalogs to the traders on-port..."

"No question, we did not display our best manners," he murmured when she allowed her thought to drift off, eyes on some point visible only to herself.

"Yes," she answered, focusing on him again. "But I cannot recall the traders of *any* port which had allowed us to dock ignoring the free catalog."

"It may have happened before," Shan replied, "but, if so, I confess the occasion has also escaped my memory."

"What could it mean?" Padi demanded. "Traders are forever curious about market and method. The catalogs provide a good deal of information for those who know how to look. It's almost as if we were invisible to them!"

Shan blinked at her.

"Well now..." he murmured.

Padi's eyes went wide.

"What is it?"

"A notion, only that. Tell me, Trader, by what method did you generate this report?"

"Why, I ... I logged into the account the port had assigned to us, and accessed the data directly from the trade database."

"Ah. And did you check the status of our listing?"

"Of course I did," she said, somewhat sharply. "It was listed as active."

"Forgive me," he said gently. "What I mean to ask is if you looked at our account on the Open Trade Board, as if, for instance, you were a trader on-port browsing the new listings?"

She stared.

"No," she said, after a moment. "No, sir; I did not."

"Nor did I. Let us do so together, shall we?"

The long and short of it was that there were no offerings from Master Trader Shan yos'Galan of *Dutiful Passage* on the Open Trade Board.

"Which makes it scarcely surprising," Shan said to Padi's infuriated face, "that we had no takers for the catalogs."

"That is ... they *charged us* for that listing!"

"Of course they did," he said, reaching for his glass. "They would hardly have been so foolish as to tip their hand by *not* charging us."

"They ought to be reported to the Guild," Padi said coldly.

Shan considered her with interest.

"For what violation?" he asked.

Padi glared at him.

"They cheated!"

"One can hardly dispute that," he conceded, putting his glass aside. "But I wonder what you would hope to gain by reporting this small divertissement to the Guild. We did not, after all, come courting Pommierport. It was merely a reasonably convenient port which would take our disaffected crew. Trade was never our first purpose here."

A shadow crossed Padi's face.

"Do you think they cheated there, too?"

"I think it unlikely, since mistreatment of personnel would quickly become known to the Guild, and would cost the port dear in fines, and possibly net them a temporary downgrade. They surely wouldn't wish to risk so much.

"However, given this other business, it would not be unreasonable for us to assure ourselves that our former crew members are safe and well treated. I will bring the matter before the captain, and request that she open a conversation on the topic with her contact on-port.

"We will not," he added firmly, as Padi seemed yet disposed to distress, "leave this planet without being certain that our former crewmates are safe, and in no danger of being harmed in any way."

She took a breath—a very deep breath—and he almost heard the focusing exercise she accessed hum in the air between them.

"Thank you, sir," she said, sounding very nearly calm.

"You are welcome. It does you honor, that you thought of this."

She gave him a dour look.

"I am in earnest," he told her. "They left us, after all, and have no further call on our protection."

"They have past credit," she said tartly. "We could not, in honor nor in conscience, leave them in peril."

"Quite right," Shan said, inclining his head. "Allow

a master a little pride, that his apprentice goes beyond what has been taught her."

"That," Padi returned, sharp again, "is nonsense, if I may be allowed, Master Trader. A master teaches by example."

It was, he told himself, ridiculous to feel himself on the edge of tears.

"I see that I am gaming out of my league," he said lightly. "Now, Trader, attend me. There is a copy of the book you kindly brought to me yesterday awaiting you in the library. Pray go and claim it, and devote an hour to its study before you present yourself to the cargo master. Your tutor in the *dramliz* arts will either be Lina or Priscilla, depending on who is available at the appropriate hour. If both are otherwise engaged, you will be forced to suffer me, which I am certain will be tedious in the extreme, so we will each of us have to hope for better."

"Has Healer ven'Deelin not improved?" asked Padi, giving the last ploy the attention it deserved.

"My best information regarding the Healer is that she rests in the care of Keriana, who is, as you are aware, fierce in defense of her patients' health. Once she is satisfied that Healer ven'Deelin is in no physical danger, she will permit Lina and Priscilla to attempt a Healing.

"I have not yet heard that Keriana has ceded oversight of Healer ven'Deelin. Neither have I heard that the Healer's physical state has declined. We must assume from this that progress is being made, if more slowly than we would like."

Padi nodded.

"Keriana is careful, but the waiting is difficult for

those of us who wish Healer ven'Deelin, and Mar Tyn pai'Fortana, well." She moved her hands, showing empty palms. "Is there anything else, Master Trader?"

"Not at present. If something occurs to me, be certain that I know where to find you."

She smiled, a trifle lopsided, and rose.

"That's well, then. I look forward to reading the book, and to discussing it with you."

"Let us plan on having that conversation on the morrow."

She bowed, and was gone, the door hissing shut behind her.

Shan, with a sigh, turned to the screen—

Pain trembled through him, panic edged his awareness: Someone was in distress—in very great distress—if he felt so much of it through his shields.

It was instinct that he cast his shields wide, and stepped into Healspace.

He saw it at once: the thread burning black against the pearlescent fog. One of the links that bound him to Tarona Rusk. The thread that she, herself, had tied when she had given him back his life.

Another shudder of pain wracked Healspace; the panic a live thing now. He extended himself and touched the link, feeling it burn—and cool.

Balance in all things, he thought, even as Healspace dissolved around him.

He blinked, and sighed, and closed his shields. Carefully, he accessed a rejuvenating exercise; felt his flagging energy revive.

Well, he thought—and tapped up his work screen.

· · · ❈ · · ·

Mar Tyn had slept, risen, and showered. Very shortly thereafter, Tima, the security guard, arrived, bearing a tray filled with all kinds of breakfast foods, and an entire pot of tea.

"My thanks," he said to her.

"The ship cares for its guests," she answered, and he noted how nice the two of them were, not to mention that the timing of the tray's arrival verified that he was monitored—a prisoner, not a guest.

"I saw Keriana, our medic, as I was on my way to you. She reports that Healer ven'Deelin is improving; Keriana is satisfied with her progress, but admits that it's not rapid. Some things, she said to me, cannot be rushed."

"Very true," he answered. "If you have the opportunity, please convey my gratitude to Medic Keriana, for her care."

"I will."

Tima tipped her head slightly, considering him.

"If you like it, I will bring you with me to the gym during my exercise period."

"That is kind," he said sincerely. "A round of exercise would be welcome."

"That will be at sixth hour. When you're done with the tray, just push that button and someone will come."

"My thanks," he said again.

She inclined her head.

"I'll leave you now to break your fast," she said—and did so.

· · · · ·❈· · · ·

"May I refill your glass, Priscilla?" Shan asked.

"Thank you," she said, and indulged herself by watching him cross the room.

He returned, one eyebrow up, as if he had heard her appreciation, and put the refreshed glass by her hand. She smiled her thanks as he settled into the chair across from her.

"I made a call to the Guild Intake Office," she said, "and was assured by Specialist Hanssen that our former crew are being treated in strict accordance with the regs."

She gave him a droll look.

"Compliments were exchanged, and we parted as very good friends. I then found where Hepster si'Neest was located, and contacted her. She has no complaints."

Shan blinked.

"Is she well?"

"I believe so. Shall I inquire further?"

"No, I think that the quality of the assurances we have received may be allowed to put our fears to rest," he said. "I hope Padi will see it in the same light, but really—Hepster si'Neest must carry all before her."

"As when has she not?" Priscilla murmured, and heard him chuckle.

"Indeed." He moved a hand.

"What news of Dyoli ven'Deelin?"

"Keriana will be doing an examination this morning. If Healer ven'Deelin is found to be stable enough, Lina and I will attempt a Healing."

"Thank you," Shan said. "I am to take Lady Selph to meet Mar Tyn pai'Fortana in a few minutes, and he will be wanting news, poor—"

The comm on Priscilla's desk chimed.

"Yes?"

"Priscilla," Lina said briskly. "Keriana has given us leave to scan Dyoli ven'Deelin and to attempt a Healing.

I think we ought both to be present for this, to back each other up. What time is convenient for you?"

"I can come immediately," Priscilla answered.

"I was hoping that might be the case," Lina said. "Immediately, it is."

The connection closed, and Priscilla rose, sending Shan a grin.

"No rest for the wicked," she said.

He considered her with interest.

"*Are* you wicked, Priscilla?"

"It must be a matter of interpretation, mustn't it? Especially for a vessel of a goddess?"

He sighed.

"The trouble with gods is that they force one to engage with philosophy. Surely the vessel is distinct from the goddess?"

She shook her head.

"We'll argue that one over dinner, my dear. I did tell Lina *immediately*."

"So you did. Until dinner, Priscilla."

"Until dinner."

· · · · ❖ · · · ·

The tea had been very good, and every dish he had tasted. He ate his fill, slowly, putting his whole attention on the meal.

When he was through, he looked wistfully at what remained, thinking what might fit into his pockets— which was a Lowporter's instinct, certain enough. Extra today was a hedge against want, tomorrow.

Well, he was not in Low Port now. He touched the button, and politely thanked the man who came to take the tray away.

When he was alone again, Mar Tyn retracted the table, set the chair straight with the walls, and made certain that no crumbs or other untidiness had been introduced into the room.

That done, matters became more difficult. Abruptly, he sat on the edge of his bunk, eyes closed and hands fisted on his knees, fighting the urge to *push* at his talent, to attempt to reach out to Dyoli along the link she had made for them, to—

He must, he told himself firmly, be patient. Above all else, he *must not* attempt to wield his gift—that way lay sorrow, as well he knew.

Need crashed through him, rocking his resolve. He grit his teeth until it receded, leaving him shaken, but firm.

He might access a meditation, he thought. This turmoil of emotion—it sapped his strength and his focus, just when he must be ready and able for Dyoli, when she came to herself and needed him.

He closed his eyes and managed a few deep breaths, and then a few more, putting his attention on a slow count to one hundred forty-four.

He took another deep breath, and opened his eyes. The desperate desire to force his talent was more bearable now. What he needed was—a diversion. He turned to the screen—a book, he thought, grimly. He would read, and be seemly. He would not—

The door chime sounded, followed by a clear, pleasant voice.

"Master pai'Fortana, it is Shan yos'Galan, come to you again. I have with me someone who very much wishes to make your acquaintance, if you will allow it."

Mar Tyn sighed lightly, for here, surely, was his own small luck in action. A diversion indeed.

"I am always glad of new acquaintance, Master Trader," he said, rising to face the door. "Please enter."

The master trader entered as he had been bade, looking much as he had previously, saving the addition of a filigreed box which he carried by a handle on the top.

Mar Tyn stepped forward, extending the table and locking it into position.

"Here," he said, and stepped back to allow the other man room.

He noted as he moved that the master trader, despite his statement to the contrary, appeared to have no companion with him beyond—

He stared at the box now safely disposed on the table with a little shudder of foreknowing.

"Indeed," the yos'Galan said sympathetically. "But I don't think she means to harm you, Master pai'Fortana. Merely, she wishes to make your acquaintance."

Mar Tyn glanced up at him.

"It *is* a norbear?" he asked, and continued without waiting for verification. "I had heard they were . . . chancy."

"As are we all—and they rarely mean harm. However, as both you and I are aware, intentions are not always proof against reality."

He pressed his thumb against the plate at the top of the box.

"For instance, while she surely would not *intend* to cause a ship-wide panic, I could not be certain that she would be able to resist going exploring on her own if I had merely carried her to you on my shoulder, as she insisted was consistent with her dignity.

"Sadly, it was necessary that we both suffer the indignity of a *cage*, for what is the discomfort of a few when weighed against the comfort of many?"

He snapped two latches, one on each side of the cage's front panel, and eased the leading edge down to the tabletop.

"I fear she may be a little out of temper. I trust that she is old enough and wise enough to recognize that I am the villain of the piece and that you are blameless."

A shadow moved inside the filigreed box, and here came a stout creature strolling down the ramp, looking very dignified indeed.

At the end of the ramp, she sat on her haunches and folded her front paws before her chest, like a stern elder sister overseeing the rambunctions of her juniors.

"Master pai'Fortana," said the yos'Galan solemnly, "allow me to present Lady Selph. My Lady, here is Mar Tyn pai'Fortana, whom you had particularly wished to meet."

He spoke to her not as if she were an animal, but as he might speak to a rational thinker. Mar Tyn therefore produced a bow fitting to a lady's honor.

"Service, Lady Selph," he said politely. "How may I best please you?"

Tarona Rusk
Her Proper Business

. . . .

SHE HAD DEBATED WITH HERSELF HOW BEST THE THING might be done.

Ought she to reach out from the shadows and take him in one blinding blow?

Ought she to make him afraid and powerless and toy with him until he begged?

Ought she to insinuate herself into the links that bound them—of creature and creator—to stop his heart, rupture his brain as he slept?

Or! Ought she strip him of his memories, one by one, until he was a husk, a nothing, until he finally succumbed to entropy, having forgotten how to breathe?

It was, after all, *revenge* that she wanted—nothing so complex, so demanding of art and honor...as Balance. There could be no Balance for what he had done.

Just as there could be no Balance—no, nor justice, either—for all that she had done.

She was what he—what they, what the *Department*—had made her—and in that, he had been true to his word. She would be a goddess, he had told her; powerful beyond words, commanding loyalty and love from the multitudes of her inferiors.

She *had* been a goddess to those she had bound. They had been loyal to her as she desired, and loved her in greater or lesser degrees, as she found prudent.

A goddess, yes.

A goddess of destruction.

He must be aware, *that* she had decided. He must *know*, as she had, the harm—no, *the evil*—he had caused. He must die—that was plain necessity—but she could make him suffer a subjective twelve thousand years of torment before she granted him that kindness. It would have been satisfying to have taken him in a duel, but there was some measure of Balance in a duel; and if there was to be any Balance at all in the matter, it would be that she would take him unaware—as he had taken her.

She had codes; she used them. Too, she was known in this place, if any saw her.

But no one would see her.

So it was that she was waiting for him in his office— in his office secured by the machines, the *dramliz* killers, which protected *him* against *her*, whom he had taken, crushed into dust, and remolded into the Department's creature, sending her forth to do likewise.

It was . . . curious . . . that he relied upon the machines. But there, perhaps he had not considered the possibility that she would touch a passing guard, and suggest to her that she was turning Captain ten'Veila's protections *on*, rather than *off*. He had never valued independent thought.

So it was that she was waiting for him when he arrived in his shielded office—and stopped, staring, struck, foreknowing his doom, even in the instant before she extended her thought and took control of his heart, squeezing it oh so gently—only enough, really, to alert him to what she had done.

He took a hard breath, and was utterly still. She would have liked to taste his panic, but he had never been one to panic, and he did not do so now. Being no fool, he was afraid, but his fear was unsatisfyingly cold.

"Going rogue?" he asked, when the pain had released him.

"Paying my debts," she answered him pleasantly. There was no need, after all, to be unpleasant. "I wish to be exact."

His fear warmed somewhat, and she felt the flicker of an idea disturb the surface of his thoughts.

Casually, she reached out and took over his motor systems, forcing him to walk across the office to the chair he had reserved for his "recruits" and sitting him, forcibly, down.

Panic did flicker then, and it was sweet.

She touched the pain center, and froze his vocal cords, too, merely for the pleasure of being cruel. The room was soundproofed; no one would hear his screams. No one had heard hers.

She increased the pain, and now—ah, now!—he panicked; he twisted; he sought to prise her fingers from around his heart, and almost she laughed. It was easy to consolidate her control, to increase pressure, only the tiniest—

Her touch slid off of the pain center; her grip on his heart eased. Her power, which had been rising in response to her prey's distress, ebbed.

She became aware . . . of a touch.

It was subtle, even gentle, akin to the touch of a comrade's hand on her shoulder.

Carefully, she explored that sensation. She followed it. Followed it . . . to the link.

The link that had been formed when she had Healed Shan yos'Galan of his imminent death.

So, he disapproved of her methods, did he? And what did Shan yos'Galan know of her necessities? He who had remade her by giving her back to herself before throwing her like a blade at the Department's heart?

It came to her, the answer to that question, in a flare of understanding as intimate as a binding.

Shan yos'Galan knew necessity. Shan yos'Galan knew Balance. He would do—see what he *had* done!—whatever Balance required.

With all of that, however, Shan yos'Galan was not a cruel man. If a life must be taken by Balance or necessity, then that life would be ended painlessly, expeditiously, and as gently as possible.

Revenge—Shan yos'Galan understood revenge, of that Tarona Rusk was abruptly certain. He merely found Balance morally superior, and less damaging to those who stood on either side of the equation.

Tarona looked at the man in the chair, his face muddy and slicked with sweat, his eyes mired in terror. The man who had captured her, altered her, and who, she saw now, had never ceased to be afraid of her.

As he was afraid now; his heartbeat fluttering in her hold; his lungs laboring; the pattern of his being a disarray of smeary, running color.

She stepped forward, bent, and looked into his eyes.

"Baz Lyr, do you know me?" she asked, and released her hold on his voice.

"Tarona," he gasped. "How not?"

"And do you know why you are going to die?"

"Yes," he answered, gasping still. "This will avail you nothing, Tarona. The Department is bigger than you, than all of us. It will win, and you will die."

"I will die," she agreed, tasting the truth of it. "But the Department will not win."

She squeezed his heart then, and held it; maintaining the link, wide open, until she felt him die.

Dutiful Passage

. . . .

I

THE HEALER'S PATTERN WAS GREYED OVER WITH DEVAS-tation, as if the fresh, healthy soul had been set afire, not once, but many times, until there was nothing left save a fine layer of ash over what once had been a proud edifice to honor.

It was possible to live—to exist—soul-struck and ashen. A terrible existence, especially if one retained the memory of what they had once been, and how they had been reduced to . . . this.

Damaged as she was, Healer ven'Deelin had yet understood that choice existed. One needn't bear with an endless, crippled, joyless future. One might simply choose not to wake to it.

Priscilla considered the grey field laid out before her Inner Eyes, and wondered if it would not be best to let the other woman go.

"It is," Lina murmured from beside her, "as if she has already died."

"And yet," Priscilla returned, still focused on that dire innerscape. "And yet, something sustains her."

"The Luck sustains her," Lina said. "His claim was for partners, so you had said. There must be a link."

"True. If there is a link, we might be able to use it to regrow..."

"Lucks are not strong," Lina pointed out. "Even if this one is an exception, it would be his life, to even begin a greening of—this..."

A pause. Priscilla felt Lina's presence draw nearer, as if she passed her hand over the cold soulscape.

"I do not believe we can effect a full Healing," she said. "She has taken too much harm. Indeed, it is a wonder that she survived the separation and the subsequent draw on her talent, even with the support of her partner."

Priscilla stirred.

"What is it?" Lina asked.

"We *saw* the indicators for separation trauma, when we made our initial examination. I didn't see anything to suggest this kind of injury—did you?"

Priscilla felt Lina's concentration sharpen until it was a blade—a scalpel.

"No. No—you are correct. The question arises—what causes this? This, *now*? Surely, nothing that Keriana had done would produce such an effect."

The medic had been focused on stabilizing the Healer physically, and bringing her to a level of health which would support a return to reality from the fogs of the coma.

Which meant that, even unconscious, Dyoli ven'Deelin had understood that her condition had changed, but not what those changes meant. Until she could weigh the new situation, she would—

"She's shamming," Priscilla said.

"What? But why?"

"She's protecting Mar Tyn pai'Fortana," Priscilla

said, certain of it. "She's trying to make us commit. *Are* we the sort of people who will attempt to end the life of a burnt-out and useless Healer? Will we bind her? Will we attempt to bind *him*, through her? Are we friends, are we foes; is she in active peril or relatively safe? She must know—and know quickly. She has very recently been living in peril not only of her life, but of her soul, if we are to believe anything her partner said to Shan."

"But what—" Lina began—and stopped. Priscilla felt her concentration shift once more.

"She is not only shamming," Lina said, after a long moment of study, "she has set a trap—a very credible trap. This is an entirely convincing illusion."

Priscilla nodded absently, focusing on that expanse of cold ash. She could *feel* something that was not ash; subtle, and formed with the intent to harm...

She narrowed her will, daring to probe beneath the ash—and struck something cold and adamantine, tasting of vinegar.

The Healer's will, she thought, withdrawing. This is not a helpless victim. She's strong, and she's taking no chances—not with her life, nor with his.

"A convincing illusion, but not a deep one," she said, withdrawing herself to speak with Lina. "The trap—I can't see it, but I can feel its presence. Whatever it is, we don't want to trip it."

She cast a thoughtful gaze over the sleeping face—cheeks sunken, eyelids translucent; her hair a swirl of pale red around the flat pillow.

"It would be best for all," she said, speaking as much to the unconscious Healer as to Lina, "if Healer ven'Deelin woke of her own will, and worked with us

like a rational woman, rather than setting traps that
are more likely to wound a friend than kill an enemy."

There was no indication that the woman on the bed
had heard her; not the flicker of an eyelash, nor even
the flutter of a breeze to disturb the illusion of ash.

Lina sighed and bent close, placing a careful hand
on the Healer's shoulder.

"Healer ven'Deelin," she said firmly, infusing her
voice with truth. "Luck pai'Fortana is safe and well.
You are among allies, aboard the *Dutiful Passage*, out of
Surebleak, captained by Priscilla Delacroix y Mendoza
Clan Korval; Shan yos'Galan Clan Korval, master trader.
I am Lina Faaldom Clan Deshnol. We mean you only
good. We offer a Healing, if that is necessary. If it is
not, yet we offer you and your partner safety."

They waited.

Nothing changed. The Inner Eyes beheld only that
gritty field of ash.

Healer ven'Deelin, Priscilla thought, had been honed
in the crucible of betrayal. It would take more than mere
names and assurances to convince her that she was safe.

"I," she said to Lina, "am going to try something.
Shield yourself."

"Try what?"

"I'm going to try to be convincing on her chosen
field."

"She will have been accustomed to displays of
power," Lina said slowly. "Such a display, now, may
drive her deeper into hiding."

"Understood. I'm only going to drop my shields,
so she can see the truth of who I am, and make her
own determination for her future."

"Ah. Perhaps that will work—though it is risky,

Priscilla. How, instead, if we have the Luck brought to her here?"

Priscilla considered that.

"I'd rather she stopped thinking of us as mortal enemies first," she said slowly. "It seems to me that bringing the two of them together before she understands the reality of her situation might...endanger the ship."

Lina frowned, inclined her head, and closed her Inner Eyes. A moment later, Priscilla felt her shields come up and gently seal.

Priscilla once more considered the devastation before her, mouth pursed. Vinegar and steel.

Then, with no fuss nor fanfare, she opened herself entirely.

Power flared; she grew, expanding out of sickbay, out of the *Passage*, into space, the galaxy, the universe—beyond. The stars sang hosanna; her wings rippled with all the colors of joy. She was beyond herself; she touched eternity; she was no mere Witch; she was Moonhawk, and a goddess.

For the space of three long breaths she allowed herself to stand fully revealed, limned against the universe.

Then, carefully, she folded her wings, breathing out glory, until she stood once more in the sickbay of *Dutiful Passage*, a Witch, a Healer: a woman named Priscilla.

She opened her Inner Eyes to look upon Dyoli ven'Deelin's soul...

...to a green and vibrant world infused with hope; flowers blooming—everything illuminated by the brilliance of the heart-link arching over all.

II

PRISCILLA RETURNED TO THE CAPTAIN'S OFFICE AT THE end of her shift, to do a final check of messages and, she admitted to herself, to recruit herself before joining Shan for dinner. Not that she expected to—or could—hide from him that she had—perhaps—overreached, but to steady herself.

It had been . . . *years* since she had expanded fully into Moonhawk's powers. Vessel of the Goddess she might be, but the Goddess had been . . . quiescent for so very long—astonishingly quiescent, for any who had read the history of Moonhawk down the centuries. She had not been abandoned—*that* she knew, deep in the core of her—only it seemed that the Goddess was content to rest, and leave any communication with the living world to her consort, Lute, who, so Shan swore, took a very delight in interfering.

She crossed to her desk; there was a single message in the queue—from Lina. Priscilla sat down and opened it.

Dyoli ven'Deelin, it seemed, had been satisfactorily situated in guest quarters. She professed herself willing to answer such questions as might be put to her regarding the Department of the Interior and Tarona Rusk, though she did make the point that neither the Department nor "the Mistress" had confided in her. She did, very properly, ask that her thanks be conveyed to the captain and master trader for their care. She refused the offer of the pinbeam, saying that she required some time to organize herself before contacting her parent and her clan—which, Lina allowed, was the very face of prudence.

Healer ven'Deelin did not ask to see Mar Tyn pai'Fortana, which might, Lina said, be thought odd by those who were unable to See the breadth and the depth of the links they shared.

That was well done, then, thought Priscilla. She wanted to discuss the matter with Shan before allowing those two in the same room.

She sighed, filed Lina's note, and pushed the chair away from the desk, closing her eyes. First a rejuvenation exercise, she thought, already reaching for—

Come to me.

* * * ❖ * * *

Shan dropped his shields and considered the young person before him. A robust child—but no, he thought of a sudden. He must break himself of that pattern. While it was true that an offspring will always seem a child to her parent, there was a disservice done both, if the child was not permitted to become her own adult.

Melant'i, Shan, he told himself. *Strive* to have some conduct.

So then, the person before him—a young adult, who had not been shy of taking on more and more of an adult's burden. Who strove with all of her considerable will toward her life goal of attaining the amethyst, and standing as a master trader. Who was also attempting to accommodate a remarkable, and unwelcome, gift. She would not, he thought, ever be an easy *dramliza*, but she would not shrink from her power, nor hesitate to use it for Balance.

In the near past, the pattern of her being had been—subdued, depressed. That had vanished with the blossoming of her gift. Now, she was radiant—one might say, brilliant—the edges of her soul not bounded so much as fading into the distant pearly shine of the empyrean.

It was, Shan thought, rather alarming to think that one had sired such a being. One hardly knew how to be worthy of her, and only hoped that the minor wisdoms gained during his longer lifetime were of use and did her no harm.

For instance, that aspect, which seemed to fade away into—or—even more disturbing!—*merge with*—the macrocosm of energies accessible to wizardkind. He had Seen many patterns and, indeed, many youths, down the tale of his years, but he was at a loss to recall if he had ever Seen one *quite* like this.

Weak as he remained, she ought to have drawn him like a lodestone, yet she did not. Her power was evident, but curiously . . . passive.

"Sir?" Padi asked quietly. "Ought we—I mean no disrespect! I only wonder if you are well enough to pursue this lesson."

"I am, I think, sufficiently well, but you must allow me to wonder in turn—whence came this . . . alteration in your gift?"

She looked at him blankly, her confusion reflecting back to him along her pattern.

"Alteration?"

"I seem to see an expansion since the last time you and I were intimate. Has Lina not mentioned this? Nor Priscilla?"

Padi shook her head.

"The concentration has been on shielding and on control," she said hesitantly. "On close work, in particular, to teach focus and discrimination. Lina says it is akin to learning the small dance, so that there is a foundation to inform the larger moves."

"Yes, we had all three discussed that, and it had seemed best—it being roughly the course of study all of us had followed. I wonder—forgive me—if you have been practicing . . . larger moves on your own initiative?"

She shook her head decisively.

"No, sir. I do not want to endanger the ship, or to cause any unintentional harm, as when I used my bowl to protect myself."

That had been rather an astonishing use of power, Shan allowed. He hadn't been able to work out quite how it had been done, which was perhaps not amazing, given his status as a mere Healer. That *Priscilla* had not been able to find the trick of the thing, never mind reproduce it—*that* was worrisome. To say the very least that might be said on the topic.

"I understand," he said. "Well. Since we are gathered together, I wonder if you will ask this"—he placed the flat disk of mottled green and blue stone that he used for a coaster on the desk directly before her—"to please rise and take up a position at approximately twelve centimeters above the desk, so that I may observe your technique."

"Yes, sir."

Shan leaned back in his chair, shields wide open, and watched. He saw the lines of Padi's pattern intensify as she brought her concentration to bear. Rather a lot of concentration, given the relatively trivial nature of the task but, there, she had already made a misstep or two with this, so was likely somewhat conscious.

He waited, anticipating the moves she would make in order to lift the coaster. He was not himself tele-kinetic, but he had watched Anthora often enough that he certainly knew the technique and the level of power required in order to—

The coaster rose, wobbling slightly. There had been not the faintest flicker of energy, nor did he see the necessary construct of will surrounding the object. Indeed, it seemed, very literally, to be floating in naked air, supported by nothing more than Padi's strong suggestion that it should do so.

"I . . . see," Shan said. "May I ask—"

Static crackled, bright and cruel, along his link with Priscilla. For a moment, she loomed enormous in his Sight, a giant, filling all his senses until—

She was gone.

No, not *quite* gone. A taste lingered along the link—a taste he recalled too well—dust, and metal, and dire intent. Weapons Hall.

He may have cursed, very quietly.

Then, he was reaching along the link—the link that was every bit as solid as it had been; running wide and true from the center of his own being, out, beyond, to the core of his beloved. The link *was* still in place, merely . . .

Priscilla . . . herself . . . was not present at the other end. Or say, rather, a shadow of Priscilla was tethered there, like a placeholder in an unfinished equation.

"Father!"

He brought himself to center, blinked into the lesser

reality enclosed by his office, and looked up into his daughter's shocked face.

He took a deep breath, and made his tone easy.

"Your pardon. Priscilla seems to have met an adventure. I will go to her."

Padi was still staring at him.

"Do you need me? Do you need Lina?"

"No..." He reached again along the links, touching the chill presence of the shadow. "No, she's quite safe in her office..." Mostly. "I think she has merely decided to...step sideways."

He stood. "I regret that the lesson must end early. Please, return the coaster to—"

"I can't," Padi said, swallowing hard.

He looked at her.

"No? Why not?"

"Because—I was startled by the—jolt of energy, and it—I threw it, I think. I'm not really certain where it may be."

· · · ❊ · · ·

"...not one of us sane. What would you? We were gods, or near enough, though none so powerful as the Mighty Iloheen, Unmaker of the Universe, Defiler of Angels. The Iloheen were careful, so very careful, that their servants were never so mighty as they. Being what they were—being *how* they were—they did not suppose that some few of their children might bind themselves together—against them.

"Thirteen was our number—that was thirteen pairs of Lady and thrall. Thirteen goddesses, let it be said. Together, we produced a Working; weaving templates of ourselves into the living stuff of the universe. We wove Names into our own essences, to anchor us to Life. This, we did in the service of Life. In that, we were nearer unto gods than our makers.

"It was our hope that we would, by these manipulations, trap the Iloheen within their own trap, and see the Destroyers destroyed.

"It was a last hope, and a feeble one. Yet we, the Thirteen, pursued it with all our art and energy, deeming any hope superior to surrender.

"There were others, our partners in deicide. Chiefest among them was Rool Tiazan, who more than any other of us could claim to be a god, and his Lady, who refused any name, and was perhaps the maddest of us all. They would see the Iloheen dead, if they might, but foremost, they would preserve Life.

"There was another of us, insatiable and cruel as the Iloheen who had made her. Her purpose was the death of the Destroyers, that she might rise into the vacuum of their power.

"There were also the children, created from the saturation of energies, the blood of angels, and the ceaseless manipulation of Probability.

"And there was Life Itself, for above all things, Life strives to live.

"Little enough, you might say, to bring against the Enemy of All Life.

"In the last hours of the universe's existence, perhaps inside the same unlikely instant that allowed Rool Tiazan to freeze the ley lines, forcing Probability and Luck into one dense, unnavigable, pool... In that instant, I Saw that, to best serve Life, if not to insure my own survival, it was necessary to weave another template—a Fourteenth for my submissive, Lute, who had, no less than Rool Tiazan, been a lord among *zaliata*—an angel—before he accepted my dominance and became part of our doomed attempt to unmake the Unmaker.

"The last instant arrived, with the universe already lost and every small life riding on one final throw of Rool Tiazan's dice.

"The throw was true, however crooked the dice; Life won through to a new universe and the Iloheen, crystalline in their perfection, remained locked in the old."

There was a pause.

Priscilla, who had been listening to this discourse with some astonishment, blinked and looked about herself.

She stood in the Witches Hall of Weapons, where she had come, in lives before, as Moonhawk and as Moonhawk's vessel. On those occasions, she had been wearing the garb of a Priestess of the Goddess.

On this occasion, however, she was suitably attired as the captain of *Dutiful Passage*. The woman before her—Moonhawk herself—held a pair of tarnished silver rings in one glowing white hand, standing tall in robes of starlight blue, breasts bare, waist bound with silver chains. Her eyes were . . . odd, as if she were simultaneously blind and all-seeing. She smiled, as if she felt the weight of Priscilla's regard.

"The Thirteen survived the destruction of the universe, though twelve had made an error. Eventually, it was a fatal error. They had failed to realize that the godhead sprang from paired energies. They had used—used up—their thralls, sparing not one thought to save them. Thus did they doom themselves. Every century, they dwindled. In these days, they are nothing more than empty Names, shadow-shreds harried among the golden threads of creation."

She extended her hand, displaying the tarnished rings.

"Lute and I survived. In fact, we have survived too long. Even Rool Tiazan was at last granted an end; dissolution. Peace."

Priscilla took a careful breath.

"Lute is surely not your slave, Lady. The histories—my own experience..."

Lady Moonhawk swayed a gentle bow, her draperies billowing starfields about her.

"The gods love Life; it is not given them to be more particular than that. I say to you that Lute is my other half; I could not survive without him, nor he, without me. Nor yet may I die without him; nor he, without me."

"My lady..." Priscilla began—and was silenced when Moonhawk raised her glowing hand.

"Do not speak," she murmured. "These matters are beyond you, as they should be. I bring them forward so that you may know what you are Seeing, and be at peace, when the moment comes. As for my purpose in bringing you here to me—there are three.

"Attend me, now."

She paused, and it seemed to Priscilla that she became more fully present, *solid* in this place that existed and yet did not.

"My first purpose is to make my apologies to the last of Moonhawk's living vessels, for the use to which I have, and will, put you, and the chaos I have sown into your life. I promise that you will soon be free.

"My second purpose is to give you—and the Lute in your time—my blessing, which is even yet a potent thing. I approve of this course you have undertaken.

"My third purpose is to grant to your child strength, and freedom. She will encompass marvels."

Priscilla bowed her head.

"My thanks, Lady Moonhawk," she murmured, and would have said more—would have asked—but the Goddess made a gesture, and whatever she might have said vanished from mind and mouth.

"Gently spoken. Your service has pleased me, as I have not been pleased in many hundreds of this universe's years.

"Go in peace, Priscilla Delacroix y Mendoza, with the gratitude of a goddess."

Weapons Hall faded.

Priscilla opened her eyes to a scrambled black and white abstract. She was cold, panting, and desperately thirsty.

"Coming," Shan said cheerily.

She blinked, reached for her center, and snatched the spinning confusion into sense by a sheer effort of will.

She was sitting in her chair in the captain's own office. Shan was at her side.

"Water for my lady," he said, extending a glass. She took it in both hands, and he hesitated for a moment, bent close, as if he wished to be certain that she had the strength to hold it.

She drank greedily, and he shortly took the empty glass away, and brought it, full, back again.

"Shall I call for a tray?" he asked.

"Yes."

He nodded. She drank the water more slowly this time, and listened to him speaking on comm to BillyJo, in the kitchen.

She finished the water, placed the empty glass on the desk and sat there, taking stock. There was, she thought, a better than even chance that her legs would buckle if she tried to stand up. Which was simply ridiculous.

"Not at all ridiculous," Shan said, leaning over to pick up the glass. "You—or someone—expended quite a bit of energy. The jolt was enough to disturb me at lessons with Padi."

He paused, tipping his head to one side.

"I fear I may have offended innocent ears."

Priscilla considered him.

"Padi served under Ama ven'Tyrlit," she said dryly.

"Very true! I was forgetting! Obviously, I can teach her nothing."

"How inventive were you?" she asked, taking the refilled glass from him.

"Depressingly mundane, I assure you. We had been in the middle of having Padi levitate the stone coaster so kindly given me by Ambassador Valeking. The jolt of power was such that I fear it has gone missing."

"Gone missing? Gone missing where?"

"Well, that's the point, isn't it? Padi's not at all certain where she sent it. Or—I suppose we must acknowledge the possibility—when. You weren't struck on the head by a flat green-and-blue stone when you were a child, were you, Priscilla?"

"No. Were you?"

"It would explain a great deal, wouldn't it? But, no. Ah, the tray."

He turned and crossed the room, the chime sounded, and he opened the door.

"Thank you," he murmured.

He brought the tray to the desk and put it down, nimbly avoiding the piles of hardcopy; removing covers with a magician's flair, pointing at the various offerings of high-caloric foods. The kitchen knew well what to send when they were asked for "Healer Mendoza's tray."

"Eat," he said.

"You, too," she said. "I can't eat all this."

He pulled the visitor's chair around to her side of the desk and sat next to her. Sighing, she leaned into his warmth, and chose a cheese muffin from the plate.

"Did I catch a taste of Weapons Hall?" he asked, choosing a muffin for himself.

"Yes."

"I wouldn't have said our case was as dire as that, but perhaps you've had a Seeing?"

She shook her head.

"I was called there by—by Moonhawk."

Shan had been to Weapons Hall; it was where he had met Lute, acquired the red gaming token, and accepted *Soldier Lore* into his heart and being. He knew it for a treacherous place, and so it was.

"Something big is going to happen," she said; then shook her head sharply. "Something big has *already* happened. But—Moonhawk is going to die."

That had been the wrong thing to say, she thought, as his horror washed through her.

"*Moonhawk* is going to die," he repeated carefully, breaking open his muffin. "And Moonhawk's—*vessel*?"

"I—said that badly," she said. "Forgive me."

She reached for the glass, drank, and met his eyes.

"Moonhawk's vessel..." she began, but he held up a hand.

"Is this event imminent?"

"I—don't...believe...so."

"Eat, then. I will contain myself."

She ate until she was sated, and the shaking had stopped. She was no longer chilled, but she leaned against Shan's shoulder anyway, for the sheer comfort it gave her.

"Moonhawk's vessel," she said then, knowing full well his feelings about Moonhawk, Lute, her dedication to the Goddess as Moonhawk-in-this-lifetime, and gods in general...

"Moonhawk's vessel *will not* die. In fact, I believe that I'm no longer Moonhawk's vessel. She called me to her as myself—as Priscilla Delacroix y Mendoza, captain of the *Dutiful Passage*. I came before her in plain ship clothes, while she stood in her starry robes, holding two old and tarnished silver rings."

"Weapons?" Shan asked.

Priscilla spread her hands.

"Everything in that Hall is a weapon," she said. "But I don't know that she came there to find them. She might have brought them with her. Weapons Hall is a place of considerable power; she could easily draw enough energy to bring me to her there."

"Stipulated," said Shan. "And she called you to her for the purpose of...releasing you?"

"That may have been part of it. She said that her purpose was threefold."

She narrowed her eyes, seeing again the glowing face, the fixed gaze...

"First, an apology, for having disrupted my life,"

she said. "Second, a blessing, for you and me together, and her approval of the *course we have undertaken*."

Beside her, Shan shifted. She opened her eyes to look at him.

"In the general way of things, no—goddesses do *not* apologize," she said, snatching the thought from his head. "And historically, Moonhawk's vessel has led a more . . . adventurous life than those bearing the other twelve Names.

"As for the course we've undertaken—I don't know what that is."

"We are, therefore, as one in bewilderment," Shan said. "Continue, please. I'm agog to hear her third purpose."

"Her third purpose was to grant to our child freedom and strength. We're to expect her to accomplish *marvels*."

He sighed.

"And here I had been hoping for a nice, orderly child, in Balance for having brought Padi to adulthood with a large portion of the universe intact."

"She might outstrip all of her kin in orderliness," Priscilla pointed out. "There are many ways to be marvelous."

"Very true. I withhold my despair until she breaks into her first locked room."

Priscilla laughed softly.

"I do not, of course, mean to pry, but was the delivery of these tidings all of Moonhawk's conversation?"

"Not quite. When I arrived, she was . . . reciting history from the Old Universe. How the Thirteen wove themselves into the fabric of the Life, and accepted Names so that they were anchored into Probability.

There was a good deal of it—what a strange place the Old Universe must have been!"

"By all accounts. I would like to hear this history lesson"—he raised a hand—"when you have the energy to recall it in fullness. Was there anything else?"

"Yes. She said that she and . . . Lute had lived too long in this universe. And the rings—I had the impression they were a set, and very old—the tarnish . . ."

"Of course," he said, and sighed.

"How did your lesson with Padi go on, before I interrupted you?"

"Surprisingly. I wonder, have you noticed anything . . . boundless about Padi's pattern?"

Priscilla frowned at him.

"I'm not sure I have."

"Well. Take a look at her the next time the two of you are in proximity. I would be interested in your analysis."

"All right," she said.

"Now, I ask—are you able to walk with me to our cabin?"

"Yes," she said, and rose with scarcely a tremor.

"Excellent."

He offered her his arm.

"I suggest we go to bed, Priscilla, and get some sleep."

· · · ❈ · · ·

Padi entered her quarters . . . cautiously, stopping just inside the door to scan the room, right to left.

Everything seemed orderly; just as she'd left it at the beginning of her duty shift. The desk was neat: styli, pads, and hardcopy placed *just so*; the keyboard under the dark screen; the chair locked into position beneath.

Farther along, the table beside her bunk displayed a framed flatpic of Quin, Syl Vor, Grandfather Luken and herself in the Tree Court, taken just before she'd left Surebleak, and also a note taker in case she should wake with an idea worthy of recording. The bunk itself was in order, the blankets pulled tight, the pillow comfortably plump.

In a word, everything appeared to be in order.

Very well.

She crossed the room, and opened the door to the 'fresher. Keeping the door open by the simple expedient of standing in the way of its closing, she surveyed the spare facilities.

Here, too, all was as it should be.

She stepped back; the door slid closed.

Crossing the small space, she opened her locker. Neatly folded clothes on neat, uncluttered shelves. Padi stepped forward and put her palm on each pile of clothes in turn, compressing each, releasing it, and watching the pile spring back into shape.

She failed to discover any hard, regular shape among the cloth.

Padi sighed, closed the locker, and sat down at her desk.

"Well where *is* the damned thing, then?" she asked the room, rather peevishly.

There was a slight clatter, as if a stylus or two had tapped the desktop. She turned her head, frowning, and the small noise ceased.

Padi bit her lip.

Where else *could* it be? she asked herself. Had

it—could she—Oh, but surely not! She *couldn't* have sent it back to Ambassador Valeking!

Could she?

For a moment, she was ice-cold. If that was in fact the case, the ambassador, who had very plainly not approved of Master Trader yos'Galan, would recognize the coaster as the special token she had presented him on behalf of her homeworld, and she would certainly find an insult in it—

But, no. No. It simply could not be. Why, she didn't even know where Ambassador Valeking *was*, except in the most general way possible. And one needed a connection, didn't one?—An . . . entanglement? In order to send things—no, it was ridiculous. One simply *couldn't* send an object—a very solid object—into, into hyperspace with a thought . . . well, really, in her case, *without* a thought! At the very least, she must have made a decision, and all she had been was . . . startled.

Frightened.

Padi took another breath—and another.

No. The idea was absurd. What was most likely, now that she had eliminated her quarters as a landing zone, was that she had simply thrown the blue-green coaster, well . . . *up*, in a sense. Very *far* up—but it would eventually come down, directly onto Father's desk where, after all, it belonged.

Yes, she thought, that was by far the most likely scenario.

So, then . . .

The lesson with Father had been the last thing on the day's duty roster. As it had been cut short, she now had time to do . . . something else.

She had time, in fact, to read the book that the

master trader had caused her to bring to him from Pommierport, and which she had done no more than glance at over a hurried lunch.

Smiling slightly in anticipation, Padi reached for her copy of *Wu and Fabricant's Guide to The Redlands*.

Off-Grid

. . . .

"OW!"

Tekelia vesterGranz spun 'round from the screen, hand on head, half expecting to find one of the youngers giggling in the shadows at the far end of the room. It was a game, after all, with the youngers—to try to approach Tekelia unaware.

But there was no delighted child pretending to cower in fear of their own audacity, not in any shadowy corner, tucked behind a chair, nor squeezed in beside a cabinet.

Tekelia thought about sunlight, and the room was replete, all shadows banished. A glance into the ambient discovered no disturbance such as might be created by someone wrapped in invisibility.

The room was empty, save for Tekelia. Tekelia—and a stone disk, cunningly cut to display glittering swirls of green and blue, lying on the floor an arm's length behind the desk chair.

Power glittered around and within the artifact. A last bit of energy flashed, playfully, as Tekelia approached, releasing a sweet, intoxicating scent before it dissipated.

Tekelia dropped to one knee and addressed the stone: *Who sent you?*

In answer, there came a flash of the thrilling signature that identified the norbear's pupil: the woman with the shields like a carnivorous flower.

Tekelia queried the disk more fully, feeling along the lines of history and intention, gaining the impression that it had been launched inadvertently, yet not entirely at random. It had not, in any sense, been *sent*, but had rather *arrived* in what could only be described as a happy coincidence.

Tekelia smiled slightly.

So then, a token had arrived from what must be considered an equal power, propelled by instinct rather than intent. Tekelia must be close in her thoughts.

Picking the disk up, Tekelia carried it to the desk, placing it by the screen.

"Bide a bit. You're quite safe with me."

Dutiful Passage
En Route to Volmer

· · · · · · · · · · · · · · · · · · ·

I

PADI WOKE, EYES STILL CLOSED, CERTAIN THAT SHE'D been dreaming—a very odd dream, where someone had been walking, walking, walking...and staring up into the sky, perhaps hiking up a hill. She had been uncertain of the identity of the walker in the dream—whether it was herself, or someone else, only that they moved with a steady and inexorable tread...

But there! The sound came again, and she was most certainly awake now—and the sound was in her cabin with her, presenting no quality of dreaming, no fey overtones of distance.

Blick. Blick. Blick.

She tried to catalog the sound, recognizing none of those ordinary to her quarters. Almost—*not* footsteps, but as if someone were impatiently tapping their fingers on a hard—

BLICK!

"That," she said, "was positively petulant."

Eyes well open now, she surveyed the dim room, catching the hint of motion above her desk.

335

A stylus—no, *two* were rising above the desk from the spot where she usually kept them to hand, and falling back with precision, each strike producing a...

Blick.

Padi rose and approached the desk. The desk light obligingly came on, illuminating the scene.

The styli were not, as she had at first supposed, striking the desktop, but rather the facsimile of *Wu and Fabricant's Guide*. The hour had been late, and while the book had not been, precisely, boring, she had abandoned it open where it was, having finished the section on ancient demographics, and not wishing to venture half-asleep into system mechanics.

"I see," she said conversationally to the styli. "The book is in your way."

The rising stylus wavered in its ascent, then continued. The falling stylus—fell.

"I will fix this," she said. "When I have done so, you will have done, and allow me to go to sleep."

Reaching out, she took the book in hand.

Both styli fell at once, struck the desktop—and remained there.

Sighing, Padi glanced down at the book. The pages were cool under her fingers, the illustrations of brightly colored crystals of quartz, amethyst, citrine, emerald. Her eye moved down the page to the text, learning that the planet Colemeno was possessed of a geological oddity known to the locals as *the ridge*, an outcropping of quartz and quartz-bearing material that might have been the remains of another planet smashed in collision a couple billion years before, spearing a world half-made.

Padi glanced again at the illustrations, seeing colors

that reminded her of Father's missing coaster, and thinking about this ridge, the local landmark. Ruefully she considered that she might have just read the only thing about The Redlands that would still be much the same now as it had been when the guidebook was written.

Her eyes were beginning to close again. Cradling the book against her, keeping one wary eye on the now-quiescent styli, she opened the desk drawer, rummaged briefly, and found a bookmark. She inserted it, closed the book and placed it on the desk well away from the usual resting place of styli.

She turned off the desk lamp and returned to her bed, pulling the blanket up with a whispered, "Sleep well," to the room, and all that might be listening.

II

"LUTE," SHAN SAID, HIS VOICE SOFT AGAINST THE FOG. "Lute, I need to speak with you, urgently."

He paused, expectant, but there was no alteration in his surroundings. The gentle fogs of Healspace eddied softly around his knees and neck; a tendril unfolding like a flower to kiss his cheek. It was tempting—somewhat too tempting—to close his eyes and just . . . go to sleep, here among the sweet mists—but that would not do. He had business here, serious business made all the more dangerous by the certainty that, if Priscilla discovered him in Healspace, shields wide, open to and receiving all, she would certainly strangle him.

"Lute," he said again. "Your attention, please. I require your presence, here and now."

For a moment, he despaired of an answer, then the fog thickened, darkened, and resolved itself into a thin tall man in black cloak and patched breeches, striding forth as if he had been walking for some time, and came to rest a bare two steps from the end of Shan's nose.

"Since you called so sweetly," Lute said. "How may I be pleased to serve you, child?"

"By telling me the truth, employing neither ambiguity nor metaphor," Shan said. "I need what is known in Terran as a *straight answer*."

Lute sighed.

"I wouldn't have come if I'd have known it was going to be as difficult as that to placate you. Does your lady know where you are, and what you are doing to yourself?"

"She does not. However, you approach my subject. It is of my lady and, as I understand it, yours—their futures together and apart—that I wish to speak."

"Even worse," Lute said, and was seen to sigh. "Ask, then, and I will attempt to govern my natural inclinations."

Shan gave a sigh of his own.

"Understand that we must deal in gods and their doings," he said. "This is not a topic I willingly take up."

"I do understand," Lute said cordially. "I am not myself a godly man."

"And yet you had told me that you were once a god."

"Therefore, I have no need to believe in anything outside myself."

Shan considered him while the mist swirled, all colors and none, cool and seductive.

"Is your lady not a goddess? Or do you not put faith in her?"

"My lady began as something very much stranger than a goddess, clever child. She has since diminished, though not so much as her sisters, as I have expanded. We stand as equals now, which we were not, at the beginning. As for faith—she has never done anything other than what she intended, and I have faith that she will continue as she began."

Shan frowned.

"I was told that you and your Lady Moonhawk love with a passion that transcends that of mere mortals."

"Now there, you open a new topic. Stories have their own peculiar truth, and gods . . . well, what would you, mortal man? Gods are beyond you. The stories teach that—and it is true.

"As for Moonhawk and myself. Perhaps we grew to

love each other down the ages and the lifetimes we shared. But the thing that binds us, at core, is much simpler than love—we need each other. We are two halves of a whole, and neither can go forward without the other."

"We now arrive at my topic," said Shan. "Are you aware that Lady Moonhawk intends to die?"

"Oh, yes," Lute said, unconcerned, "I know that."

"She has spoken of her intention with her vessel in this lifetime, my lifemate Priscilla. She has extended thanks and blessings, and she has shown two tarnished silver rings."

"In that case, she is well advanced to her goal, and I will gladly join her in seeing it completed. We were not meant for this universe, and ought to have quit it long ago."

"Why didn't you?" Shan asked. "Leave."

"We had left a door open, child," Lute said gently, "and as best as we could know, we two, and Moonhawk's sisters, were the only protections this universe might have, did our enemy step through behind us."

Shan frowned, feeling slightly askew, and shook away the thought that it would be...comfortable... to lie down on the fog and rest.

Instead, he forced his attention to the man before him, and gazed into frank and knowing dark eyes.

"Was it *probable* that...the enemy from the Old Universe might come through?" he asked.

Lute shrugged.

"We judged that it was not impossible. Unlikely, yes; there we agreed, but we could not prove an absolute to our own satisfaction; therefore, we remained."

"But now the door has closed."

"So it has. And we are free, at last, to go."

"Will Moonhawk's death murder Priscilla?"

There, it was asked, more harshly than he had intended, and there was something... glittering in the mists, at the very edge of his vision.

Lute appeared amused.

"Is *that* what frets you? Be at peace. Moonhawk and I will return to those elements which spawned us. Say that we will die—it may look, a little, as if we had died. But that won't be true; it will be a sweet release, and a return to what we were meant to be.

"Your lady Priscilla has been, so I gather from this talk of blessings and gifts, likewise released to her full self. Though you don't ask for it, I freely give you assurance that no harm will come to you from our parting."

Well, it *hadn't* occurred to him, Shan admitted. On the other hand, he was scarcely the vessel of a god. Or possibly he meant only *very* scarcely...

"Stay," Lute said, placing his hands on Shan's shoulders. "Allow me at least to replenish that which you have spent."

He smiled, sardonic.

"After all, prayer must be rewarded."

"Prayer," Shan said, but he placed his hands on Lute's shoulders, and looked into his eyes. The mists swirled; he felt energy flow, sparkling, in his veins, and his eyes drifted shut, for a moment only.

When he opened them again, he was sitting in his desk chair, shields closed, and heart at peace.

Well, he thought.

And spun his chair around to address his work screen.

III

SHAN CONSIDERED HIS SCHEDULE. PADI WAS DUE WITHIN the next minute for their trade discussions. After that, he needed, most urgently, to have a word with Dyoli ven'Deelin. After that—

The door chimed, and Padi entered at his call, note taker in one hand, and a scowl on her face.

"Good shift to you, Trader," he said, spinning his chair so that he faced her. "Did you have a pleasant off-shift?"

For a moment, she didn't answer, and he followed her gaze to the spot on his desk where the blue-and-green coaster had been accustomed to repose.

"It didn't come back," she said, her tone somewhere between irritated and disbelieving. "I was *certain* it would come back."

"Well," Shan said, extending a hand and placing it, palm down and fingers wide, in the very location, "at least it hasn't come back *yet*."

"Blast," Padi said comprehensively.

"Indeed, it must be a sad disappointment to all who wish it well."

She threw him a black look.

"The point is," she said, with exaggerated patience, "that we *don't know* where it *did* go. It might have hurt someone. It might have—it might have gone back to Ambassador Valeking!"

"That might be amusing," he offered, at the risk of yet another angry glance. "What do you suppose the odds are of it having actually struck her?"

"I don't know!" Padi answered, clearly frustrated, though her voice was quieter. The effect was of a subdued scream.

"I don't *know* where it went—or, really, how I sent it . . . wherever it went! I—could I have sent it back *in time*? What happens if Ambassador Valeking never gave you that coaster?"

"I think we can dismiss any concerns regarding temporal displacement. Even your Aunt Anthora can't charm time."

"But Uncle Ren Zel can," Padi said, her face rather pale. "Can't he?"

"No. Or rather—perhaps. Ren Zel has a certain affinity for the fabric of the universe and the energies that influence cause and effect. I believe that there is *not* a temporal element, save what may be bound up in the distances involved."

He extended a hand, showing her the empty chair, and when she had seated herself, he rose and walked across the room, taking his wine glass with him.

"What will you have to drink, Trader?"

"Cold tea, if you please."

He poured for both of them—the requested cold tea for her, ice water for himself—and carried the glasses back to the desk.

"Peace," he told the scowl that persisted on her face. "You probably threw the wretched thing into a sun, and if so, your instincts are most wonderfully appropriate."

She half-laughed. Sighed.

"It's only that it would be good to know—for certain. If I am *capable* of throwing something into a sun, then . . ." She sighed again, and sipped her tea.

"I would only like to know," she repeated.

"One should know one's own strength," Shan said softly. "I've spoken to Priscilla about the matter of the coaster, and you, of course, will bring it to Lina when next you meet with her. In the meanwhile, we have matters of trade before us. Tell me what you thought of *Wu and Fabricant's Guide to The Redlands.*"

"Useless," she said crisply.

Oh, dear, Shan thought, sipping water.

"Please continue, Trader," he said politely.

Padi considered him thoughtfully.

"The guidebook was published nearly three hundred Standards ago. At that time, The Redlands had not yet been engulfed by Dust. We are told that there are three planets in-system: Metlin, the scientific base; Ukarn, a mining operation; and Colemeno, agriculture and system administration. At the time the guidebook was written, Colemeno was the port planet, receiving goods from outside the system, and placing goods and information from its sister planets into the trade routes."

She paused.

Shan lifted an eyebrow.

She continued.

"All of this information predates the arrival of Dust in the Redland System. Not only has considerable time passed since the publication of the guidebook, but the Dust is only just now moving away. The Redlands—who can tell what has survived of The Redlands?"

"Ah! You suspect a descent into savagery!"

She frowned.

"I suspect," she said, more moderately than her frown would predict, "*changes*. The Redlands would have been thrown entirely onto their own resources once they were engulfed. It would not be wonderful if the scientific station had been closed, for instance."

"You don't think that Rostov's Dust is worthy of study?" Shan asked.

"I question the effect on the instruments," she said, "but I concede they may have found an answer to that, and continued as a scientific station. Likewise, the mining operations may have continued, but where would the ore go? The Dust would have cut off outside trade."

"Would it have done?" Shan asked, leaning forward. "Would it *necessarily* have cut off all trade?"

Padi's frown eased somewhat—perhaps it was surprise.

"As a pilot, you have surely seen Dust warnings. I've studied the calibration problems attached to Jumping into any large manifestation of Dust. As for bringing—well, the *Passage!*—into a Dust zone—"

"The Carresens Syndicate maintains a station at Edmonton Beacon, which rides the Dust. Or did."

Padi stared at him.

"Yes," she said slowly. "The Carresens operate *Hacienda Estrella*, serving family Loop ships, small freighters, and others who come out of the Dust. You think that The Redlands have a similar arrangement, trading with small shippers who can more easily navigate Dust conditions?"

"I am," Shan said modestly, "well-known to stand as an optimist."

She laughed, which was, he admitted, something of a relief.

"Though," he added pensively, "I have never actually *witnessed* a civilization descended into savagery. Perhaps that would be interesting."

"Between us, it sounds quite tedious," Padi said. "Plus, you know, we might be moved to *do something.*"

"Our besetting sin, yes. Are we then agreed that we will find three worlds doing well enough, and perhaps in need of what we can bring them, now that the Dust has released them to larger opportunity?"

"Yes, agreed."

"Excellent. We will therefore plan on putting in to Colemeno, where we will respectfully propose ourselves to Admin. Does this plan meet with your approval, Trader?"

"It does," she answered slowly, her mind perhaps on something else.

As if conscious of her lapse, she raised her eyes to his.

"Forgive me, Master Trader. I only wonder how we will choose, at Volmer?"

"You anticipate my next topic!" he said gaily. "Let us by all means consider between us what cargo we might usefully bring to The Redlands, not, perhaps, to answer any particular need, but to display the range available to us, while informing everyone we speak to that we are eager to learn what they most need, so that we may provide it to them."

Padi sat up straighter, and opened her note taker.

"I wrote down some things that occurred to me over breakfast," she said.

Shan leaned back in his chair and smiled.

"Did you? By all means, Trader, enlighten me."

IV

THE SHIP HAD BEEN GRACIOUS, DYOLI ACKNOWLEDGED, as she finished the meal she supposed must be her nuncheon.

She had been given medical attention; Healed, and prescribed a high-caloric diet. She had communed, briefly, with a goddess, and been granted her own quarters, with a door that locked from the outside, her rescuers not remotely resembling idiots. Her clothing was from ship's stores, so that she was clad as seemly as any ranking member of the ship's company, save there was no Tree-and-Dragon on the breast of her jacket.

Neither was there Ixin's Moon-and-Rabbit, and that—that was very nearly an omen.

Not that Dyoli ven'Deelin believed in omens. Not *as such*.

She believed in luck.

She believed in the power of the Code, both sorrow and joy.

And she believed in her own abilities.

They were not, granted, the abilities most valued in a child of Ixin. It had been a blow to her mother, when her heir had come Healer, but a blow only to the ego, as Dyoli was all too able to see.

There had been no need to mourn the loss of a trade-bred daughter to the *cha'dramliz*. Ixin did not lack for traders. Indeed, Til Den, her younger brother of the same mother, had stepped into the void created by Dyoli's departure for Healer Hall, achieving the garnet handily, and last seen, had been well along the path that ended at amethyst.

Dyoli finished her tea and put the cup on the tray.

Dutiful Passage had, among its other generosities, offered her use of the pinbeam, so that she might report her whereabouts and condition to her delm. Certainly, she ought to do something like, and soon; but she was . . . disinclined. What, after all, might she say to her delm, that would begin to make sense of—

The door chimed.

Dyoli rose from her chair.

"Who comes?" she called.

"Healer ven'Deelin, it is Shan yos'Galan. May I join you? I fear we have matters to discuss."

Matters to discuss, by the gods. Almost, Dyoli laughed. Instead, she composed her face, and said gently, "Please enter, Master Trader. Indeed, we have much to discuss."

"I wonder," Shan yos'Galan said, after they had done with the pleasantries, and she had assured him that she wanted for nothing—a polite mistruth—"I wonder how long it has been since you had news of home?"

Dyoli frowned. Truly, time had moved . . . oddly in the Mistress's care, and while she was in possession of this day's date on the homeworld, the precise date of her . . . recruitment eluded her.

"I believe on the order of two Standards; it may have been more, but not, I think, less."

"I see. I must give you information pertinent to your case," he said. "You will not, for instance, have heard that the Council has banished Korval from Liad."

Dyoli stared at him, strongly suspecting some attempt at humor.

His face was quite composed, however—all that was polite and well-bred—and she opened her Inner Eyes, meaning to be certain.

A shield met her Sight, supple and silver, and shimmering as if with some inner light.

She sighed, closed her Inner Eyes, and met his politely curious gaze.

"Forgive me," she said, her voice moderate, though her face was warm. "I had suspected a jest. Of course, you would not make light of such a thing. But you must allow my astonishment, sir. Korval banned from Liad? Has the Council run mad? For what imagined cause?"

"Yes," he said, "and yes, again. Aggression against the homeworld, which I must be the first to tell you is quite true. Merely the Council refused to entertain evidence that the act of aggression was brought against an enemy burrowed beneath the planet surface."

"And so the Council has run mad. I see."

"I am," he said, as gently as the High Tongue would allow him, "bound to say that, of course. I introduce the topic only so that you might understand why you must contact your delm immediately, and find a way off of this ship. Ixin will not want to be entangled in Korval's difficulties, or be seen to associate with us."

Dyoli shivered.

"Did Ixin . . ." she began, and caught herself on the edge of impropriety, raising a hand. "Your pardon. I do not need to know that."

Because so long as she did not know if Ixin had voted to expel Korval from Liad, she could remain an honored guest of an occasional trade ally.

She glanced aside, and he waited, allowing her time to think.

"I understand, I think, the relative positions of our clans," she said at last. "However, my personal situation is far from simple."

"I have spoken at some length with Master pai' Fortana," Shan yos'Galan said.

"Then you are informed."

She met his eyes.

"Master Trader, I would speak with my partner, so that we may plan together."

He considered her, and she braced herself. Lucks were despised and mistrusted on Liad. If Master Trader yos'Galan had spoken *at length* with Mar Tyn, he would not have failed to notice that the High House ven'Deelin claimed a partner who was plainly of the Low Port; a clanless rogue, as the High Port counted such things.

She considered the link that bound her to Mar Tyn, comforted to feel that he considered himself both well and well treated.

"Master pai'Fortana," Shan yos'Galan said at last, "admits a partnership, and a regard, forged in the fires of shared misfortune. He also allows me to know that your talents have an affinity for each other. That, in fact, they *mesh* into something which is neither Luck, nor Healing, nor Short-Sight, but something—else. Do I have that correctly?"

Dyoli blinked, taking a moment to master her surprise.

Mar Tyn had told Shan yos'Galan the secret of her second talent. Mar Tyn, therefore, trusted this man. That...was telling.

"Yes," she said. "We are...uniquely compatible."

"Given that this is the case, you will understand

my reluctance to allow such a meeting," he said. "I do not willingly—or, one hopes, at all—risk my ship, nor my kin, nor my crew."

"I understand," she said. "You may scan me, if you wish. Mar Tyn and I mean you and yours nothing but good. You saved our lives. We are in your debt."

"Luck," he said slowly—and raised a hand, as if he had heard her flicker of anger on Mar Tyn's behalf. "I mean no disrespect! Indeed, I *have* spoken with Master pai'Fortana, as has my associate, Lady Selph. We find him to be a very good sort of person. Merely, you know, I have some experience of luck, and I am aware that it moves to its own rhythms."

"Yes," Dyoli agreed, "and it is precisely on this point that I can reassure you. The affinity of our talents somewhat modifies the . . . random effects of both. In fact, there is less risk to the ship, if we are allowed to meet, than kept apart."

His eyebrows rose. "Is that so?" he murmured, and held his hand out to her.

She took it in hers, and felt a light, cool breeze pass over her soul.

After a moment, Shan yos'Galan slipped his hand away.

"That," he murmured, "is very interesting."

He rose.

"Pray humor me," he said, as she rose in her turn. "Be assured that you and Master pai'Fortana will be allowed to meet. I will, however, for my own peace of mind, put such arrangements in force as seem necessary, for the good of the ship."

"Thank you," Dyoli said. She bowed—respect and gratitude.

He turned to go, and, daughter of a trading clan that she was, she belatedly realized that she lacked one final important piece of information.

"Master Trader!"

He turned, eyebrows up.

"If you please, what is our next port of call?"

"Forgive me; I should have said immediately. Volmer is our next stop, Healer. Very soon now."

Tarona Rusk
Her Proper Business

· · · · · · · · · · · · · · · · ·

SHE HAD FINISHED WITH THE LAST OF HER PRIVATE BUSI-
ness, having learnt yet another lesson from Shan
yos'Galan. The last one . . . she had not the heart to
taunt her; found that she cared nothing for the other
woman's fear. Her death—oh, yes, there was nothing
for it but that Chona pel'Bisit should die. She had
earned death, many times over, but Tarona found it
in herself—that she cared more that Sub-Commander
pel'Bisit be prevented from performing any more
atrocities, than she cared about putting paid to those
committed in the past.

So it was that Chona pel'Bisit died in her sleep—an
aneurysm in the brain—and the universe was spared
any more of her particularly loathsome cruelties.

Surely, Tarona Rusk thought, ironically, the universe
was grateful.

In the meanwhile, she was wanted at Daglyte
Seam, the Commander's own base. Kethi vay'Elin had
called for her, and she admitted to a mild curiosity
as to what she might be wanted *for*. Possibly, Kethi

had seen the wisdom of eliminating the Commander, and wished Tarona to undertake the task. She would of course willingly murder the Commander, though this particular Commander had done much less evil than her predecessor, if only because she had been in the position for so short a time.

Kethi's belief was that the download had been incomplete, or that the vessel had been in some subtle way unfit. In any wise, it would seem a dire case; best for the universe, the Commander, and the woman the download had destroyed, if an end were made.

Indeed.

Her boots rang as she went up the gangway to her ship. The pilot admitted her, and she gave her instructions.

Then, she retired to her quarters, to review the remainder of her plans.

Dutiful Passage
Private Meeting Room

• • • • • • • • • • • • • •

THE ROOM WAS SMALL, MEANT FOR ONE-ON-ONE MEET-
ings, or partnered work. A table and two chairs filled
most of the available space. A modest tea had been
placed on the table—a pot, two cups, and a plate of
small sweet things.

Mar Tyn did not sit down at the table. Instead, he
ranged 'round it, ill at ease; wondering exactly what
he was doing here, and for whom that other cup and
plate had been provided.

He was wanted at a meeting—that was what the
security person who had brought him here had said.

As his gift made no protest, he followed where he
was led, and entered the room when the door was
opened for him, the first to arrive.

His talent remained quiescent, and he was encour-
aged by this, despite his uneasiness. It was true that
his talent was a small thing; Luck did not conquer all,
or even most, though it deflected much. And certainly
his gift was no proof against his own bodily harm.
It was likely the captain who was soon to arrive, or

perhaps the ship's Healer, whom Lady Selph had shown him during their small soiree. The Healer looked a sensible woman, even kind. Perhaps—

There came a distinct *thud*, as of someone throwing a bolt, and the light over the door snapped from red to green.

Mar Tyn spun to face the door, dancing two steps to the right, so that whoever entered would see him immediately, and made himself stand meek, round-shouldered, open-handed, and unthreatening.

The door opened, and his meeting partner came into the room.

His breath left him; his heart slammed into over-action. Despite Lady Selph's kind assurances, he had not—he had not *truly* believed that this moment would come.

Her face was thinner than it was meant to be, but radiant with good health; her pale red hair had been pulled back into its usual neat tail. Her light blue eyes were bright, her gaze unclouded. The ship had given her crew garb, rather than the sweater and slacks that had been found for him. That said something subtle about her *melant'i*, and his, but he had no inclination, just now, to parse *melant'i*.

"*Dyoli*," he breathed, as if his blood were not rushing, hot, in his ears.

Two steps and she was upon him, gripping his arms and looking into his eyes.

"Mar Tyn! You are well? Unhurt? Have they taken good care of you?"

"Peace, peace," he said, and did not laugh at her questions. There were few enough people in the universe who cared that Mar Tyn pai'Fortana was unhurt and well treated. Dyoli's concern was a warmth that he cuddled to himself, even as he made answer.

"I've been treated very well—exceedingly well, now that I have been provided with my last desire. *You* are well, I see, though badly in need of a meal."

"Bah! You sound like the medic. Let her have her way with me for a week and you'll see me round-faced once more."

"Then, I will be in the medic's debt," he said sincerely, and looked beyond her shoulder to the security person standing there.

"Sir?" he murmured.

"I am given to say that you may enjoy this space for an hour. It is monitored remotely. If you should require aid, say *assistance required*, and the system will send a member of ship security. The phrase for requesting additional food or drink is *catering please*, followed by a list of your needs. Should the temperature grow uncomfortable merely say *cool* or *warm* or *scent*."

"Thank you," Mar Tyn said.

"You are welcome," the man said. "I will return to guide Healer ven'Deelin and yourself to your quarters in one hour."

He bowed, and stepped back into the hall. The door closed; the light went to red, indicating that they were locked in.

Dyoli looked into his face, lips parted, as if she—well.

He slid away from her hands, drifting a bare step back.

"Mar Tyn?" she asked, but he spoke over her.

"Dyoli, the risk you took! My life is not worth half of yours!"

She froze, then her gaze flickered as she glanced

at the walls. Yes, he thought, seeing her understand:
The room was monitored; someone heard them or
could access the record of what they said.

More, he thought, if the room could deliver cool
air or a scent, it could deliver other, less amiable
things. Apparently, they were not...wholly trusted.
And why should they be? A captain did not dice with
her ship—and a Korval captain least of all.

"I had no choice," Dyoli was saying now, speaking,
as he had, for the shadows. "If there was the least
possibility that I would survive that...blow, your talent would bend it to our benefit. If I kept you alive,
the odds were that we both would live. Care only for
myself, and we both died."

She moved her shoulders.

"Or so I reasoned. It was a risky throw, Mar Tyn;
well I know it. But one uses the dice in-hand."

"And it came out well, you'll tell me."

"Well?" she answered, saucy. "Did it not?"

He sighed.

"Your point," he acknowledged. "We are not dead,
we stand together in good health and"—he moved his
hand, showing her the table—"there is food. Perhaps
you should have some tea, and a cookie—to please
the medic."

"Because my first purpose must be to please the
medic," she said crossly, but she did go to the table
and allowed him to seat her.

"Now," he said, after she had been persuaded to eat
two cookies and drink a cup of tea. "What's to do?"

"Very much is to do, my Mar Tyn. The Larger
Plan under which we labored while in the Mistress's

care bore fruit—Korval was cast out from Liad, their honor impugned."

"We had heard whispers of that, here and there, recall it?"

"Barely—what were whispers to us then? Now—*now* this becomes important, for Korval must have me off this ship quickly, with all propriety and honor, so as not to earn Ixin's frown."

She paused. Mar Tyn poured more tea into her cup.

"Where do they propose to put us off?" he asked, as if it were of no great importance, which, on the one hand, it was not, but—

"Our next port is Volmer," she said, watching him.

He moved his shoulders, the name of the largest hub in Clarion Trade Space meaning precisely nothing to him. But, there, Mar Tyn was not a trader.

"Volmer is a hub. It is advantageously situated in a busy sector, and along half-a-dozen well-established trade routes. It is said that all ships stop at Volmer—and that is closer to being true than most such maxims are. Ixin stops there, and Ixin's allies. Korval stops there, and Korval's allies. The Carresens stop there, and others of the Terran syndicates. The odds are—very much in favor of there being a ship at Volmer which will be pleased to succor me, and win the Rabbit's smile."

Mar Tyn sipped his tea, watching her.

"They will take you back to Liad, these allies?" he asked.

"Or to a port where they may meet an Ixin ship."

Dyoli was looking harassed. Mar Tyn considered pressing another cookie upon her, but decided that would only add to her stress. So far, he was hearing only good news. Dyoli would be returned to her clan, which would hold her safe and care for her. What more might a Luck in love ask for?

Across from him, Dyoli sighed.

"You don't ask where you come into this plan of Korval's," she noted.

"There's no need to plan for me," Mar Tyn said. "We claim partners. Korval will assume I go with you." He smiled at her. "And so I will, to a point. From what I hear you say, Volmer will suit me well."

She glared at him.

"You would remain at Volmer?"

"I believe I won't be given a choice, once we meet an ally of your House," he murmured. "I can provide no lineage, nor do I have skills that might make me acceptable as crew."

"I will insist that you are boarded with me," Dyoli said, stubborn.

Mar Tyn sighed to himself.

He had known that it would come to this, in those moments when he had been able to think of a life beyond the Mistress's care.

"And then? When we arrive on Liad, will you take me to the door of your clanhouse—the *front* door, Dyoli? How will your delm deal with that?"

It was harsh; he was not accustomed to taking that tone with her. She had depended on him, and he on her—and they had survived. Together. Now, it was time to part.

Truly, he had not thought to live long enough to arrive at this necessity, to be the one to force their parting.

"I would prefer," he said now, and softly, "not to return to Low Port. Volmer will suit me well enough."

Dyoli's lips were pale, but she met his eyes firmly.

"Our talents," she said. "Together, we are unique."

Mar Tyn looked aside.

This was worse than he had ever imagined. He was not a cruel man, despite having had ample opportunity to become one. And it was *Dyoli*, whom he would never willingly hurt.

Except to save her life.

He raised his eyes again and met hers.

"Will you tell your delm then—and the Healers—about your other talent?"

"For you," she said, "I will make the trade, and together we will transform Low Port."

He spared a thought for those monitoring this conversation, and shrugged. This was no plot against the ship, and he might find an ally in the yos'Galan, if these matters they told over were made known to him.

"Dyoli," he said urgently. "I cannot see you in Low Port." He did not make the mistake of thinking that she could not survive Low Port. He had seen what Dyoli ven'Deelin could survive.

"No," she said, quite firmly. "Nor will you see me there. We are not going to Liad."

There was *that* look on her face—that *particular* look. Mar Tyn slid his hand toward the center of the table, palm up, fingers gently curled.

"Tell me, then—where *will* we go?"

Dyoli put her hand in his, and he felt the crackle of connection along the strange pathways from which his luck operated. They were joined, and operating on reality in a way he tried not to think about too closely.

"We are going to Civilization," Dyoli said her voice ringing with certainty. "We are needed, and we can teach much."

"Civilization," Mar Tyn repeated. "And how will we arrive there?"

"This ship. This ship will take us."

"Will it? And what will convince the yos'Galan and the captain?"

Dyoli smiled, her face flushed.

"An Ixin ship will come into Volmer," she said. "Master Trader yos'Galan will send us to them."

Her eyes closed, and Mar Tyn felt the connection snap. Across the table, Dyoli sagged in her chair, but he was already out of his, kneeling, catching her as she slipped toward the floor, easing them both down and holding her in his arms.

She was asleep, her head on his shoulder, and he recalled what the yos'Galan had told him, that she had overspent her strength, and that he would need to be vigilant on her behalf.

Well.

He should, he thought, call out to their auditors, but it was a comfort to hold her, and he sensed nothing wrong aside from a profound weariness. He would hold her a moment more before he called, and take his comfort.

And trust that whatever they had done between them had been done well, and would cause no harm.

Volmer

· · · · · · ·

I

THEY WALKED, THE THREE OF THEM HAVING AGREED that it would be pleasant to stretch one's legs and to see what there was to see, which, on Volmer, was usually a great deal more than one could properly encompass in even three strolls from dock to Trade Bar.

This was not Padi's first time on Volmer, of course; one could scarcely trade without stopping at Volmer, even if only briefly. It was a hub, and more than that, it was used by some ships as a recreation stop, others for resupply, still others as a wayport. The trade at Volmer—there was that, just as there were ships that supplied her—but that was not, so Padi had always felt, the *point* of Volmer.

The plan for the day was that Trader Padi yos'Galan would accompany her master trader to the Trade Bar and be made known to Trader Janifer Carresens-Denobli. After introductions, Padi would take to the trading zones, with Karna as security, while Master Trader yos'Galan and Trader Carresens-Denobli sat together and discussed...whatever it was that they would discuss.

Padi and the master trader had talked at length
regarding the goods they might add to the inventory,
with The Redlands in their eye. They had done their
research, made lists, compared them, made new lists.
The venture was exploratory, but there was no reason
not to show courtesy and forethought.

While Padi was eager to be out and trading, she
regretted that she would not be attending the meeting. To be privileged to sit at the table and listen
to the discussions between Korval's master trader,
and a senior trader from one of the oldest and most
successful Terran Syndicates—*that* would be beyond
price. Who knew what she might learn?

On the other hand, to be wholly in charge of the
trade side while the master trader was in negotiations?
That spoke of a trust in her abilities and trade-sense
that could only gratify.

Perhaps the garnet was not so distant, after all.

"Here we are, my children," the master trader
announced. "Arrived in good time, with merry hearts!
Let us find what delights await us."

He swept through the doors into the main floor,
Padi on his right, Karna on his left and one step
behind, her head moving alertly.

Despite the fullness of the room, the master trader
appeared to be neither tallying the number of occu-
pants, nor keeping a particular eye out for familiar
faces or favored colleagues.

Indeed, he strode forward, deliberately visible,
more so even than a master trader's usual entrance
onto what amounted to his floor. It was as if Thodelm
yos'Galan had arrived, Padi thought—and corrected
herself immediately.

No. It was as if Thodelm yos'Galan *and* Master Trader yos'Galan had arrived at one and the same time. And together, they drew every eye. There could be no doubt that everyone in the Trade Bar was made aware of his arrival. Nor any doubt, but that he wished this to be the case.

Padi put her chin up and followed, making her own effort to be visible, though certainly she could not hope to eclipse the master.

They arrived at the counter. The master trader placed his finger on the bell. Padi glanced up at the board, seeing the names of ships she knew as well as those that she did not, and—there! There was the particular ship she had been hoping to find.

Nubella Run out of Tradedesk.

Senior Trader Janifer Carresens-Denobli's ship. Padi sighed quietly. It had been her secretly held concern the proposed meeting would be revealed as another strike against the *Passage*, but no. The meeting had been made in good faith.

She sighed again, gently, just as the barkeep arrived in response to the bell.

"Service, Trader?"

Master Trader yos'Galan beamed at her.

"Good-day to you. I am Shan yos'Galan, master trader on *Dutiful Passage*. I believe you are holding a meeting room key for me."

The nearby hubbub died, and Padi saw heads turn in their direction. Karna noticed, too, and gave the impression that she had straightened to a new height. Vanner, who had frequently been their on-port security, had done the same thing when he felt interest focused on his charges—a subtle reminder that there was security present, active, aware, and ready to answer any threat that was proposed.

Amazingly, the tactic usually served to divert interest—as it did now.

Curious faces turned away, voices took up their interrupted conversations, and the barkeeper spoke.

"Yes, Master Trader. Here is your key." She produced an iridescent metal card, and placed it in the transfer tray. "Shall you wish a guide?"

The master trader took the key in hand, glanced at it and bestowed a smile upon the barkeep.

"Thank you, but no. I am familiar with the facility."

"Very well, then, sir. On each floor, spin-side, there is an infobooth, in case need should arise."

"Thank you," the master trader said again, and turned from the counter. "Trader yos'Galan," he said. "With me, please."

"Sir," she murmured.

Together, they passed down the quiet room, Karna at their backs, Padi feeling the weight of speculative stares.

The lift stopped at the seventh floor, and the door opened briskly. Karna stepped into the hallway first. Over her shoulder, Padi saw the door of the lift opposite open. Two dark-haired traders in pale blue uniforms stepped into the hall, and paused, the elder, standing slightly to the fore, tipped his head gently to one side.

The master trader strode off the lift, stepping past Karna to the elder trader, sweeping out a big hand in a gesture that was, Padi thought, a sort of bow.

"They arrived together from their separate starts, and the hour-song had yet to die," he announced.

The trader laughed, and flung his hand out in precisely the same gesture.

"You know it! But what else! A good omen, yes? In poetry or in life-time."

"A good omen, indeed," the master trader said, with his true-smile. "Trader Denobli. Good-day to you."

"And to you, Master Trader yos'Galan. A fortunate meeting, though we should, I think, have met before. I see you have our key in hand. Please, admit—ah, but no, my wits! First, you must allow me the pleasure— here I bring to your attention my 'prentice, Vanz Carresens-Denobli, soon to wear the garnet!"

"I am gratified," the master trader said, and 'prentice Vanz did very well with a bow in the Liaden style, perfectly recognizable as honor to the master.

"Master Trader yos'Galan, I am honored," he said, face and voice displaying sincerity.

"Trader Carresens-Denobli, well met," the master trader said affably. "Good fortune to you in your pursuit of the garnet."

He moved a big hand, sweeping Padi forward with the sheer force of his personality.

"Allow me to enjoy presenting to you my 'prentice Padi yos'Galan, also soon to wear the garnet."

Padi bowed to the elder trader in the Terran style, fingers fluttering *well met* in the oldest dialect of Old Trade. "Trader Denobli, I have heard stories."

A shout of laughter greeted this.

"So, so. And we traders, we know what to make of stories! Hah! I am honored, Trader yos'Galan."

He paused and tipped his head once more.

Father moved a gentle hand.

"I bring Karna Tivit to your attention, Trader. She

stands an honored member of our ship's security team and will be accompanying Trader yos'Galan on her tour of the markets."

"Ah, prudence," said Trader Denobli, his face regretful—and in the next moment bright with animated good will.

"But wait! Do I hear that Trader yos'Galan will be enjoying Volmer's markets?"

"You do hear it," the master trader said solemnly.

"Then I must ask of Trader yos'Galan a boon. Perhaps she will not mind so very much to have another trader with her? For this is a splendid notion you have, Master Trader! Why should business wait upon us, when we are both assisted by very able traders who are each soon to wear the garnet! Let them walk the markets together and see to the necessary! It would be a fine thing, and generate happiness all around."

"I would be pleased to tour the markets with Trader Vanz," Padi said, giving him a smile, which he returned.

"I would welcome the opportunity," Trader Vanz said. "We can learn from each other."

"So! Master Trader yos'Galan, what say you?"

Master Trader yos'Galan inclined his head.

"I say that I wish the traders success in the markets."

"It is done, then!"

Trader Denobli turned to his 'prentice.

"You know everything that I know," he said with a weighty seriousness that Padi would have found suspicious in Father on such an occasion. "You know where we are bound; you know our inventory. You need no instruction from me. Go, Trader. Do well for the ship."

"Sir."

Trader Vanz faced Padi in turn, bowing very slightly, and gestured for her to proceed him.

"Trader."

"Certainly," said Padi, and moved to the lifts, Trader Vanz at her side, and Karna behind them. Padi pressed the button, the door opened, and the three of them entered.

The lift door closed.

"Now," said Trader Denobli, with an outright grin, "the key, Master Trader. Ply it well!"

· · · ·✷· · · ·

The room lights came on as they crossed the threshold. Shan put the key on the shelf by the door, and turned to survey the room. Trader Denobli walked toward the table, round in the traditional manner, then turned on his heel.

"Well, Master Trader, what *do* you think?" he asked.

"I think," Shan said with feeling, "that you are beyond me, Trader Denobli."

Black eyebrows rose in an expression of faint disbelief.

"This comes from the trader who sent me Theo Waitley, and her so very interesting ship?"

"Ah." Shan moved farther into the room, watching the other man's face. "The ship—I had not been . . . *certain* about the ship, you understand."

Janifer Carresens-Denobli raised both hands chesthigh, showing his empty palms.

"It happens that I understand this well. The ship—we have no claim on the ship, though longago captains were invested. In the hour of murder and treachery—if the ship had come to us, gladly we would have extended the protection of family. That was not the choice made. We honor the choice made by an individual acting to preserve their life."

"Which brings me to the subject of news," Shan said, approaching the table. "You are aware of the field judgment rendered by Scout Commander yos'Phelium, on behalf of the Independent Logics?"

Denobli smiled gently.

"Indeed, indeed. The Scout Commander's field judgment was the cause of much celebration in our family, and continues to make us all very happy. Our own *Disian*, of which there is nothing better in all the worlds, I am given to know, than to stand as *Disian*'s own captain, she is in a state of optimism. The family, we are more conservative, and we ask her to be happy—but to wait. She has, perhaps, agreed to this."

He paused, and cast a droll look.

"She has many friends, our *Disian*."

"It pleases me to hear that so many find happiness in the judgment—and especially that *Disian* is optimistic," Shan said sincerely. "I believe *Bechimo* and his captain share her happiness and her optimism. There are those among *Bechimo*'s crew, however, who are of a more . . . conservative nature."

"So, they are not without counsel. Good. That is good."

Another smile.

"And Scout Commander yos'Phelium—what a work he has made! What repercussions he produces, up and down the universe! It is his *Envidaria*, is it not? All is changed, in an instant. It is only left to do the work."

Surprised, Shan laughed.

"Yes, exactly! And who could complain? What are we here for, Trader, but for the work?"

"Precisely. And, as we find ourselves yet again of one mind, let us sit and consider the work. I have information for you, Master Trader."

"I had hoped so," Shan said. He unsealed his jacket and pulled out a pouch made of space leather. This, he put in the center of the table.

Trader Denobli took his jacket off, draping it over the back of a chair before he sat down. Shan followed suit. When he was seated, he put his hand flat on the pouch.

"I brought these," he murmured. "I was uncertain of custom, and thought it best to be prepared. If you have your own, or they are deemed not needed..."

He opened the pouch and allowed a few to spill out—glancing up when he heard the other man's sharp intake of breath.

"The *aequitas*?" Denobli whispered. "May I see them?"

"Certainly." Shan handed the pouch across the table.

The trader poured the polished rounds out with soft reverence, fingered them, weighed them, then gently returned them to the pouch.

"They are rare and beautiful. We have nothing like. I thank you for your generosity in allowing me to see them." He leaned back in his chair.

"As for custom—we teach them, and rarely we use them in trade. But for this—I think we have each the measure of the other, you and I, and very much to discuss. The coins might only slow us."

Shan inclined his head. "I agree," he said. "Though

I propose they may perform one traditional service, if you agree. Shall we draw to find who speaks first?"

Denobli smiled, and sat forward.

"Yes, it is a good thought. We will draw."

"Have you a specific quarter of the markets you wish to visit, Trader Denobli?" Padi asked as they came out onto the public way. Their passage together through the Trade Bar had generated an expanding circle of silence. She wasn't certain yet what to think of that, but she was glad of Karna's solid, professional presence just behind them.

"I would ask you to lead, Trader," the Denobli said, with a bow that was rather less precise than the one he had offered Father. "And I would also ask, Trader, if it is not an impertinence, that you allow yourself *Vanz*, or perhaps *Trader Vanz* more properly strikes the note. We are partners in this scheme of our elders, after all."

Padi turned to face him, seeing an honest, open, and earnest lad—an effect that a trader soon to achieve the garnet would find no challenge to produce.

On the other hand, this was a mission of good-will, as she had understood from the master trader, and certainly the tenor of the meeting between the two elders had approached, if not achieved, frank playfulness.

"I may allow Vanz," she said slowly, "but only if you may allow Padi, Trader. It is a question of Balance, you see."

Something flickered across his face, arriving as a smile.

"I do see, yes. I have no impropriety. Padi, I allow myself."

"Splendid, Vanz. We ought to move, I think, before those people in the window chairs fall over from the strain of pretending not to look at us."

"Lead us please, Padi," Vanz said, sweeping his hand out in a gesture that recalled the elder Trader Denobli.

"I to the textiles then," she said, turning in that direction.

"We'll see more interest as we move around the markets," Vanz said, somewhat gloomily, as they mounted the slideway. "It's what they wanted, I guess."

Padi slanted a glance at his face.

"Is it," she asked, "what they wanted?"

"It would have been easy enough to keep us apart— you to your trading and me to mine. It was a brainstorm on the trader's part; I've been with him long enough to know the signs. And *your* master picked right up on it. They want Tree-and-Dragon and Denobli seen walking together; trading together. It'll serve ... something. Maybe the trader will know by the time I ask him."

Padi swallowed her laugh.

"Is Trader Denobli your father?"

"No, worse! He's my mother's double-brother—from Carresens *and* Denobli! Great deeds are expected of me daily, if not by the hour."

He shook his head, and looked to her.

"The master trader—is *he* your father?"

"He is, indeed, and I am his heir. You understand, great deeds are not expected from me, for it is no great thing to achieve the amethyst, when *so many* others have done so."

Trader Vanz did *not* withhold his laugh.

"This other matter...of crew jackets on the port. The traders are here to negotiate, certainly. Possibly they wish a collaboration. But to send us out together before they even sit to talk? What if negotiation fails?"

"That's where the trader and his brainstorms play in," Vanz told her. "I have never known him to be wrong in a brainstorm."

"So, they not only both wish for the deal, they wish to make a...sensation...of the deal."

"My mother says that gossip makes the market."

Padi looked at him with interest.

"Does she? Our recent experience would be the opposite."

"Every coin has two sides," said Trader Vanz, who apparently had his quotations by heart.

Padi gave him an agreeable nod. "So we say, as well. Here is our ramp, I think."

. . . .❖. . . .

The draw had favored Trader Denobli, who appeared momentarily overcome by his good fortune. He sat, head bent, as if lost in admiration of the old token.

"Water?" Shan murmured, glancing to the tray.

"Of your kindness," Denobli replied, sounding nearly absent.

Shan poured and placed a goblet with ice chips gaily swimming by the trader's right hand, and another for himself.

Denobli looked up with a faint smile, reached to his glass and raised it.

"To a frank and profitable discussion," he said, which set the tone nicely.

Shan raised his own glass.

"To alliances," he answered.

Denobli smiled subtly—very nearly a Liaden smile—and nodded.

"Our thoughts run yet together. Good. That is good."

When they had sipped water and replaced their glasses, he leaned back in his chair and sighed.

"There are several points of discussion," he said. "In keeping with our shared thoughts and hopes, I bring you Hugglelans Galactica, Master Trader. You are aware?"

"I am aware that they have decided now is the time for a bold move of expansion," Shan said. "They see opportunity for themselves in the misfortune of others." He moved his shoulders. "It is a fact of trade that there is often profit to be found in the misfortune of others."

"These . . ." Denobli nodded at the pouch, "they would make a line between the risks of the trade, and manipulation of misfortune, would you say?"

"The *aequitas* are exacting," Shan admitted. "Perhaps the masters ought to make a push for their revival."

Denobli laughed.

"If you wish to go a-grailing, Master Trader, I am not the one to stop you."

"Should it come to that, I will welcome your support. For this moment, your point is good. There is a difference between seizing an opportunity created by market conditions, and manufacturing misfortune with an eye to profit.

"What I have heard from our agents is that Hugglelans walks a line. They have observed a third party being destructive, and have also placed a coin on that square. They have not, so far as I am made aware, initiated a wager."

"We," said Denobli slowly, "have seen otherwise, with sadness. With great sadness, I do not hide it. Myself, I have done business with Grandfather. We, the Family, have done business with certain others as well. Hugglelans was solid; we honored them. Occasionally, we made partnerships. Not often, for our routes cross rarely, but there was no question, when those crossings occurred.

"Now—a sadness, as I have said. The children— they do not honor their training. Or only they honor profit before their training, which Grandfather—I, a full trader, seated before you now, I tell you frankly that I tremble here in my chair, to even think what Grandfather would say to such things as we have observed."

He had recourse to his goblet, briefly looking as chastened as he had claimed. Shan waited, enjoying the skill of the storyteller, if not the story he told.

"Briefly, I will tell it briefly, sad as it is," Denobli said, pushing his glass aside. "Hugglelans Galactica has three times attempted to undercut us with Family. You understand that we, the Carresens-Denoblis, we have our yards and our suppliers—as does Tree-and-Dragon and—yes!—Hugglelans. Does our Syndicate approach the Hugglelans supply master and suggest that she will profit more by selling to us *first*, even before family—at a rate so slightly higher than Hugglelans insider rate? We do not! These support arrangements are in place—have been in place, for a long time, for reasons made by long-heads . . . and those reasons are still valid.

"Did we find only one Hugglelans supply master willing to accept our deal, and to subvert the chain for reason of short profit, the Hugglelans system trembles, a small route—not so important—crumbles. And what then, I ask you?"

"Once destabilized, the system continues to tremble and small routes continue to fail," Shan said, as if this were not a rhetorical question. "I have observed that it is far easier to destroy than it is to build."

"Yes, you understand it! Of course, you do. And do you know, I wager Hugglelans understands it, too."

"Yes," Shan said quietly, "I'm certain that they do."

"I grieve, I can tell you. Especially I grieve for Grandfather. These circumstances must distress her. Her honor is intact, but she will not see it so, I think."

Denobli sighed and shook his head, his gaze resting briefly on the pouch where the *aequitas* slept. He lifted his head and met Shan's eyes.

"You and I, we are traders," he said. "We may be sad, and grieve for lost honor, but we must not let sadness blind us to opportunity."

"Certainly not," Shan said.

"Our thoughts continue together, so I hear," said Denobli. "That is encouraging. If the *aequitas* allow, I would hear the master trader's voice."

Shan inclined his head.

"I, too, have several topics in my pocket," he said, and produced a wry smile. "I believe you are correct, Trader."

"Of course I am correct. In what way, this time?"

"We ought to have met sooner."

"Hah. Well, but we are now met. We may rectify."

"Do you say so? I wonder that we dare continue."

"Now you are playing with me, eh?"

"Never," Shan said, and raised a hand as if a sudden thought had occurred.

"A question, if I may, regarding your *Disian*."

That earned him a sharp glance before the trader folded his hands on the table.

"Ask," he said.

"Merely a matter of connections. You say that your *Disian* has many friends. This must make her very happy. I only wonder if one of her friends might be Tinsori Light."

Black eyebrows lifted.

"*That* one? It is a sad thing I must tell you, Master Trader. Nobody, so I hear it, is friends with Tinsori Light. It is perhaps happiness of a kind, as I also hear that he wishes no friends. Even our happy *Disian* might be made sad by Tinsori Light."

"Then I have good news for you, and for *Disian*. I am informed by my delm that Tinsori Light is now a Tree-and-Dragon station. The former unhappy person has ceded his position to Korval's daughter Tocohl Lorlin, who I believe to be someone of serious but generally pleasant disposition. It may be that your *Disian* will value her, to our Tocohl's benefit. She does have some friends to support her, but I feel certain that she would rejoice in more. She is quite new, to the universe as well as to her duties."

Denobli actually blinked.

"So, so. I will send word. Our *Disian* would be delighted, I think, to make the acquaintance of a station; and to one newly born, she can offer much helpful advice. Also, there is the matter of her other friends, who might also wish to befriend a station. I will exactly send word, Master Trader. And now that you have brought to me this, I wonder—"

"Yes?" Shan murmured.

"There was not only the difficulty of Tinsori Light being so unhappy a person. He was also, as I recall it, situated in a very strange place. Sometimes, he could not be found at all, though not many, understand me, sought him out. There were papers written, and piloting warnings issued, regarding the space around Tinsori Light. It was not, I think, the Dust—or not only the Dust—that made it chancy..."

"An anomaly in the fabric of the universe," Shan murmured. "I am informed that the condition has been repaired."

"Has it? That is welcome news, indeed. And, as our topic was opportunity..."

"Exactly," said Shan with a smile. "The station of course falls within my honor as Korval's master trader. My experience of administering stations is small, and I will need to sit with my charts, being unfamiliar with that section of space, and where we might look for custom.

"I wonder if one of the senior administrators from Tradedesk might be able to meet with me in consultation, at Tinsori Light."

"We might arrange; it is not impossible. But first, as you say, the charts."

"It is not an immediate project. My delm bids me attend to it at my earliest convenience."

"Do they say so? Well, then you have time to study and become fully informed."

"Exactly," said Shan, and frowned slightly, there was something, just there...

"Master Trader?"

"A moment," he murmured. "We are speaking of opportunity . . ."

"We were; I recall it."

"Yes, and it seems to me, Trader, that there is a flaw built into how we accomplish trade. While there is benefit in Loops, and in being expected—known ports and known goods—our predictability lays us open to the very mischief you were just discussing regarding the Hugglelans. Certainly, we have found it to be so."

He paused, allowing the thought to come to the fore. No snatching, no pushing, just—there.

"I wonder," he said slowly, teasing the idea into words. "I wonder if there isn't room for some collaboration between established traders. How, for instance, if a Carresens ship were to run part of a Tree-and-Dragon route, bearing its usual cargo, armed with the names of contacts in port, while a Tree-and-Dragon ship does turnabout with Carresens cargo . . ."

"Hah!" shouted Denobli, striking the table with his fist. "Who then will they file mischief against! I follow you. This is . . . unusual—exciting. Master Trader—let us explore this notion of yours more closely!"

· · · ❖ · · ·

"Delivery to *Dutiful Passage*, Canister Six-Nine-Oh-Two-South-Axis, name Trader Padi yos'Galan. That's paid in full. Here's your chit, Trader. Thank you for your business."

"Thank you," Padi answered, taking the chit and tucking it into her belt.

She turned to find that Vanz had already concluded his business with the vendor across the aisle and was awaiting her at the edge of the booth.

"Good trading?" she asked, as she and Karna joined him.

"It's possible that even my uncle will allow it to have been tolerable trading," he told her, with the wry grin she had come to understand was his irony indicator. *Some*one had done well for himself.

"Where now?" he asked.

"I am of a mind to visit this specialty shop the entire market has been talking about," she said.

"Madame Zoe's Whimsies?"

"Yes, exactly. She is said to stock *unusual* textiles."

"She is also said to be a very small vendor," Vanz pointed out.

"True. But that is, I think, in line with an artisan. We do well with art, and artisan, goods."

"Do you? We find art . . . difficult—except at the Festevalya. It would seem people buy art when they are festive, or the occasion is already special in some way."

"Well," Padi said, "we are hoping that our arrival at the next port will be a special time, so perhaps art fabric will do well."

"As you say, and as the trader often asks—though not expecting an answer, you know: How can we succeed, if we do not strive?"

Padi smiled.

"This is amusing?"

"It is—evocative," she said. "We say, Who will dare for me, if I do not dare for myself?"

He grinned.

"I hear it! Nearly alike, and not for the first time. Could Tree-and-Dragon and Carresens-Denobli be Dust-cousins?"

"Dust-cousins?"

"Kin separated by the movement of Dust, who rediscover each other when the Dust turns aside."

"Is that a . . . common occurrence?"

"In fiction, eh? And in plays. In real life—well. I guess it must have happened at least once, so everyone saw what a grand story it made."

Padi shook her head. "Tree-and-Dragon keeps close track of our bloodlines," she said. "Perhaps we are traders, and the trade has taught us similar lessons."

"That is more likely," Vanz agreed, producing a sigh. "But how unromantic!"

"I fear I may not be very romantic," Padi said. "It is entirely a failing of my own character."

"No, I don't allow you to have a failing. It is only exactly who you are, correct on your own terms."

He paused, then said, in a more serious tone, "May I ask a question? It bears on trade. If I am impertinent, I will withdraw."

"I hope you mean that you will withdraw the question, not that you will yourself leave me," Padi said, keeping her tone light. "I think that this notion of the elders has worked out very well, never mind *their* reasons. Being able to discuss various offerings with a colleague has been pleasant and useful."

"So it has! I think we have had good trade today, each complementing the other. I promise I won't withdraw from our company if my question is awkward, only that I'll withdraw the question."

"Fair enough, then," Padi said. "Ask."

"I wonder after your next port," Vanz said slowly. "I see you buying wide . . . but you are not buying deep. I wonder . . . well, I wonder *why*, there's the short of it."

He was a perceptive lad, Padi thought. Of course he was! Great things were expected of him, and he was 'prenticed to one of the major traders in the Syndicate.

The master trader had not given her any instructions regarding the limits of frankness, or if there was any secrecy surrounding their next port of call. She must therefore suppose that there were no secrets between herself and Trader Vanz.

"My master trader," she said, "is opening a long-dormant market. We are therefore bringing a wide range of goods, but as you notice, we are not deeply invested in any one offering. Once we have seen what is needed, talked to the merchants, and tested the markets, then we will know better what to bring on subsequent visits."

"Excitement!" said Vanz, his eyes sparkling. "We'll be reopening ports as well, with the Dust thinning in sectors we haven't seen in nearly a hundred Standards. I'll tell you that I'm very much looking forward! The Loops are well enough, and without the Loops how would we live? But to open what is essentially a new port? To discover what is needed, what is wanted, and engage to bring it? That will be exciting, yes!"

"Yes," Padi said. "It will be—exciting. I am looking forward to seeing my master trader at work, of course, but I also am anticipating this new port. What will they have on offer? What can we fulfill for them? How best can we get to know each other?"

Vanz sighed, smiled—and pointed.

"Here. Do you think this is your artisan?"

Padi followed the direction of his nod, finding a pavilion draped with silks; the entrance was narrow, and there was a length of ebony fabric hung from a rod at the top. A flag fluttered in an artificial breeze, teasing the eye with a pattern, until one had seen enough to realize that the pattern was, instead, a word: WHIMSIES.

"It certainly looks as if it might be," Padi said, feeling her expectations sharpen, for surely here was an artist in textile. She would, she warned herself, need to keep her wits about her, and to recall that she was not buying deep. For all and everything that she knew, the folk of The Redlands were wizards with silks, or they revered synth.

"Shall we?" Vanz asked.

"Of course," Padi answered.

"Together?" This with a mischievous glance she was beginning to know.

"Why not?"

The inside of the pavilion was strangely dim, with here and there a spotlight on an artfully tumbled avalanche of silk; a heavy banner woven from some oily, dark thread, that gave back pure gold where the light struck; a gay tail of ribbons, fluttering before an air vent, changing colors as they moved.

So much were they allowed to see. Six steps into the shop, Padi stopped. The displays were admirable, and she admired them, but the rest—

"Ah, is it too dim?" came a languid voice from deep in the darkness. "Forgive, Traders, forgive. Too much light and I am blind. Too little light and you are. I cannot seem to achieve a level that is well for all. Here, now let us see if this will do..."

The light brightened slowly, like a compact, slightly blue sun rising. Padi blinked as display racks dripping with textiles began to glitter and beckon under the caress of the light.

"Tell me, does it yet offend?"

"Thank you," Vanz said from slightly ahead of Padi, "it's just right now."

The corner from which the voice had emanated was still darker than the rest of the shop, but some portion of the darkness moved and separated itself, resolving into a bipedal form draped in dull black. A long silver braid fell, gleaming, across one bulky shoulder.

Her face was pale and pointed, her eyes very large and very dark.

"Greetings, Traders. I am Madame Zoe," she said, her eyes on Vanz. "How may I assist you?"

"We were told of your shop in the textile quarter," Padi said when Vanz said nothing, "and knew that we must do ourselves the honor of visiting."

Madame Zoe turned her head, the large black eyes focusing—or so Padi thought—on her.

"And so we are all honored. Please, Trader, look at your will. If you have questions, I will do my humble best to answer. My fabrics are unique. They have been treated with my special dyes and emulsions. You will find them irresistible."

Irresistible? Padi frowned, and moved to the right to inspect a jumble of what might have been scarves. Madame Zoe apparently felt that her wares showed better in disarray than in tidy rolls or folds or bundles. Padi, considering the display, thought she might have a point, but such showmanship made it more difficult to understand what one was seeing.

She moved closer, wanting to get her hand on a bit

of that silk, to feel the texture of the cloth, to test the weight of the dye, to...

There was an...aroma. A scent.

Padi sniffed absently. Had the silk been treated with perfume, too? That would be unfortunate. Scent was so individual. What was sweet bliss to one was a dreadful stink to—

She stopped, her hand extended, and licked her lips. She recognized the scent now.

Vya.

No wonder Madame Zoe's goods were irresistible.

Padi turned on her heel, half expecting to bump into Karna—but her security was not at her back.

Karna was standing by a table piled with bright tapestry, her hands buried wrist deep.

Padi strode over.

"Security, attend me!" she snapped, with all the force she could put into the Command mode.

It was enough—just.

Karna jerked to attention, blinking.

"Trader?" she gasped. "I—"

"Remove your hand from those textiles and attend me!" Padi snapped, going with what had worked.

Karna did as she was told, though her fingers lingered on the last bit of fringe.

When Padi was certain of her, she turned to look for Vanz.

And swallowed.

Madame Zoe was standing under a fall of sapphire light, and her formerly impenetrably black robes were now...transparent, putting her on full display.

Vanz was, apparently, entranced by the view, oblivious to everything else.

"You like what you see, eh?" Madame Zoe was crooning. "I am irresistible, am I not?"

"Irresistible," Vanz repeated, but not, Padi thought, like he . . . entirely . . . believed it.

Madame smiled and leaned forward slightly.

"Tell me your name."

Have they taught you yet, Lute whispered in memory, *that names are to conjure by?*

Vanz licked his lips. One boot shifted against the floor, as if he were trying to move aside. Madame's eyes narrowed; she raised a hand.

Padi's vision twisted, showing her a silver cat, paw up, claws out, looming over a cowering mouse.

She caught her breath, and stamped forward.

. . . to conjure by.

"Vanz! It's time to go! We must meet your uncle!"

It was an enormous breach to speak to an equal in Command mode, but it would be an even greater breach if she left a Denobli trader in the hands of a . . . an unscrupulous person.

Vanz's shoulder twitched. He turned his head—and Madame Zoe flung her raised hand out, toward Padi.

The air crackled; Padi staggered, her vision greying under the sudden stabbing pain of a headache. She caught her stumbling feet with a move out of *daibri'at* and thrust herself forward.

"Vanz!" she snapped again, and grabbed his arm. She felt a frisson; he gasped, leaning just the slightest bit toward her.

She pressed her advantage.

"Your uncle!" she snarled. "We don't dare keep him waiting! You remember what happened last time!"

"Don't I just, just remember what happened last

time," he stammered, his voice shaking, but he was moving—he was moving *with* her.

"Vanz, come here to me," Madame said calmly.

Padi shivered; Vanz groaned softly, but he kept moving, with her, toward the door.

"Don't let go," he muttered, and Padi kept her grip on his arm.

They made it to the door, out of the pavilion, and into the market proper. Padi guided them down the aisle and around the corner. Vanz was shivering, but he kept her pace, pressed close to her side. On her other side Karna walked, silent.

"Karna," Padi said. "Status?"

"I'm able, Trader."

"Good. There's a tea shop," Padi said, seeing the sign glowing halfway down the aisle. "We'll stop there and take stock."

"Too close," Karna said. "If Trader Denobli is able, it would be best to keep moving to a known quarter."

"Vanz?"

"Security's advice is good," he answered, his voice unsteady.

"We go on then," Padi said.

• • • ☼ • • •

"So that, for the business managers," said Denobli, sitting back in his chair and smiling at the shared work screen with an air of satisfaction. "There will be astonishment, I predict."

Shan smiled. He was pleased; he was exhilarated; he was, just a bit, weary. They had done good work at their round table already, and he was confident that they would do even more before this day was out. Really, it had been too long since he had met an equal in trade. Trader Denobli was not audacious. Not *particularly* audacious. Merely, he did not recognize the boundary between possible and impossible. It was a trait that made for stimulating conversation.

"How long shall we tarry at station?" Shan asked now. "Agents need time to work."

"As do traders! So we have made it that agents know where and how to find us, eh? Between us we have built a strong outline. Our intentions are clear, and we have given thought to which routes may bear the test. It would amaze me, Master Trader, to learn that our agents would discover any difficulties in marshaling mere details."

"Very true," Shan said, reaching for his glass.

"Are you well, Master Trader?" Denobli's voice lacked its usual note of slightly mad exuberance.

Shan glanced at him, eyebrow up.

The other trader raised his hands, showing empty palms.

"I mean no offense. Word had reached us of the attack at Langlast. Gossip has it that you were injured—not slightly."

"Ah. No offense taken. I am moderately well, and continue to recover myself. Slowly. Which is maddening. I believe we may find ourselves as one mind on this topic, as well."

"Do we not! What is this *rest* that the medics are so much invested in!"

Shan smiled. "Exactly." He put his glass aside, and inclined his head. "I wonder if I might speak to you, frankly, regarding our next port of call."

Denobli cast him a reproachful glance.

"Master Trader, you must know that I am eaten up by curiosity on the subject of your next port. Trader yos'Galan shops the market of Volmer—ably and with a true eye, I make no doubt! But—Volmer? Everyone stops at Volmer. There may be finds, but are they worth the profit?"

"Who can know, when you have your eye on a port at the new edge of the Dust?"

Denobli looked thoughtful.

"We ourselves maintain a station at Edmonton Beacon," he said. "At Dust-edge."

"I have heard this," Shan assured him solemnly. "Which is why I particularly wish to hear your opinion of The Redlands."

"Hah! The Redlands, is it?"

He sat, eyes narrowed, perhaps studying the table-top, though Shan rather thought not.

"The Redlands...we have not much seen," Denobli said slowly. "I will tell you that some who are newly emerged feel no need to rejoin the universe in any way. Some are thirsty—parched!—for news. Others are shy, they need to be wooed, to be shown the benefits of trade and the distribution of goods and ideas. The Redlands..."

He sighed.

"The Redlands were...difficult before Dust came between them and everything else. In truth, they have not sent word to the universe, though the Dust has been spinning away from them for some years. It may be—I tell you frankly—it may be that they will not want you, Master Trader, no matter how sweetly you woo."

"That is always possible," Shan said. "It is also

possible that they are simply awaiting a particular suitor."

"True. How, if another trader might ask it, did you hit upon The Redlands?"

Shan hesitated, and into that hesitation came a sharp three-toned chime.

He snatched at the comm on his belt, met Denobli's eyes, said, "Security call," and into the comm, "yos'Galan."

· · · · ❖ · · · ·

"Do not, I beg you, let me go," Vanz whispered.

"I swear it. Not until we find your uncle or your ship. Tell me which."

"Uncle."

"At the Trade Bar," Padi said, to be certain he understood.

"No! Gods . . ." He shivered again.

"Karna," Padi said sharply. "How do you go on?"

"I'm able, Trader. I have a headache from the *vya*. But Trader Denobli was getting special attention, I think."

"Yes. Call . . ." She hesitated. It was no small thing to disturb the master trader at his work, and such work as he undertook with the Denobli—it was scarcely to be thought of. And yet Vanz—it might well be Vanz's life in play.

"Call the master trader," she said to Karna. "Give him our location; tell him we have a situation and require an immediate meeting, himself and Trader Denobli, at a discreet location."

"Yes, Trader."

"Trader," Vanz whispered.

"It is Padi, had we not agreed? What may I do for your comfort?"

"Do not let me go."

"Not until your uncle takes you into his care. I swear it, on my honor and Korval's."

He was shivering still, but she *felt* relief wash through him.

"Padi," he murmured. "This was not your blame. I know it. Security Karna knows it. My uncle will know it, from my lips. You—*you* should know it."

"I—"

"It was a setup," Karna said from behind them, her voice clipped. "The master trader directs us to Finley's Corner Bar, three aisles to spinward. We're to ask for Charlie."

"Yes," said Padi. "Vanz. Do you hear?"

"I hear."

"Tell me true, can you manage the walk? Shall I call for a chair?"

"No! I can walk. I *will* walk. Only hold me, Padi. Do *not* let me go. I—there is something, pulling..."

Padi swallowed, remembering the strike against her head—

No, she thought suddenly. Against her *shields*.

"I understand," she said. "Come. Let us to Charlie."

Vanz's shivering became acute, and his pace began to drag, the more hallways they put between themselves and Madame Zoe's Whimsies. Padi began to think that they might need a chair, after all, when Karna stepped to the trader's other side and slipped her arm through his.

"Merry we go, eh, Traders?" she said, looking far more grim than merry.

"M-Merry wanderers of the port are we," Vanz quavered, not at all on-key.

"That's the ticket," Karna said approvingly, and capped his line, her singing voice unexpectedly fine.

Padi did her bit with humming, being unsure of all the words, and by holding onto Vanz's arm until it seemed a good possibility that she might break it.

But, there, at last: FINLEY'S CORNER BAR glowed in friendly amber letters at the far end of the aisle they had just entered. Padi dared increase their pace, fairly pushing Vanz along, and Karna pulling, and there at last the door, opening as they approached into a dim, crowded, and noisy foyer. Stepping out of the crowd toward them was a tall Terran woman in a pair of clean, but well-worn coveralls, sporting a breast tag that read "Charlie."

She stopped close to them, her smile at once rueful and fond.

"There you are! Your party's waiting for you."

Padi hauled Vanz with her to Charlie's side.

"Are we terribly late?" she asked.

"I don't think you've crossed into *terribly*, yet," the woman told her, maneuvering them deftly out of the foyer and down a modestly lit hallway, "though you're definitely into worrisome."

The babble of voices faded behind them, and Charlie spoke again, her voice lower.

"Are there special requirements? We've got a medic on site."

"We will know better after we've joined our party," Padi said. "May we call?"

"Sure thing. There's a panic button in the booth. Here we are."

She swung sideways, and put her hand against the doorjamb. The door opened, and Padi pushed Vanz in ahead of her, still keeping a grip on his arm. Karna came after, and the door slid shut behind her.

Father and Trader Denobli were seated at a table laid and provisioned for nuncheon, both wearing trade-faces, waiting.

"Uncle!" Vanz said. "I'm struck."

"I see it," Trader Denobli said easily. "Come, sit, and tell me."

"Yes," Vanz said, shuffling forward a step. Padi loosened her grip—and his hand flashed out, fingers tightening around her wrist.

"Padi, don't let me go!"

"No, I won't," she said softly, and held his arm firmly while he moved to the bench and sat next to his uncle, she on his other side, facing Father, who pierced her with a look, eyebrows up.

"I'm all right," she said, to the eyebrows, and added, "I think."

"Your ability to soothe a father's fears is remarkable," he commented, and looked beyond her.

"Karna, have you taken harm?"

"No, sir. Just a headache."

"From what cause?"

"Breathing in too much *vya.*"

"So? You will please apply to Charlie for a medic. When you are cleared, you will have a meal in the staff room, and wait for us to call."

"Yes, sir."

Karna turned, pushed the call button, and then triggered the door, stepping out into the hallway.

"Now," said Trader Denobli, who had one arm

around Vanz's shoulders, and was leaning in, close and comfortable as kin. "If Trader yos'Galan will be so good as to tell us what happened?"

Padi told the story down, as neatly as she was able. During her discourse, a handwich was set on a plate before her, and a glass of lemonade. She ate and drank, one-handed, finding that she was hungry. Vanz turned his face from food and lemonade, though he thirstily drank two glasses of water.

"We left, quickly, and called in aid, whereupon you find us here," she finished.

"It was a setup," Vanz said, his voice stronger now, though the arm Padi still gripped continued to tremble. "Several of the vendors on-market described Madame Zoe's Whimsies as a specialties shop that couldn't be missed, which is how we happened to arrive there."

"The names of these so-helpful vendors?" Trader Denobli said.

Padi stared at him, her mind a blank, then reached into her belt, pulling out her receipt chip.

"They will be on here," she said. "Your pardon, Trader."

"It is a small thing," he assured her. "We will look later. And it may be that Madame Zoe will be helpful, in her turn."

"If she's still there," Vanz muttered.

"Do you think she won't be?" his uncle asked with interest.

"I think it possible that she'll remove herself."

"Hah. But such a shop, so prettily made; and the scent—the *vya*—it will linger. It is equally possible that she will brazen it out. Now, this fear that you will seek the shop, or the lady, if left alone. From what is this born?"

"From the drag against my center, and the conviction that I must return, now, immediately."

"And you would obey this urging?"

"I fear so, Uncle."

Trader Denobli sat quiet. Father spoke.

"I may be able to rectify this problem. At the very least, I may make an examination and provide a comprehensive report of the damage."

Padi ... didn't gasp. Didn't *quite* gasp, but Trader Denobli was perceptive. He turned to her.

"It will be dangerous for the master trader, this rectification?"

Padi met his eyes.

"Not if he will accept my assistance," she said, suddenly seeing—suddenly *knowing*—how this could be made to work without exhausting Father utterly, and with the best chance of Healing Vanz now, before this—*compulsion*—took any deeper hold upon him.

She turned to look at Father.

He sighed.

"They grow up," he said to Trader Denobli.

"They do, and we should not impede it, though we know it's possible that they will not always be perfectly happy."

"It's both of us in the soup, then," Father said, looking back to her.

She nodded.

"I've been in the soup before," she said, "though I realize it will be a new experience for you."

Father laughed.

"Wretch. Very well, Padi yos'Galan; I accept your

assistance. Pray do *not* open your shields until I ask you to do so. I will be making several preliminary examinations."

"Yes, sir."

"Now, she finds her manners," he murmured, and she was about to make answer, but he had already turned his attention to Vanz.

"Trader, I am a Healer. I believe that I may repair or, at the very least, mitigate this trouble that afflicts you. In order to test this proposition, I must have your permission to proceed. Will you allow me to examine you, and give you what ease I may?"

Vanz took a hard breath.

"Yes. Please, sir. Make it stop."

"I will endeavor to do so. First, I will examine Padi, as she was struck also, but reports no ill effects. We all wish to be certain that there *are* no ill effects. A moment only..."

He turned to Padi, his eyes holding hers. She took a breath, feeling as if she were floating, and time seemed suddenly to stop. Into this period of timelessness, Father spoke.

"Janifer."

"Shan?"

"You will please call whomever you know in station security. There is a very powerful *dramliza* on this station. She is enslaving the unwary, and she has attempted at least one murder during this station-day."

"What?" Padi said, shaking her head. "How—"

"I go now to do this thing," Trader Denobli stated. "Vanz—"

"Padi has promised not to let me go," Vanz said. "Quickly, Uncle. That person is dangerous."

"Yes."

He was gone on the word, the door snapping shut behind him.

"Murder?" Padi demanded.

"*Attempted* murder. I know you have lamented your shields, child, but anything less would not have stopped the blow you were delivered. As it is, I can see the image of the strike on your shields, and fissures in the fabric. Had Madame been given the opportunity for a second blow, she may well have killed you."

He took a breath, and inclined his head.

"Well done, Padi. Now, let us continue."

He turned his attention to Vanz.

"What is your name, Trader?" he asked gently.

"Vanz Carresens-Denobli, sir."

"How would you prefer me to name you?"

"Vanz, please, sir."

"Vanz, my name is Shan. As we have discussed, it is probable that you have had a compulsion placed upon you. I See that you are distressed by this event, as you should be—but you have had some very good luck. The person who sought to control you was interrupted before she could do very much more than begin her work—I can See that it is unfinished—and that what she did accomplish is less than two hours old. This means I will be able to remove it with relative ease.

"I am going to tell you what I will do, so that there are no surprises.

"In a few minutes, you and I will seem to meet in a very peculiar place, filled with soft fog. I find it a pleasant space, and soothing. I hope that you will also find it so. Once we are together in this space, I will remove the compulsion from you. Nothing I do

ought to hurt you or frighten you. If you are hurt
or feel threatened, you will tell me so *at once*, and
I will stop.

"Do you understand?"

"Yes, sir."

"Good. There is one more thing that I must ask,
before we begin. Do you wish to remember this incident? I am able to . . . allow you to forget, if you wish."

"Forget—no! No, sir. I can't forget this. We need
to be able to *tell* people."

"Very well, then. As soon as your uncle returns—"

As if on cue, the door opened to admit Trader
Denobli, face somber. He resumed the seat next to
Vanz, and again put his arm around the younger
man's shoulders.

"Events move," he said to Father, who inclined
his head.

"That is well. We are about to begin here. I have
explained the process and discussed the outcomes with
Vanz. He has chosen to remember what transpired with
Madame Zoe. My part is therefore limited to removing the compulsion which has been laid upon him."

Trader Denobli inclined his head.

"I understand that you will follow Vanz's wishes.
What is my part?"

Father smiled at him.

"Your part is to watch and call for help in the
unlikely event that one of us seems imperiled. You
will also deal with the outside world should someone
knock on the door. We three will be . . . elsewhere for
a time."

"Does the time have a distance?"

"One minute beyond a full hour is too long."

"Understood."

Father extended his hand, and met her eyes with a smile.

"Your part, Padi, will be to open your shields, and accept what comes. I will require also your hand, and your very good will."

"Yes, sir."

She took a deep breath and imagined flinging the heavy, rough panels of her shields open, felt a warmth like sunlight, and a crescendo of what might have been music, fading, as she put her hand in his.

"Freely given," she said, and smiled.

Father's hand was warm, his grip firm and comforting. Padi sighed, content, glanced down at their linked hands, and blinked.

Surely, she could *not* be seeing their linked hands wrapped in silver threads? And yet, she *did* see that, so plainly that she looked to Trader Denobli, to find if he also saw—but Trader Denobli was watching Vanz's face, his expression tender.

Padi looked down again. The lines bound her to Father, and then led—somewhere. She couldn't quite follow where they went, after they passed the point of her fingertips. She squinted; the thread blurred . . . and blurred again, into a soft fog, faintly pink, and there just before her were Father and Vanz, their hands on each other's shoulders.

Between them, the fog boiled, thick and silver-shot. Padi brought her attention closely to that space. A . . . diagram . . . no, an artwork . . . a tapestry . . . a . . .

It was Vanz, she realized abruptly. Vanz as she might have seen him with her Inner Sight. She focused more tightly still, and heard a sharp *snap*. She blinked, feeling Father standing quite close beside her.

"Ah, there you are," he said. "Attend now, child; I will do and you will watch."

Before her, the tapestry continued building out of the fog, a thing of heartbreaking complexity, bright and potent. There were, Padi saw, a few dark threads, but for the most, it was brilliant, focused, cleanly, and sane.

"Splendid," she heard Father say, and then, "Now, what have we here?"

It was a flower, Padi thought—a delicate, dark bloom, exotic. Padi felt its allure, even through the cushioning fog, and she also felt that it was incomplete, that there ought to have been many more than one single set of petals. That the mature flower would be so endlessly fascinating that one could happily lose oneself forever within its pattern.

"And that," Father murmured, "is precisely how Madame operated. She ensnared the vulnerable into an eternal meditation upon her construct, whereupon she might access their will, and motivate them to accomplish any deed or task. This, my child, is unethical. Now, attend."

Her attention sharpened on the weaving that was Vanz, his heart, his soul . . . There, the ebon flower, incomplete, ineptly twisted around half-a-dozen thick bright strands. A second glance revealed rather that the placement of the flower was no accident, and that the seeming ineptness was rather a subtle hand at weaving. The threads entangled by the alien flower felt strongly of honor, love, conscience, purpose . . . and Padi felt her stomach clench. If Madame had finished her construct, it would have required a master, or two, to address it, and even then, they would only have pruned it, leaving some of the Other within Vanz's pattern. Cutting it entirely away held the very real possibility of killing Vanz, though someone who thought himself Vanz would still continue.

"So we see that the lady has skill, for these knots are firm. But they have not cut into the threads that they are intended to replace. The compulsion is woven into the base pattern, as insurance against this very eventuality—if a victim slipped away before the weaving was complete, they would—they must—return to Madame, whereupon she would finish what she had begun.

"If we beheld the entire construct, we would see that the first threads placed would have grafted themselves onto the threads natural to the pattern, and strangled them. If it had gone so far as that, it would have been beyond any repair I might effect. This, however..."

The fog stopped its boiling; the tapestry was revealed in its entirety, the black flower a...blot, a...wrongness...

"Vanz," Father said, "I am going to remove the compulsion that has been set upon you. This will not hurt. Indeed, you may feel a pleasant warmth, a lassitude..."

The fog swirled lightly around Vanz, who smiled slightly.

"This is a delightful place."

"It is, I agree. One moment only..."

From the depths of the fog came a knife, its thin blade the very ideal of *sharp*. It slid along the surface of the tapestry, steady and sure. The black flower fell away, melting into the fog, which flared—and began to disperse.

"We are done here," she heard Father say. "Let us return, all three."

Padi blinked, and looked down. She was still holding Father's hand, but there were no glowing threads binding them.

"Ah!"

She turned her head, and met Vanz's eyes. He smiled.

"You can let me go now, Padi."

II
Sosacilli

TIL DEN VEN'DEELIN WAS EATING BREAKFAST AT HIS DESK, vanquishing the last bit of paperwork that stood between him and a proper leave, when the comm gave tongue to the particular tone that indicated receipt of a high-priority communication.

Of course, he thought, crankily.

Cup at his lips, he spun to the screen—and choked, having inhaled a mouthful of hot tea.

The high-priority message was from Master Trader Shan yos'Galan, *Dutiful Passage*.

Recovering his breath, and his wits, Til Den ven'Deelin looked at the screen again.

Master Trader Shan yos'Galan, Dutiful Passage.

One could wonder what Master Trader Shan yos'Galan might want of new-made master Til Den ven'Deelin, but it wasn't likely an invitation to tea.

Or not *only* an invitation to tea.

He reached to the screen, the light glinting sharply off the edges of the amethyst, and tapped the letter open.

On the matter of Dyoli ven'Deelin.

Til Den blinked again.

Dyoli? What in the name of the gods—Dyoli had been missing for every minute of three Standards. The delm, to the best of Til Den's knowledge, would not declare her dead until the traditional six Standards had passed, but it was believed within the family that Dyoli his sister was dead.

He had himself subscribed to that melancholy theory, but now, here—*On the matter of Dyoli ven'Deelin.*

Had yos'Galan *found* his sister?

Breathless, he read the letter—read it again...

Dyoli ven'Deelin and her companion... in distress... Pommierport—Pommierport? Whatever had Dyoli been doing on Pommierport?—*would he see to their proper care?*

See to her proper care? His favorite sister? What else did yos'Galan imagine that he might do?

He snatched open a reply screen and typed, rapidly.

III
Dutiful Passage

PRISCILLA SAT UP, AND LOOKED TO THE CONSOLE ACROSS the darkened room. It was halfway through her sleep shift; and the console was dark. Whatever had wakened her, it had not been the ping of an incoming comm call, nor any sort of alarm.

No . . .

What had waked her was—Shan.

She opened her Inner Eyes; the links they shared were blazing bright, Shan himself a lambent presence.

"No . . ." she whispered, for he could not, in his present state, have conjured so much power save by burning his very life.

Horror melted in the brilliance of his will; she had already flung herself as wide as she could, reading the flow of power, finding another silver-charged presence, quiescent, but burning bright. Priscilla placed her attention on that second presence, finding with a certain amount of relief that it was Padi, open, quiescent; allowing what really must be a modest draw upon her considerable resources.

What in the name of the Goddess had transpired to put them both at peril, linked, and working . . . working . . .

She focused on Shan, drawing closer, until she felt the fogs of Healspace swirling nearby. A Healing. An *emergency* Healing, given the suddenness, the deliberate disregard of plain common sense, and the best health of both.

Priscilla flung back the blankets and stood, pulling on a robe as she crossed to the console.

"Tower. Service, Captain?"

"Please patch me through to Karna Tivit, Tower."

IV
Finley's Corner Bar

AT LEAST, THEY HAD ALL HAD SOMETHING TO EAT BEFORE Volmer Security arrived with a request that Trader Padi yos'Galan and Trader Vanz Carresens-Denobli come with them to lay personal evidence against Zoe Martenegsburg, registered deck-holder and licensed vendor of Volmer.

There was a small silence before the elder Trader Carresens-Denobli spoke.

"The vendor stands accused of mind control. My 'prentice is dear to me, so I ask—how is she held harmless?"

"We have enlisted the services of the Blades of the Goddess, a registered mercenary unit certified by the adepts of Chaliceworks," said the guard with the two white stripes on her dark blue sleeve. "They have the skills to hold one possessing the abilities Zoe Martenegsburg has been accused of abusing."

Father tipped his head, but said nothing.

Trader Denobli actively frowned.

"I have heard rumors of this company," he said slowly, and Padi noted that he refrained from passing on dockside gossip. Instead, he rose, and Vanz with him. "This trader is both my blood-kin and my 'prentice. I accompany him."

"Of course," said the two-striper, and turned her attention to Padi.

"Trader Padi yos'Galan."

Padi sighed and rose, and Father rose as well.

"I fear you find a like situation in us," he said to the guard. "The trader is my 'prentice and blood-kin. I will accompany her."

"Of course," the guard said again, and stood aside to allow them, one by one, to exit the booth.

Karna rose when they entered the waiting room outside of the Community Standards Hearing Room.

"Master Trader," she said, approaching them. "Captain Mendoza called, sir, to ask if reinforcements are required."

Father looked faintly amused.

"How very good of Captain Mendoza," he said brightly. "Did you assure her that we are quite complete in ourselves?"

"Not in those exact words, sir. I gave her a précis. She advises that she is in communication with Captain Denobli of *Nubella Run* and that they are monitoring."

"Hah! I join you in the soup, my friends. The only one of us who escapes is Vanz."

"No, sir," said the trader firmly. "I insist on joining the soup, in solidarity."

"That's a good lad you have there, Janifer," Father said solemnly.

"When have I ever said otherwise?"

Vanz met Padi's eye, looking droll, but wisely said nothing.

The door opposite opened, to admit a security guard with four stripes on his sleeve.

"Trader Vanz Carresens-Denobli. Trader Padi yos'Galan. Officer Karna Tivit. The Community Standards Committee will see you now," he said. "You will be required to face those whom you accuse."

"My master trader accompanies me, as witness for the ship," Padi said firmly.

"My trader will stand at my side," Vanz stated, every bit as firmly.

Karna stood with her hands folded, and said nothing.

"The witnesses may be in the room. They may not accompany the accusers to the floor."

"Understood," said Trader Denobli.

Father inclined his head.

The four-striper turned and led the way through the door. Padi followed, Father walking beside her.

"Be wary, daughter," he murmured in Low Liaden. "Virtue is your sword and shield."

"Yes, sir," she answered and guiltily closed her shields.

There was a long table at the front of the room. Three persons in Volmer Admin livery sat behind it. Before the table, to the right, stood Madame Zoe, flanked by two mercenary soldiers, faces grim. Beside Madame were the two vendors Padi recalled having mentioned the specialty shop to her.

"Stand forward and face the committee," the four-striper said.

Padi walked forward, Vanz on her right, Karna on her left.

"State your names for the record."

They did so, and the questioning was opened by the woman seated at the center of the table. She led them neatly through the account of their day, with no words wasted, gathering corroboration between them, and finally put the question.

"And do you see before you, Trader Carresens-Denobli, the person who attempted to bind you?"

"Yes, Committee Chair. It is the woman with the long braid, standing between the two soldiers."

Madame's eyes narrowed, and for a moment, Padi feared—

But the soldier on the left shook her head, sadly, so it seemed to Padi, and Madame gasped, hand half-rising, as her shoulders slumped.

"The accused will comport herself according to the customs of law-abiding persons," the committee chair said calmly.

"Now, Traders, we also received information that you were both injured in a manner peculiar to such adepts as Madame. The committee of course wishes to verify this, and we have therefore asked Master Healer sig'Endra from Volmer's Healer Hall to make an examination, and report the nature of these injuries to those of us who are unable to see and assess them for ourselves."

The door at the back of the room opened, and it was all Padi could do not to turn around and look for who had just come in. Out of the corner of her eye, she saw Vanz twitch, but he, too, maintained a proper decorum.

There came the sound of footsteps that Padi recognized as belonging to the four-striper, but no others.

The footsteps stopped.

"Healer sig'Endra," the four-striper stated.

A leather-clad figure stepped silently onto the evidence floor, and bowed gently to the committee.

"Ter Ans sig'Endra," he murmured, "Healer and Scout, attached to the Volmer Hall."

"Healer," said the committee chair. "These traders accuse Vendor-Resident Zoe Martenegsburg of mind control and murderous violence. The committee requires verification of these statements."

"Certainly."

He bowed again and turned to face them; an elder Scout, Padi saw, with lines at the corners of his eyes, as if he spent much of his time looking into bright lights.

"Traders, as you have heard, I am a Healer. I will require your permissions in order to examine you. I will not hurt you. I hope that I will not alarm you. All I will do, as the committee chair has said, is look at you using senses which are available to me, but which may not be available to you."

He glanced at Padi, and his eyebrows lifted, very slightly.

"Trader, may I have your permission to make an examination of your private self?"

"Healer, you have it."

"I thank you. One moment."

Truly, she felt nothing. Healer sig'Endra's eyes may have widened, or it might have been her fancy, but in the next heartbeat, he was bowing to her, and turning to address Vanz.

There was a pause . . . long . . . and longer, until the Healer sighed and turned to face the table.

"Regarding the accusation of a violent attack, my examination reveals that this trader," he moved a hand to indicate Padi, "has been the recipient of a massive blow. The marks I Saw upon her persuade me that the force utilized in this attack would have killed or unminded her, had it landed . . . fully. Happily for the trader, and for those who hold her in esteem, it went aside."

He paused. "There are technical details, Committee Chair, if you require them."

"The committee will require a detailed report to enter in the files of the proceeding," the committee chair said. "For now, we take note of your assessment. What can you tell us regarding Trader Denobli?"

"There, Committee Chair, I am in quandary. I can . . . see that the trader was Healed recently, and deftly. So deftly, in fact, that I cannot say what it was he was Healed *of*."

Vanz drew a breath, but before he could speak, Father did.

"If I may address the committee. My name is Shan yos'Galan, and like Healer sig'Endra, I embrace two vocations. I am both a trader and a Healer. It was I who Healed Trader Denobli of his distress. If the committee allows, I will open myself so that Healer sig'Endra may witness what was done."

There was a small pause.

"Is this possible, Healer?"

"Very possible, ma'am. Healer yos'Galan and I may establish a rapport, so that I may have access to his memory of this event."

He paused.

"It is a very generous offer," he added. "It is not an easy thing, to submit to such an intrusion."

The committee chair sighed. "Pray establish this examination."

Father stepped onto the floor, offering his hands palms up. Healer sig'Endra placed his hands, palms down. Both closed their eyes, and the moments stretched. The two Healers stood motionless, linked, breathing as one. Padi fought against the need to open her shields, to See—and at last, Healer sig'Endra stepped back to address the committee.

"I confirm that an artifact, which created an... unnatural compulsion, was placed upon Trader Denobli. Had it been completed, this compulsion would have subverted his will and made him the slave of the artificer. The construction was interrupted before it was complete, but the first effect was an order to return to the creator. This..." He took a breath.

"This is not civilized behavior, Committee Chair," he concluded, his voice stringently calm.

"Thank you, Healer. You may go. The Committee will require your technical report."

"Yes," said the Healer. He bowed and left them on soundless feet.

The committee chair glanced up the table and down, before addressing Padi and Vanz.

"The accusers may return to their lodgings on-station or to their ships. Do not leave Volmer until you have received a determination from this committee."

"Thank you, Committee Chair," Padi said, and Vanz, too.

They turned and stepped off the floor, Padi slipping her hand into Father's and deliberately opening her shields.

"Drink," she said in Low Liaden. "You are tired."

V
Trade Bar

SECURITY OFFICER TIMA FAGEN ESCORTED THEM TO A private parlor in the Trade Bar, and left them there with a jaunty bow, assuring them that she would be on the door until Master Trader ven'Deelin dismissed her.

Mar Tyn scarcely had time to study the control panel, from which he learned that the room was set to "private, passive monitoring only," when the door chimed slightly, and slid open.

Dyoli's brother was very like her, Mar Tyn thought. He matched her in height, and had his pale red hair pulled back into a tail. His face was round and personable, with a firm chin and a soft mouth. His eyes were dark brown, rather than blue; he wore two white, glittering gems in each earlobe, and one ring between both hands—an amethyst. The badge on the breast of his jacket was a stylized rabbit silhouetted against a full moon, *Sosacilli* embroidered in a curve above the moon, and *ven'Deelin* countercurving beneath the rabbit.

"Til Den!"

Dyoli rushed to him, lifting her hands to his face— and froze.

"Til Den?" she asked, hands descending to perch on his shoulders like small golden birds.

The trader looked earnestly into her eyes.

"Do you remember," he said, with a melancholy lilt to his voice, "when we had used to slip away from the house at night and go down to the docks to watch the ships unloading?"

Her eyes narrowed, slim brows pulling together in a frown.

"We never did anything so daft! First of all, the house would have whistled us gone before we had opened the front gate. Second, we were so utterly worn down from being at the docks and the warehouses and shadowing our mother in active trade all day that we slept the night through!"

The plump trader laughed, then threw his arms around her waist and spun them both about.

"Dyoli!" he cried, when he had set her on her feet again. "Where have you been? Mother is . . . well, you know . . . Mother. But Ixin is beside himself, poor fellow, between worrying after you, and fending off Aunt Gruin, who wants your shares brought back into general funding."

Dyoli laughed, breathless, and shook her head.

"Gruin would sell her left ear for an extra cantra in the general funds," she said. "But tell me, Brother, how long have I been absent?"

"Three Standards and a *relumma*," he said. "So you see, Gruin really is before herself."

"The delm decides when and who has died," Dyoli said, sounding truly annoyed. "Six Standards is traditional, and she surely knows that. She only wants to devil Uncle Vis Dom; she takes perfect pleasure in making him unhappy."

"And always has done. Now! Enough of this dancing about in the meeting room as if we were strangers! Let us get you on board and situated, and—"

He blinked, as if he had only just then come back to himself, which, Mar Tyn thought, might actually be so. A man might be made temporarily unthoughtful on the occasion of his sister's return from the dead. On the other hand, Til Den ven'Deelin was a trader—a trader who wore an amethyst ring. The last person Mar Tyn had seen wearing such an amethyst had been addressed as *master* trader.

"Your companion," Til Den ven'Deelin said, his voice not quite faltering. "Forgive me, I should have asked you to make me known."

"Yes," Dyoli said. "We were both caught up. I am as much to blame as you."

She spun and caught his hand, pulling him forward.

"Mar Tyn, please forgive me."

"There is nothing to forgive," he assured her. "I would be surly indeed if I begrudged you a proper reunion with your brother."

"You are too easy with me," she told him, and looked to that same brother, whose plump face displayed an expression entirely amiable.

"Til Den, this is my partner, Mar Tyn pai'Fortana. Mar Tyn is the reason I survived the last three Standards and a *relumma*. Mar Tyn, here is my brother Til Den ven'Deelin, who will not dare to disapprove of you."

Mar Tyn bowed as she had taught him, accepting an introduction to an equal.

"Master Trader," he murmured.

The bow he was returned duplicated his in every particular.

"Master pai'Fortana," answered Til Den ven'Deelin—and met his eyes.

There was sorrow there, and Mar Tyn sighed. He had expected anger. Sorrow would make it harder for Dyoli's brother to do what he must. Though he would bow to necessity, Mar Tyn thought. He depended on that.

"Dyoli..." Til Den began, but she had snatched his hand up and was gazing down at his single ring, her eyes narrowed as if she stared into a sun.

"You have captured the amethyst! *Ge'shada*, Brother! I know that Mother must be very... Mother."

He laughed.

"That she is, exactly! Dyoli—"

She raised her head and met his eyes, her grip tightening on Mar Tyn's hand.

"Til Den, do not tell me that I must forsake Mar Tyn now, given what Ixin will not allow. I know full well what Ixin will not allow, and I have no wish to break Uncle Vis Dom's heart."

"What will you then, Sister? Leave the clan?"

He glanced to Mar Tyn.

"Master pai'Fortana, forgive me, I beg. If my sister has not explained to you—"

"Bah!" Dyoli said. "The two of you would have me embrace nothing but propriety! It won't do! And you—Til Den, you have earned the amethyst! That means—that means—"

She stumbled, her words slurring for an instant. Mar Tyn shivered as his gift wakened, and he waited in breath-caught horror to see what his feet would choose to do—

Dyoli's fingers tightened around his.

"That means," she said, her voice suddenly sharp and clear, "that you may go to Master Trader yos'Galan and offer to become a partner with him in his newest venture. It will be of benefit to Ixin, of benefit to Korval, and of benefit to Civilization! He will want

Ixin in person, and you will offer me. I was trained
as a trader. I will not shame the clan."

"Dyoli."

Her brother slipped his hand free and put both
hands on her shoulders, looking into her eyes. After
a moment, frowning, he looked to Mar Tyn.

"A Seeing," he began and sighed sharply. "*Is* this
a Seeing, Master pai'Fortana?"

Mar Tyn inclined his head, the feeling—that feeling—
when his Luck was engaged and was moving him toward
an event . . .

"A Seeing, yes, sir. We—our talents enhance themselves, when we are together."

Understanding washed over that round, amiable face,
and he looked again to Dyoli, who was beginning to wilt.

Mar Tyn stepped forward, still holding her hand, the
grip of her fingers slackening.

"She overstrained herself," he said rapidly to her
brother. "She must sit, and if there is something to
eat—sweet tea, at the least . . ."

"At once. Here—let us have her to the couch. Pray
you keep watch while I call for a tray." He paused.
"Medic?"

"I think—" Mar Tyn began, and Dyoli snapped,
low-voiced.

"No medic."

Til Den and Mar Tyn exchanged a glance.

"No medic," Til Den said, and moved toward the
intercom. "I *am* calling for a tray, and then—you will
tell me everything."

"Yes," said Dyoli, settling back against the sofa. She
looked at Mar Tyn and smiled.

"Everything."

VI
Dutiful Passage

THEY WERE MET AT THE HATCH BY SECURITY OFFICER Grad Elbin.

"Master Trader, Trader. The captain wishes to see you in her office, immediately."

"Thank you," Father said composedly. "We will, of course, honor the captain's wishes. In the meanwhile, please see to Karna. I fear we have not given her an easy shift."

"Yes, sir," Grad said, and looked past them. "Karie? Cup of coffee and a chat?"

She smiled tiredly. "Just what I need."

"Excellent!" Father said brightly. "Pray continue. The trader and I will find our way to the captain."

"Sir. Trader."

Father waited until they had exited, the door closing behind them, before he sighed and looked to Padi with a wry smile.

"Well, Trader. I fear not so much soup as stew. Shall we?"

"Best not to keep the captain waiting, if she is so much tried before us."

"True, true. To the captain then, bold hearts to the fore."

. . . ❖ . . .

The door chime sounded, and Priscilla raised her head.

"Come!"

The door slid aside. The master trader entered, trader on his heels. He approached the desk without hesitation and bowed.

"Captain, you wished to see us. We are here at your word."

Hungrily, she read him, finding him tired, but not dangerously so, and no signs of having depleted himself yet again.

Padi—but Padi was a burning bush, too bright and chaotic, still, to read with any accuracy.

"Sit," she said to both of them, and they did, facing her across the desk like good children, faces attentive, hands folded in their laps.

She wanted to shake the pair of them. She wanted to hug them.

She wanted to weep.

"The captain," she said, "was made aware of an incident on the port. Is the ship compromised or under restraint?"

"Station Admin has asked the ship to remain at dock until such time as an official finding has been filed," Shan answered. "The traders and Security Officer Tivit may be called again to witness before the committee, but the chance of that is, I believe, small. The hearing was thorough, all necessary experts were speedily called and made their examinations. The accused is held, firmly I believe, by a mercenary unit styling itself Blades of the Goddess, and I believe will be undergoing a thorough examination by an extremely competent Scout Healer."

"How long is the ship to hold dock?"

"Until the investigation is completed and the sentencing made. Based on what we observed, I would venture to guess that the entire matter will be brought to a close in a matter of two or three days, whereupon the ship will be free to pursue its destiny. As it happens, the master trader has continuing business with Trader Janifer Carresens-Denobli, which may easily encompass most of two days."

The captain inclined her head.

"Are the traders compromised or under restriction?"

"We of course share the restrictions placed upon the ship, but are free to move on-port, and pursue our lawful business."

He sighed suddenly.

"The traders are, I believe, justly wearied from their work upon the day. It was an exhilarating day, and would have been so, even without the intrusion of rogue *dramliz* into the markets."

Priscilla closed her eyes briefly.

"Is the captain satisfied?" Shan asked gently. "If there are other concerns, I will happily continue, but I really think that Trader yos'Galan ought to be allowed to seek her bed."

Priscilla opened her eyes.

"The captain is satisfied," she said, and took a breath.

"The *pair* of you . . ." she said, allowing her feelings rein at last.

"We're neither of us competent to be allowed on-port alone, clearly," Padi said unexpectedly. "But no harm was done, Priscilla. I know that you and Lina are cautious about my lending Father energy, but it was an emergency."

Priscilla met Padi's eyes.

"An emergency?"

"A *cascading* emergency, if you will have the worst of it. Vanz—Trader Carresens-Denobli—and I were sent to the markets by the combined word of the elder traders.

I was to increase inventory for The Redlands, and Vanz was to...show his jacket alongside the Tree-and-Dragon, and set the port a-twitter, or so he believed. He made some small purchases of his own, but it was my will that guided us, and I was buying textiles."

"And these emergencies rose from textiles?"

"The first did, yes. Several vendors made certain to mention Madame Zoe's Whimsies as a specialty shop worthy of our attention. We went, and Karna with us. The shop was...very strange. Dim. The goods seemed to have been dyed with *vya*. I was bemused, Karna was very nearly overpowered—and Madame Zoe had *utterly* beguiled Vanz. I created a diversion and snatched him and Karna away.

"It was only after we were away that we realized that something very bad had happened to Vanz. We called in an emergency to the elder traders and met them at a safe place, some distance from Madame's shop."

She paused, and Shan took up the tale.

"A compulsion to return to Madame Zoe at all costs had been attached to the boy—Padi had snatched him away before it was completed, at great risk to herself. I examined him, realized that the construct needed to be removed at once, if only for Vanz's peace—"

"And *that*," Padi interrupted, "is when the second emergency arrived. It was clear that Father *was* going to do something. It was also clear to me—because I have, truly, Priscilla, *paid attention* to you and to Lina—that he would make himself dangerously ill, if he did so without assistance."

Priscilla met a pair of hot lavender eyes.

"*I* couldn't Heal Vanz, or I would have done. *Father* had the skill and the knowledge to do what was required; certainly, he had the will. All that was required was sufficient energy to see the thing properly done—and that I could offer him."

"Padi was seemly and professional, Priscilla," Shan continued. "She did precisely as she was asked; she merely made herself available. I controlled the flow. The lad was freed, and neither of us took the least harm, as you *can* See."

She could, Priscilla admitted, her anger cooling. Merely . . .

"I was frightened," she told him.

"Forgive us," Padi said, with surprising gentleness. "But somebody had to do *some*thing."

Priscilla laughed, sharply.

"The trouble with Dragons," she said, her voice not quite steady, "is that they *always* do *some*thing, no matter their own danger!"

"That's fairly said," Shan answered. "I believe that may be why there are so few of us."

"Goddess . . ."

She frowned and looked to Padi.

"What sort of *risk* to yourself?" she said.

"Oh, Madame was angry because I was robbing her of Vanz, and she threw—I really don't know what she threw, but my shields turned it and—"

"Goddess forfend!" Priscilla interrupted, opening her Inner Eyes to survey the carnage. "She did that? A second strike—"

"Yes," Padi said very patiently, "but she didn't *get* a chance to do it again. Whatever it was. I am *quite* unharmed."

Priscilla closed all of her eyes.

"Padi?"

"Yes?"

"Go to bed, child. Go to *sleep*. See Lina at your first possible opportunity tomorrow; your shields must be repaired before you venture out on-port again."

"Yes," Padi said, and rose. She bowed gently, appropriately, between clan members.

"*Chiat'a bei kruzon*," she murmured, and left them, the door whispering closed behind her.

There was silence in the office for several heartbeats. Priscilla sat with her eyes closed, seeing in vivid memory the damage done to Padi's shields. If *Shan* had been struck with the same blow—

"My shields," he murmured, "are tricky."

She opened her eyes and met his glance.

"So they are. Shan—"

"Priscilla," he said, leaning forward in his chair. "Will you sleep with me tonight?"

She half-laughed.

"You are impossible," she told him, and stood abruptly, unable to stay seated.

"Yes," she said, holding her hand out to him. "By all means, let us sleep together tonight. We'll particularly celebrate the fact that you're here for me to hold."

• • • ❖ • • •

Padi all but fell into her bunk, half-asleep until her head struck the pillow, whereupon she opened her eyes.

"But *how long* will it take to repair my shields?" she demanded of the dim air. From the desk came a faint rattle, as if a stylus or a notebook, or both, had taken to the air.

"Behave yourselves!" she snapped, and heard three distinct strikes against the desktop.

It was not a trivial question, she thought. It had taken *hours* to form the shields in the first place; hours *more* to learn how to maintain them. If they were only to be at Volmer for two more days—she would lose the opportunity to do more trading. Specifically, since today she had been buying on behalf of the ship, she would lose the opportunity to increase her own inventory, which, with the master trader intent on opening a new market—if she chose well, she might make considerable gains in her march to the garnet. Not only that, she and Vanz had been discussing a collaboration, working off of his idea of introducing novelty to *Nubella Run*'s current Loop, and if she were confined to the ship . . .

Quite simply, she *didn't have* hours to set her broken shields right—

She blinked up at the hidden ceiling.

Broken shields.

Shields that required, in a word, Healing.

Was it possible, she thought, that she might find her own way to that foggy country where Father had Healed Vanz? She had . . . the impression—no! the conviction!—that the fog had bolstered Father's efforts with Vanz as much or more than Padi's freely given energy. In fact, he might have been counting on the fog's assistance, when he had determined to Heal Vanz. Father was not, in her experience, a fool; he would have accepted risk—even grave risk—but he would not have traded his life for Vanz.

Yes, Padi thought, abandoning that line of thought to focus on her immediate needs. If she could recall the way to the fog-filled land, perhaps she might *Heal* her shields, and there would be nothing to do tomorrow, save show herself to Lina before she went out a-trading.

Closing her eyes, she tried to recall how it had felt, that space into which Father had retreated, effortlessly drawing herself and Vanz with him. She recalled the softness of the fog, the faint tint of pink in the busy clouds, the taste of the air—

Something cool and damp stroked across her face, and she opened her eyes—to a parlor, complete with two chairs and a tea table bearing an entire service. Sitting in the chair on the far side of the table was the person she had twice met, with Lady Selph's assistance. In this time and place, the rough hair was loosely braided; the face seemed not so much fierce as . . . simply curious. The eyes were mismatched still— tonight, in this place, one was grey, the other green.

"Ah, there you are," they said, voice reflecting a certain bemused whimsy. "Pray sit. The tea is fresh, and the cookies made by my cousin Entilly. You will taste no better, travel where and how you might."

Padi glanced around her. The room—well, there *was* no room. There were the chairs, the table, the tea service, and the little plate of sweet things, but the room . . . faded away, until at the far edges, where perhaps there ought to be walls, there was simply a gentle roiling of . . . fog.

"Am I inept again?" asked her host. "Did you not mean to come here?"

It was, Padi allowed, a fair question. It came to her that this person might, indeed, be a teacher. Certainly, they were relaxed in this odd situation and the others where they had previously met.

"I believe it is I who am inept," she said, sitting in the chair left for her. "I had wished to arrive at a space filled with fog, which would enhance my ability to perform a Healing."

A tip of the rough head to the right, and then to the left, brought her attention to the misty might-be of the walls.

"Yes," she said doubtfully. "But the place I was in . . . earlier . . . was *only* mist and fog, myself, and the persons involved in the Healing."

"I see. Well, perhaps we might sort it out together. Tea?"

"Thank you," Padi said, suddenly realizing that she was intensely hungry.

Her host poured, handed the cup across, and nodded to the plate of cookies.

"Please, have what you will."

"Thank you," Padi said again.

She sipped her tea; the host sipped theirs. They both reached to the plate at the same time, fingers brushing. It seemed the very air crackled, and Padi felt a thrill of delight along nerves she had not previously known she possessed.

Raising her eyes, she met an interested mismatched gaze.

"Are you well?" the host asked.

"Very well," she returned, composed, and withdrew her hand.

The cookie her wily fingers had captured was iced in lavender. It was delicious, and she had eaten the whole thing before she realized what she was about.

She raised her eyes, but met only an approving nod.

"Please do not stint yourself," her host said—and abruptly frowned.

"But what has happened to your beautiful shields?"

She frowned in turn.

"I believe you have confused me with another of your wide acquaintance."

"No, that would be quite impossible, I assure you. What *has* happened to your shields?"

Padi reached for her teacup, sipped, and put the cup down.

"As I am given to understand it, what happened is— they worked. Someone threw . . . something . . . I am very ignorant and I do not know what, precisely, was thrown. However, my shields turned it, exactly as they ought.

"But here is the dreadful thing—I must see to their repair before I may go out on-port again!"

"Certainly you must do that!" returned the host with feeling. "Someone is clearly trying to kill you."

"No, but only see what will happen—I will not be able to go on-port again, and *quite aside* from the fact that I will not be able to increase my personal inventory with an eye toward our next port, *and* that I will be forced to forswear myself, they will—that is to say, if there are others, who are with that person—they will think that I am afraid!"

"I see," said the host, and leaned close to choose another cookie. Padi waited until they had leaned back before taking another for herself. She ate it with somewhat more decorum than the first, and sighed when it was gone.

"I can quite see that it will not do for them to think you craven," the host said.

"No, it won't," she said more calmly. "However, we are only a few days at Volmer, and I fear it will take at least that long before my teachers are satisfied with any repairs."

She gave her companion a conscious glance.

"I am not very apt with my lessons. To form the shields at all took . . . a very long time. My teacher is patient, but she was worn quite thin by the time I managed a credible result, unbeautiful as they are."

"No, I do not allow that. Your shields are lovely— they may, in fact, be poetry—and I am lost in admiration of them. Of course, they must be repaired, for your own safety. But there is no need to spend days, or even hours, laboring over them. I think that between us we may do the needful speedily and with good result within this very hour."

The host glanced from one side to another.

"Do you know, I think you have come to a correct location, after all? So, tell me, what do you wish from your shields?"

Padi blinked.

"Well, that they should work as well—or better!—as they did today." She paused, thinking.

"Better?" asked her host, picking up the pot and warming their cups. "Have they not performed well enough?"

"They performed admirably," Padi said. "I honor them, whatever I may think of their aesthetics. But, if they can be made better and I am able to hold them firm, that would be desirable. Everyone who has seen the damage immediately flies into alt, imagining what might have happened, had there been a second assault."

She moved her shoulders. "It is quite disconcerting; there was no second strike."

"One must always plan for the second strike, however. At least, this is what my cousin tells me. As he is put in charge of the safety of a great number of people, I expect he knows something of the topic."

Padi chewed her bottom lip, still considering her own shields.

"If it were possible, I would also like them to be...beautiful and flexible, but—I will not give up functionality for grace."

"Nor should you. Your shields are perfect as formed. They reflect yourself—as even one who has known you only briefly may see—and they produce an effective warning."

The host struck a pose. "Behold me, a feral flower! Admire, but do not try me!"

Padi laughed.

"Yes! If I may suggest, you will want to lay in layers, given the possibility of a second, or even a third, blow. They may be as light as laughter, or mist, and if you can love them, it will be all the better. Only see how they cherished you!"

Padi sighed. "There's another problem. I can't really See them. Only I sometimes can manage glimpses, around the edges. Enough to know—"

"Enough to know nothing at all about them!" the host interrupted passionately, rising all in a rush. "Here!"

Abruptly, the table vanished, replaced by a tall, ornately framed mirror.

"Look, then!"

Frowning, Padi stared into the mirror, expecting to see herself in her familiar uniform, but finding instead a smear of pewter, swirling—and snapping into sharp focus.

She was looking at her shields, Padi thought. They *were* beautiful, in a toothy, louche sort of way. The arching planes reminded her of the wings of Megelaar, the dragon who guarded Korval's Tree. The fretwork evoked knots of lavender flowers. There was a significant dent in the upper right quadrant, with shock lines radiating out and down—

Padi took a sharp breath.

"She *was* angry, wasn't she?" she murmured.

"And surprised, I think we must believe."

"Yes, which was why there was only one strike."

Padi looked over the mirror, into a pair of interested, mismatched eyes. "Are you able to hold this for me? I would like to see what I am doing."

"As long as you like," said the host gallantly. "I am completely at your service."

"Thank you," she said, studying the image more closely.

Light as laughter, she thought, and as surprising.

She nodded, and said meditatively, "I am going to preserve the dent."

"A poetic choice. If it is not impudent, I approve."

Padi frowned. "I would have thought it the choice of a port tough."

"Poetry is in the eye of the beholder. Indeed, it might be understood as a challenge—*Only see what I have already survived! Need I fear you?* Others might see a fair and friendly warning. Still others, an appropriate modesty."

Padi laughed. "Modesty?"

"Indeed. *Look! Look here! I know my limits to a fine millimeter. Do you know yours so well?*"

Padi laughed again. "What is your name?"

"My call-name?"

"If it is not impudent of me to ask."

"Not at all. Call me Tekelia, and I will come."

"And is that poetry, or a threat?"

"Merely fact. May one ask—a name for a name?"

Have they taught you yet that names are to conjure by? Lute whispered from memory once more. Padi hesitated.

"If I am impertinent, I offer regret—"

"No," she said, "you are not impertinent. I was only remembering something a friend had said to me, about names. But I see that, here, is no discrepancy."

She inclined her head. "You may call me Padi."

"And so I shall. And now—again, if I am not impudent!—may I suggest we give our attention to your shields?"

"It is time, isn't it?"

She looked again to the mirror, to her reflected shields, and felt a certain, sudden fondness for them. They had saved her life; they were well-made, graceful and strong. They were worthy of her gratitude, and her love. They deserved nothing more or less of her than to be made into the best shields she could possibly craft.

Light as laughter, she thought again, surprising and strong.

She glanced 'round at the room that faded away into the friendly brume—and suddenly, she knew exactly what to do.

She reached out, took up a handful of mist, and began, very softly, to polish her shields.

Lina considered Padi, frowning.

Padi stood, waiting.

"I was told," Lina said finally, "that your shields had been damaged and required repair."

"They were—damaged," Padi said. "But I repaired them."

She paused.

"I'd appreciate your opinion of them, Lina."

The other woman threw her an amused glance.

"Have you been my student thus long and not understood that you will receive my opinion of your work, whether you ask for it nicely or not?"

"No," Padi told her honestly. "I knew that you'd do a thorough examination. I only wished to let you know that I welcome your expertise and value your care."

"Worse and worse! Ah, but I know! The trade calls, and you are disallowed the markets until your repairs pass scrutiny. Please hold yourself at peace, and I will make an inspection."

Padi closed her eyes, took a deep breath, and tried to think of nothing. She was not particularly successful in this, her thoughts kept wandering to her list of intended buys, the Festevalya collaboration she had discussed with Vanz, and the intriguing advertisement she had just seen in the *Volmer Trade News* . . .

"Had you assistance in making these repairs?" Lina asked, interrupting all of these wayward schemings.

"Yes—no . . ." She sighed sharply.

"I had—advice. Also a mirror was held for me so that I might See what damage had been done."

"What sort of advice?"

"Aesthetics mostly and . . . support of my need to repair the damage quickly so that I might go about my proper business with as little delay as possible."

She thought for a moment.

"Also, tea and biscuits."

"It sounds entirely convivial. May I know the identity of your aesthetic advisor?"

"Tekelia."

"And it was on Tekelia's advice that you preserved the scar?"

"It was my idea. Tekelia merely offered approval." She half-smiled. "If it was not impudent."

"As I see it was not. Well. And Tekelia's other advice?"

"Only a suggestion that I love my shields, and not resent them. They had, after all, preserved my life, when no one would have wondered, had they failed."

"Do I know Tekelia?" Lina asked.

Padi frowned.

"Perhaps you do. We met through Lady Selph. The stranger I told you about—recall?"

"The intruder whom you pushed away."

"I've become more convenable," Padi said, slightly shamefaced. "Lady Selph does not *approve* of bad manners."

"Certainly, she does not," Lina said, and sighed.

"I find no weakness in your shields, nor any failure in the repairs that have been made."

She stepped back, and bowed.

"You are released to the markets, Trader. Fair fortune and profit to you this day."

Padi swallowed a cheer, covering her glee with a bow of respect for the instructor.

"Thank you, Lina."

"Yes, yes, all you like. Thank me by avoiding any more terrible danger, eh? And come back with your shields intact."

"Yes!" Padi said. "Good-day."

A moment later, she was gone.

Lina sighed, and went to find Priscilla.

VII
Trade Halls

VANZ WAS WAITING FOR HER AT THE ENTRANCE TO TRADE
Hall L. He grinned when he saw her and raised a
hand, as if they were cousins in truth. Padi raised her
hand in return, smiling as she met him.

"Forgive my tardiness," she said.

"*Are* you tardy?" he asked.

"Well, I must be, mustn't I? You are before me!"

"I'm early," he told her. "The trader says, if you're
always early, you can never be late!"

"That's . . . difficult to argue with," said Padi.

"Isn't it?"

She half-laughed.

"Well then, are you prepared to be bold?"

"As much as I can be. Will you lead us?"

"Oh, I intend to," Padi told him seriously, and
turned down the hallway. "Coming?"

They had discussed this tour yesterday—a tour of
the luxury, artisan, and artist supply aisles with an
eye toward the unusual, unique, and uniquely useful.

"For one person's luxury is another's necessity,"
Padi said. "I doubt that either of us will grow rich
offering uniquities and pretties among our more
usual items. However, I can say that a solid twelve
percent of my profit comes from art and luxury
sales. Nor is it a percentage that I could make up
in another line, if I were to drop those items from
my offerings. Some number of persons want, or

need, a whimsy, and nothing will do until and unless they have one.

"Ideally, any such items you take on ought to be easily stored, easily shown, and amenable to long storage. Like slide whistles."

Vanz tipped his head.

"Slide whistles?" he repeated.

Padi smiled at him.

"One of my first independent buys was a case lot of slide whistles. I made the mistake, at first, of offering them in lots of themselves—they didn't sell. Eventually, I learned that they went best as a single item, or as part of a mixed lot of small practicalities. More often than not, it was the whistle decided the sale, if the customer was unsure."

"It sounds worth a small investment," Vanz said, as they walked together down the aisles, considering the items on offer.

Not infrequently, Padi would see speculative eyes on them, or hear whispers nearby.

"We're still creating a sensation, are we?" Vanz murmured.

"So it would seem. I hope the elders wanted this much attention on their business."

"The elders are up to something, mark me!" Vanz said, moving forward to scrutinize the dance of a bulky spool down a bit of string no more substantial than a thread of spider's silk, that was suspended between two frighteningly flexible posts only slightly longer than Padi's hand.

He took a quiescent toy from the merchant, listening seriously to the pitch even as he studied the construction, and pulled on the posts to make the spool spin.

"Unpowered?" he murmured, and got an affirmative, along with the information that the posts were made from recycled plastics, and the string likewise. The spool was carved from scrap wood.

Vanz gave the sample back, struck a deal for one hundred forty-four of the toys to be delivered to his storage pod, and stepped back to Padi's side, tucking the receipt into his belt.

"The master trader promises me several contracts for light reading, once the last details have been set in and the signatures affixed," Padi said, as they resumed their tour.

"My trader has made a similar promise," Vanz said. "He hints great things are afoot, that will change the very nature of trade."

Padi blinked, recalling Master Trader yos'Galan's casual, almost bored introduction of new contracts about to arrive in her life.

"You have to understand that misdirection is one of the trader's greatest pleasures," Vanz said, reading her face with alarming accuracy. "When it finally comes to the contract, it will be something on the order of supplying ice toast to the commissary at Hacienda Estrella."

"That may be so," Padi said carefully. "However, the master trader takes a similar delight in understatement."

Vanz stopped and looked at her.

"That's . . . unsettling," he said.

"Yes. Isn't it?"

They stood another heartbeat or two, gazing into each other's eyes—then Padi shook herself.

"It is very nearly impossible to predict either of them, acting alone. Together—together they form a new force entirely."

"Even *more* unsettling," Vanz said, and blew out his breath. "Well, nothing for it. We'll have to accept the moment and the lesson that rides it."

His lips quirked.

"As my trader *often* tells me."

Padi swallowed her laugh.

"Trader Denobli, you have my heartfelt sympathy."

"I hardly notice it, anymore," he assured her earnestly.

"It does me good to hear you say so. Now! May I suggest that the market lies before us, offering promise, profit, and momentary surcease from the trials placed upon us by our elders."

"Business," said Vanz, "must go forth. Shall we, together, or meet at the end of the hall?"

"Oh, why not together?" Padi said. "We did well, yesterday."

A shadow crossed Vanz's face, replaced almost immediately by a smile.

"We did, didn't we? Together, then."

Padi nodded, and swept her hand out.

"Lead on, Trader."

They finished their tour of the hall in high good spirits, each having added several hopeful items to their personal inventories, and at last sat themselves down together at the Trade Feed for a quiet lunch.

The trade feed from which the eatery took its name ran down the center of the table—the newest prime offerings, auction listings, private sales, and service ads.

Having sent their orders in to the kitchen, Vanz stretched back in his chair.

"That was fun!" he said, giving her a grin. "Thank you, Trader, for an enjoyable morning."

"And you, as well," Padi said. "May we both find profit in the wake of today's pleasure."

"What are your plans for the rest of the day, if I'm not impertinent?"

"I am entirely free to tend my own business," Padi said. "I'll be touring the other side of the market with our upcoming port in mind. I have some few notions that I would like to test—and given that it *is* Volmer, they ought not come *too* dear.

"Have you plans?"

"My instructions from the trader were to do well for the ship, and not to skimp on my inventory. I have the offer of an extra half-pod, if it's needed."

"That's generous."

"It is—and not at all how he generally approaches Volmer. I think your master has stirred him up."

"He has that effect on people," Padi said as their lunch arrived, via autobot.

She had finished her slice of cheese-and-egg pie, and was reaching for her salad, when a line running under the table surface caught her eye.

AUCTION: HIGHEST BID TAKES ALL. YARD LOT POD ADAPTERS 1240 SERIES TO 1530 ALL SIZES BETWEEN FORWARD AND BACK-WARD COMPATIBLE. ON DISPLAY VIA LIVE FEED AUCTION CHANNEL BIG LOTS. HIGH-EST BID TAKES ALL. BIDDING CLOSES STATION DAY 132, 1400 HOURS.

"What a peculiar thing," she said, dragging the ad into Vanz's half of the table. "Surely, there can't be so many running the twelve-forties any longer? And yet it looks as if this vendor had deliberately stockpiled adapter kits."

"Hm?" Vanz frowned, squinting, and put his finger on the ad to stop it.

"Oh. Well, I guess it is a little odd, here at Volmer," he said. "We—that is, the syndicate—keep some adapter kits at Hacienda Estrella, though mostly for when a ship coming out of the Dust wants a retrofit. The adapters are for those who'll go back—"

He stopped, raised his eyes and met Padi's gaze. She saw him realize what he had just said.

"We're taking charts and the latest edition of the ven'Tura Tables, world books, and guild updates with us to The Redlands," she said slowly. "Those will be wanted, with our market having just emerged."

"Yes," Vanz said. "The trader intends to push the Dust himself, once business here is done."

"And it is not impossible," Padi said, "that a ship that has been trading in the Dust, having achieved new charts, might raise Volmer, in search of markets."

"Yes, and if they wish to continue—to bring their markets with them, Dust-bound as they might be, they'll need to keep the old pod mounts, and make certain they can accept the new pods."

Vanz pushed his chair back, and looked gravely at Padi.

"Trader, it is your find. Will you—?"

"I think we both must," Padi said calmly. "Not only have we both understood what this may be, there is the matter of capital. I do not have unlimited funds, though you might."

"Hah."

He eyed her speculatively.

"You're proposing a collaborative buy—*between us*."

"Yes," Padi said with a smile. "*Between us*. Why not?"

"I can't think of one reason," Vanz said, and outright grinned.

"What?" asked Padi.

"I think your master trader isn't the only one who stirs things up!"

It was fortunate, Padi thought, that both the Carresens Syndicate and Tree-and-Dragon had business offices on Volmer. It was also fortunate that there had been knowledgeable juniors in each office able to assist, as it seemed that the senior traders were occupying the senior managers.

So! She and Vanz had created between them Out of the Dust Limited Trade Partnership, which had bid upon and purchased at much less than Padi had feared, the yard lot of pod adapters. The inventory was split three ways—each of the partners receiving their investment in pods, the larger portion to be available for sale through Volmer channels. The partnership had appointed the two juniors who had assisted in the transaction as caretakers of the Volmer portion of the business, for a percentage of the profit.

In all, an amazing and fulfilling day's work.

She smiled as they walked into the Trade Bar.

"So, Trader," she said to Vanz, "you will need that extra half-pod."

"A good thing it was offered, too!" he retorted. "If it hadn't, I'd be lashing adapter kits to the outside of the *Run* . . ."

She laughed.

"We ought," said Vanz then, "to seal the deal."

Padi frowned at him.

"The paperwork..." she began, and paused when he moved his hand.

"No, I mean—there's a custom. When a successful deal's been made, or a partnership formed, the partners drink together."

"Ah, of course! I had forgotten!" Padi shook her head at her own lack of manners. "Forgive me. I will stand the wine, if you will rent the booth—"

She stopped once more at the slight shake of Vanz's head.

"May we follow the custom of my family?"

Padi did not hesitate. She had come to know Vanz well, not to mention having seen the state and condition of his whole self in Healspace. She not only liked him, but she trusted him; their dealings this afternoon in the business offices had only reinforced those feelings.

"I would be pleased to follow the custom of your family," she said.

"Excellent! For this we will sit at the bar."

"In full sight of everyone," Padi noted. "The elders will be pleased."

"Do you think so?" asked Vanz, guiding her to two empty stools near the center of the main bar.

"Service, Traders?" asked the 'tender.

"Yes," said Vanz. "We have just concluded a lucrative deal—the first of many, so we fondly hope—and to that we will drink!"

"And what *will* we drink?" Padi asked breathlessly, in order to honor the dramatic moment.

Vanz's smile was brilliant.

"What else but a Trader's Leap!"

"Two Trader's Leaps on the way!" the bartender called out, loudly enough to be heard by the entire bar. A gong sounded as she moved down to the mixing station. Padi dared a glance at the wider room—to find all eyes on them.

The drinks arrived as she turned back—tall and frozen and sporting at least a dozen small charms. She lifted her glass. Vanz lifted his.

"To our mutual profit!" she said, projecting her voice as if she were an auctioneer. "yos'Galan and Denobli!"

"To our mutual profit!" Vanz repeated, every bit as loudly. "Denobli and yos'Galan!"

VIII
Trade Bar

THE LAST MEETING OF THE DAY WAS WITH MASTER TRADER Til Den ven'Deelin, at a private booth in the Trade Bar. Shan arrived with a spring in his step. He was tired, it was true, but he was also exhilarated. Really, this stop had been fruitful beyond even his most optimistic flights. He had parted with Denobli only an hour ago, at the business center, where they had signed the contracts detailing the several agreements they had come to over these few short days.

They had promised each other to keep in touch and—more audacious yet!—had planned three face-to-face meetings across the coming Standard.

So now, the last meeting of the day: in fact, his final meeting on Volmer. The *Passage* had already filed for departure, in—he glanced at the time board as he entered the Trade Bar—eight local hours.

He did not expect his meeting with Master Trader ven'Deelin to last nearly so long.

Indeed, he expected he would be with the trader no longer than it took to hear a pretty speech of gratitude for the return of the trader's sibling, and to drink a glass of wine to their mutual good health.

Shan spared a small sigh for Mar Tyn pai'Fortana as he crossed the main floor toward the private booths. It was not to be supposed that he had long been allowed to linger with his Dyoli. He should perhaps find what had been done for the lad, and make it his business to do somewhat more. Lady Selph had quite liked him. Shan

might have offered passage to Surebleak in exchange for
general crew work, had Mar Tyn embraced any other small
talent. A Luck—a Luck on a Korval ship. It was beyond
risky. Really, it was wonderful that nothing even remotely
untoward had happened between Pommier and Volmer.

Well.

Master Trader ven'Deelin had proposed Booth 11
Spinward. Shan picked the key up at the counter and
continued into the private hall.

The light was on at Booth 11; Master Trader ven'
Deelin had arrived ahead, as befitted the host. Shan
slid his key into the door slot and entered.

"Master Trader yos'Galan."

A young man bearing an extreme resemblance to
Dyoli ven'Deelin rose from his seat at the table and
bowed.

"I thank you for agreeing to meet at such very
short notice."

"Master Trader ven'Deelin." Shan returned the
bow. "I am pleased that we were able to agree so
easily on a time."

"Yes . . ." the younger man said, and moved his hand,
showing the table, with its still-sealed bottle of wine
and two glasses.

The wine, Shan saw, seating himself, was not one
of those on offer at the Trade Bar. Rather, it bore
the reserve label of ni'Mauryx Vineyard; clearly, a
bottle from the young master trader's own cellar. A
pleasing vintage, though extravagant for the occasion,
Shan thought. On the other hand, which bottle might
he be moved to offer, were Nova, or even Anthora,
unexpectedly returned to him after he had thought
them lost?

"Please," said young ven'Deelin, "open for us, Master Trader."

Obligingly, Shan used the wine knife from his own pocket, slit the seal and removed the cork. Then he set the bottle back in the center of the table.

They sat together a moment in respectful silence, allowing the wine to breathe.

"Will you pour?" Shan asked, and ven'Deelin did so, with pretty precision.

Both raised their glasses, and sipped. Shan sighed, pleased, and heard an echo from the far side of the table.

They put their glasses down with reluctance, and ven'Deelin inclined his head.

"Master Trader, please allow me to thank you for succoring my sister. She had been long away from us, and—frankly, I had despaired. It was unlike Dyoli to simply...vanish, with no word. Well. I will say, with no word to me, at least. We have lived in each other's pockets all of my life. Dyoli is the elder, you see."

He sighed sharply, reached for his glass, and held it for a long moment of meditation, which it surely deserved, before he sipped.

Shan took the opportunity to address his own glass, and when he again put it aside, found himself confronting a pair of earnest brown eyes.

"In a word, I am grateful to know that she did not simply cast us away. Though I confess I find the true cause of her disappearance...disturbing in the extreme."

Shan raised a eyebrow.

"She told you all?" he asked.

The soft mouth tightened somewhat.

"Not a full measure; she would spare me the worst, so she had it. But between herself and her partner, I believe I have information sufficient for many nights of ill dreaming."

"Her partner is still with her?"

"Well, what would you, when he was, so she insists, the instrument of Dyoli's survival? I have also been assured that you, yourself, found him a very good sort of man, as had Lady Selph." He paused, and cast out a whimsical glance.

"Pray enlighten me: Who is Lady Selph?"

"Lady Selph is a norbear, very old, well-connected, and wise. I have never known her to be wrong in taking the measure of a heart."

"Hah."

Another taste of wine; a brief moment of closed eyes. Shan sipped, giving the wine its proper appreciation, and waited.

At last Master Trader ven'Deelin opened his eyes again.

"This," he said, "is difficult for me. I will say that I am guided by my sister, who had been given a firm grounding in trade before she came Healer, and chose to follow that life-path. In addition to having been trained in the business of our House, and being, from what I understand the masters of the Guild to say, an extremely capable Healer, she has one other talent which I am told is considered *small*." He produced an ironic glance. "This being, I apprehend, a technical term."

"Yes," Shan said, intending to spare him any more embarrassment. "She has Short-Sight. It is rare, and not much . . . appreciated by the masters of the Guild, because it is considered unstable. Had your sister had only that one gift, she would have not been admitted to the Healer's Guild, nor would she have received training in the use of her gift."

"Precisely. Which is why Dyoli neglects to mention the existence of this second gift. I know of it, but we lived, as I said, in each other's pockets, and this . . . small talent . . . manifested some years before her Healer abilities."

He paused, glanced aside, and met Shan's eyes again.

"It is . . . quite remarkable, what she Sees. It is very specific."

"Yes," Shan said again.

"It comes about—but you know this, of course—that Mar Tyn pai'Fortana also possesses a small talent—he is able to influence random events within a certain range around him. He represents this gift as being very little in his control and says, rather, that it largely controls his actions."

"That is, I believe, the way of it," Shan said. "There are very few old Lucks. It is a difficult gift."

"It is a terrifying gift!" Til Den ven'Deelin said hotly. "Especially so, when it is paired with my sister's *small talent*."

He took a hard breath.

"Do you know," he asked, as Shan refreshed their glasses. "Do you *know* what they can do—together?"

"Survive?" Shan murmured.

ven'Deelin gave him a conscious look.

"Yes, survive. I do not wish to seem ungrateful. But, also, Master Trader, what they can do is . . . bring their gifts to operate simultaneously and on the same plane, whence they may, in a very small way, so Dyoli assures me, influence upcoming events."

Shan took a careful breath. "Does Master pai'Fortana

also believe this?" he asked. "He is the elder in these matters, I believe."

"Yes, so I believe as well. He is less certain of their effect, though he allows me to know that, when they are together engaged in a...working, the sense he has is very much as if his gift had woken and is exercising itself."

"I...see." Shan sipped his wine. Really, an excellent vintage.

He sighed, and looked to young ven'Deelin.

"You are telling me these things for a reason," he said. "If you wish an...intervention, I may give you an introduction to a very able Healer resident in the Volmer Hall."

"I may wish that, but first allow me to conclude the particular business on which I wished us to meet."

He looked wry.

"I swear, there is only a little more."

"Pray continue," Shan said, and gave him a smile. "I admit that it is a compelling narrative."

"Perhaps. Briefly, then, with her partner's assistance, my sister has Seen that ven'Deelin and Korval may be of use to each other, and also some third party, which she styles as Civilization. Her instruction to me is that I offer partnership in your efforts to bring Civilization into trade, and give you Dyoli as Ixin's representative in this venture."

He paused, and added, as one making a point perfectly clear, "Master pai'Fortana would, naturally, accompany her."

"Naturally," Shan said, when he could speak again. Really, the thing was audacious. It solved Dyoli ven' Deelin's problems neatly enough, and certainly a partnership, with Ixin as the junior, would do much to repair Korval's reputation with the old Liaden trade families . . .

"You need not hold shy," Til Den ven'Deelin said dryly, "from telling me it is entirely self-serving, and mad besides."

"Not *entirely* self-serving," Shan said, reaching for the bottle and dividing what was left between their glasses. "I see . . . opportunity, in fact, for Korval, and also for Ixin. Your sister has good instincts. I cannot speak to the benefits possible for . . . Civilization, yet. One intends to open a new market, you see.

"However . . ."

Shan sipped wine, sighed, and shook his head.

"Are you willing to listen to a business proposition, Master Trader?" he asked.

"I am always willing to listen to a business proposition, Master Trader. The more so when it comes to me from one of the most highly skilled of those who wear the amethyst."

ven'Deelin raised a hand, his own ring glittering. "I offer no idle flattery."

"No, I see that you do not, though it does not save my blushes."

Shan finished his wine with another sigh for the vintage, and put the glass aside.

"Here is how I think we ought to go forward. You will call for a meal, a pot of tea, and a light bottle for us here, to be charged to *Dutiful Passage*'s account. In the meanwhile, I will call my ship. There is someone I must consult regarding the . . . compatibility of the gifts involved. This is an added complexity, and I feel it must be addressed."

"I understand," said the young master.

"Do you? I hardly think *I* do, but let us meet as traders on this, and find how far we may walk together. Are you willing?"

Seated as he was, Til Den ven'Deelin bowed.

"Master Trader, I am willing."

· · · ❈ · · ·

"They do *what*?" Priscilla stared at Shan's face in the comm screen. "Is that... possible?"

He moved his shoulders.

"The two people with the most experience of this melding of talents believe that it is. They also believe that neither the *Passage* nor its crew will take harm from them. I wish I could be so certain. The question comes down to—do we believe them and, if so, are we willing to gamble all and everything on what we have chosen to believe?"

"Do either of them know *why* they are destined to take part in this benefit to—Civilization, was it?"

"Civilization indeed. Aside that such a remote placement honorably guarding Ixin's interests allows Healer ven'Deelin and Master pai'Fortana to stay together? No. They both swear that benefit will be received by all three participants, and again we come to our question: Do we believe them?"

Priscilla took a breath.

"I have Long-Sight," she said quietly.

Shan went still.

She nodded.

"Do you and Master Trader ven'Deelin still have something to negotiate, if we refuse Healer ven'Deelin and Master pai'Fortana as Ixin's representatives?"

"I believe so. I will put it to him. He's a sharp lad, new to the amethyst and eager to stretch himself. I believe he sees benefit aside from what might accrue to his sister and her affairs, or he would not have brought the matter to me at all."

His smile was rather crooked. "What do you propose?" he asked.

"Tell the master trader that your analyst on board requires some time to research the question thoroughly and fairly. Their answer ought to arrive within the hour. In the meantime, if it is acceptable, the two of you may begin negotiations."

"It sounds well enough," he said. "I wonder, though, how my analyst will go about her thorough and balanced research."

"I will pray," Priscilla said calmly, "and open my eyes to the future."

· · · ❖ · · ·

The table had been set for a working dinner: small plates and a tea service, with the wine and glasses set to one side awaiting the conclusion of negotiations, successful or no, when they would drink together to demonstrate that no good will had been lost.

"So," Shan said, sitting down, "I have spoken to my analyst, who needs time, naturally enough, and will call with her results within the hour. Before we commence—if necessary, can Ixin provide a representative to the market who is not Dyoli ven'Deelin?"

"Ixin can provide a very able trader to stand for its interests, should we find ourselves moving forward in a collaborative effort. The inclusion of Dyoli ven'Deelin is not necessary to a successful outcome."

"Excellent," Shan said, around a pang in his chest.

ven'Deelin reached for the pot and poured tea in order of precedence—Shan's cup first, then his own.

That done, he settled back comfortably in his chair, and gave Shan a blandly interested look from amiable brown eyes.

"So, Master Trader—about this market you are seeking to open..."

· · · ·✦· · · ·

Priscilla marked herself unavailable for the next hour, locked the door, and brought down the lights. She took off her jacket, loosened her shirt, and took off her boots.

At the temple where she had been trained as a priestess, she would have placed sweet-smelling candles at the thirteen points, and herself in the center of that circle, naked and upright, hands raised over her head as she clapped—once, twice, three times—to gain the attention of the Goddess.

None of that was *necessary* to prayer. Any space occupied by a pure heart and a willing spirit was a temple, after all. Nor was it *necessary* to pray prior to opening her Long Eyes. But unlike the sweet cloying candles, and the inevitable cool breeze raising goose bumps on naked flesh—all of which was the merest stage dressing, as Lute so famously had it—it was *prudent* to pray before looking upon the shapes of the futures.

Priscilla stood tall in the center of her office, closed her eyes, raised her hands over her head, and clapped—three times.

Who is it? asked a voice out of the gold-laced ether.

"It is . . ." she faltered, and caught herself up. "It is Priscilla Delacroix y Mendoza."

The golden strands blew slightly, in a gust that sounded like laughter.

Do you know yourself so little? We wonder that you dare pray.

"I've recently been returned to myself alone," Priscilla told the voice. "And I dare to do very much more than pray."

I remember you, said the voice of the Goddess. *For what, then, do you pray?*

"I pray for a clear sight of the most probable future."

No future is guaranteed.

"I am aware. I pray for clear sight of the most probable future."

Hah. So you said. Open your Eyes then, Priscilla Delacroix y Mendoza, and Look.

Priscilla felt her faraway body shift, as if it had taken a deep, fortifying breath.

She opened her Eyes, and Looked.

For a heartbeat, all her Sight brought her was a confused roiling of black and gold. Abruptly, the view steadied and she was looking slightly downward, as if she floated above a lens or a window.

On the far side of the window, she could see the *Passage*'s familiar lock, ramp running down to the dock. Shadows moved across her Sight—other, less probable futures; souls brushing by on their own journeys with fate . . .

Below her, at the base of the ramp, two shadows solidified, wearing the livery of Clan Ixin. Each carried a ready-case; both were well-groomed, and walked with confidence. One was taller, plumper than the other—and Priscilla recognized Dyoli ven'Deelin's pale red hair.

The two of them walked up the ramp, and were admitted to the *Passage*.

The lens darkened.

Priscilla waited, deliberately keeping her mind thought-free and receptive.

The lens brightened, and there again was the *Passage*, at dock. Down the ramp came Shan and herself, Padi, the two from Ixin, and one of the *Passage*'s security personnel, face indistinct. At some small distance from the end of the ramp was a group of strangers, two standing forward of the rest.

The lens darkened, brightening again almost immediately, this time showing a hillside beneath a twilit sky, glowing ribbons unfurling in a slow dance with the meager stars. She saw Shan's distinctive white hair among the group, standing next to a woman she thought might be herself. No one else of the surrounding group was familiar—neither Dyoli ven'Deelin nor Mar Tyn pai'Fortana was present, and if Padi was there, she was well-back among the crowd.

Priscilla bent closer to the lens, but the scene was already fading—vanishing in a snap, like a switch had been closed—but not before she had seen Shan crumple to his knees.

· · · · ❖ · · · ·

"It sounds the most wonderful venture possible," Master Trader ven'Deelin was saying, with an enthusiasm better suited to his youth than his ring. "I declare myself desolate, not to be accompanying you myself."

Shan laughed.

"You do realize that it may all end in ashes?" he said. "Truly, Master Trader, this is the maddest throw of my career."

"Better yet," ven'Deelin said, and reached for his cup and the dregs of his tea.

"I believe we have an accord, sir. Your terms are acceptable to me. If an office is established, Ixin will do its part. If it happens that Dyoli will be our representative, we will both be very fortunate; she is a wizard with inventories, but her real gift is for just-in-time scheduling."

"The identity of Ixin's representative being the sole detail left to us . . ." Shan glanced down at his notes and nodded. "Yes, let us send this to the business office, and have it drawn up properly—there will be an extra fee for expedited service. We will manually fill in the identity of—"

There came a loud click, and a voice spoke through the room's intercom.

"Master Trader yos'Galan, you have a call at Screen Nine. I'm to say from *Dutiful Passage*."

Shan rose.

"This will be my analyst. Your pardon, Master Trader."

"Certainly."

Shan left the room, and crossed the hall to the comm screens. His particular screen was blank. He placed his palm over the pad, felt the scan—and was looking at Priscilla's face.

Her too-pale face, and tight lips.

"Shan," she said, a note in her voice that he was not at all accustomed to hearing. Priscilla Mendoza was not a woman who frightened easily.

"Priscilla, what's amiss?"

"Amiss?" she repeated, with a sense of shaking her head. "Nothing's *amiss*... Not—now."

"Excellent," he said, still wary. "What has your analysis shown?"

"I have Seen Dyoli ven'Deelin and Mar Tyn pai' Fortana enter this ship wearing Ixin livery, and each carrying a case," she said slowly. "I have Seen you and I and Padi; ven'Deelin, pai'Fortana, and one of our security people arrive—someplace, where we are met by an indistinct group.

"I have Seen us—you and I only—among a great group of people on a hilltop in the gloaming."

"This all sounds innocuous enough," he said. "What troubles you?"

There was a pause, an in-drawn breath.

"As my Sight was fading, I Saw...I thought I Saw—you, on the hilltop...beginning to—fall."

"I...see." Shan closed his eyes. This was what came of scrying the future. Who could possibly parse cause and effect from those disparate glimpses that were not, in any wise, guaranteed?

Still...

He bethought himself of Dyoli ven'Deelin, of Mar Tyn pai'Fortana; of the *Passage*, and the unreliability of Luck.

Prayer must be rewarded.

He blinked.

"Shan?"

"I will make the leap," he told her.

She bowed her head.

"I'll assign them each a crew cabin," she said, looking up to meet his eyes.

"Thank you, Priscilla," he said gently. "Master Trader ven'Deelin and I are almost done here. I swear I will be on board in time for departure."

"That would be useful," she said, sounding more weary than wry.

"Even the most probable future may change," he said, meaning it for comfort.

"Yes," she said, and pressed her lips together.

"Priscilla, it will be well."

"You always say that," she answered.

"Well, I'm bound to, you know. If brashness doesn't come with the amethyst, it surely comes with Korval."

She laughed then, a half-laugh, at least, and some color returned to cheeks that had been too pale. Shan smiled, a small warm glow around his heart.

"Hurry," she said. "The ship leaves in five hours, and we won't wait for laggards."

"Yes, Captain," Shan said. "yos'Galan out."

Civilization

. . . .

THE FIRST DUTY OF THIS DAY, AS EVERY DAY, WAS TO SPEAK with the Oracle. As every morning, Bentamin brought her a cup of tea, carried in his own hand.

The head of housekeeping let him in, with a smile and a bow.

"She's in the library, sir."

Bentamin blinked, felt the cup move in slackened fingers and spared a thought for its contents.

"The library," he repeated, inclining his head. "It must be the change of season."

"As you say, sir."

It had been a full seven years since he had last visited Aunt Asta in her library. On the occasion of that visit, the books had all been tidied away in their shelves, and the Oracle to the Civilized had been dozing over a word puzzle at the table.

Today . . .

As on that former occasion, Aunt Asta was seated at the table. A tea service sat on a tray next to her, and before her was a perfect muddle of books. They were all of them open, each exposed page displaying a flatpic of some exotic landscape.

"Good morning, Bentamin," she said without looking up from the volume she was perusing. "Please pour for yourself. I'll be with you in a moment."

Bentamin looked down at the teacup in his hand, returned it to his kitchen counter with a thought, and bent over the tea service to pour for himself.

He pulled out the next chair at table, returning a volume that had apparently slid to the seat to the company of its kin, and sat down, slouching comfortably, ankle on opposite knee.

He sipped his tea and considered the Oracle. She looked well, her cheeks positively dewy, her gaze firm, and her eyes a-glitter.

He felt a stab of guilt. He had known that the universe's supposed peril had weighed upon Aunt Asta, but until he was confronted with this concentrated, vibrant person, he had not marked how heavy that weight must have been; nor realized how far she had traveled within herself. He *should have* known that; should have found some way to ease her.

"Well!" she said, pushing her book a little away on the table and picking a cup off the tray.

She sipped, and bestowed a smile upon him that was positively benevolent.

"I think it only proper," she said, "that you should be the first to know. You may then take the news to the Council."

"But what news is this?" Bentamin asked, a little ball of ice beginning to form in his belly.

"The Great Ones will be arriving among us, very soon now. I will of course stay on as Oracle until they are settled, which I don't imagine will be very long. After, I will be retiring—and I intend, Bentamin, to *fully retire.* I will not be contained. I have been a hothouse plant long enough."

"Will you leave us alone, without your wisdom to guide us?" Bentamin asked carefully. Of course, the Oracle could retire at any moment she chose. What she could not do was give over being a hothouse plant. Oracles and Civilization did not—

"Of course," Aunt Asta continued, "I wouldn't dream of placing anyone in peril, or of embarrassing you or the Warden's office. I intend to travel."

"Travel, Aunt Asta?" Bentamin eyed the tumble of books before her. "Travel where?"

"That is precisely what I am trying to decide! So many possibilities, but frankly, none seem to require me. Perhaps I'm simply not required anymore. Or perhaps I need to wait. The possibilities are still unformed. Once the Great Ones are settled, my Sight will become clearer."

"What will you do," Bentamin wondered, "as you travel?"

Aunt Asta warmed her cup and sat back in her chair.

"Do you know, I think I might teach."

"Teach?"

"I feel that I may be wanted," she said. "Nothing so definitive as a Seeing. Well! As I said, the futures have yet to be fine-sorted, the impossibilities eliminated. Once that has happened, I am confident that my path will grow clearer."

She gave him a sympathetic smile.

"You might tell Tekelia, too, dear."

"Yes, certainly."

Bentamin put his cup down.

"Aunt Asta, you know the Council will not simply

allow you to walk away. The Oracle is so very important to Civilization—"

"Balderdash," she said calmly.

He blinked.

"Your pardon?"

"You know as well as I do that the Oracle is considered a danger to Civilization. There are never very many of us at one time, so it's been easy to keep us sequestered, and take what benefits may arrive, but I think..."

She paused, and there came that arrested look, her eyes focused on something beyond the room, the present, or both.

"I think," the Oracle said slowly, "that Civilization will end, and the Haosa, too."

Bentamin shivered and sat up.

"You are speaking of an apocalypse," he said.

The Oracle blinked.

His Aunt Asta smiled, leaned forward, and patted his knee kindly.

"Only of change," she said, and sat back.

"Go away now, Bentamin; you have better things to do than listen to an old woman dither over her retirement plans. You look quite worn out—perhaps you might take a nap."

Tarona Rusk
Daglyte Seam

. . . .

THEY HAD NOT NEEDED HER AFTER ALL. ONE OF THE
old machines had engaged to do Kethi's work for her.
The Commander had gone willingly to her death hours
before Tarona arrived at headquarters.

No, it would appear that Kethi's plan was for
Tarona's own rehabilitation. She was to stay with
the Healers who had assumed the care of headquarters. There was a Scout team expected, and
a new commander who would protect the interests
of those who remained. So much had been Seen,
and headquarters was in shape to receive this new,
benevolent commander.

"Mistress, we need you."

"Kethi, you do not need me. And I have my own
business, yet, to attend."

"What business?" asked the Healer, tears in her
eyes.

Tarona cupped the distressed face between her
hands, as if the other woman was her child, in truth.

"My business, child," she said softly, and leaned

to kiss damp cheeks, before stepping away. "I will remain," she said, "until the new commander is come."

And with that Kethi was apparently satisfied, for she said nothing else, and Tarona left the room.

Dutiful Passage
Rostermin Breakout

∙ ∙ ∙ ∙ ∙ ∙ ∙ ∙ ∙ ∙ ∙ ∙ ∙ ∙ ∙ ∙ ∙ ∙ ∙

I

THEY BROKE OUT AT ROSTERMIN POINT TO DOWNLOAD news, update the navigation databases, and collect replies to the letters the master trader had sent before the *Passage* Jumped out from Volmer. Or so the master trader hoped.

They had a busy time during Jump, the master trader, the 'prentice trader, the trade-wise daughter of Ixin, and her astute partner. The master trader, of course, had his letters to write. In addition, he had held himself available for consultation in the matter of sorting their current inventory into trade lots, and was the final sign-off on the lot descriptions and order of offering.

Young ven'Deelin and pai'Fortana had together taken it up to edit the ship's catalog into a Redlands Edition—and very attractive it was—while Padi had produced a history of Tree-and-Dragon Trading, not stinting on the reasons for their relocation from Liad to Surebleak, nor standing shy of spelling out why the arrival of the *Dutiful Passage* in their space was an unparalleled opportunity, not only for the Redland System, but for their current trade partners.

Good work, done well by all, and now—well, *now*, Shan thought, he very much hoped that he would find useful answers to his previous letters on the screen.

He poured a glass of the red and approached his desk, a positive spring in his step, sat down, lifted the glass—and glanced over his shoulder at the sudden person in the chair opposite.

"To what do I owe the pleasure?" he asked mildly.

Lute smiled.

"Now, there's a sweet welcome."

Shan turned his chair so that he fully faced his visitor. He looked . . . different. Less shabby, perhaps, and somehow more definite. Also, his big, clever hands were folded on his knee, fingers quiet, the sense of power palpable.

"Our time in this space is limited," Shan said slowly, "and, while I know you disdain it, yet I do have work that must be accomplished."

"Nay, then! Whenever did I disdain work? I merely said that a wise man does not allow his work to kill him."

"So you did," Shan said, with a small bow of his head. He met Lute's eyes.

"To what *do* I owe the pleasure?"

"It's not so large a thing. Merely, I ask to be released from the geas you laid upon me."

Shan eyed him.

"And that geas would be?"

"It's a poor witch who fails of recalling his obligations," Lute chided. "Still and all, you've been ill and beset. I forgive this small lapse."

"I am, of course, grateful. Does forgiveness encompass revelation? Under what obligation of mine do you labor?"

"You had lain it upon me to guard your daughter," Lute said. "Mind, it has not of late been an onerous task, nor even unpleasant. Only, I will soon be unable to fulfill your charge, and I would not break an obligation when I might instead be honorably released."

Shan shivered.

"Your dying," he murmured. "It is—imminent?"

"It approaches. You will see me once more, I believe, before it is done."

He tipped his head, and extended a hand across the desk. Shan took it, feeling firm, warm flesh.

"I am at peace with this thing, child," Lute said softly. "Do not mourn me."

"One does mourn the loss of the usual," Shan observed. "Whether I willed it or not, you have become usual."

"More sweet words! I fear you are mellowing."

"It is possible," Shan said modestly. "The universe is wide."

"So it is. So it is. May I be released? I don't wish to seem precipitate . . ."

"Not at all. I daresay we are both busy. I hereby release you from all and any obligations I may have wittingly or unwittingly placed upon you. Specifically, I release you from your obligation to guard my daughter."

He paused to take a breath and added, "If it is permitted, and will do you no harm, I also offer my thanks for the meticulous manner in which you performed that duty."

"Child, child! My blushes!"

Warm fingers exerted pressure before Lute withdrew his hand.

"You're a good lad," he said, with a pure and open smile. "It is a blessing to have known you in your wholeness, and an honor to have seen what I have grown to be."

The chair was empty.

Shan closed his eyes.

After a long moment, he turned back to his screen.

In fact, there were three replies to his letters sent at Volmer—and two more, which were both unexpected and gratifying.

The first of the unexpected letters was from Janifer Carresens-Denobli. He opened it, his face relaxing into a smile.

> *You will soon hear this from other sources, but I wished very much that you hear it from me, first.*
>
> *You must allow me to praise Trader Padi to you. She is everything that her elders want to see in those who follow—she is fiery, she is courageous, she is compassionate, she is canny. I am not, I think, her most ardent admirer, but admire her I do, most sincerely. I am impressed by her trading acumen from my own observation of her, and of her work, at Volmer. I took it upon myself to read her records, and I am impressed even more. Were she independent, or of other Family and seeking a more expansive berth, I would offer her a daughter's contract.*

This, so you understand the full scope of my admiration, which I had arrived at on my own.

Having become an admirer, I was content to remain so. She was a breath from the garnet. Matters would proceed as they would.

Only then did I speak with our Vanz, who showed me this collaborative venture he and Trader Padi have built. I hide nothing from you— my admiration overflowed. But I did not allow it to inform my judgment as Senior Trader. Vanz and I went over this deal line by line, intention by intention, he explaining to his heavy-headed elder all the particulars. An expansion is built into this agreement, so if—no, I will be as bold as they are—when another opportunity is seen, it may be added into their collaboration.

It is an art form, this deal. I say this to you— the two of us having made similar art so recently together. What our juniors have made is worthy of us, were we still wide-eyed and youthful.

I sat and I thought about all I had seen, and all that I knew. I reviewed, again, Trader Padi's records on file; I reviewed her work at Volmer.

Having done these things, I wrote to the Guild, and put Padi yos'Galan's name forward as a young trader worthy of the garnet, detailing my reasons, and my personal observations of the trader, her skills, and her demeanor. I asked, because the Guild, as you know, demands this clarity, that my letter of recommendation be placed in the trader's records on file, and that a copy also be forwarded under seal to her master.

So! You are now made aware of my actions. I regret nothing, and I urge you not to delay this matter, which will—I am an old trader, and I must think this way—greatly benefit your own goals in approaching The Redlands.

All this said, I remain Janifer Carresens-Denobli, Senior Trader, and your willing partner in our own small collaboration to redefine the art of trade.

Shan read the letter twice, grinning, and had a celebratory sip of wine before he cleared the screen back to his inbox.

Yes, there was the copy of Denobli's recommendation, under seal. And just above it in-queue, the acknowledgment of the Guild's receipt of Shan's own recommendation for Vanz Carresens-Denobli.

Still grinning, he tapped up a blank screen and began to type.

My dearest Janifer.

Truly it is said that old traders think alike...

II

THE COMM PINGED AS PADI WAS ATTEMPTING TO FINISH her assigned piloting sim. As she was running solo, she swept a hand out to press the toggle.

"yos'Galan," she said crisply.

"Good-day to you, yos'Galan!" Father's voice came gaily out of the speaker. "How delightfully *sharp* you sounded just then."

"Thank you, sir," she said, her hands moving over the board. The sim required that she dock before signing off, and this particular docking, at stationside, was being decidedly difficult.

"Was there a particular reason you called?" she asked, when she had hit another pylon and had to retreat to try again.

"Why, yes, now that you mention it, there was! The master trader would like to see you in his office directly you've finished with the sim."

"Thank you," Padi said. "Please allow the master trader to know that I will wait upon him immediately after I make a successful docking at Lasilati Station."

"Ah, Lasilati Station!" Father—or possibly Master Pilot yos'Galan—said, with a certain fondness in his voice. "I believe it required two dozen attempts, my first time there on sim. Be of bold heart, Pilot; it can be done."

"Thank you, sir," she said, keeping the ship steady under her fingers.

"You're quite welcome, Pilot. I leave you now. Good luck."

"Good luck," she muttered, eyeing the instruments. She made a fine adjustment and started the approach again.

· · · ·✵· · · ·

Shan turned his attention to the last of the letters he must write before they made their last Jump to the unknown. He doubted Val Con would be pleased, but, there—he had already written to the delm. His brother was forewarned.

Denubia—

To say that I am astonished by the news contained in your last letter would be to understate the case by many factors. I hereby utilize this excess of astonishment as the excuse for my own woefully belated correspondence.

I trust that Ren Zel and Anthora are fully recovered by now, and that the babe is secure. I have nothing from Anthora, but that is not wonderful, as you know. I follow my usual practice of failing to write, lest I be seen as an overprotective elder brother. I also receive nothing from Nova, which is slightly more wonderful, but I gather from your letter that she is markedly busy, even by her standards. Boss Nova! It suits her, I swear.

News of returning cousins is always welcome; I look forward to embracing all.

As for us—it has been a trip of parts, Brother. The number of ports that will not receive us, or will receive us only to cheat us—a circumstance Padi finds particularly egregious—is lowering.

The worst affront came to us at Langlast, where we met with unpleasant company from a source well known to you. We were beset, and won free, but not without paying Balance her toll.

I believe you were acquainted with Vanner Higgs, and trust that you will grieve his loss, as I do.

Padi was thrown upon her own resources. I hasten to assure you that she prevailed, and, despite having learned a salutary lesson, which is never pleasant, was unharmed.

Among the company which importuned us was an individual who had been much oppressed by circumstances. A highly trained, and extremely powerful dramliza; a recruiter, and very well placed in the organization. Her pain was acute, and I undertook to Heal her. When last seen, she was swearing revenge upon her Department and all within it. I trust that she will do well for us.

I must now report stupidity, which, as you know, rankles me, as I always wish to stand the infallible elder. However, there is nothing for it but to make a clean breast—I was an idiot.

In the course of freeing the above-said recruiter from her illness, I overreached. I hasten to assure you that I am physically well. Merely, I overspent my reserves as a Healer, and must now engage in rest, which I do, faithfully, whenever I have time.

I am at one with your desire that I return home to clan and kin, but I fear we must both anticipate a homecoming for some while more.

Having met with so much rejection and deceit in the course of our recent travels, the Master

Trader has found for us a bold move. We are even now approaching The Redlands, as the Dust has chosen another partner with which to dance. He hopes to open trade, and to set up a base from which to move into sectors that have long been constrained by conditions.

Prior to our excursion to the edge of the Dust, in what must be seen as a superfluity of boldness, the Master Trader met with a representative of the Carresens-Denobli Syndicate. Several projects have started from this meeting, contracts signed. The Master Trader has forwarded all particulars to the delm, and to dea'Gauss.

I will write again after we have concluded what business we may find at The Redlands— there's a solid promise for you! In the meanwhile, please be assured of your continued place at the center of my heart.

Priscilla—and Padi, too!—join me in sending their steadfast love to you, and to Miri, and of course to my niece, pretty Lizzie.

Be well, and try not to wish the boredom away, denubia. There is something to be said for a lack of adventure.

Shan

P.S. I had nearly forgot! We are soon to witness the death of gods, as both Moonhawk and Lute have stated their intention to leave us, now that a certain door has been closed.

• • • **⁂** • • • •

Padi put her hand against the plate, heard the chime and the call from within to enter.

The door slid aside and she stepped into the master trader's office.

"Well met, Pilot," Father said, looking up from his chess problem. "May I offer you a glass of wine?"

"Do you know?" she answered, with a sigh. "I believe you may."

He gave her a sympathetic smile.

"How many approaches?"

"Eighteen," she said, hoping that she didn't sound quite as aggrieved as she felt.

The smile became a grin.

"You have, in fact, bested me! I agree with you absolutely, Pilot; a celebratory glass is very much in order! Sit! Sit! I will pour."

She sank into the chair, surprised to find a grin on her own face, but there, he was right. She had shaved six from his twenty-four. *Clearly* a victory!

"Here you are, Pilot."

She received her wine. He propped a hip on the edge of the desk, and smiled down at her as he raised his glass.

"To the heady achievements of pilots!" he declared.

She laughed lightly, raising her glass in turn.

"To figuring out the damned angle at last!" she answered.

They drank, still grinning, and sat for a moment, quietly, remembering, perhaps, other heady achievements. Then, Father sighed, and stood, and moved 'round behind the desk.

Padi had another sip of wine, and set the glass down.

"So then, Trader, I have some news for you," said Master Trader yos'Galan.

She waited; he sipped and put his glass aside.

"Firstly, your cousin Gordy—I should say, Trader Arbuthnot—has been detached from *Sevyenti* and will be the Tree-and-Dragon trade presence on Tinsori Light. What do you say to that?"

"I say that it's a very good thing!" Padi said warmly. "He's been having the most dreadful time imaginable with Trader per'Cadmie. The restrictions he's placed on Gordy's lines of trade would be appalling were they put upon a fresh-made 'prentice. To constrain a full trader in such a—petty—manner—it's simply spite."

She bit her lip, and met a pair of serious silver eyes.

"In my opinion, Master Trader," she added.

He inclined his head.

"Your partiality for your cousin is noted. Also, it happens that we agree with regard to Trader per'Cadmie and the extent of his abuses. That issue will be addressed in good time, but our first object is remove Gordy from the good trader's influence. Thus Tinsori Light. Do I infer from your comments that you approve?"

"I do approve, most heartily."

"Excellent. We proceed to my next topic."

He opened his desk drawer, withdrew some small object, and extended his hand across the desk.

"Honor me, Trader, with your opinion of this."

Three jewels glittering red fire set in a plain silver band. Padi's chest tightened; she kept her expression trade-calm.

"It is a full trader's ring," she said evenly. "Quite new."

"As the trader who will receive it," the master trader murmured. He withdrew his hand, and stood to move around the desk.

Padi rose to meet him, tears stinging her eyes, as he took up her hand and slid the ring home.

"Trader Padi yos'Galan, welcome to the fullness of our art."

She looked up at him, noting his eyes, too, bright with tears.

"Art?" she asked.

"So Trader Denobli would have it. You have made a conquest, there. And before I forget, there is also this."

This—her license.

She took it from his hand, read that Padi yos'Galan was a certified trader, backed by the Guild, and constrained by its rules and guidelines.

"It is advisable at times like these," Father said, after a moment, "to breathe."

She gasped a laugh, tucked the precious card away in her sleeve and extended her hands. Father, and the master trader, received them and held them warmly.

"Well done, Padi. I note that you have achieved this goal ahead of both your revised schedule and your eighteenth nameday."

"Well, that's so," she agreed. "I will need to improve my planning skills."

Father laughed, drew her into a hug, and the two of them stood thus, until she had recovered the knack of breathing and broke the embrace.

"This brings me," said the master trader, "to my third point."

She looked up at him.

"Yes, sir."

"I wonder if you would consent to hosting a small celebration, once we clear Rostermin. It will lighten the time in Jump, I think."

"Yes," she said. "I will gladly share my joy with the crew."

"Splendid," he said, and bowed her back to her chair.

"Come, let us finish our wine together. We do, after all, have much to celebrate."

Civilization

. . . .

PORTMASTER KROGERSLYTE CONSIDERED THE REPORT
from Director qeenLemite at the Metlin Science Station. The Council had decided that it was too risky
to announce The Redlands to all of space. There was
considerable concern regarding pirates, especially with
the recent example of the Reavers before them.

The Council, so it was understood, wished very
much that the Dust would return and keep them safe
from all and everything.

It was a point of view with which Portmaster
krogerSlyte had...some sympathy. More sympathy, at
least, than the Warden had, considering his speech
at the last Council meeting, reminding them all
that life was risk, and that they could not remain
hidden forever.

The Council, as Portmaster krogerSlyte saw it,
believed otherwise.

In any case, a compromise, so-called, had been
struck. Metlin Ear had been instructed to expand
its range, and listen to space. The Council's thought
was that, eventually, something in the way of useful
information would arrive, which would then be given

480

to Trader Isfelm, who would be responsible for taking what risks there might be.

It was, Portmaster krogerSlyte admitted, a disappointing decision, but at least they were doing something other than freezing under a bush and hoping that danger would look away.

Thus, Director qeenLemite's report . . . which was—provisionally—disappointing. The Ear had so far heard nothing—not, so the portmaster was given to understand, "nothing of importance," but "nothing at all."

The director, who was inclined to regard orders from Colemeno Admin as suggestions, had also stretched the station's Lesser Ears as wide as they could accommodate, and had begun cycling through the frequencies—listening only, she assured Portmaster krogerSlyte, though she also gave it as her opinion that they might safely risk a low-beam handshake. The station would not proceed to that step yet, but it was in the protocol.

Portmaster krogerSlyte nodded approvingly. Let the results of listening continue to bring nothing, she thought. The Council would become impatient sooner rather than later, especially as Trader Isfelm was due to arrive very soon on her usual schedule, hoping for news of charts or contacts.

The Council, risk-averse as it was, could not risk losing Trader Isfelm. Which, the portmaster thought, they might do, if the trader found the motion of Dust gave her a viable option to go *out*. One received the very clear impression that Trader Isfelm was feeling . . . confined.

She returned her attention to the report, noting that Director qeenLemite had added an addendum to her official report.

It seemed that, in her capacity as director of Metlin Scientific Station, qeenLemite had made a decision some half-year before Trader Isfelm had made her case for going *out*. Noting that the Dust was thinning, she had measurements taken, and consulted with her staff. They had together agreed that it should be possible to contact Metlin's bounce station, one light-year distant. If the bounce station was still functional, Metlin might speedily resume communication with the wide universe.

They had therefore sent a signal, and were now awaiting the bounce-back.

The portmaster sat back in her chair.

Metlin Station had sent a query to its bounce station. If there were ears nearby—attached either to pirates or honest traders—that signal would be perfectly audible to them.

The Council, thought Portmaster krogerSlyte, was not going to be pleased. She, herself... inclined toward pleased. Yes, there was risk, but as the Warden himself had said—life was a risky enterprise, even at its safest. And, while Colemeno had no space force, it was not wholly unprotected.

In any wise, the report with the addendum ought to be sent to the Council. Perhaps it would spur them toward more... definitive action. She would craft a cover letter, pointing out qeenLemite's efforts, and suggesting that approving the handshake protocol was risk at its most minimal.

Yes. She would write that letter and pass on the report—after her tea break.

She pushed back from her desk, stood, and turned toward the door.

A chime sounded, three notes, ascending.

The portmaster turned to stare at the console across the room. She had heard that tone before, during scheduled system tests.

Three chimes, ascending—in theory, they meant...

...message incoming.

· · · ·✸· · · ·

Bentamin stared at the message that had been pushed to his screen by the portmaster.

Dutiful Passage out of Surebleak, owned and operated by Tree-and-Dragon Family, requested permission to dock. Their purpose was trade. A catalog was offered, and a history of Tree-and-Dragon Trading, for the portmaster's perusal.

Bentamin blinked thoughtfully.

Tree-and-Dragon had a special place in the history of The Redlands. It might, in fact, be said that Tree-and-Dragon had made The Redlands what they were today.

There had been two high clans willing to risk themselves and bring the *vas'dramliz* of Liad away from certain danger into an uncertain future. The Dragon and the Rabbit, so history had it—Clans Korval and Ixin—had made themselves responsible for the safety of the persecuted small talents, with the majority of ships and pilots coming from the Dragon.

It had been the Dragon who had found The Redlands, thereby providing the small talents with a home that suited them as no other could.

The Redlands, Bentamin thought, were very much in debt to Clan Korval.

His screen pinged, signaling another push message.

This one, not unexpectedly, was from the Chair of Council. A meeting was called in two hours in the Council Chambers, the topic of discussion the tradeship even now entering orbit around Colemeno.

Bentamin sighed, and sent his acknowledgment.

Dutiful Passage
Colemeno Orbit

. . . .

"SO FAR, WE ARE FORTUNATE," SHAN SAID, HANDING PRIS-
cilla a glass and taking the seat next to her on the couch.

"In what way?" she asked. "It can't be because
we're uneaten; we haven't gotten near enough yet to
seem tempting."

"But we have been granted permission to approach,
thereby moving closer to the possibility of being eaten.
And Colemeno Portmaster has kindly accepted our
catalog and the history of Tree-and-Dragon Trading,
which is really a great deal more trouble than simply
telling us to go away and leave them alone."

"Yes," Priscilla said, somewhat faintly, "I can see
that's a hopeful situation."

Shan frowned.

"Priscilla, what is wrong?"

She didn't deny that there was anything wrong—
which was worrisome in itself. Instead, she put her
glass aside, untasted, and brought her hands to her
lap, fingers twisting together.

"I . . . feel," she began—and stopped.

Shan put his glass down, and reached out to take her hands. The busy fingers were cold, and as he leaned closer he could see tears at the ends of her lashes.

"What do you feel, love?" he asked gently.

She took a hard breath, and looked up to meet his eyes.

"I feel that I must go with you, down to Colemeno. Moonhawk—I feel her... pushing. There's a place—a particular place—that she wants—needs—to go. Immediately." She smiled, wry and pale.

Shan lifted one hand and cupped her cheek.

"I thought your time as a vessel was done."

"Apparently, I am needed for this one last thing," she answered.

"I don't suppose we can just call the pair of them a taxicab and let them go where they will?"

"That would be convenient—but no, I don't think so."

"Then I would suggest to Moonhawk, that *immediately* is not possible," Shan said tartly. "We must make an orderly approach. We must not frighten the Colemeno portmaster, nor those to whom she reports. If we are not to be eaten—which, I now confess, was never part of my plan—we must be seemly. Moonhawk may have what Moonhawk requires, but she may not be first in this."

Her fingers trembled in his, and that was a strike to the heart. She was afraid. Whether it was her damned Goddess that she feared, or himself, scarcely mattered. He did not allow his lifemate to be afraid.

"My dreadful temper," he murmured. "Scolding the vessel for the demands of a Goddess—"

Priscilla jerked her hands away from his and sat up straight, her eyes meeting his.

Her eyes that were ebony stars, hard and bright, set in a face of alabaster, smooth beyond both youth and age.

"Would you scold a Goddess, mortal man?"

Shan felt his lips part, and heard himself—no, not *quite* himself, after all—speak.

"Gently, my lady. He speaks from the heart, *for* his heart. You overburden your vessel, having promised her freedom."

"She will be free. It can be done—now! I feel the place; I long for the ending."

"As I do. Only think—we have waited long years for release. Can we not wait a few hours more? It becomes gods, I'm told, to be gentle with their servants."

"We were not born gentle, nor did gentleness win us through."

"But we may die gentle, having done everything we set ourselves to do."

A breath, a sound, unmusical and ragged. Perhaps, Shan thought, it was the laughter of a goddess.

"An answer for everything, has my Lute."

She leaned forward then, the Goddess in her vessel, and touched cold lips to his cheek.

"I will strive to be gentle," she said. "Until soon."

"Until soon."

A flash of bright pain sent Shan back against the cushions. He gasped, and forced his eyes open, the agony already forgotten. Priscilla was limp against the sofa, her eyes opening even as he reached for her.

"Shan?"

"Yes. And before you demand it, I swear—never again will I scold a goddess."

He swept forward, putting his glass in her hand.

"Drink," he said. "I will call for Healer Mendoza's tray."

Colemeno
Portmaster's Office

• • • • • • • • • • • • • • • • • •

IT WAS A RAUCOUS MEETING OF THE COUNCIL, WITH THOSE most easily alarmed demanding to know what they wanted, this Tree-and-Dragon tradeship—and how, if they were Reavers come again?

"The Reavers came in secret, to enslave," Chair of Council gorminAstir said. "Also, we have the template for the Reaver pattern." It had been graciously provided to the Council by the Haosa, though that was not mentioned. "We will not be surprised again."

"As to what they *want*," said targElmina, "assuming, as I do, that they are *not* Reavers—they say that they want to trade. As this is the most common business of tradeships, I see no reason to doubt them. I have read the history they provided, and I see that they have been ill-treated by the Liaden Council of Clans, as our forebears were. They are now seeking to make routes which are profitable for the new homeworld. All of this is consistent with a stated intent to explore markets, and trade."

"The archives may be a resource in this," said

ivenAlyatta, the librarian. "I will be pleased to pull relevant documents for those who are interested."

"Also," said seelyFaire, in her soft voice, "they may be coming to check on our progress, now that the Dust has cleared. Tree-and-Dragon—Clan Korval—and the Rabbit—Clan Ixin—were responsible for uniting the ancestors with The Redlands. It would not be unreasonable for them to have some curiosity regarding us."

She paused for a sip of tea, and looked around the table, a half-smile on her face.

"I confess to having a curiosity regarding Tree-and-Dragon, after all."

That produced a flutter of laughter and some loosening of the tensions 'round the table, after which decisions were quickly made.

The first decision was that a message be sent immediately to Trader Isfelm, informing her that a tradeship had arrived at Colemeno from *out*.

The second decision was to allow *Dutiful Passage* docking and to entertain its representatives as befit the first honored new visitors to Colemeno since the Dust had gone.

A committee was formed to put together that entertainment, while Portmaster krogerSlyte opened communication with the ship to find who those representatives would be.

The meeting had gone well, eventually, Bentamin thought, at his apartment some hours later. If they were fortunate, Trader Isfelm would arrive in time to prevent the port market manager from selling the entire Redland System to the Tree-and-Dragon trader. *Dutiful Passage* would have charts—new, accurate charts of the universe beyond the Dust. That realization might speed Isfelm's arrival. Once seated at the same table, perhaps the two traders might craft an arrangement that would benefit themselves, and The Redlands, all together. That would be the happiest outcome.

Bentamin drew a hard breath, and realized that he was smiling.

There would be problems, he reminded himself, in an effort to defeat that smile of hopeful anticipation. Spacers would bring new customs, new talents that might not mix well with Civilization.

"But after all," he said aloud, "the traders and crews can be kept to the port, and we can employ the Deaf—"

His comm chimed.

He frowned, glancing at the time, hoping that it was not, at this hour, one of his more easily alarmed colleagues from the Council, calling for yet another dose of reassurance.

The comm chimed again. He touched the button. "Yes."

"Bentamin, I hope I didn't wake you," his Aunt Asta said.

"No, a Council meeting went late, and I'm just home," he told her. "How may I serve you, Aunt Asta?"

"By bringing me with you to the reception for Master Trader yos'Galan and his entourage two days hence, in the Great Hall at the port," she said calmly.

Bentamin stared at the comm, wondering which question he wanted to ask first. But really, he thought, the Oracle could easily have Seen the tradeship, Heard the name of the master trader—even Seen the Great Hall bedecked for celebration.

Which left him only one thing to say.

"Aunt Asta, I cannot bring you into a public gathering."

His aunt sighed, gustily.

"Do you know," she said, her voice tart, "I really have no desire to have an argument about this, Bentamin. That being the case, I will instead provide you with an ultimatum. Either you bring me with you to the reception, or I will take the bus to the port and walk the rest of the distance to the Hall. I leave it to you to decide which action will pollute Civilization more readily."

"Aunt Asta..."

"And if you think my staff will prevent me from leaving my apartment, you are quite wrong," she interrupted.

That gave him pause. And in that pause, thought stirred. Aunt Asta might threaten him with a bus, but in sober reality, she need only call upon Tekelia for transport and support. And the thought of his chaotic and charismatic cousin in the midst of a reception for off-worlders chilled the blood far more than the prospect of the Oracle to the Civilized riding a public omnibus through the city.

"If I knew more...?" he suggested.

"I have Seen that I will be needed," she said flatly.

Well then. Who was he, after all, to argue with the Oracle to the Civilized?

"I will be pleased to escort you to the reception, Aunt Asta," he said.

"Excellent," she answered cordially. "Call me tomorrow and we will arrange our details. Good-night, now. Sleep well."

She cut the connection.

Dutiful Passage
Colemeno Orbit

• • • • • • • • • • • • • • •

"I'M GOING TO BE MEETING VERY MANY PEOPLE," PADI WAS telling Lady Selph. "Eventually, they'll come into your collection."

Lady Selph allowed it to be known that, while she appreciated Padi's exertions on her behalf, it would be far more satisfying if she were herself part of the trade party.

"Perhaps once we know how Colemeno feels about norbears," Padi temporized. "But, you know, we don't want to overwhelm them just at first."

Lady Selph sighed, and wriggled to be let down.

Padi obediently bent over the pen and placed the elderly lady on the sand. Master Frodo immediately bumbled over, bearing a fresh bit of greenery, which he offered to her.

Padi had already said her good-byes to the rest of the norbears. She lingered a few minutes more, making sure that the fountain she had just refilled was clean and free-running, that the greens were perfectly fresh, and the bowl was filled to the top with dry food.

492

Lady Selph was chewing on her leaf, Master Frodo curled next to her, his side touching hers. Delm Briat and Tiny were napping together at fountain side.

It was time to go.

Padi turned as the door to the Pet Library cycled, and Priscilla stepped into the room.

"Excellent," she said, giving Padi a nod. "May I have a moment of your time, clan-daughter?"

Padi blinked. Priscilla never—well. Priscilla *very rarely* addressed her as clan-daughter, though it was both perfectly true and perfectly proper. The few times she had done so in the past, the address had been in Liaden and driven by circumstances. Here on the *Passage* . . . one could only wonder what it meant.

And, of course, she was being given the opportunity to find out exactly that.

"Certainly, I have a moment," she said cordially. "Do you prefer to talk here, or shall we to the cafeteria or—"

"The library, if you will. I have reserved a privacy booth."

A privacy booth? Curiouser and curiouser.

"Lead on," she said. "Please."

They settled into the booth, Padi on the left bench, Priscilla on the right, the study screen folded away. Priscilla's hands were in her lap, and they were clenched, Padi noted; the knuckles were ice-white.

"I must ask you, as the daughter of my lifemate," Priscilla began, her voice stringently calm, "to guard him most nearly, as we come onto Colemeno."

Padi blinked.

"Are we going into danger? Have you Seen something?"

"I have Seen—something," Priscilla said. "You should understand that Seeing something is often more trouble than having Seen nothing. Seeing requires interpretation, and the Seer is left perplexed, having Seen—*something*—without context."

"What does the Seer—do?" Padi asked. "Try to forget what they've Seen?"

"No. We watch carefully, for context, and stay alert for situations that might lead to the event we had Seen. That's what I would be doing in this... upcoming instance, except—there's a complication."

Padi frowned.

"A complication? What complication?"

Priscilla's lips curved into a shadow smile.

"Me," she said. "Or who I was. Do you *know* who I was, on Sintia?"

"You were a priest in a religious order," Padi said promptly, having gathered so much in the way that children do, through this dropped word and that mentioned event, over a period of years.

Priscilla's smile grew somewhat more definite.

"Simply put—yes. More fully, on Sintia, I was not only a priestess of a Goddess, I was what we called a *vessel*. That means I willingly gave permission for another—intelligence—to overrule my spirit and my self and use me for Her own purpose. When that happened, we would say, *the Goddess has filled her vessel*."

Padi stared at her in horror.

"You *agreed* to this?"

"I was twelve," Priscilla said apologetically. "And it was a very great honor."

In Padi's opinion, it sounded like very great fraud.

She refrained from saying so, and instead, asked a half-question.

"But—you left Sintia."

"Yes. The religious order cast me out. But the Goddess did not relinquish her hold on me."

She paused, and added, "Apparently, good vessels are hard to find, and are not to be cast aside because of small differences in doctrine. And, truly, Her requirements were not a burden. For years, it seemed as though She had . . . faded, if not withdrawn entirely. But now—there is one last thing that She must do in this life, on this plane."

"And she needs you in order to accomplish this . . . one last thing," Padi said, sternly repressing a shiver.

"Yes. Which is why I am telling you this. This last task—I may not be able to guard Shan. I may not be . . . precisely . . . present."

Padi took a breath.

"Allow me to review. You're asking me to be particularly alert to any danger, and to watch Father carefully. I—yes, of course, willingly. May I know what you Saw?"

Priscilla frowned.

"I struggled with whether or not I should tell you more, because, as I said—context. But, it may help. What I Saw was a large gathering of people, most of them strangers, atop a hill in twilight. I Saw myself in the crowd. As my Sight was fading, I Saw Shan fall."

Padi's breath caught in her throat.

"But—"

"Context," Priscilla said again. "There is one more thing."

Padi eyed her. "If one may ask—how many one more things are there in this?"

"This is the last. May I proceed?"

"Please."

"If it appears that I am the cause of your father's distress, you will not hesitate to act against *me*—against the Goddess, that will be."

"What! Priscilla—" She stopped.

Priscilla waited.

Padi took a breath.

"Am I," Padi asked calmly, "strong enough to kill a Goddess?"

"You're certainly strong enough to get Her attention," Priscilla answered.

"Marvelous. And if I do—get Her attention—what harm might I do to *you*?"

"Perhaps none. Perhaps more than none. It will be an adventure, and we'll all find out together."

"Priscilla . . ."

"Padi."

Priscilla leaned forward and took her hands. Padi found herself gazing into luminous black eyes.

"Please," said Priscilla.

Padi sighed.

"Yes," she said. "Of course. I'll do whatever I can."

II

TODAY, PADI THOUGHT, WAS HER EIGHTEENTH NAMEDAY. She glanced down at her hand, where the garnets glittered. She'd written Gordy to tell him about the garnets, and gotten a vigorous congratulation in return.

She'd also written to Vanz, her letter crossing his, bearing similar joyous news. Her nameday, however... Sadly, the arrival of her nameday had... paled, not only against the garnets, but their imminent arrival at Colemeno.

Well, and one could not live in alt all the time. She finished pulling on her boots and crossed the room to her desk, tapped the screen up—and took a step back, blinking at the multiple warnings of messages in-queue.

At the top was a 'beam packet, unfolding into a dozen letters—from Aunt Nova and Syl Vor, Grandfather Luken, Aunt Miri and Uncle Val Con, Quin, Cousin Pat Rin and Natesa, from Jeeves and the cats, too—there was a whimsy!—and, oh, everyone!

Padi smiled, opening each quickly and skimming their nameday wishes. She would read each more carefully later, and write her return notes, but for now—they would be leaving soon for the planet surface and she needed to be quick with the rest of her correspondence.

There was another pinbeam, from Ms. dea'Gauss. That, Padi thought, would be her adjusted quartershare amounts, reflecting both her increased worth to the clan as a full trader, and as one who had achieved her eighteenth nameday without, as Father would have it, something catastrophic having occurred. Eighteen was not a marker year—not like twelve or, indeed, thirty-five—but it was the year by which she was expected, by Korval's own laws, to be a confirmed contributor to the health of the clan.

She opened Ms. dea'Gauss's message, revealing the expected documents. She read them over, noting that the increase in her quartershare was somewhat larger than she had anticipated, appended her initials and her signature in the indicated places, and sent the letter into the outgoing queue.

There was also a letter from Vanz, who opened, rather surprisingly, with a well-wish for her nameday before moving on to business. He had found a market for a lot of six adapter sets at a general repair facility orbiting one of *Nubella Run*'s usual stops.

They get a ship or two out of the Dust every year, so the tech let me know. He'd been in the way of fabricating his own sort of adapters, which worked well enough, but took time. He was pleased to see ready-mades, which will save time for him and his customers.

I'd been looking forward to seeing how the units will go nearer to Dust-edge, but that might mean rationing sales, close in, which will be no great pleasure.

I hope the trading goes well for you at The Redlands. I'll tell you that I'm looking forward to hearing the whole tale, next we're on-port together.

Padi smiled and closed the letter, glancing again at the queue, but Vanz's was the last letter. She marked it to be answered, along with the well-wishes from her family, and straightened as the comm chimed.

"yos'Galan," she said, wincing as she caught sight of the time.

"Trader yos'Galan," said Mar Tyn pai'Fortana gravely. "The master trader wonders if you will join us in the atrium meeting room for a working meal before we descend."

Padi bit her lip.

"Thank you, Master pai'Fortana," she said, matching him for gravity. "Pray give the master trader my regards, and assure him that I will arrive within the next six minutes."

Colemeno Portmaster krogerSlyte had been kind enough to forward an agenda and a letter from the Colemeno Administrative Council.

The Council was pleased to welcome Tree-and-Dragon tradeship *Dutiful Passage*. It was understood that a small group would arrive on-port from the *Passage*, that delegation to include Master Trader Shan yos'Galan, Trader Padi yos'Galan, Captain Priscilla Delacroix y Mendoza, Healer Dyoli ven'Deelin, and Master Mar Tyn pai'Fortana, as well as Security Officers Grad Elbin, Tima Fagen, and Karna Tivit.

Colemeno Council was pleased to host a small reception in order that Council members and other persons of interest to the Tree-and-Dragon delegation might be introduced to one another.

Though it had not been requested, the Council stated that they were not at the moment able to open Colemeno port to shore leave for general crew. Council members were looking forward to speaking with the master trader and the captain on this and other topics, to find what accommodations might be made. The Council was excited by the possibility of new trade, its members particularly pleased to welcome a Tree-and-Dragon tradeship.

"Well, Trader?" the master trader asked from his seat at the head of the table. "I recall that you had hoped for a descent into savagery. Are you disappointed, or fulfilled?"

Padi met his eyes.

"I am—puzzled," she admitted. From the side of her eye, she saw Dyoli ven'Deelin incline her head slightly.

"What puzzles you?" inquired the master trader.

"Well...they have followed the forms," Padi said slowly, frowning at the letter projected onto the screen above the table, "and they have said nearly all the correct things. The leap to deny shore leave, which we certainly did not request, this being as strange a port to us as our ship is strange to them—"

She sighed sharply.

"I would say that they are...considerably wary of us."

"As anybody would be," the master trader said. "We've made no secret of our recent past, after all."

"True."

"We may still withdraw," the master trader said. "What say you, Trader?"

"Withdraw?" Padi stared at him. "Of course we cannot withdraw! We will attend the reception, display our manners and our acumen, and sweep all before us."

Dyoli ven'Deelin actually smiled.

The master trader looked around the table.

"Does anyone find reason to disagree with Trader yos'Galan's summary or the plan she has put forward for our success?" he asked.

No one spoke.

"Well, then. Bold hearts, forward. Our shuttle, I believe, awaits."

Colemeno Port
Great Hall

· · · · · · · · · ·

THE PORTMASTER HAD GONE TO MEET THE DELEGATION from the *Dutiful Passage* and escort them to the Great Hall.

In the meanwhile, the rest of the Council, with the market manager and his second, had forgathered in the hall and were talking among themselves.

"I don't see our Warden," tryaBent said to ivenAlyatta. "Do you suppose he won't be coming, after all his mocking and hard words?"

"I think he will be here," said ivenAlyatta. "Possibly something has kept him in the office—or he may have gone to consult the Oracle."

"That would be prudent," said azieEm, one of the Council's more timid members. "The Oracle will be able to tell him if these people have given their true intentions."

"Why would they not have given their true intentions?" asked ivenAlyatta interestedly. "Or have you returned to the pirate camp?"

"There was never a pirate camp," azieEm said,

frowning. "Merely, it is a very easy thing to lie the door open, and only show your true nature once you are inside the house."

"Have you seen that pin seelyFaire is wearing?" tryaBent asked, too brightly. She looked to ivenAlyatta. "She says it's from the time of our relocation to The Redlands."

"Trust seelyFaire to have something from the Relocation! I would be disappointed if it were not jewelry. Is it worth anything, I wonder?"

"I wouldn't—"

There was a slight *whoosh*, as if a small breeze had gotten loose in the Hall, or the Warden had arrived via teleport. Those gathered turned toward the sound automatically—and azieEm spoke, her voice loud in the sudden, shocked silence.

"Who is that with him?"

The lady—agreeably plump, with grey-stitched dark hair and a soft dreamer's face—turned her head as if she had heard them. Smiling, she came forward.

The Warden had apparently not expected this; he had to hurry to reach her side.

"Hello, children," the stranger said as she reached their group. "I am Bentamin's Aunt Asta. Bentamin, introduce me, please."

It was a perfectly ordinary request, tryaBent thought, and no reason for the black look that the Warden bestowed upon the lady, his aunt. Though there was the question of *why* the Warden had brought his aunt to a Council function. Well, he certainly must have cleared it with the Council Chair—

"Councilors tryaBent, ivenAlyatta, azieEm," the Warden said austerely, "allow me to present Asta vesterGranz, my aunt, as she says. You will know her better by her official title: Oracle to the Civilized."

· · · · 🞷 · · · ·

The air was...tingling, Shan noted, as he stepped out of the shuttle. In fact, the air was *crackling*. Wu and Fabricant had ascended into eloquence regarding the *invigorating environment* of Colemeno, and Shan had done them the disservice of believing it to be hyperbole.

He took another, deeper breath, and mentally begged the research team's pardon.

If he were himself prone to hyperbole, he would say that his blood fizzed. He noted a glistering along the edges of his shields, and opened them, very slightly.

Every nerve sparked; where he had become accustomed to muddy colors and a dull, background drone, suddenly he—

He could See again.

All around him were colors, brilliant, sharp, nuanced. He perceived textures. He heard music.

"Shan," Priscilla said from beside him.

"Priscilla," he answered. "Open your shields—only a fraction, mind."

He Saw her open—no wider than a cat's whisker—and felt her shocked delight in the moment before she closed herself again.

"This is a dangerous place," she said.

"Perhaps," he answered, opening his own shields wider. "But I will tell you, Priscilla, that I am *well*. Look for yourself."

He felt her scan him; felt the prick of amazement through their links.

"Dear Goddess."

Padi stepped out onto the ramp beside them.

"Why is the air—sparkling?" she asked.

"The guidebook's invigorating atmosphere," Shan said, and felt the weight of her gaze fall on him—on *all* of him.

"Why are your shields open?"

"Because I am weak and prefer to be wholly myself," he said promptly. "Why are *your* shields open?"

"I am searching for context," she told him primly.

Farther up the ramp, Mar Tyn pai'Fortana leaned close to his companion and murmured, "Dyoli, I feel—odd."

"I feel it too, my Mar Tyn," she responded, reaching up to touch the Ixin pin her brother had placed on her collar, testimony of her place in the clan. "As if something were...enhancing us."

"Escort approaching," Grad Elbin called from the bottom of the ramp, where he and Tima stood between them and the docks.

"So it is," Shan said, turning to the left and sweeping a hand out, to show the rest of them the delegation moving purposefully down the dock—four persons in what appeared to be a uniform—possibly security personnel—pacing three jitneys.

"Places everyone," Shan said gaily.

He and Priscilla went down the ramp first, followed by Padi; then Dyoli and Mar Tyn, with Karna Tivit bringing up the rear.

The jitneys stopped and a tall, brusque woman stepped out of the passenger's compartment of the first. She, too, was wearing a uniform, subtly different from those worn by the security people. Coming forward, she produced a bow faintly reminiscent of a formal bow of welcome.

"I am Urta krogerSlyte, master of Colemeno Port," she said.

Shan bowed in answer—trader to portmaster, whether their host recognized it or not.

"Portmaster krogerSlyte, you honor us. I am Shan yos'Galan, master trader aboard Clan Korval's *Dutiful Passage*. Allow me to present Captain Priscilla Delacroix y Mendoza. Also, here is Padi yos'Galan, trader and my second; Healer Dyoli ven'Deelin, representing Clan Ixin, and her assistant Mar Tyn pai'Fortana."

"We welcome all," the portmaster declared sturdily.

She stepped to one side and gestured, showing them the jitneys.

"Will you be pleased to ride? There is a small entertainment in your honor at the Great Hall. You will meet the members of our governing council, and also the managers of the port markets."

"Splendid!" Shan said, feeling positively exhilarated. Carefully, he closed his shields—not fully. It would not do to become inebriated on Colemeno's fine atmosphere.

"Let us aboard then," the portmaster said, opening the door of the jitney she had recently vacated. "Captain Mendoza, if you will do me the honor?"

· · · · ❉ · · · ·

The invigorating atmosphere was acting on Moonhawk. Priscilla could feel her growing stronger, even as the jitney lumbered through the port.

She had felt this sort of thing before, when power was raised in temple to create a working, to access one of the Names, or to gain the attention of the Goddess.

Raising that kind—that much!—power took the concentrated and coordinated effort of many talents. Who could conceive of an entire world where power existed at those levels naturally? Goddess knew how this environment had worked upon the small talents in the time since they had been set down here. The portmaster had betrayed no particular talent to Priscilla's quick scan, merely an increased brightness of her soul, and a structured feeling to her pattern, which became one who was responsible for enforcing regulations.

Moonhawk, however...

Moonhawk was growing stronger. Priscilla was *also* growing stronger, but that availed her nothing for her own defense. She was the vessel of the Goddess; everything that was hers was Moonhawk's to claim.

The jitney pulled up before a large building, its façade bright with mosaic. The door was opened, and the portmaster slid out, then Padi, and Shan. Priscilla debarked last, taking Shan's offered hand and feeling a spark leap between them.

"Priscilla?" he murmured.

"I am—well," she said, and did *not* add "*too* well." Rather, she turned aside to consider the mosaic. "What fine work," she said truthfully.

Portmaster krogerSlyte rose to the occasion.

"This art was made by Ming tawEllir, and depicts the Arrival of the Outcasts at Colemeno. It is noteworthy for both its accuracy and its beauty. There are lectures given on the history contained in this mosaic. If you are interested, we will arrange for you to attend one. Very quickly, if you look just here—"

A heavy hand gestured toward the lower portion of the scene, just off-center, to the left.

"Here, you see the ships that brought the Outcasts, two marked with the Tree-and-Dragon, and one with the Rabbit-and-Moon."

"Clan Korval," Shan murmured from beside her, "and Clan Ixin."

The portmaster sighed lightly. "It demands study; it *deserves* study—especially from those so intimately involved in the event. Captain, we will, I swear it, find time for you to commune with the art, and to attend a lecture."

"You are very kind," Priscilla murmured, as Shan turned to beckon Dyoli.

"See here, Healer ven'Deelin—a ship of your clan."

"Beautifully rendered," Dyoli said with commendable enthusiasm. "See you, Mar Tyn?"

"I do," he answered in his quiet way. "The artist had an eye."

"Exactly," agreed the portmaster, visibly gratified by this plentiful praise.

"For now, the Council's reception awaits us. If you will kindly follow, just through this doorway..."

· · · ·✵· · · ·

The portside door opened and the babble of many voices ceased as if cut with a knife, everyone in the reception room beyond turning toward the widening portal.

First came Portmaster krogerSlyte, and three persons accoutered and uniformed befitting security persons entered. Security ranged themselves advantageously and promptly faded from conscious sight. The portmaster, having stepped to one side of the open door, made a wide sweep of her arm.

"I am pleased," she said to the room in her large, carrying voice, "to present to the assembly our honored guests from the Tree-and-Dragon Trade Family.

"Here is Captain Priscilla Delacroix y Mendoza."

A tall, slim woman, short black curls framing an oval face—she bowed to the room, and stepped to the portmaster's side.

"Master Trader Shan yos'Galan."

A match for his captain in height, and her perfect foil in coloring. He bowed to the room, and stood aside.

"Trader Padi yos'Galan."

Not quite so tall as the captain or the master trader but, for all of that, long in the leg, light brown hair worn in a neat tail at the back of her head. Her face, with its bold nose and decided chin, suggested that she was not merely kin to the master trader, but *close kin*. Like captain and master trader, her jacket bore the Tree-and-Dragon sigil on the breast.

"Healer Dyoli ven'Deelin."

A woman of normal height, with fewer angles, her hair pale red; her jacket showed a Moon-and-Rabbit patch on the breast.

"Mar Tyn pai'Fortana."

Here was the least imposing member of the trade party—slight, small, and instantly forgettable. His jacket bore no patch at all.

Zeni gorminAstir, Chair of Council, stepped to the center of the room.

"The Council of the Civilized is pleased to welcome our guests."

She bowed, the entire room following suit.

The guests bowed likewise, then Master Trader yos'Galan stepped forward to engage with the Chair, while the remainder of the guests moved forward, to mingle and to make themselves known.

· · · ❖ · · ·

"Ixin!" a voice said excitedly at Dyoli's elbow.

She turned, a pleasant expression on her face, and bowed slightly to the woman before her.

"Indeed," she said, "Ixin." She touched the pin on her collar, and the other woman raised her hand to touch the pin on *her* collar.

"Cousin?" Dyoli said, which was flattery—perhaps. Or perhaps not. The other woman had . . . something in her face, something familiar. It was not entirely an Ixin face, but very nearly so.

"It may be," the other said. "According to records held by our kin-group, we *were* Ixin, relocated with the others. The clan—this is in my long-ago grandfather's diary—the clan had protected him and his heir. They would have continued to do so, but he would not have it. In the diary, it says that fear of exposure had already made him weary, and soon would make him reckless. He wanted better for his heir—a life without fear; a life in which she could live to the fullness of *all* her talents.

"Here, where are my manners?" she exclaimed suddenly. "I am Betya seelyFaire. Come, let us at least find you both tea, and perhaps some pastries . . ."

· · · ❖ · · ·

Padi had drifted away from the center of the room, her eye on Father, who was positively boisterous. Priscilla was speaking politely to a sternly groomed man and a soft elder lady. She seemed subdued, though how that was possible with the very air crackling, Padi could scarcely understand.

Farther across the room, Dyoli and Mar Tyn had been captured by a woman who was guiding them to the refreshment tables.

She—

Padi . . . turned, and very nearly walked over a young woman with short-cut brown hair, merry brown eyes, and a fetching grin.

"Good-day to you, Trader Padi yos'Galan," she said, her voice high and sweet. "I am Saru bernRoanti, assistant manager of the port market."

"Aha!" Padi said with a grin of her own. "*Just* the person I was wanting to talk to!"

"I'm glad to hear you say so," said Saru bernRoanti. "Why don't we find some tea and cookies and a quiet place to coze?"

"There, for an instance?" asked Padi, nodding toward a curtained corner at the far back of the room.

"Trader," beamed Saru bernRoanti, "I believe we have made a perfect plan."

· · · · ❋ · · · ·

"But you are a Healer, not a trader," Betya seelyFaire was saying. "Do you attend the trade mission in your official capacity?"

"As I am needed," Dyoli said, taking comfort from the presence of Mar Tyn at her side. The effervescence in the air was acting upon her in a disquieting fashion. She ought, perhaps, to seal her shields, but she did not care to stand blind in a roomful of people who were, as Padi yos'Galan had so succinctly put it, considerably wary of them.

"I am with the trade mission as a partner on the trade side, representing Clan Ixin," she continued, focusing on Councilor seelyFaire, whom she read as genuinely interested *and* on the lookout for her own profit. "If the master trader's plans bear the fruit he desires, I may be based here for some time."

"But how exciting! What does the master trader plan?"

Dyoli cast her eyes down.

"It is not my place to speak for a master trader," she murmured.

"No, of course not!" said the other, abashed.

Dyoli looked up and smiled.

"You might assist us with a matter of local custom and law, if you would be so very kind. You understand that there was very little information available to us concerning The Redlands. Are there prohibitions regarding talents? Will it even be possible for us to be based here?"

"Prohibitions—not as such," said Councilor seelyFaire, serious now that she had been asked an official question. "You would each need to have your talents evaluated by the proper experts. I may perform a quick scan as we stand here, if you permit."

Dyoli inclined her head and heard Mar Tyn, beside her, murmur, "Of course."

There was a brief, not unpleasant, weight against her soul, and the very lightest of spicy breezes wafted over her Healer senses.

"So!" said the councilor with a smile. "A brief scan gives me no cause for concern. You are both entirely unexceptionable—Luck, Healing, and a tiny bit of Sight, is it? So long as you're not an oracle, you need have no concern there!"

She laughed.

"When our ancestors arrived, there were tests administered. To tell truth, it has been so long since we had any-one wishing to settle, I don't know if tests are—or should be—any longer required. Something else for the Council to discuss in the light of the changes the Dust has made."

Mar Tyn stirred, and the councilor looked to him.

"I wonder," he said slowly. "Would it be possible for us to be evaluated—fully—now? If there is something that has eluded your surface scan, we ought to know it, before the master trader puts all in train."

Betya seelyFaire frowned slightly, then nodded.

"Yes, I see your point—very astute! If you don't mind a ride in a jitney, I can take you to Evaluation Expert ringZun, and you can be examined immediately. One moment, only..."

Her thin, pleasant face went briefly blank. Dyoli drew in a sharp breath, but before she had exhaled, the councilor was smiling again.

"Yes, we are fortunate! He is available, and we may see him at once."

"Excellent," Dyoli said, rising with their host. Mar Tyn was slower, and she tarried for him, whispering in his ear as they followed the councilor toward the door.

"Mar Tyn, what is this?"

"We are better out of this room," he said. "My Luck would have it so." He paused, turning his head to look fully into her eyes; his dazzled.

"Dyoli. My Luck—it's changed."

· · · ·✳· · · ·

"Bentamin, fetch the captain a nice cup of tea, do, and some of those delightful fruit bars."

The person so addressed, who had been made known to Priscilla as Bentamin chastaMeir, Warden of the Civilized, considered the elder lady for a long moment before he bowed very slightly.

"It will of course be my pleasure," he said, with an edge to his soft words. "I will be only a moment, Captain. Aunt Asta."

He walked away toward the refreshment table and the elder lady laughed softly.

"Well, that's fortunate," she said, low-voiced. "He's perfectly capable of 'porting an entire tray full of cakes from there to here, and holding them for an hour or so. I could see him considering the possibility, though he finally decided to be seemly. Quickly now, my dear, tell me how I may assist you."

Priscilla felt Moonhawk grow heavier on her soul.

"Assist me?" she said, trying to strengthen her inner defenses.

"There is no time to be coy!" the elder lady snapped. "Bentamin will be back in a moment. Let us be plain. I am the Oracle, and you are the Great One who is in need."

Priscilla drew a breath even as a whirlwind of energy swirled her away to a distant part of herself, and she heard Moonhawk's voice.

"I seek the Hill, Oracle. I must be there in twilight."

"I can show you the way. Is it you alone who travels?"

"There is another. He will follow. He must."

"Then we go—now, for the Warden is returning. Are you able to travel by the Ways?"

"Yes."

"Take my hand then. I will guide you."

Priscilla struggled for control, and felt a soft touch, as though someone had put a gentle hand against her hair.

Peace, child, said the voice of the Goddess. *I promised you freedom, and freedom you will have. But you must not distract me now. Sleep.*

Returning with two cups of tea and a plate of cookies

balanced between his hands and his thought, Bentamin saw his aunt—No. He saw the Oracle to the Civilized take Captain Mendoza's slim hand, and lean confidentially forward. There was a moment of disorientation, as if the lines of reality had blurred and run.

Reality reasserted itself, sharp-edged and unequivocal.

Save that Captain Mendoza and the Oracle—were gone.

• • • • ❖ • • • •

"Of course," Shan was saying to Chair gorminAstir. "I will be most delighted to speak with Trader Isfelm. It is, if I may be candid, exactly what I had hoped for—that there was an established, inward route, so to speak, that had The Redlands as one of its anchors. When is the trader expected?"

The inside of his head itched; his chest was constricted, and the link to Priscilla was—hot, hot—

Cold.

He jerked around, saw her standing with an elder lady, talking with calm seriousness, even as he felt her—felt his lifemate struggling.

"Your pardon," he said to Chair gorminAstir, and moved toward the two ladies who were speaking so calmly together. The elder extended a hand; Priscilla hesitated, and he felt her struggle increase.

"Priscilla!" he cried, pushing his way through a knot of conversationalists.

He reached for their link—but it slipped out of his grasp, Priscilla herself nothing more than a shadow, dreaming.

Four steps away, Priscilla—Moonhawk!—took the elder lady's hand.

Shan leapt, stumbled as the room tilted sideways, recovered his stride—

They were gone.

And he was face-to-face with an astonished man who had just dropped two cups and a plate of cookies.

"You!" the man snapped.

Shan felt the surge of his will, Saw the restraints forming—and it would not do, at all, for him to be taken, just when her blasted Goddess had snatched Priscilla away. He felt a round smoothness between his fingers, too familiar and too useful. He took a breath, and thought himself invisible.

· · · ✳ · · ·

Priscilla and the elder lady—who Saru named the Oracle—vanished.

Padi leapt to her feet.

"Run!" she snapped at Saru, who didn't wait to be told twice.

Father had very nearly reached the spot where the two ladies weren't, and there—*there*, the strong-willed man—the Warden, also according to Saru—Padi Saw him create restraints, his will a visible thing, snapping toward Father—

Who faded gently against the air, vanishing completely.

Padi did not wait to see anything else.

She ducked behind the curtains, abandoning both cups and cookies—and only then realized her error.

The Warden was shouting for *the others, find them and hold them!*

Padi bit her lip. Priscilla had asked her to protect Father by any means necessary—and her best means of doing that was to remain uncaptured. If she was taken, she would be the Warden's bait, to bring Father into his net.

Unfortunately, in her haste to hide, she had trapped herself, for the little alcove behind the curtain had no exit save back into the main room.

Padi sighed. She was not a teleport—she thought—nor was she able to vanish into thin air, as Father had done—and very unnerving *that* had been, to observe!

I need help, she thought, and suddenly understood why norbears kept—and kept adding to—their index of useful persons. Who did she know, who might be able to assist her in what was quickly becoming a battle between *dramliz*?

One grey eye and one green eye in a pointed, half-wild face. *Call me Tekelia, and I will come.*

She closed her eyes, pushing aside her immediate peril, the inadequate curtains, the danger in the room beyond. She stepped back—back into the memory of a comfortable room, a tea service, an affable host...

Tekelia, she thought. And repeated the name aloud, in a breathy whisper.

"Tekelia."

· · · ·✳· · · ·

"Lock the doors!" Portmaster krogerSlyte ordered, which wasn't, Bentamin allowed, a bad idea.

It was merely useless.

Captain Mendoza and the Oracle had not troubled themselves with doors, nor had the white-haired master trader. The other three—

He scanned the room hurriedly, catching no hint of Healer ven'Deelin or her companion.

"Warden."

He turned to see timid Councilor azieEm at his side.

"Healer ven'Deelin and Mar Tyn pai'Fortana left the reception in company with Betya seelyFaire."

He frowned at her.

"Where did they go?"

"Warden, I don't know. I happened to look up as they passed through the door."

"Thank you," said Bentamin. "Please inform Chair gorminAstir of this circumstance. She will be able to contact Councilor seelyFaire."

"Yes," said azieEm, and went away.

Bentamin drew a breath, heard a small clink, and glanced down at the mess of broken dishes and spilled cookies and tea. With a sigh, he banished it into the Hall's prep area.

Then he began another scan of the room, seeking one signature: the one person yet to be accounted for, the slim, neat young trader with her air of pleased competence . . .

He Saw something, at the edge of his Vision.

Something . . .

. . . just . . .

. . . *there.*

He turned toward the curtained alcove.

· · · ·❊· · · ·

"I admit," a low familiar voice murmured, "that I had hoped you would call me farther."

Padi took a careful breath.

"Tekelia?"

"So you did call me, and so I did come. But, really, Padi, *only* to Colemeno's own port?"

"How was I to *know* you were on Colemeno?"

"That's fair," Tekelia acknowledged; "and I *am* pleased that you called. May I know *why* you called?"

"I'm in trouble," she said, peeking 'round the edge of the curtain.

"Is that rare?"

"Sadly, no. But I'm about to be discovered, taken, and held hostage."

"That sounds wonderfully dire. Who would dare hold you hostage?"

"Do you see that man with the broken cups on his shoes?"

She felt a movement behind her, heard a slight snort.

"I do, yes."

"He—" Padi began—and stopped, staring. The pool of tea, the smashed plates, and soggy cookies were gone.

And the man was walking toward the curtains.

"He's found me," she whispered, despairing.

"Very likely. He's quite good. If he got even a glimpse of your signature, he will certainly find you. Especially, if I may, *your* signature."

"Can you help me escape?"

"Escape? Well, I suppose I could, but he's looking rather peeved already. I suggest it is not in your best interest to make him angry. He's much easier to deal with when he's cool-headed. Best to meet him now, I think." Tekelia paused.

The man—he did, indeed, look peeved, Padi thought— was nearly to the alcove where the two of them stood behind the curtain.

"Would you," Tekelia asked delicately, "have any idea what has happened to annoy him?"

Padi took a breath.

"He's going to find both of us in a minute," she said.

"Yes, that's foregone. Why is he annoyed?"

"Captain Mendoza, who is also my father's lifemate, stole a plump lady who was this man's escort, and took her elsewhere. When he tried to—capture—my father, who had tried to prevent the abduction—my father vanished in turn."

"Poor Bentamin," said Tekelia, around a breath of what Padi very much feared was laughter.

"You know him?"

"Everyone knows the Warden of the Civilized. As it happens, I know him better than most, as we're cousins. His name is Bentamin chastaMeir, and I believe that the plump lady must have been our Aunt Asta, Oracle to the Civilized. Do you know for yourself that Captain Mendoza stole her?"

"Do you think otherwise?"

"Well, it is possible that Aunt Asta wanted the captain for some small this or that—a private chat, for instance—and whisked them both off. Aunt Asta is rarely allowed parties, so does not often meet new people. If Captain Mendoza proved interesting, as I'm sure she must have done, it's perfectly possible that Aunt Asta became . . . a little . . . greedy."

"Captain Mendoza is a very powerful *dramliza*," Padi said slowly.

"Yes, certainly. So is Aunt Asta. Ah, here's Bentamin at last. Don't squeak."

"I never squeak!" Padi said indignantly—and the curtain was yanked aside.

"Trader yos'Galan," the Warden of the Civilized stated coolly, "may I have—"

"Hello, Bentamin," Tekelia said from behind Padi's shoulder.

The cool-voiced man blinked, and looked, his expression going from peevish to stunned.

"How did you get in here?"

"I asked Tekelia to come to me," Padi said.

"*You* asked Tekelia to come to you," Bentamin repeated, his gaze back on her face. "How are you acquainted with Tekelia?"

"We met in charming and unusual circumstances," Tekelia said. "Is Aunt Asta here, cousin? I haven't seen her in such a time, I was quite looking forward."

"You cannot be here," Bentamin snapped.

"I was invited," Tekelia replied mildly.

"And I," Padi said, with emphasis, "am tired of being pent in." She stepped out of the alcove, and the Warden gave ground.

Tekelia looked over Bentamin's shoulder.

"No one seems to be taking the slightest interest in me."

"That is because none of us is here at the moment," Bentamin snapped. "Tekelia—go away. You cannot be in Civilization."

"Can I not?"

Tekelia directed a glance downward, and Padi did, too, taking in a rough sweater, heavy pants and boots.

"You aren't really dressed for a formal reception," Padi said. "I ought to have given warning."

"So that I could tarry to change into something more appropriate? No, you felt yourself in peril, you called, I came. That is a perfectly proper sequence, and there is nothing to forgive. In fact, it is precisely what I hoped would occur, ever since I received your token.

"As for clothing appropriate to a reception—that's a small thing. Here."

There was a slight shimmer; Tekelia went misty, and was solid again in the next moment, wearing a ruffled and wide-sleeved red shirt under an embroidered black vest. The scarlet flowers on the vest repeated down the side of the deep black pants until they broke at the arch of shiny black boots.

"There now," Tekelia's smile was pleased. "Am I not wholly civilized?"

"Not quite wholly," Padi said. "Your hair wants attention. Here, I have another tie."

She walked behind.

"Stand still," she said, fishing in her belt. Carefully, she reached up, gathering up the warm, rough mass, combing it with the small comb she had also taken from her belt, smoothing it, and at last confining it with the tie.

"There!" she said. "That looks very well."

She stepped up again to Tekelia's side. Bentamin was staring.

"Have I committed a social error?" she asked.

"In no way," Tekelia assured her with a smile.

"Your pardon," Bentamin added. "I had been under the . . . obviously mistaken . . . impression that no one was permitted to touch Tekelia's person. Where is Captain Mendoza, if you please, Trader?"

Padi pressed her lips together.

The Warden of the Civilized sighed.

"Very well. Where is Master Trader yos'Galan?"

"Padi," Tekelia said gently. "Bentamin is your friend in this. He *must* find the Oracle. The whole of Civilization depends upon her Sight, and she is Bentamin's specific and most particular charge. It will go very bad for him, if he loses her."

Padi did not quite throttle the laugh.

"Yes," Tekelia said approvingly. "It is *exactly* that dire."

Bentamin glowered—and Padi held up a hand to forestall more bad temper.

"No, we are *all three* in the soup! Bentamin has lost the Oracle. I have lost my father, after his lifemate had me *particularly* promise to protect him with my life. And Tekelia—"

"I—" Tekelia interrupted, "have missed my Aunt Asta, of whom I am quite fond."

"Why would Captain Mendoza steal our Oracle?" Bentamin demanded.

"It is . . . possible that . . . *Captain Mendoza* . . . did not," Padi said slowly. "In her youth, Captain Mendoza willingly agreed to serve as a receptacle for another intelligence. I do not quite understand how, but this intelligence may, at whim, fill the captain, override her will and—perform acts in the physical world."

She paused, waiting for either of them to laugh. There was instead a thoughtful silence before Tekelia said, "I believe we have found Aunt Asta's Great Ones, cousin. Or at least one of them."

"I fear you may be correct. Trader yos'Galan, any information you have regarding the intentions of either Captain Mendoza or the intelligence which occasionally commands her may be vital to the safety of Civilization."

"And the Haosa, too," Tekelia added, voice dry.

Bentamin moved a hand, fingers fluttering.

"That goes without saying."

"Which is well, since it is said so little."

Padi cleared her throat—and stared at the cup of tea Bentamin was offering her.

"Thank you," she said, and took the cup from his hand, sipping gratefully.

"Priscilla—Captain Mendoza—has Long-Sight," she said slowly. "She had Seen herself and my father on a hillside at Colemeno as day faded, a crowd of strangers ringing them 'round. She Saw my father fall, as if struck."

She paused for another sip of tea.

"She told me that she had felt the—the Goddess, as she had it—growing stronger and feared either that the Goddess was the source of his distress, or that she herself would be so depleted by the Goddess's use that she would not be able to assist him."

She took a breath.

"She told me these things so that I could be aware and guard my father from—anything or anyone—that might seek to harm him."

She looked at their faces, saw that they were listening courteously.

"Priscilla did say that Long-Sight is unreliable due to a general lack of context."

A smile broke the severity of the Warden's face.

"Now, there's a particular accuracy," he murmured. "Please, continue."

Padi took one more deep breath, and told out the last of it.

"I asked her if she thought I was strong enough to—to destroy a Goddess. She said that I was at least strong enough to distract one."

Tekelia laughed. Bentamin inclined his head.

Padi finished her tea.

"It seems the Great One seeks Ribbon Dance Hill," Tekelia said. "Certainly, Aunt Asta could take her there."

"But for what cause?" asked the Warden.

Both looked to Padi, who moved her shoulders.

"Priscilla said—no context."

"Oracles," Bentamin said, looking to Tekelia, "very rarely See all."

"Oracles exist to tantalize us," Tekelia said. "We know where they will be, Bentamin—and when."

"At least we know where the Oracle and the Great One will be. Master Trader yos'Galan however—"

"Master Trader yos'Galan seems a clever man. If he is required on Ribbon Dance Hill as the day turns to twilight, I think that we can trust him to be there."

Bentamin glanced at the cup in Padi's hand.

"More tea, Trader?"

"Thank you, no."

The cup vanished, with a little puff of cool air against Padi's fingers.

"I must inform the Council," Bentamin said. "I will be part of the circle on Ribbon Dance Hill."

"Naturally," Tekelia said.

"I may be constrained to bring others. The entire Council is not beyond the possible, though I will make my best efforts to limit their enthusiasm."

"I understand," Tekelia said. "You to yours, and I to mine. I will bear Padi with me, and gather the Haosa."

Bentamin frowned.

"Why?"

"It was Seen, was it not? A circle on the hilltop at twilight. The councilors may form a mob and witness, if they must, but the evening's work will fall on the Haosa."

"I agree that the Haosa must be a part of it. However, I will take charge of Trader yos'Galan."

"No," Padi said. "You will not. I will go with Tekelia."

"Trader, I guarantee that no harm will come to you while you are under the protection of Civilization."

"Which," said Tekelia, sotto voce, "has just lost its Oracle."

Padi drew in an unsteady breath. Bentamin looked black.

At that precise moment, she felt a hand slide into hers, warm and big and reassuring, and felt a slight, hard pressure against the side of her palm, like the band of a ring.

"I am going with Tekelia," she said again, tightening her grip around those sudden, surprising—and invisible—fingers.

She looked to the left, meeting Tekelia's interested gaze.

"I am going with you," she said firmly. "To Ribbon Dance Hill."

"As you wish," Tekelia said, extending a hand.

Padi bestowed her unoccupied hand, felt strong fingers close around hers. There was a moment of scintillant delight before the reception room was gone, lost in a swirl of darkness and light.

Tarona Rusk
Her Proper Business

. . . .

SHE HAD FULFILLED HER LAST PROMISE.

She had dismissed her pilot.

It was now time to complete her last piece of business.

She had found a place to be alone, where her actions would harm none but the intended target.

It was time.

Closing her eyes, she began to gather herself to herself.

Immolation was no more than she deserved.

Ribbon Dance Hill

· · · · · · · · · · · · · · · · ·

PADI FELT SOLID GROUND BENEATH HER FEET, AND HER hands held firmly in two very different grips. The air displayed a slight, glittering turbulence, as if they had emerged into a flurry of ice crystals.

The crystals continued to swirl, obscuring their surroundings, even as they slowly faded. When they were gone, Padi looked up into a vaulting dark-blue sky, and down on distant trees, and what was perhaps the shine of a stream between the flutter of leaves. The air was cool despite the sun, which, to be fair, was not high in the sky, and the invigorating atmosphere pinged audibly against Padi's shields.

Father's grip slackened, and his hand slipped away from hers. Padi knew a moment of panic, that she might lose him, which was only foolishness. Priscilla would be here at twilight, at the behest of her Goddess, and Father would surely be here to meet her.

"Ribbon Dance Hill," Tekelia said from her side, fingers still entwined with hers. "The ambient is concentrated here. You might open your shields, if you wish to. Even the Civilized are welcome here."

Padi turned to look into mismatched purple and brown eyes.

"Am I Civilized?" she asked.

There was a moment of silence.

"I hesitate to classify you, Padi yos'Galan. You are near enough to the Haosa that we were able to meet inside the ambient, despite the distance between us. Yet your presence failed to distress any of the Council, who are the most Civilized on all Colemeno. Furthermore—"

Tekelia raised their linked hands.

"This...*this* cannot happen to me, lest we court grievous harm to you. And yet, here we stand, neither of us flung into the ether by the force of our connection."

Tekelia's fingers tightened, and for a moment, it seemed to Padi that both eyes were the same dark shade of brown.

Then came a grin, eyes mismatched and merry. "In fact, you are a puzzle."

Padi sighed.

"That would seem to be my role."

"And who can say but that you're fit for it?" Tekelia looked again at their linked hands, gently raised them and kissed Padi's knuckles. "Thank you."

Padi drew in a hard breath, unsure of what answer she might make as her hand was released, and Tekelia made a show of looking 'round the sunny hilltop, paused, and spoke.

"If you please, sir, I must know if you are a Reaver."

There was a pause, then Father's voice, speaking out of thin air, "Naturally, my first impulse is to say *certainly not!* But perhaps I will have more credibility if you tell me what a Reaver *is*."

There was a sudden impression of fog clearing, and Father was standing only a few steps away, his hair mildly disheveled, and the red counter moving across the back of his hand.

"We called them Reavers, having no better name," Tekelia said. "They were talents, enslaved, come here at the will of their master to steal any of us that they could."

Father tipped his head, white brows drawing together.

"Something about this rings strangely familiar. To your point, however—no, I am not a Reaver."

Tekelia took a deep breath, and met Father's gaze squarely.

"Then I fear I must ask worse—are you the puppetmaster?"

Both brows shot up.

"You have a reason for asking worse, I assume? May I know what it is?"

"The Reavers each bore *this* as part of their signature."

Fog boiled briefly, and there it hung in the crystal air between them, a sleek, dark thing at once repellent and attractive; twisted, like a tesseract.

"My reason is that I see this, in you," Tekelia finished.

"What?" Padi cried, and Tekelia glanced at her.

"Open your Eyes and Look. I would be pleased to be mistaken."

"You are not mistaken," Father said, even as Padi threw her shields down, opened her Eyes and Looked.

For a moment, the intricacies of Sight threatened to overwhelm her. She—blinked—and stared and there—*there* was the wholeness of Father, very much more complex than Vanz, wider, deeper—*older*; informed by a life lived on so many levels—

Jewels glittered among the weaving; some threads brilliant, others dull—

But none so determinedly, willfully black as the two threads woven deep into the core of him.

"Who?" she wondered and did not realize she had spoken aloud until she heard Father's voice in answer.

"Tarona Rusk, the *dramliza* broken and subverted by the Department, who in turn broke and subverted others."

He paused, then added quietly, "I saved her life, and she saved mine, which is why there are two threads. For there was never a Healing made that did not bind both Healer and Healed."

Padi closed her Eyes, and turned to Tekelia.

"What happened," she demanded, "to these—Reavers?"

"They died."

"What killed them?"

"An interesting question," Tekelia said, turning to face her. "We believe that they had been bound so tightly, that when they were cut free—the links that tied them to their master broken all at once—the shock of liberation stunned them. The links sustained, as well as imprisoned—and they died before they could surmount the shock and repair themselves."

Tekelia looked aside.

"Your pardon, sir?"

"How many?" Father said, his voice harsh. "*How many* died?"

"Dozens—all that were sent to us."

Father took a hard breath, another—and closed his eyes, but not before Padi saw the tears.

"That, I do own," he said, scarcely a whisper now. "I was the knife that cut their links. I knew that some would not be strong enough—but—gods! *All* died?"

"All that we knew of, here," Tekelia said softly. "If there were others..."

"There *were* others!" Padi snapped. "Dyoli and Mar Tyn survived. Surely—"

"Mar Tyn is a Luck," Father interrupted, "and Dyoli is an enormously determined person." His face was wet; his breath unsteady. "I *knew* that some would not survive, but—she was bound to *hundreds*—"

He stopped and visibly composed himself.

"Your pardons," he said, and stepped—aside— remaining quite visible to the outer eyes, and more completely absent for all of that.

"Where has he gone?" Tekelia asked sharply.

"Healspace," Padi said, never doubting it. "Will he—*can he*—call her to him there?"

"Healspace is what you were looking for when you came to me for tea?"

"Yes."

"Then I would say—yes, he can call anyone he shares a link with to him—there."

Tekelia's face was somber.

"Should we," Padi asked, "support him?"

"No," Tekelia said slowly. "I think that we would only—be in the way. However..."

A pause, as Tekelia turned 'round there atop the hill, the thick air following in streamers of translucent color.

Ribbon Dance Hill, Padi recalled, and glanced up to the cerulean sky.

"How long," she asked, "until twilight?"

"Not very long, though the light lingers longer here on the hill."

Padi brought her gaze down from the sky. Tekelia was standing, hands on hips, scowling. Father remained as he had been, loose limbed and absent.

"How long do you think this meeting will take?" Tekelia asked.

Padi moved her shoulders.

"I—one minute past an hour was too long for him to be absent in a Healing, is what he said to Trader Denobli, when we undertook to rescue Vanz in that place."

"So we have both a time frame and a warning. Can you follow him there, if necessary?"

Padi bit her lip.

"I—" she began, meaning to deny it—and stopped, seeing the silver thread that bound her to Father, shimmering like a guide line in the busy air.

"Yes," she said to Tekelia's interested eyes. "I can."

"If it does become necessary, that will be your task. In the meanwhile, I ask your indulgence while I call the Haosa together. We must, after all, give the Great One her crowd."

Healspace

· · · · · · · · · ·

"TARONA RUSK."

Shan heard his own voice boom and roll away into the mists like thunder, accompanied by sharp flares of lightning. There was a sense of pointed activity in this iteration of Healspace; the fog roiling so energetically that he had, for a heart-stopping instant, thought he had come to some other place entirely.

But, no—it *was* Healspace. He felt it welcome him as an old and valued friend; the fog that immediately supported him obligingly shading to pink.

Apparently the invigorating atmosphere—what Tekelia-*dramliza* styled the *ambient*—was acting upon Healspace, too.

There was, Shan thought, a certain amount of sense to that. It was taught that Healspace existed in a dimension accessible to those who were talented, and that each Healer and *dramliza* was their own doorway into that shared dimension. Merely, he had utilized the doorway of himself, and entered a Healspace informed by Ribbon Dance Hill and the ambient enclosing Colemeno.

It came to him, as if a gift from the energetic fogs, that Wu and Fabricant's "invigorating atmosphere" was precisely why Priscilla's Goddess had chosen to come here to die.

Which brought to mind, too vividly, that there were other deaths in the Balance.

"Tarona Rusk," he said again, his voice rolling away into the fogs.

For a moment, he knew despair; she would not answer. Why *should* she answer? Even as he asked the question, he felt a—tug at the core of him, a stab of pain in his heart.

Before him, the fogs darkened, as if they were become thunderclouds indeed. A wind whipped the leading edge into a froth—bleak, dire, and toothy. The link that bound him to Tarona Rusk was burning, burning cold, singeing the stalwart pink fog that supported him.

At the heart of the storm, a darker shadow moved, and a voice rode the cold froth to him.

"Are you with me, Little Healer?"

"I am," he returned.

"Now, I wonder why?"

The dark clouds blew, and she was there, straight and edgy, and lethal as any dagger. The links that bound them all but froze his breath in his lungs.

"How many of yours did I murder?" he asked her and, impossibly, he heard her laugh.

"More than a dozen and less than twelve hundred," she said, darkly flippant. "The brights and the small talents—the *innocent*, you might say—they were lost to a soul. The stronger talents—Healers, nearly all, from the middle range to master class—were able to preserve themselves, and in some cases to assist their juniors."

"Did you send recruitment teams to Colemeno, on the edge of the Dust?"

"I did—and they died, but those were at risk in any wise, Little Healer. Lavish no guilt upon them."

"I cut the ties."

"You did. And Colemeno is too strange to survive. We had to try, but we never thought we would succeed."

Shan took a breath—Tarona Rusk held up a hand.

"You will perhaps wish a report, having released me as your agent into the heart of the Department. Those who survived their liberation have arranged a defeat from within. The Commander has been vanquished, and Headquarters is even now being turned over to the Scouts, working through a transition team.

"Your revenge is complete; the Dragon has prevailed. Are you not pleased?"

"Relieved, let us say. You have done exemplary work."

"I have done nothing, save exact my own revenges and lend my support to those who had shaped and seized the plan for the Department's defeat. Now, I am needed no longer, my purposes are fulfilled, and there remains one more task before me."

The storm clouds billowed. He heard her resolve, tasted her intention, and shouted, with all the power available to him.

"NO!"

The murmuring paused, bleakness tempered somewhat by . . . chagrin.

"Now what it is?"

"Tell me what benefit accrues from self-murder," Shan snapped.

"Aside from ridding the universe of the cancer that is myself?"

"Far better to Balance the ill you have done in the past, with good in the future. You have the capacity. You have the means."

There was a pause, as if his words had struck her heart, prompting her to reconsider.

"I agree," she said then, and it was humor he caught from her, and a certain grim eagerness. "I have the means to do some small good. I merely need to divest myself of that which is no longer required.

"Little Healer, I make you a gift."

There was a distant sense of forces gathering.

And of forces being released.

He Saw it, a wave of dark, brilliant energy, boiling through Healspace, a tsunami of power.

He spared no thought for his shields; rather, he grasped the links that bound them. He felt her surprise, stilled her instinctive withdrawal even as he formed that which he would give her—a gift for a bold and damaged soul; a payment to the future in Balance for the past.

The fogs of Healspace were gentle no more; they boiled, merciless. He might deflect them, but what harm would he cause?

With a breath he opened himself utterly, accepting the download of power.

And in the last moment before he was engulfed, he pressed upon those links that bound them, and instilled them with his gift.

The Healer's penultimate mercy: forgetfulness.

The wave struck, bearing him up into a boiling sea of energy, smashing him out of Healspace, and down onto his knees, in the center of a circle of staring faces.

· · · · ❖ · · · ·

"Father!"

Padi lunged forward—and stopped, staring at the taut figure stitched in black flames, his outline fluid, melting. She felt a flicker from the base of her spine—the seat of her power, so Lina had always insisted—as if she, whom her elders had found so bright and unwieldy, was being drawn into this greater conflagration.

From those in the circle—the Haosa, summoned by Tekelia—there came a shout, half in wonder, so Padi thought, and felt one foot slide toward Father, who was burning—burning—into ash.

She took a breath, opened her shields, and extended her hand, sliding another step forward...

"What will you do?" Tekelia asked beside her.

"My intent is to siphon off—enough..."

"Excellent. Take my hand."

She did, feeling their fingers interweave. Then she took a deep breath—and reached out.

· · · ❊ · · ·

It was instinct, to try to filter the power, to clean it, absorb it. He might, Shan thought painfully, actually survive the process, but if he did, would he any longer be himself? So much power, so much potential for good or for evil; so many things that he might simply solve with a thought...

"Father?"

Padi. Gods, no... Powerful as she was, still he would draw her like a moth—and immolate her.

"Stand back!"

"Father—do you *want* all of that?"

Shan shuddered.

"No! But I daren't release it. There are—" Belatedly,

he saw them, a dozen signatures and more. He was surrounded by talent, not to mention—ambient conditions . . .

"Take my hand," Padi said, horrifyingly, and before
he could snatch himself away, her fingers were around
his, her grip firm and sure. The power howled, and
flowed—he cried out once and saw it flowing—flowing
away, through their linked hands, through the links
they shared, father and daughter, master and 'prentice;
links of affection, links of—

He saw her take fire.

. . . . ✦ . . . .

Padi felt the power fill her—hot and cold, joyous
and despairing. It swirled, and passed on, past her
open shields, into her *self*—and onward yet, across
that other bridge of two hands tightly held, and
Tekelia was living flame, free hand flung toward the
glittering sky—

It began to snow, upward, black flakes dancing in the
glittering air, fading as they danced, until they were
gone, indistinguishable from the ambient. Overhead,
brilliant against the twilit sky, ribbons of light flamed
brightly—red, yellow, blue—and went out.

"Ribbon Dance Hill," Padi murmured, and beside
her Tekelia said, "Yes."

Padi felt a tug on her hand, and turned to meet
Father's dazed silver eyes. Dropping Tekelia's hand, she
stepped forward to help him rise. He was as disheveled
as she had ever seen him, rumpled and exuberant.

"All's well?" she asked him, low-voiced.

"All is, I believe, very well," he answered, and
drew her into a hug. "And well done. Though I have
a question for Tekelia-*dramliza*."

"Sir?"

Tekelia stepped forward.

"Why put Padi in the middle?"

"It was the most fortunate thing that Padi was available to be the conduit," Tekelia said earnestly. "If I had touched you, those of us gathered here would even now be searching the ambient for the disconnected pieces of your self, to return you to your proper plane, and body.

"Padi centered you while I gathered only the excess energy—a *much* simpler process!"

"So I apprehend."

He looked to Padi.

"Well, daughter?"

"Yes, sir. Very well."

"Then, perhaps—"

"They come," someone said sharply from the circle.

Tekelia spun on one heel. Padi turned her head.

Across from those already gathered, the dim air shimmered, and four people stepped forward onto the hilltop, as if they were exiting a lift.

Padi recognized Tekelia's cousin Bentamin, with Chairman Zeni gorminAstir; the other two were councilors, but she had forgotten their names.

They paused, and Bentamin spoke to Tekelia.

"Speaker for the Haosa, I greet you. These councilors and I are the representatives of Civilization. We will witness the action of the Great Ones foretold by the Oracle. We will assist, if asked. When we leave, the Oracle will accompany us."

"Civilization's Warden, we welcome you and the councilors as witnesses, and will accept your assistance, should it be needed," Tekelia answered in the same formal tone. "We have with us one of the Great Ones who was foretold. We await the other, with the Oracle. When their matter is settled, the Oracle will decide for herself where and how she will go."

There was a gasp from one of the councilors, which Tekelia and Bentamin alike affected not to hear.

From among the Haosa, someone cleared their throat and said, very softly, "They come."

Ribbon Dance Hill

. . . .

THEY STEPPED OUT OF THE SHROUDS BETWEEN MAYBE and Was, to the top of Ribbon Dance Hill—two women, hand in hand.

One was elderly, plump, and rose-cheeked; her eyes a-glow and her hair snarled by the exertions of her journey.

Her companion was tall, slim, and pale. Stars were caught in the floating strands of her night-black hair. Her dress was a blue that matched the color of the twilit skies, strung with crystal beads, like stars. A silver chain embraced her waist, and in her hand she held two bright and lambent silver rings.

She bowed to the elder lady, and gently kissed her cheek.

"My thanks for your guidance, for your friendship, and your care. Go, now, to your kin."

Released, the elder lady genuflected. She turned and walked into the circle, pausing at the Warden's side.

Padi, her arm pressed against Tekelia, watched the woman who was not Priscilla, and shivered.

"Have you never seen her thus?" Tekelia asked.

"Never," Padi answered, "though I have seen another god, now that I think about it. He is utterly different."

The woman—the Goddess—turned 'round slowly where she stood.

"Sweet children, have you come to sing us to our doom?"

There was a pregnant moment, as if everyone gathered had been breath-caught at once. Then, the Warden of the Civilized stepped forward, and made a formal bow.

"Lady, it was foretold that you would require a service from us. We have gathered for that particular purpose."

"A service? What should I want aside this hill, the forces that birthed us stretched, potent and living, above?"

Bentamin bowed again.

"Lady, only know that we are here to serve, and to witness, and to ease whatever you would do."

"To witness," she repeated. "Yes, you will want to witness this, and recall it, and tell your children down through the ages that you saw the proof, the final proof, that the Enemy is defeated on their own terms."

Bentamin bowed, and stepped back into the circle.

The Goddess raised her face to the sky where a few shy stars were beginning to show, between The Ribbons dancing. When she lowered her face, she was smiling.

"Lute," she said then, her voice soft and caressing. "My fierce angel, my support, my perfect opposite. The final door is sealed and forgotten. The power has been raised, and there are dancers in the wind. I say we are bid fair to go. How say you?"

Padi gasped—and looked toward the center. Father—

Father was gone, a shimmering shadow in the place he had been standing.

"Lute!" the Goddess called again, and the shadow blew apart in a blare of gilded white.

All around, those watching gasped as the white cloud continued turning—once, twice—

Three times.

A man stepped out of the fading glory, and bowed, with an edge of irony.

It was not Father, Padi saw with a small jolt, but Lute himself—though for all that, a Lute transformed. Gone were his tatters, replaced with elegance and quiet glory. His cloak fell flawless over one shoulder, showing a lining as bright as a sun. His long black hair was braided with silver bells, and there were the shadows of wings at his back.

His hands, he held before him, fingers moving with subtle grace. Padi saw the red gaming counter walk across the back of his hand once—and fall off into the deepening air.

"My Lady Moonhawk, first among the Names, who created us a Goddess; she who won us free of despair, and found for us both life and hope. The door has passed out of memory, and we are free. Only one task remains us, before together, we may go."

"One task, my Lute? What task is this?"

"We must ask a boon of these gathered, who are, after all, our very grandchildren."

"Ask then," said the Lady.

Lute bowed and turned, graceful, his cape belling, and his arms outstretched as if to embrace the circle entire.

"We ask the boon of your forgiveness," he said, his voice carrying. "You are ours, children of the children of our wills and our thoughts, whom we did not protect. We were, I fear, rather bad gods. Born as we had been, we could scarcely have been otherwise."

He paused, but there was no movement, no question from those in circle, who stood, scarcely breathing.

"We ask," Lute continued, his hands folded, unnaturally still, before him. "We ask also that you witness our return to the elements that birthed us. While it is true that I was born from starlight, and my lady from crystal itself, these precise elements are not native to this universe. Be vigilant, children; take care that we do no damage as we leave you. Though we brought you here in turbulence, we would leave you here in peace."

There came a murmur from the circle, then. Tekelia stood forward, and Bentamin.

"Our forgiveness we give freely, though we know of no wrong done to us," Bentamin said, bowing.

"Our thanks," said Lute, and turned to Tekelia.

"We will watch and be vigilant on your behalf, Lord and Lady," Tekelia said gently. "You may pass in peace."

"Sweetly spoken."

Lute stepped to the Lady's side.

"It is time," he said, and extended his hand.

Moonhawk slipped one of the rings onto his finger. It blazed, limning him in silver, striking the shadows of his wings into glory.

He took the second ring up from her palm, and slid it onto her finger.

Bells sounded, high and cold, like ice. Or crystal. The Lady blazed like a promise, the two of them a benediction.

A miracle.

For long minutes they stood, side by side, casting their gleaming shadows against the twilit air, while overhead The Ribbons danced in mingled joy and sadness.

"Blessings, children," the Lady cried. "May all of your endeavors bring you joy."

The air gusted then, and they were gone, melted into the grass, the sky, The Ribbons brightly dancing.

Crystals like embers blew briefly on the bright wind, a single feather drifting among them until, all at once, they were gone.

The circle as one breathed in—and breathed out.

Lute and Moonhawk were gone. The center of the circle was empty.

"No!" Padi cried, and took one step forward—

Thunder boomed, the hillside shook, reality blurred into illusion—and became real again.

In the center of the circle, holding hands, stood a man and a woman, wearing respectable trading clothes, the Tree-and-Dragon showing bright on the breast of each jacket. They turned to look at each other. The woman smiled. The man did.

"Hello, Priscilla," he said gently, and lifted her hand to his lips.

Colemeno Port

. . . .

IT HAD BEEN A LONG, EXHILARATING DAY, TOURING THE markets, meeting with the vendors as a group, and privately with the market masters. Padi owned herself by turns fascinated, excited, frustrated, and by the end of the last meeting—tired to the bone, and looking forward to a quiet dinner.

Indeed, she was ordering her thoughts in the direction of that goal when a man in the livery of the market staff came hurrying 'round the corner.

He smiled when he saw them and lengthened his stride.

"Master Trader yos'Galan, Trader yos'Galan. I'd been afraid that I was too late! Trader Isfelm has just arrived, and hopes to have a word with you."

It was surely not worthy that her first reaction was dismay, Padi thought. And then she caught Father's consternation, followed by a ruffle of resigned humor.

"Certainly, I will be pleased to stop for a word with Trader Isfelm," he said. "Trader yos'Galan?"

"A word," she allowed, "or perhaps three. We ought to compare schedules and mark out a time for an in-depth meeting."

"Excellent," the master trader murmured, and turned to the messenger.

"Will you, of your kindness, lead us to Trader Isfelm?"

"Of course!" the man said. "Just down here, Traders, in the short-term meeting room."

"It would seem that Trader Isfelm has the same notion as you, Trader," the master trader murmured as they followed the staffer back up the hall.

"It would," Padi returned, with composure. "Perhaps we will continue to find ourselves as one on all matters of interest."

"Now, wouldn't that be odd?"

The staffer opened the door, and bowed them energetically inside, which meant that the master trader stepped to the right, while Padi went to the left.

The short-term meeting room was large enough to hold a small round table, four chairs, and a modest refreshments bureau. A keypad sat in the center of the table; the screen suspended on the far wall showed the port stats screen—ships in, ships due in, departure times filed...

There were three ships in—Research Boat *Ayjak*, out of Metlin; *Dutiful Passage*, out of Surebleak; and *Ember*, out of Dallimere.

Between the table and the buffet, back to the door, apparently quite intent on the screen, was a tall, slender shape wearing a space leather jacket in a style Padi had never seen before.

"Trader Isfelm," their guide said, somewhat breathlessly, "here are Master Trader yos'Galan and Trader yos'Galan."

"Ah, thank you."

The trader turned as the door shut, the room light falling full across her face.

Padi took a quiet breath, and said nothing.

"I have a wager in place with my brother," said Trader Isfelm conversationally, "dating from the time we were learning our first board drills."

"Really? What was the wager, I wonder?" Father asked in the same tone.

"Whether it would be Tree-and-Dragon or another of the trade clans that would arrive at The Redlands first, after the Dust had blown aside."

She paused.

"He favored one of the lesser clans, reasoning that they would have more cause to be bold."

"And you?"

"I? I would have nothing other than Tree-and-Dragon *would* be first. And here you are."

"And here we are," Father agreed gently. "We had cause to be bold, you see."

Trader Isfelm laughed.

"And when has that not been the case?"

She raised her hand, so that the many gems in the Jump Pilot's cluster flickered and flared in the room's light, like a miniature galaxy. "You'll be wanting this back . . . cousin."

"I am not the delm," Father said. "Keep it until it can be returned in proper style."

Trader Isfelm inclined her head.

"You may have heard that we—the Isfelm Trade Union—are principals in the Iverson Loop. The Redlands are one anchor; the other is still deep in the Dust. We, of course, wish to expand outward."

"And we wish—to expand," Master Trader yos'Galan said. "It appears we have much to talk about, Trader."

"I agree," said Trader Isfelm. "Perhaps we might arrange for a proper meeting."

"An excellent idea. Let us consider our schedules."

They were able to block out the whole of the next afternoon for Trader Isfelm and the Iverson Loop by shifting two meetings with local vendors to the following morning. While Padi was finalizing those arrangements, Trader Isfelm bespoke a so-called project room, and ordered catering.

"It seems our work here is, temporarily at least, done," said the master trader, beginning to rise.

Trader Isfelm held up a hand.

"In fact, there is one thing more, if you have time, Trader yos'Galan."

"A *little* time," said Padi, and Trader Isfelm smiled.

"I swear it is one question only. The adapter kits you have on offer—will they bring twelve forty-twos into compliance with the pods I see on *Dutiful Passage*?"

"Fifteen-thirties," Padi said. "Yes, they will." She paused, and added, "It was a lucky find."

Trader Isfelm smiled gently.

"Of course it was," she said.

Off-Grid

. . . .

"WAS THIS NEW—COUSIN—UNEXPECTED?" TEKELIA ASKED.
They were on the balcony overlooking the forest,
dawdling over their wine.

It had come dark while they were eating dinner,
but there were The Ribbons, which gave their dancing
light, besides that the trees themselves gave a small,
self-satisfied illumination. Padi sighed and sipped her
wine, and was . . . content.

"The new cousin," she said slowly, "was neither
expected nor unexpected. It's the Luck, you see—and
also the family. *Isfelm*, and the Pilot's cluster—one
assumes this particular cousin is out of yos'Phelium.
Korval *did* have a part in bringing the small talents
here from Liad. It would not be at all wonderful, that
a yos'Phelium pilot decided to indulge herself with a
bit of exploration. I expect we may have the whole
history from the trader, tomorrow."

"What is Trader Isfelm's signature, I wonder?"
asked Tekelia.

"Hmm?"

Padi considered for a moment, and produced it,
shining in the dark air before them.

"Ah." Tekelia sighed. "You know, I had someone suggest that signature as being connected to you, a little time ago."

"Who was that, I wonder?"

"A norbear named Eet. You may well meet him, if you come often to the village."

Padi laughed.

"Lady Selph was adamant that I make her part of the trade team; it had almost been worth my life to refuse. Shall I send for her?"

"I see no reason why not, though Bentamin might."

"Bentamin holds no sway in the village surely?"

"Well, but one must bring the lady through the port," Tekelia pointed out. "There's the test that she might fail."

"True. Well. Perhaps after we've demonstrated how mannerly and—and *civilized*—we are."

Tekelia laughed, and Padi did, and when merriment was done, they sat quietly, sipping wine in the cool dark.

"What do you foresee?" Tekelia asked eventually.

Padi tipped her head.

"I don't know that I have any sort of Sight," she said.

"But you don't know that you are blind," Tekelia countered. "So near the Hill, even the smallest inclination to a particular talent will be magnified. But I was merely asking after your thoughts—how do you foresee the master trader's mission resolving?"

"Well, that. The master trader came prepared to establish a trade hub here, with Ixin as the junior partner. I think he will achieve that, easily. Once there is a hub in place, other traders will come—from *out*, as Portmaster krogerSlyte has it. Now that the Dust is cleared, The Redlands are not so distant as they had seemed, before.

"It's apparent that Trader Isfelm means to go *out* by whatever means. She asked about the adapter kits—but I believe she would go as a 'prentice in hydroponics, if only she *was* going *out*."

"The master trader will, in his turn, want to go *in*," Tekelia suggested.

"The master trader will want *one of his* to go *in*," Padi corrected. "And that will be me, as I am proximate, and wear the garnet."

"And will you go?"

"Yes, of course, I will go," Padi said, a little surprised by the question. "We must learn what we can bring to Colemeno for itself, and for the Iverson Loop, to the profit of all."

She turned suddenly, to consider Tekelia's face in the glow from the trees.

"There is a thing we say, our family being both, you know," she said slowly. "Pilots choose, but traders leap."

"And so you will leap," Tekelia said, "and land where the Luck will take you."

"It sounds mad," Padi said apologetically.

"Not at all," Tekelia answered politely.

Padi extended a hand. Warm fingers met hers, and they sat, content, together, while The Ribbons danced brilliant above.